T0365663

THE DEVIL'S CLAW

PATRICK JAMES

Order this book online at www.trafford.com/07-3022
or email orders@trafford.com

Most Trafford titles are also available at major online book retailers.

Illustrated by: Ben Didier
Cover Design by: Ben Didier

Note for Librarians: A cataloguing record for this book is available from Library
and Archives Canada at www.collectionscanada.ca/amicus/index-e.html

Printed in Victoria, BC, Canada.

ISBN: 978-1-4251-6540-6

*We at Trafford believe that it is the responsibility of us all, as both individuals
and corporations, to make choices that are environmentally and socially sound.
You, in turn, are supporting this responsible conduct each time you purchase a
Trafford book, or make use of our publishing services. To find out how you are
helping, please visit www.trafford.com/responsiblepublishing.html*

*Our mission is to efficiently provide the world's finest, most comprehensive
book publishing service, enabling every author to experience success.
To find out how to publish your book, your way, and have it available
worldwide, visit us online at www.trafford.com/10510*

www.trafford.com

North America & international
toll-free: 1 888 232 4444 (USA & Canada)
phone: 250 383 6864 ♦ fax: 250 383 6804
email: info@trafford.com

The United Kingdom & Europe
phone: +44 (0)1865 487 395 ♦ local rate: 0845 230 9601
facsimile: +44 (0)1865 481 507 ♦ email: info.uk@trafford.com

10 9 8 7 6 5 4

Chapter 1

"And the second angel poured
His vial upon the sea, and it
Became as the blood of a dead man."
Book of Revelations. **Apocalypse.**

Plague? No way! I simmered, wanted to blister someone—anyone—for stuffing up my tour.

Eloise Pringle caught my ineffectual glare; wrinkled her nose; stared beyond with acquired indifference. Jake's old Toyota troopie rattled and careened up the River Road, aggravating my physical discomfort, notably the monster bruise on my butt. Diesel infused heat and a dead air conditioner reduced sleep to a rude, sweaty stupor.

Through midday haze the great flood plains of the Ord River passed by. Boab trees, like bloated sentinels crowned with antler branches, dotted the landscape. As we droned eastward, termite cities towered everywhere across parched bushland; each aligned in primeval worship, east, west, avoiding unnecessary sun expo-sure. How long ago did some archaic intelligence work that one out? A perfect harmony; unlike calamitous humanity busy de-vouring and squabbling its way through 2013.

Sascha, my greedy tent mate, wormed in claiming dozing space amongst the chaos of luggage and legs. Her fluoro fingernails posed, suspended in mid air, as if making a cautionary statement.

Late in the second day we crept through the stench of flood stricken Katherine. Saw the macabre spectacle of cruising crocs still prowling mud-choked streets as storm waters subsided. "It's August, not bloody rain season, mate." One local bit off words as he shovelled muck out of his shop, but then one expected the unexpected these days.

"We've gotta tell them." I recalled Stella saying as she bull-dozed Jake, her easygoing husband. "It's bloody over." And it was. So much for the Pringle Super Outback Tour.

Jake yielded, canned the last and best parts, the Geiki and Cathedral Gorges, the amazing Bungle Bungles; made me mad as a cut snake. She was to blame. It meant returning to an odious school term with awful, hoop jumping I'd learned to loath.

Mum didn't help. She bordered on workaholic as senior nurse and expected me to dance to her tune. Dad was now a rare echo in my life; spent months embroiled in Europe and Africa as a *United Nations* executive in the *World Health Organisation*; or was it *UNESCO*? At any rate, they also ate their own.

Plague. Okay, there'd been heaps of strife. Wars. Starvation televised; enough haunting eyes and festering sores to jade a billion lifetimes; this latest I reluctantly sensed was different. "Wake up - time to buy the farm." I remembered some sci-fi character leering as he dispatched a hapless victim. "The secret's not minding the pain."

"This plague thing; it's mushroomed everywhere. Hundreds of cases." Jake said, as we devoured hourly news reports. Our mobiles were either out of cash, or out of juice. Now we were scurrying homeward like frightened rabbits. I still wanted to regard it the same way we'd ho-hummed about deadly bird flu. Such epidemics killed elsewhere, not Australia. Is it human nature to minimise danger to one's self like cracking up through a silly B grade horror film?

We drove hard south along the Stuart Highway into the land of the 'Never-Never', a parched plain ancient beyond the age of the Bungle Bungles. Raw red earth, archaic dust baked against a bleached blue sky issued the scape a strange quality, like being in a time warp; dimensions drawn to the heavens; beyond comprehension. Alien.

The hours dragged as our motley crew mauled bush songs and fumbled bad jokes. My best offer, pirated from my science teacher fell lame; a "blonde moment", as gay Ralph quipped. "Some people say I'm a horrible person, but that's not true. I have the heart of a young boy - in a jar on my desk." Bree Price strikes again.

Our party. Three gays. Two blushable churchies. Haley and Trev, newly marrieds. Big Bruno Bug-eye we called 'Donuts'. These were our fellow adventurers. Sascha, my opposite in most ways, jet haired and outrageously cheeky, rescued the social patter. She'd made the tour as oddball. Now all of us brooded, searching for words, occasionally plucking at scraps, notions, to come to grips with the unspeakable.

4

"Science is on our side." Said Haley.

"They beat that Ebola thing. Didn't they?" Bruno lisped, nodding his anxiety. "Well, didn't they?"

"You wish! Not so. It mutated. Two days after the first symptoms appear you're as good as dead." Gay Graham said; his voice tinged with melancholy.

I saw their bravado as empty as the ineffectual power of most antibiotics. Nothing touched this virus, so authorities said. They weren't even sure where it came from let alone how it appeared across the world at the same time. Like mushrooms; none in the evening, a forest by morning.

My memory of junior history served up images of bloated, rotting bodies, "the end of the world", a desperate monk scrawled on a church wall. "Pitiless, wild, violent." Worry Walker, ghoulish by nature, did a great job of scaring the stuffing out of me. Sascha's stories from the 'stiff lab', compliments of her mum's ex-boyfriend, Mortie, the mortician, made us feel all the pricklier.

※

Arrival in Sydney came late Sunday night. Conversations remained subdued, such an anti-climax after exciting days in the Outback. Jake explained we should arrive when things were quieter. Newscasts hinted at pending *Martial Law*. Severe curfew.

The others, bar Hugo, Stella and Jake quickly whisked away, scuttling into the night, waving furtively, as if already pursued by the disease.

A family huddled together cowering against the chill; kept as far from us as possible. None spoke.

Sascha stared forlorn at a swirling Macdonald's chip box. A tendril of ripe garbage wafted by; made me snuffle.

Hugo was flummoxed when we suffered a parting kiss, just a peck. Stella mumbled apologies, well wishes. I gave Jake a hug, whispered thanks for a great time.

"Oh, before we go. I found this by your tent. That was the oddest thing I've ever seen." Jake said. He held out a small paperbark package tied neatly with vine. "I peeked," he grinned. "There's a mix of leaves, grasses, umm, mosses and some roots. Must be a dozen kinds. Figure that old Aborigine couple slipped it in during our last night at the billabong."

"That's too weird. I thought we left them far behind." The

5

hackles on my neck stood up. I shook my head. "Wish I could thank them. I'll be sure to keep it."

How they expected a bush dumb girl to use it was a mystery.

They'd appeared wraith-like out of gully scrub near Wolfe Creek meteor crater five nights previous. Both were as ancient as the land, cured, reduced to wrinkles. He'd shuffled into camp propped on a bent cane. She stooped, lost in a faded daisied dress.

I remembered his words. "You got bad fever, missy. Bad stuff. Bush fever."

Somewhere in that night I recalled his toothless grin. And they'd vanished like a dream.

I'd sweated litres, slept a sticky mess, but whatever brew they'd concocted worked by the following morning. I still felt vague, weakened by the shakes.

❊

The bus sub-station hung, suspended, a ghostly plain cocooned in pallid fluorescent light. Wind swept newspapers scuttled about as if whispering secrets. Shadowy figures loomed between trees in a nearby park.

"This is worse than hanging on a cliff face." I muttered. A squad car prowled by, eyeing us as if to say, "this isn't a cool place for the likes of you."

"Promise you'll call." Sascha said.

I nodded; bit my lip. "Stay with us. Your mum too."

"She'd never move." Newtown's her space."

"If it all falls apart?"

"It won't. She'll be right, mate. You'll see." Her eyes betrayed her smile. "We'll meet in town—soon."

We'd clicked from day one. I, shy, she being capricious; flouncing through the camp's routine, a gossip's gossip. Now, the shell of fun blown away, she appeared lost for words, eyes moist.

Sascha departed leaving me forlorn. Shortly after I caught a bus to Central Station, transferring to the Northern beaches Line. On board I sat close to the driver. A woman and child were the only other passengers. They clung together at the back; a Gumby balloon bobbing overhead.

"What'sa girl your age doin' out in this town so late?" he said abruptly. The accent was Mediterranean, the manner, fatherly.

He smelled of garlic.

"Don't you know what'sa goin' on? He added, face wrinkles deepening. "The whole cities' public transport, she's shuttin' down for good at midnight. Lucky you caught the ten-to-twelve. This is the last bus," he emphasised. "Soon they set roadblocks. Sheesh!"

I sighed. "I've been out in the bush for weeks. Is the plague really *that* bad? I heard hundreds."

"Is it bad?" He shook his head. "Yeah. Bad." He fell silent, his knuckles white on the steering wheel. "It got away from the authorities. Maybe twenty-thirty thousand got it here, could be more. Thousands dead. All cities the same," he gestured.

The chilling thought of mum swept up in the thick of it suddenly turned my stomach. What if she'd caught the virus - was dead? Our regular mobile phone calls ended just before our return. She'd never mentioned anything distressing about work in our last words, but then mum kept a lot to herself. Dad's mobile wasn't on, just a text six days old and cryptical. *'Imperative you make plans to escape. Will call. Love, dad.'* Escape? Where?

Downtown was darker, muted. Once teeming with nightlife, show fronts lay in shadow. Pink Tips, a notorious burlesque bar still neoned its leggy product, suggested feverish signs of life. Few people were on foot elsewhere. Traffic seemed furtive, skulking along as if the vehicles themselves were threatened.

I knew after we crossed the bridge I'd be only a few kilometres from mum's hospital. The temptation to get off grew unbearable, but I sensed it was seriously foolish to attempt going there first; tried imagining the unimaginable chaos. Getting home was my only real choice no matter how strong the desire to see her. She'd phone.

We crossed the Harbour Bridge, Sydney's great 'Coathanger', and moved north.

Sirens cut the air raising a mournful din in the distance. Another screamed nearby, shrill with urgency.

Rain began to fall adding the swish of wipers to the diesel's throaty drone.

"Been wailin' like that for days," he said, jarring my numbed senses. "Don't know what I'm gunna do for work. Whole city is a mess. Strangled. Love, you won't be goin' to school tomorrow. They shut them all down on Friday."

The super coolness of that notion shrivelled away like my en-

7

ergy. Gods' I felt wrung out.

"Isolation is the heart of the experience," Jake once said. Now I sensed there was a new and desperately real isolation; Uncertainty; a sinking feeling, foreboding.

Media hype struck me as unusually measured and terse. Figures offered were suspect, at odds with one another. Newscasters remained optimistic flashing glib comments; I sensed, tight smiles. A few patches of information indicated how deep in the dung humanity appeared to have fallen. Was the government masking medical reports? It was clear enough the *Great Pandemic*, as alarmists coined it, had managed to mysteriously cross the world to muck up all my plans.

I dozed, as we swept northward. The child at the back of the bus whimpered tiredness.

Rain rattled against the coach, enveloped the city in a shroud. Shadows cast an eerie fantasy through skeletal trees I glimpsed lining what I imagined was a cemetery. The dark shimmered in shifting curtains of silver drops, bleaching out colours; hues of grey.

We hissed to a stop at the top of our hill.

"You take care, love," he said. "Stay away from crowds. You hear me? Good luck."

I wished him the same and stepped into the night. Pack on back, I trudged a soddened kilometre through bush suburb down to our tiny cul-de-sac. The only street lighting by our house was still out, making it hard to see much. The gate was locked. I thought that strange. Using my pack as a step I peeked over the brick wall. One glimmer of light came from the lounge room.

"Anyone home?" I shouted. Ace, our border collie, whined somewhere in the back of the house. Nobody.

I focused on the Ramira's flickering porch light next door. Soaked to the bone, and resentful not one wretch welcomed me; I entered their yard resolved to abuse hell out of the first social reject found.

Chapter 2

The door opened. Cris, the Ramira family's noxious son peered out, indifferent to my misery. Jeff pushed him aside.

"Jeffie, I'm back." I hugged him. Unlike his normally wooden response, he shocked, squeezed, pulling me hard against him.

"Easy, Godzilla! I'm hoping they'll grow."

Cris stared sullenly, side on, head hung under a shock of unkempt curls. Nothing changed there. Our relationship sat firmly on the rocks, had done so for some time. Couldn't stand his smart-ass antics, always trying, always blundering.

"Why didn't you answer on the mobile?" I snapped.

"Mine's busted. Ace knocked it flying into the pool," Jeff said releasing me. "We've stayed the day with Cris and Millie. Arie's sick."

"Is mum at the hospital?"

"Yeah, she phoned Thursday night. Said she was sleeping in the cafeteria. They've brought in beds for the staff. Everyone's needed." Jeff became animated, agitated. "She says the place is a madhouse with plague cases—even using the underground car park to isolate them from the other patients. Stacking the bodies there too. She's dead set worried. Sounds so tired. Says she has to stay."

"Has to?" I said.

Jeffrey looked totally dejected, matching the hole infested tracksuit pants and plaid shirt he regarded as cool. Lines etched his face. Freckles drooped.

"She's got to come home *some* time," I said.

"Bree!" Zoe poked her face into our midst and launched into my arms. She clung like a limpet to a rock.

"How's my little elfette?" I said, planting kisses on her hair and forehead. I blew a 'raspberry' against her neck. Zoe squealed and squirmed, paying me back with a wet kiss, her 'Slobberella' special.

"Why didn't you come sooner?" She whined. "I'm petrified."

That was her favourite negative regarding emotions and food, whatever. Cabbage was petrified, so were most teachers who ranked below veg level.

With Zoë still clinging I turned on Cris. "Don't *you* have something better to do than stare?"

"No." He stared by me, dark eyes glinting.

That figures. He'd have to be the most useless guy in an emergency. No. Millie, his sister, made it as Queen of the Airheads. Hormones had done an express job on her at fourteen. Millie was far too shapely for her own good, and aware of it. Cosmetics, tacky magazines, gross music like Spazo Mainline, and miscellaneous post-Ken sham-boys made up Millie-world.

"Jeff, what about dad? When's he coming home?"

"He's stuck in Europe, Bree. The airlines shut down except for emergency traffic. America's the same."

"You mean we're on our own."

"Yeah, in more ways than you can imagine. It's Cris and Millie's mum. We think she's got it."

"The plague? How do you know? You're not a doctor," I quavered. My stomach turned queasy.

"She came down with a weird cough and a fever two nights ago. She's got red and purple blotches now, all over her body. The fever's heaps worse. It fits what they say happens. It must be plague. She ordered us to stay away from her - screamed at Millie."

I eyed Cris. "Didn't you phone for a doctor or get an ambulance?"

"Yeah. It took ages to contact anyone. Nobody would come. That's in-your-face *no* in my books. Keep her isolated, they said. Everyone to stay well away," he said, asserting authority, but his face sagged.

"That's crazy. She has to have water. What happens when she needs a toilet?" I said, incredulous that he'd overlook such a thing. "When did you last go in?"

"Every time we go down the hall she howls at us." Cris said.

Jeff said. "I peeked. She's thrown up everything. Blood. Dry-retches like a cat does. You know, fur balls. She heaved and retched all last night. We're wiped out listening. It's scary."

"Mum's too weak to get up," Cris said. "Nobody has the nerve to go in. It's highly contagious."

"You mean you can't find enough guts to help her? She's your mother," I said, glowering, forcing him against the wall.

10

"Go easy, Bree," Jeff wedged in. "None of us can handle it."

"It can't possibly be that bad," I said.

"I'm going to throw up." Millie threatened, dove for the garbage pail.

Insensitive brain. Emotional stomach.

Something had to be done. I couldn't stand knowing she was suffering. If the boys couldn't face it then I'd have to pluck up courage to nurse her somehow. Surely there was hope. If I could clean her up, give some fluids and encouragement. I could think of nothing worse than being so ill and all alone.

"Get me cleaning stuff. Disinfectant. Sponges. Towels. I need gauze and rubber gloves, Jeff. Find mum's supply - and her surgical gown and mask. A spray bottle, better still, the garden spray applicator; the one with the long shaft."

Cris rummaged through the kitchen in haste almost as if trying to make up for past stupidity and insults to me. Moon faced Millie sat whining in the kitchen wiping vomit off her sun top; her eyes big; staring at our sudden burst of activity.

"Aspirin. Painkillers. Anything strong," I demanded. "Millie. Move."

Still dazed, she stumbled off to search. There was soon an assembly of makeshift equipment crowding the table. It was twenty-three past three, the middle of the night; strange how particular details remain fixed in your mind.

Zoe was wide-eyed while I struggled to dress. For once she was silent, face clouded, brow furrowed. Jeff and Cris tried rigging me up using masking tape to seal joins so that no skin was exposed. They sprayed disinfectant all over me and on gauze pads before stuffing these into the facemask. Jeff's hands shook. The mask stank of something between ether and mothballs making me gag again and again before tolerating the brew.

My sadistic history teacher, the scare merchant, told us about medieval doctors. They used long beak-like masks crammed with cloves, crushed rose petals and powdered worms, so they got the name 'quacks' from all their harebrained remedies. History was repeating itself. Most of them died. Maybe I was up for it now.

"From the frying pan into what?" I muttered. Slowly opening the door to Arie's bedroom was like entering a nightmare. Faint light flooded the bed from a table lamp, leaving the rest of the room dim. A statue of the goddess *Celestial Girl*, stood posed sensually over the bed, the feeble light making her shapely body

11

glint, almost alive. The statue surveyed what was once equally as beautiful.

For a long time I couldn't will myself to move beyond the threshold. Her breathing fluctuated, coming in rasps and sudden bursts.

A whiff of her sickness penetrated my senses, defying disinfectant. This was an odour that chilled me out, as if death was there in person filling the room, each wave of it curling, fingering my body.

Arie lay unclothed on a sheet. I stared disbelief.

Several islands of angry skin bore festering boil-like secretions. Some patches intensified, glowed, possessing an alien life of their own. Other larger areas formed lines like veins of cracked glass. These radiated out seeking new flesh to spoil.

Aries' eyes lay sunken; the whites now inflamed pink surrounded by shadow. Her face distorted with pain.

She was attractive once, skin a golden cinnamon. How could any disease take over like this? I was not prepared. Pity. Anger. Fear. All churned up. My skin crawled. I winced; fought the urge to run, forced my mind to function.

"Arie," I whispered from a distance. "Can you hear me, see me?" No response came other than a horrid rasp, as if she was about to drown. "I'm going to try and give you a drink and wash you." Gods. This was useless.

I'd dissolved two strong painkillers and two anti-biotic tablets from some previous crisis, mixing them into warm, honeyed water. It was wrong medically, pathetic, stupid, but there was nothing else we could think of. My idea of helping fell lame.

By propping Aries' head up with a pillow, careful not to touch her, or come in line with her breath, I forced the spray nozzle into her mouth. The first efforts resulted in her coughing it up, but after several attempts some went down. She laboured to swallow.

Washing by touch and a sheet change was impossible. Arie was fused to the sheets. Bits of dead skin hung, shed after the eruptions of body fluids. With diluted Detol and the spray device, all I did was spread a warm mist over the corruptions until each of the buckets Cris ferried inside the door lay empty. Pleas to "be careful" filtered in.

Our effort in masking up was no guarantee of defence, that much was obvious. Arie radiated contagion.

12

Four fallen faces stared at me from the end of the hall as I exited.

Yapping mina birds announced dawn arrival, chilly and wet, matching my feelings.

"What do you think?" Cris said, backing away, stumbling, as I made for the sink fighting the urge to retch.

"Nothing to think," I said, focusing through misted goggles. My will not to break down centred on a delicate seahorse ceramic Arie created for the kitchen wall.

"It'll run its course no matter what we do. I can't go in there again, and neither can any of you."

Zoë rose to help me.

"Don't touch me. Stay away. I could have virus all over my smock. Everything I've worn. Burn it. You can't risk touching *anything* Arie handled, like in the kitchen, the bathroom."

Jeff sprayed strong disinfectant over my outfit.

Millie sought solace in coffee, shook, spilling it.

On my blunt instructions she set to work removing the smock by cutting the back ties with a hooked fish knife taped to a stick. She and Jeff wore gloves and masks. I held my breath as the gloves peeled away with the smock.

I became aware of Cris gaping at me and realised my underwear was up my crotch, but couldn't be bothered to adjust. I peeled my saturated top off, slipped downstairs to the pool shower, rummaged a change of clothes from my pack and scrubbed until the hot water ran out, but her corrupted body never washed from my mind. Driven by fear, we left the Ramira home for ours.

After a second hot shower, I joined the others gathered in the lounge. Millie and Zoe crashed, curled up under a quilt by the fireplace. Dejected, and exhausted, I sat alone too hyped up to sleep. Embers radiated a faint and friendly glow in an otherwise dismal setting. My emotions and body sagged; the room narrowed, strangely distorted.

"What can we do now?" Jeff said, hungry for any reassurance. "You look terrible, Bree."

I turned to Cris. "Helping your mum's out. She's in a horrible state. It'll get worse." I saw his eyes water; felt pity, saw softness I'd never seen.

"I'm sorry, really sorry I snapped at you. I'd no idea it was this bad."

"She'll die," he said, more a statement than a question.

"Somebody must have advice. Maybe we can get serum - an injection. I'll try the medical centres again."

Sascha and Bruno's plea echoed through my mind. Surely science would find an antidote. Could any of us survive such a horrifying infection? Who amongst us was next other than me?

Ace, who'd scratched and whined for hours downstairs, raced into the lounge room, turning inside out with joy. Although she was Zoë's dog, Ace usually adopted my bedroom if there was any kind of disruption to routine. Black and white patched, Ace was an endearing hound. She sported ears that flapped at any disturbance, and an angled way of looking at you belying the sharp intelligence of the breed. She was a doing dog, bordering on neurotic, and a perfect match for Zoë.

Ace headed towards my bedroom. I found her lying on a patchwork rug at the foot of my bed, tail thumping.

I held no recollection of hitting the pillow.

※

Mid afternoon brought no hope. Jeff and Cris tried every possible source for help. Most phone numbers remained busy. Cris, who had his red P driving license, drove to several local centres and came back dejected, said they'd offered nothing for treatment.

"One masked medic told me to piss off," Cris grumbled. "There were heaps of patients. Kept my distance. Hey, saw a dead dog on the way back."

"That could mean other animals catch it and carry the virus." Jeff said.

The bus driver's words returned to haunt me. "Thousands dead." But nobody seemed to be offering clues about surviving. A treatment.

Evening reports confirmed the part animals were beginning to play spreading the contagion, including birds, house pets, rats and mice. Winter was the season rodents migrated into homes. Plague would see stricken animals on the move seeking refuge. Our bay had its share of rats.

"Any of you thought about food, eh?" Jeff said.

That added another dimension to our situation.

"There's signs of a run on food already. The markets. We've gotta act fast." Jeff waved his hands like a conductor.

"We're strapped for cash." I said.

"Nowhere near enough, Bree. Mum stocked the freezer two weeks ago. We need to get our act together, use credit cards. Anything. What if the whole bleedin' city falls to pieces? Where'll food come from?" he added. "Could face starvation in a month. There'll be big mobs around before long. We'd better be ahead of them."

He was right. Newscasts raved about *Martial Law*. Roadblocks.

Jeff could bring up the most awkward questions sometimes like the time at the ripe age of ten he asked what my periods were like. His bull-headed insistence infuriated me. Typical Leo. I could only think of belting him with a pillow and screaming him down. He could be so damn nosy.

Now, his questions about survival compelled. It had to be dealt with. What if the government put restrictions on supply or even shut stores down? I numbed thinking of the threat.

Millie and Cris, smocked, masked and gloved, were hard at work hunting for food of every sort within their household. We'd agreed it was wise to abandon their home. Arie must have con-taminated some areas, even though Cris said she'd gone straight to bed on arriving home. Millie said she'd returned from an art seminar that Thursday, the day before schools shut down. Maybe she caught it at the seminar or in some earlier contact. Perhaps simply a friendly exchange with someone infected at the library where she worked.

It must be around the Ramira household in patches just wait-ing for someone to brush against it. Was it already teeming through my body, multiplying by the minute, readying soon to erupt?

News reports throughout the day added to all our additional worries, and a few new ones. S.B.S. television carried world news specials on widespread riots for food in Rio de Janeiro and many countries already deep in crisis. The Middle East, India and South East Asia were especially hard hit, considering the spin-off from local conflicts and massive refugee movements.

World stock market reports reflected the collapse of confi-dence as stock values tumbled daily, and food prices soared.

In America any stray animals in cities were to be shot on sight. Soon it'd be stray people.

We sat dejected by each report. People must make a living. If cogs in any machine stop the whole structure will grind to a halt, and the World Village was such a complex machine of interlocking needs and forces.

✤

I vividly remembered one interview with an Indian medical expert in communicable diseases.

He was asked. "How had the virus spread so fast?"

"This new strain appears to be able to gestate, or develop for as much as four weeks in a hosts body," he said. " Oh, yes. Also, the number of refugees and people travelling has been at record levels," the doctor added.

"Do we have any firm evidence where the epidemic began? It has been suggested Africa or South America are the most likely origin," the commentator queried.

"U.N. health authorities are sure the World Environmental Conference that took place in Brasilia city has unwittingly spread the plague far and wide. The virus spread through air conditioning to many of the forty thousand delegates attending. Oh, yes. There were many thousands more in support of the conference," the doctor said. "Is it not ironic?"

"You mean they've taken the virus home to nearly every country?"

"Yes. We now know mice were original carriers, driven out of their habitat by land clearing in the Amazon. Feeding on grain. These have invaded the cities as food supplies have been trucked in. In effect, we've become perched on a biological time bomb. It is surely devilish work, oh yes," he added.

Images of Arie's skin erupting, the claw-like veins radiating, searching. I convulsed, showering Ace with coffee. She thumped her tail, appreciating attention.

The interview droned on.

This wasn't entirely new to me. Human invasion of the once impenetrable jungles of the Amazon was "disturbing ancient ecologies", as my father said. "Upsetting nature's darkest corners," I mused. Though a bookworm by nature, my naivety about these events became obvious.

"There's a price to pay for everything." My stern grandfather used to say. How wise he was.

✤

Arie died early Wednesday. Gaping at her now from the doorway, she was not recognisable. Her bloodied features lay distorted, almost melted.

Burial. We were traumatised. Tears came in unpredictable bursts during the preparations and the next morning. Jeff and Cris found a place next to Arie's favourite frangipani tree. They dug an incline into the grave so that her body could be slid in and keep some shred of dignity rather than allowing her to tumble in. It was hard enough giving her the respect she deserved.

The boys shrouded her using a pole and with a snake noose snared her feet. In that manner the beauty that had been a striking blend of Sri Lankan and Scottish features was dragged out of the bedroom, down the hall and down the stairway. With each jarring thump, it was difficult to keep her shroud in place.

Jeff, Zoë and I stood close, arm-in-arm, each adding tears to the soft rain. Millie stood alone blubbering a farewell.

"Mum - I can't find words - you were so special to me. I wanted to be a perfect daughter for you - but I'm different," she sobbed, "You *are* my mum." She stuck her chin out. Her eyes shone pink. Each time she broke down we joined with our heart-torn feelings.

Cris remained closed off, dark. He stood rigid on the opposite side of the grave, his fists clenched.

A wreath of winter flowers, golden orange sprays of teardrop-like Cape Honeysuckle and deep, royal purple tibouchina's covered the shroud. Magnolia blossoms added soft white and mauve to the mix. These were Arie's favourite colours.

Her death cut deep, made me ache for news from mum and dad. Zoe, who was clinging to my side, popped the question.

"We've got to find mum, Bree. Can't you go to the hospital today? I want my mum home."

Chapter 3

Zoë always needed reassurance ever since the year dot. She was a funny little thing, often a royal pain. But now she hit a nerve centre I couldn't ignore. She became relentless; a verbal thug when something bothered her. I tried placating her about mum all evening after the burial.

Something in the back of my mind, call it intuition, told me wait before acting, to find out what was going down in Sydney. News bulletins, I sensed, were now heavily screened and reading between the lines proved difficult. Surely mum would phone soon.

"I think she's safe, Zoë. Mum's so busy and off duty she's exhausted." I knew it was scrappy guesswork. My efforts didn't satisfy her.

Ever since I'd ventured into Aries' room I suffered fear and depressed. The recesses of my loft offered little comfort. And late at night it terrorized my dreams shocking me awake.

I made self-examination in front of the mirror looking for any symptom that meant the beginning of the end, like red splotches and tenderness or infection-like weeping. Zoë's arrival in an over-sized pullover nudged me out of mind-lock.

"Why can't someone phone for mum if she can't do it?"

"Newscasters warned days ago - avoid calling hospitals. They've enough to worry about," I said. Later that evening, rummaging around, I found mum's mobile tucked deep in her carry bag. Still, she could use someone else's phone.

I resolved to do something bordering on the foolhardy, to suss out mum. The more news digested from television, the stronger my desire became.

Television and radio hotlines ran round the clock. These were swamped with callers, and each report added bad news. Restrictions were already established for food purchasing. I wondered what else could possibly complicate our lives more than that.

Regional fighting in Burma and Philippines ground to a halt after years of senseless slaughter. This and economic crises sent shock waves far beyond their borders. Runaway inflation put hungry people in grave danger as prices soared.

Famine and declining health conditions made the spread of this new plague so much easier. News analysts pointed to the movement of millions, desperate people streaming across Asia, spilling into the South Pacific.

According to one dour announcer, "*The Four Horsemen of The Apocalypse*" was loose. Fancy putting that comment to air. I figured there was a fifth rider. *Stupidity*.

Australia was under siege. Thousands were washing up on our northern shores, dead or alive, open season, and crocodiles bound to fatten up.

Jeff switched into high gear pre-dawn Friday.

"We can kill two birds with one stone, eh. If Cris and I do the Co-op store first we'll drive into the city and find mum."

"I'd rather you didn't say kill," I said.

We pooled all our money to the tune of nine hundred and fifteen dollars, a depressing amount, but credit cards were worth using. In all there was about six thousand dollars of purchasing power, if the cards were still accepted.

The city authorities placed a nine til one trading time for all food suppliers. Just four hours. Each quarter of the alphabet by surname had one hour to buy using coupons with ID. I couldn't figure out how anyone could enforce it.

The boys struck pre dawn Friday morning sneaking in behind Poppa Alvareze's Co-op store. Jeff and I regularly worked there so pleading for Pop's help gave our food situation a huge boost, which proves that who you know can pay big time.

Jeff, looking haggard and relieved said, "we figured on bein' sneaky, like in the dark, eh. Somebody saw us. Well, hell, you should've heard the commotion. They went ape-shit. Lucky we'd finished loading."

Cris said, "The buggers chased after us. Figure they'd lynch us."

This news made me twitchy. The high brick wall surrounding our home suddenly gained importance. Nobody could see what we were up to. Out of sight, out of mind.

Zoë and Millie found themselves dragooned into weighing up the food. Jeff and I decided this was a good way of taking their minds off Aries' death.

We then turned to Cris concerning our second objective, the trip to hospital. He was the only one who could legally drive with a P plate. But there were roadblocks closer in the city to slow the spread of virus and put a lid on feral activity.

"Jeff, if I go into town to find mum, you have to keep a watch on Zoë and Millie - and our supplies. They can't stay here alone. Cris, you drive me in as far as possible and wait. We'll take the bike in case."

"That makes sense," Jeff said. "But if there's any sign of violence you promise me - turn around and forget reaching mum for the time being."

"Do you think things are getting that much out of hand? I said, wishing, rather than wanting to face reality. Reports of riots and gang rampages were on the increase. Looting was widespread.

Both of us turned to see Cris's reactions. He sat stone silent to this point.

"What do you think?" Jeff said.

"What's wrong?" I asked. "Are you afraid to risk finding her?"

"It's not fear. I can cope. We haven't much fuel left, only one-eighth in the tank, or less, so if we go in the old bomb may not make it home again."

"You're telling me you've run out of diesel fuel? How could you be so damned stupid? I fumed." They've put a freeze on all petrol supplies. Midnight. Last night. Remember?"

Cris turned beetroot. He hated me bagging his dismal behaviour, which I found revolting. He'd put his foot in the cow pack, big time.

My first blue with him erupted two years back on a hot January afternoon. Everyone dragged off bargain hunting for fire sale specials, an event always slavishly followed by mum. I declined to go. Christmas wiped out my savings. Besides, I hated the masses of women turned storm troopers, all fixed on grabbing more than they needed. Tight-mouthed credit freaks on a mission, and heaven help anyone in their way.

Our narrow side courtyard with its high walls draped in masses of jasmine served as my outdoor hideaway, a slice of privacy ringed with hibiscus and palms.

Being vain at fifteen, I didn't want white skin splotches ruining the effect of my black cut-away party dress. This was all for the fantasy masquerade dance, my first serious social venture.

Masques were the latest in thing with my generation; a modern version of a fad dating to the seventeenth century, now, costumes were risqué, politically incorrect, full of teen angst.

I'd sun baked starkers in the courtyard. Tanning was easy. Dad said there was some "dark stuff" in the Welsh side of my genes, far back in time. "Iberian, dark and bedevilling," he said.

There is something deeply sensual about lying exposed. It was private and safe. Towel over face, I dozed off. The next sensation was an explosion of ice water across my body. Shrieking, arms and legs flailing, I flew into the air to stand transfixed, a spectacle.

Cris's maniacal laugh, no, hyena snigger, came from somewhere over the wall.

"You rotten little ratbag," I snarled. "Deadshit!" He'd been perving on me, and for how long?

From that day on, I carefully contained the event. I admit. There was a raw thrill in the pit of my stomach long after, but I, Bree Price, would even the score as I saw fit. He began to understand this, especially considering he catcalled, "don't get yer tits in a tangle." Called me "Ice Castle." I fumed, speechless, since I didn't have much to be tangled, and that hurt most. What I wanted to say remained just off the boil for later, like now.

Jeff knew when to duck. Cris's absence of mind bugged him too, but to me he was a wipe-out, a boofhead.

"So, mister, what do we do now?" I said tartly.

Jeff coughed, rather than say anything. Even he could be such a dill, sticking by this fool for whatever reason.

There was no luck in getting a taxi. Few were game to operate. That left me with two choices, walk or bike in. Jeff and I exchanged a short, sharp discussion about who would go. My emotion and logic finally won out. They'd guard the house and girls. Age packed weight. I ignored Cris as a candidate for hero status; sensed his puppy fat would slow me down. We agreed the vehicle should stay put for short trips, like back to Papa's.

"If there's any trouble, you promise to turn back without delay," Jeff said for the umpteenth time.

"I've no intention of being a heroine," I replied. "I'll leave tomorrow - Saturday, first light, rather than risk an afternoon trip now. There should be little traffic. Could reach the hospital by eight."

Sleep eluded me. I cursed suffering bouts of insomnia. Zoë added difficulty by crawling in for a cuddle. She writhed under

21

the covers. Ace added her own racket, groaning out dreams at the foot of the bed, regularly stenching the air. Dog walk neglect. I sat in the bedroom window alcove waiting for first dawn. It came sharp and cold. After a quick bite I readied to venture.

As I departed, Cris fumbled with a bundle of sandwiches, stuffing them in the saddle pouch and mumbled something that sounded like "good luck." A faint acknowledgment was all I could give, a tight smile short of sour.

Chapter 4

Setting out for town by bike tempted the fates, dangerous even on a good day. In the dawn it seemed easy streaking along Pittwater Road, now bearing only scraps of traffic. My calves ached under the hard grind, pumping up the twisty hill of Wakehurst Parkway. It looked a safer route to take. Much of this stretch still passed through bushland reserves. My fear of making contact with anybody bordered on manic.

It wasn't long before smoke, the distinct gum leaf stench of bush fire, made my eyes smart. Its origin came in sight minutes later.

There, slewed into the bushes, was the skeleton of a late model car, still smouldering. Fire crept down into the gullies beyond. No brigades tended it. Shortly after, four army vehicles passed heading for the city. The rear trucks carried soldiers with the telltale slouch hat. They were armed. One gestured to me, waving his arms implying I go back. He was shouting, but words dissolved in the thundering diesels. This did nothing for my state of mind. I caught a whiff of smoke and choked.

A few cars skulked by. One accelerated as if I came from the damned.

Something else out of place made me uneasy. Pedalling through Seaforth and descended to cross the Spit Bridge, what bothered me since starting surfaced. The sirens, which howled all day and night since my return, were silent. I heard the rattle of halyards on the yachts moored in the marina a hundred metres to my left.

There was a strange spatial, physical sensation, a discord between the freshness of the sea front, and the growing malaise of the city. Sailing craft always suggested freedom, the ability to go anywhere, to venture, something immediate and compelling, making the prospects of people in the city appeared bleak, trapped.

The slap and ring of yacht rigs pealed like shrill bells, but happy or sad, that metallic ring and flutter of lines beckoned me to break away. Some people were busy loading gear. A lone yacht slipped out of the anchorage.

Apart from patches of traffic, few people braved heading city bound. Manly Road, becoming Military Road closer in, saw some furtive human activity on foot. A few wore padded masks. I'd donned an improvised cover after crossing the Spit Bridge.

Some stores were brave enough to open.

On spotting what appeared to be a manned roadblock, I veered off using side streets before dashing across Military Road into Cammeray.

Twice before a faint, sickly smell stood high in my nose. It grew in strength as I peddled my way past Primrose Park overlooking Middle Harbour. Something dark lay beneath a park bench. Two Indian minas regarded the corpse, one exploring an eye socket.

Minutes later death confronted me directly beyond the barricades cordoning off road access to the hospital. I could see police and military vehicles and personnel strung out at every entry junction off the main road. All were dressed in sealed red uniforms, including face shields and a large breathing apparatus, like a grotesque gas mask.

Beyond, strewn across the hospital lawns were scores of bodies in tents. Some lay exposed to the sky. Many of these were shrouded. Others appeared lifeless, covered only by yellow emergency blankets. The bulky white suits of medical staff moved amongst them, as if in a dream world. Police car lights flickered blue. The overhead traffic light winked green, amber and red to traffic banished days ago.

Five of the men looked up, staring at me as if I'd come from another planet. One was a woman, judging from the feminine bulges of the suit, which was too small for her. She approached and was the first to speak, her voice muffled and remote.

"What are you doing coming to this hell hole? This is a 'Level Five' zone. The place is rotten with plague, love."

"I'm here to find my mother," I said, trying to be assertive, but sounding rather weak.

"My mum, Anika Price, works there," I pointed. "She hasn't phoned home in more than a week. We're worried she might be ill."

"Love. There's no way you can enter this place. You go in without protective gear and they'll bury you. See that pit over the far side?" She pointed. "It'll be full soon."

In contrast to her massive gear, my clothing suddenly felt terribly thin, exposed to anything air borne.

A bobcat gnawed away at the ground beyond the green encampment. Raw earth heaped high edged a trench line perhaps thirty metres long. I shivered.

"Would you please try to find her? We need to know she's okay."

"We're too busy for any personal contact," the masked woman said. Her voice carried the edge of authority and now a measure of annoyance. "We can't abandon our posts. There are strict orders to bar any unauthorised entry."

Two of the others moved forward. Facing three beings with bulbous visors overwhelmed. Red Aliens. Their imposing size dwarfed me.

The third interjected, "look princess, you can't hang around. It won't do any good. There's sick arriving all the time. Anything you touch around here could have the virus. The air." He waved.

"We want you out of here and away." The other stated.

"I've brought a note. Could one of you please find a way to give this to her?"

They were right. What could I do even if there was a way to get in?

A shift in wind brought a whiff of sickly smell, ranker than sewer stench, washing away flimsy notions I clung to about seeing her. My stomach threatened to heave. The woman took the note.

"I'll see it gets to administration. They'll pass it on. Now, get on your way."

I turned away angry, but relieved in one sense. Seeing her, even at a distance, would've been enough. Now, she seemed even more distant and home was suddenly too far away.

As we'd talked, several individuals arrived at the far barricades. These were ushered in to the hospital green by guards. Even at a distance two looked unwell, the subtle signs in their feeble walk foretelling their fate.

My thoughts shifted to Sascha. She lived in Newtown about ten kilometres away. Several phone calls Friday had ended in a cheerful "Hello, we are unable to take your call." I left an urgent text to contact me. The image of her smiling face on the phone screen and sound of her bubbly voice added to my sense of aloneness. My E-mail bounced back. I suddenly felt the urge to re-arrange Cris's testicles.

I retraced my route dejected. My head throbbed. Thinking made it worse.

Hunger? Food was the answer. Cris's sandwiches tasted especially good. Prawn salad was a surprise.

Once in a while I've felt particularly nervous about entering a street, especially an empty one at night, but in broad daylight? That wired feeling wouldn't go away. I pushed harder to make a swift return, again dodging the roadblock.

I narrowly avoided running into trouble rounding the downhill bend to the bridge. Several men were piling goods into vehicles. Two were still crossing the road. My sudden presence caught the two stragglers by surprise. One flailed around wildly as I veered behind him, streaking by. His blow clipped my back. The impact nearly knocked me onto the pavement. I braked, struggling to regain control, managed to keep momentum up and accelerated.

"Hey. Bitch! We'll catch ye in a minute," one bellowed.

Another goon hollered crudities. Catcalls.

That was enough to put fire under me, driving me up the long hill beyond the Spit Bridge. Thankfully, the drawbridge wasn't open for boat traffic.

At the top I was a lathered wreck. My butt ached. Legs wobbled. Shoulder throbbed. It was exactly like those wretched school cross-country runs where my stomach wanted to heave everything up, and the rest of the body didn't want to communicate.

There was just enough time to dive into a driveway with a box-hedged front when the looters roared by. My instinct proved right. They'd meant what they said.

Their thievery was done in broad daylight within a few blocks of the road barrier. I'm sure the few drivers within sight of me must've seen the attack, but nobody appeared to care. I'd spotted one police presence on the whole stretch of road. Where on earth were the rest?

The idea of carrying out this self-imposed mission proved more than foolhardy. I felt like a total dunderhead.

There were people home. The curtains moved. Nothing more. I'd learned. Fear was a great isolator.

Trembling, my clothing glued to me, the best strategy was to take a rest. Time would put some distance between the marauders and myself. It was then I felt the pain from his blow. Blood oozed from a gash just above my left shoulder blade, felt stickiness in the small of my back. "You damn bastards. You've ruined my sun top.

26

My cycling jacket!" I shouted, the only audience being a nervous dog limping by hastened by anger he thought was meant for him.

Around three I pushed off. Jeff and the others expected me back by now. It'd be stupid to be found out after dark when more raiders would prowl.

The Wakehurst Parkway still held light traffic. Maybe the police were setting up road checks further west. They'd be looking for troublemakers, that is, if there were enough police alive to enforce order. Police numbers were seriously down just from resignations.

Most of the route was now flat or downhill. Again, the stench of rotting flesh whiffed across the bushland from suburbs kilometres beyond. Acrid smoke columns told of new happenings, adding a menacing backdrop to an already bleak setting. A lone siren, the first all day, cut the air far away.

※

The same band of scum I'd evaded earlier appeared out of a gravelled side lane in an open jeep.

I'd begun the downhill plunge towards the coastal flatlands by Narrabeen Lake. They were too close. I heard burnout, gravel spitting and rattling. The chase was on.

How could anyone accelerate a bike fast enough with only legs for pistons? In tenth gear within seconds, the speedometer rose quickly above seventy kilometres as I careened downhill, the wind whistling in my ears. But it was useless trying to outstrip them. Jeering and catcalling, they accelerated onto broken bitumen, making the tires squeal protest. They bore down on me. If their bumper rammed my wheel I'd be gone, go head over heels.

"Where ya goin' bitch?" one taunted.

"I'm into feather fluff," another said. "Gotta taste watchya got, honey."

Adrenalin spiked, made me pedal harder. My stomach churned. I wanted to pee.

A tight curve bought a scrap of time as the driver lost control on gravel. The rest cursed as he braked hard, slewing around, then revved, accelerated. Whoops and howls filled the air. Tires shrilled.

"Yer cummin' off bitch - won't have to strip ye."

I barely noticed the land cruiser lumbering around the bend fifty metres ahead. In a flash I swung across its path, sweeping by the far right side, missed his fender, tore the side mirror away, grazed the guardrail, and hung on. I glanced, saw the driver veer towards the jeep.

A grating crash filled the air as the vehicles struck. Two piercing screams, one chopped off, the other an agonising howl like a banshee announced someone's departure. Hubcaps, glass and plastic sprayed the roadway. A chunk of metal skittered alongside. I knew one of the vehicles careened over the guardrail, shattering, tumbling end over end down the embankment.

There was no chance to make much out; rather, every bit of concentration was needed to stay on. Too weak to brake and gasping for breath, I reached flat ground, wobbled to a stop, and sat down in the dirt; realised I'd peed my pants.

A few cars skulked by in convoy; fearful faces pressed hard against glass. None stopped to offer help.

Minutes passed. The approaching scrape and grind of tortured metal on rubber told me one vehicle survived. The battered grill and fender of the land cruiser ground to a halt.

"What the hell did you pull that boner for, eh?"

There was only one irate guy that used boner in his speech.

"We'd better get the hell out of here. That lot are minced meat. Don't want cops on us," Jeff said.

Jeff and Cris hoisted me into the jeep, flung the bike on the roof rack. We raced off.

Homeward bound was fifteen minutes of distorted time with little said. The boys were subdued, buried in thought. The old troop carrier rattled along, smoking, metal howling on rubber at each turn.

My energy zeroed, leaving me in a dream-like state. Events of the past few hours swirled through my mind. Ghostly images of a hospital turned graveyard stuck, wouldn't fade. The hospital barriers loomed, mocked my hope of seeing mum in the flesh. Jeff cut my glumness short.

"You right, Breezie?"

This was his way of prying into my feelings, sussing me out when I looked sour. It was risky. He sparked warm memories of Sascha. She had called me Breezie in our gab sessions.

As we pulled into the driveway I said, more angrily than I intended, "we've got to do something. Living where we are is a dead end."

Both turned, taking a hard look at me.

Chapter 5

Zoë sat cross-legged, her back against the brass bed head. She helped peel off my top, examined the stain.

"So. Why'd you two waste fuel hunting for me? We agreed not to..."

"You were late," Jeff said, straining to remain patient. "Besides, don't you think there'd be stuff-all chance you'd shake those ratbags?"

"I intended leaving the road. The bike track we used—you know."

Jeff was annoyed and hurt. I knew better than criticise being rescued. Misery guts. Totally one eyed, that's me, but my body hurt, every muscle abused, especially my legs.

I remained still while Jeff sponged caked blood. He gingerly daubed the gash with ointment sealing it with a large bandage to hold the wound together.

"It'll scar. You're damn lucky he didn't shove it in. Look at your leather pack strap - the buckle."

I knew of the damage. "Sorry for being so miserable. It's a crap day."

I'd briefed them. In turn they cross-examined what was going on in Sydney, every detail, especially the number of victims. My opinion of the future impacted on them, imaginations did the rest. I'd managed one thin message handed to a woman, cold and faceless.

"What did you mean when you said *dead end*? Jeff persisted. "We've a lot of food stashed."

"And what happens when we run out?" I said. "It *will* happen, even with rationing. How long before we scrounge for scraps like everyone else? You described the Co-op shelves as empty?"

"What do we do? Wait? We could see if this blows over," he said. "Go bush?"

I persisted. "We can't stuff around. If we stay put you can bet we'll dig each other's grave. Animals carry this thing. Birds.

The wind. It's all around us. Look at me as our death warrant. It incubates."

Silence, except for fireplace hiss and crackle echoing down the hall. Sharp eucalypt scent cut the air.

Zoë broke in, sighed, lost in her mix of feelings. "I wish we could all sail away from this. I miss my friends. Can't go anywhere."

I dismissed Jeff's argument. "The bush is no answer. All the food and supplies, you couldn't fit it in. The jeeps' nearly sucking air thanks to..."

"Bollox to you." Cris said, sticking his nose around the door. Millie trailed. Both appeared fierce with one another.

I persevered. "We get more food, and quickly."

Cris fidgeted, tapped. "There's no point in leaving here."

Millie nodded automatically. That vacant brain was a marvel I couldn't come to terms with.

"Are we? Crap on." I said, jumping up, ignoring the pain. "How could we stop looters taking every scrap we have?"

"Cris and I'll make defences," Jeff said, trying to argue the un-arguable. "There are rolls of chicken wire. We rig up the walls like netting. I've got an old recurve bow with some arrows."

"I've dad's old shotgun, a slingshot and my crossbow," Cris said.

"That's illegal, dummy," I said.

"That's illegal," Cris mimicked. "Who gives a damn?" He turned away, muttered. "Fucking know-it-all."

Legal lines were beginning to distort, so how far could our actions go beyond the norm? Law? We'd just left four guys mangled, most likely dead. I felt shock, but not remorse.

That night I collapsed in deep sleep. The council of war continued next day over scorched pancakes, maple syrup and whipped cream.

※

"Food. This is numero uno on our list, whether we stay here or not," I said. "Maybe we can hold out for four or five months before hitting bottom. We'll starve." The girls gaped wide-eyed. My lips set tight. None argued.

The boys ventured for supplies early next morning. They managed to purloin extra goods from what Papa squirreled away. He'd hoarded tinned beans, flour and vital toiletries for us. Ten packs of pads and tampons were a welcome surprise. The girls screamed with laughter as they measured and secreted items away. Neither shared the joke. I couldn't tickle or threaten what it was that sent them rolling on the floor.

Millie and Zoë eventually grabbed centre stage with a tally sheet. Sitting cross-legged, both rattled off encouraging figures.

Speaking of figures, Millie's tired sun top reflected nature's hormonal binge.

I wished my genes would do something equally spectacular. A hay fever sneeze on her part guaranteed them an audience.

All grizzled, but agreed to rationing. If we followed a strict diet it meant survival for several more weeks.

Millie's awkward little girl voice, I thought of as 'Barbie-like', tersely summed up the situation. "We've got nearly four hundred and fifty kilos of food. Most of it I don't like, except the box of chocolates from mum's birthday." She lapsed into staring at her empty breakfast dish. "It *is* diet time," she said.

Millie humour? Feeble. I raised an eyebrow at this notion, shrugged, and turned away.

Zoë's brassy voice chimed in sharp contrast, striking me as funny. "We'll have to become gourmet cooks. A kilo a day keeps starvation away."

We chuckled. It was an echo of my grand dads' warped saying, "An apple a day keeps fartin' away." I wondered if starvation would do the same.

"Maybe we'll tighten our belts til there aren't any notches left," Millie whinged."

To my surprise, the following morning the boys raised the existing barrier to three metres high with an addition of chicken wire stretched across the front wall and down each side as far as materials permitted. The brick wall reflected my parents' desire for privacy, and to us became a fortress. Old two-by-three timbers with bits nailed on for length made enough height for the uprights. Hex head bolts screwed into large wooden plugs sunk in the wall made these frames secure enough to resist being easily toppled. The tangle of wire, twine and rope had the appearance of a mad spider's production. Struts were positioned at right angle to stiffen the uprights. Anybody trying to push the mesh down would find it tough going.

Our weapons materialised as an antique Remington, single barrelled 410 gauge shotgun with six shells of unknown vintage.

The recurve bow, arrows and string were battered and frayed. Cris's real baby was the crossbow. He bragged it was powerful enough to send a bolt straight through a body.

Fat chance, I thought.

By day three's efforts we had a makeshift defence.

※

That night dad phoned from Switzerland. Jeff took the call. We were ecstatic, but anticipation and desire to hear his voice inevitably killed my patience. Jeff droned on in his peculiar short-hand of "yeps" and "nopes," delivering a patchy picture of our plight. I snatched the phone away.

"Dad. It's Bree. I can't contact mum. We're stuck, holed up here. Don't know what to do."

"Babs, you've got to get out of Sydney, and soon. The plagues' on the loose. It'll happen there the way we've coped it. Everything's falling apart in Europe. A royal bloody mess." His voice resonated anxiety.

"Please come home?"

"I can't fly—no regular flights. It's chaotic. Everyone's terrified, either holing up, or running around spreading it."

"But, how can we get away?" I pleaded.

"What's wrong with the old cutter? It's a strong boat. The sails and engine are reasonable - well, fair. Use it to find isolation. Remember my charts in the study, the pilot charts for the Pacific? Oh, there's a new battery in the garage."

"We've never been far out to sea, only up coast. We'd be like sardines in a tin, and a damn sight unhappier."

"It's safer to put to sea than wander along the coast with all the reefs. You don't want people contact. Remember the tiny island I used to tell you about where your mum and I had our honeymoon?"

"Motu - umm, what?" I said stunned.

"*RIVA*. Motu-Rivas' a small island south of the Society Island group, very isolated."

I remembered dad showing a speck on the South Pacific pilot charts I'd mistaken for a cockroach dropping, a miniscule one.

"It's so far away, thousands of kilometres across the ocean, a pin dot. You expect us to find that?"

"The Global Positioning System should still be working.

That'll do you. Jeffrey has that tiny GPS unit we used for bush walking in Tasmania. See if you can loan old Harry Trumble's sextant and navigation books."

"I'm still not convinced, dad. There are five of us now, with Cris and Millie. Arie died of the plague."

I neglected to frighten him by what I'd done out of sheer ignorance.

There was stunned silence. "We're all living in our home. Theirs is contaminated."

The rest hung glued to scraps, every snippet of information. Pacific? A speck of an island?

Dad covered a lot of ground about the disease, food and boat talk. I knew he was super stressing about us, begging me to consider escape. He became apologetic for not being able to get home. His voice in itself injected new hope, lifted my spirit. Hanging up sickened me.

The upside-down side of it was his insistence we leave home, and fast. That put me in a bind. In the end instinct and fear dictated we abandon home.

I resented being shouldered with the headache of Cris and Millie. Could I survive them in tight quarters on a small yacht, or anywhere for that matter?

Over the next few days we tightened security. The perimeter was reinforced with anything likely to hinder penetration, including a comical network of transparent nylon fishing lines attached to tin cans. Each was designed to crash to the patio if disturbed.

Every night and early morning either a curious possum or magpie toppled a booby trap. It gave us the jitters, creeping around with a flashlight on a moonless night looking for culprits, like 'forty-four home', a version of hide-and-seek. Cris tripped over one of his own creations, landing in a rose bush. I learned how little he liked gardening.

We decided to take watch shifts of two hours from ten until six in the morning. Zoë was relegated to the Sandman's care, despite her protests.

Marauders came to our neighbourhood around two a.m. This night a fresh wind scattered leaves across the courtyard, made branches rattle. We heard a truck revving beyond the hill.

There was little to see in the murk. Minutes later, somewhere beyond, a growing commotion of muffled shouts erupted. Piercing howls walls couldn't contain spelled disaster. It rose to a pathetic, prolonged howl of outrage, and suddenly stopped.

Silence claimed the night, stretching tension, and our sense of dread. Shadows played across the wall, reaching out, as if mocking us. We were imprisoned within our cage and scared stupid. Flames soon silhouetted the skyline, bathing the area in angry light and acrid smoke.

Wailing sirens announced the arrival of fire trucks and police. We remained fixed, unwilling to stick our necks out.

A permanent pall of smoke settled over the coastal region, while the sickly sweet stench of death, the foulest of odours, forced its way in.

Our scant observations were useless to the police. Encased in bulbous blue suits, they stumbled and mumbled exhaustion. Demoralised.

"It'll be us next," Zoë said, matter of fact.

None of us spoke.

Chapter 6

The boys continued barricading us in, assumed we'd stay. Dads' anxiety and advice were at odds with the way we were coping, clouding emotions. The more they dug in the harder it'd be to accept any other solution. Staring at the boat swinging on its mooring in the bay below did nothing to quell my fears.

The catalyst that changed our mind-set lay within, having already invaded our sanctuary under our noses.

Cris did a door lock check the morning after the raiders came. He'd found a broken pane from the french doors leading onto our private courtyard. The following day someone raided the fridge, plundering food. Missing sausages and crumbs made Jeff and I focus on Millie as chief suspect.

"No way!" she whined, wide eyed. "I'm on a diet, practicing for the real thing, Bree."

Both needed a diet after Arie's exotic cooking.

We did a search. Found our rat.

A smear of sauce on dads' study door handle gave away the villain. He lay asleep on the couch next to a dead computer. Food scraps littered a side table. Picky eater, I thought.

Our quarry was the image of what city life washed up these days. A shock of long, unkempt hair framed his sallow, underfed face; a straggling wisp of juvenile beard revealed a weak chin. Shadow rimmed his eyes, accentuating life wasted, like the army of drugged human refuse seen hanging around downtown parks. A tattered leather jacket, once a quality garment, stressed his slight features.

Jeff reached out to poke a foot clothed in a frayed orange sock; the other mouldered green. "Hey!"

Our apparition sat bolt upright, eyes unfocused, as if not knowing where he was.

"Yer trespassin' kid. Yer' a thief. How'd you get past our snares, eh?"

He hesitated, said sleepily, "Jeez. Needed a place to hole up

35

- not frickin' safe where I came from."

"How'd you get here?" Jeff accused.

"Walked, man. Got into your 'dive' from the water side." He yawned. "The reserve. Easy."

We'd been outflanked, our defences rendered useless by a mere weed.

"You're gettin' out," Jeff said.

"Haven't had scoff for two days. Good sausages," he said, feigning an apology.

He looked up directly into Millie's soft, blue eyes. Avoided mine. I sensed his cunning. City instinct honed to a sharp edge.

"We'll feed you, then you go," I said, matter of fact. "What's your name?"

"Malcolm. The Olivers of Newtown," he jested waving a hand.

"And your parents?"

"Ain't got any alive," he said evasively, fixing me with a sad, mocking smile.

The more we probed the less dangerous he became, except as a possible plague carrier. Should we eject him? If we did so, what fate would he suffer? How hostile did we have a right to be?

Millie already flushed, purring, and Zoë wasn't far behind. Malcolm was the newest stray, like a manged dog with a bad limp. And he did limp.

The idea of having him as excess baggage was intolerable, messing up our situation. I felt Cris would spite me if I froze this guy out. Jeff remained hostile, glowered, so we prevailed. Malcolm slouched out of the house the way he came, but not before we gave enough food for the next few days. Millie offered clean socks, and too much attention.

※

The question of escape reared its ugly head.

"Dad says use the old boat. Is it seaworthy enough to take us a long way?" I said.

Jeff shrugged. "Maybe. He did some repairs. The sails are scabby. It's big."

She was Elysius, an eleven-metre long, beamy ferro- cement cutter, dad's escape machine that never escaped.

She was once a pretty boat, sporting a clipper-like bow, white hull and cream topsides. Teak trimming added a warmth and charm. She'd become shabby with neglect. Her single mast was massive, rigged in stainless steel.

Elysius was named after the fabled Greek plains of Paradise where wine, golden women and song were the norm.

Diplomatic work overseas in the *United Nations* often kept him away, putting his dreams as far away as the Elysian Plains.

Our hope of escape was to cast ourselves on the ocean. The notion of leaving land for the deeps brought heaps of bleating from Cris and Millie.

Seasickness dogged both on the one short trip they'd made with us to Port Stephens. Millie's face transformed becoming a horrible grey-green against the red bucket. She'd bussed home. Cris hung on, typically macho. I felt sympathy for him then, before his ice water stunt.

I knew both panicked, were desperate to remain behind, prepared to go it alone, but if we threatened sailing off they'd be terrified into risking the voyage. Millie would just have to tranquillise that peanut mind until she was catatonic.

When pressed for a decision she resignedly said, "If I'm roaring drunk I won't know I'm sea sick."

"Brilliant idea," I said.

Jeff lifted the conversation tone and topic. "Five on board is a squeeze. Nowhere to get away."

"Our rations will change all that," I said. " We'll have a new emaciated look. Check us out sideways and you won't see a thing."

"Knock it off. We need room. Another boat?" he said.

"Oh, don't be ridiculous." I said.

"Remember old Harry's boat Limpet? It's been for sale over a year. We can't buy it. Maybe we can borrow it like we did when Elysius was out of action."

"But it's old. It leaks," I said, "besides, how could we stay together at sea? Who'd sail in a sieve?"

"Not me!" the other three said in perfect chorus. We howled with laughter—needed to laugh.

"Then we sail in Elysius," I said. It came out rather more a statement of fact than how I actually intended it to be taken.

"Can it carry everything like enough water and fuel?" Cris said.

"Full, she's got about seven hundred litres of water and three

37

hundred for diesel," Jeff said.

"For five of us using maybe two litres each a day we've got about two months worth. No showers included," I said. "We'll just have to shower and do laundry in public whenever it rains."

"I'll need a shower curtain," Millie said, her face stricken with thoughts, eyed Jeff, glared at Cris.

If it weren't such a serious situation, the cornered look plastered on Millie and Cris would crack me up.

"Transparent, I bet," Jeff said, winking at her.

"We've got to think about packing everything useful on board. Food. Clothing. Tools," I said. "There's no point in hanging around here much longer."

Sorting gear became a headache. Zoë and Millie succeeded in creating a clothes mountain.

"This isn't good enough," I said, casting a jaundiced eye over Zoë's collection. Millie's carnival of fashion statements defied description.

"Pick a dozen items each. No more." I ordered, hands on hips.

"Aw, Bree. Get a life."

"Or I'll cull the lot for you," I glared. Round one over, nine to go. They'd smuggle things on board.

On the third dawn of preparations, Malcolm's scruffy profile appeared slouched against the ramshackle jetty shed. At a distance he blended in with the wharfs' weathered ruins, hair like matted strands of decayed seaweed. He slept, a battered haversack under his arm.

"Why are you still here? We gave you food."

His eyes opened, slowly climbed my frame, staring into me sleepily, pausing, as if peeling away layers of my person.

"Yer real tall. Nice legs. Like the short-shorts." He grinned.

I bit my lip. Said nothing. Felt my face flush. He made me feel physically frisked.

"What do you want from us?" I said.

"Heard yer leavin' town. I'm desperate to go with ye'. Ain't goin' back to that bloody hole," he said, tongue clicking. "Got no mates in Sydney. Nowhere."

My resolve to be rid of him sagged. His whole seedy bearing spoke of experiences beyond his age. It was harder to say no when death already distorted our thinking. He was even more a refugee than we were about to become, and a damn sight worse off. Whatever his faults, if given a chance, he must have some redeeming features.

Still. Millie presented worry. Those two were instantly in heat, her hormones a chemical bomb.

Much to the annoyance of Jeff and Cris, the arguments shifted in Malcolm's favour with the proviso he'd be dropped off at the first safe landfall. Maybe New Zealand's North Island. That feeble notion could prove to be a bad joke.

Chapter 7

Everyone worked in fits and starts as if uncertain about the reality of leaving.

Malcolm drifted about in a daze. I'd lay a bet he was doped. Cool Hand Mal simply didn't want to move his scrawny arse except when he sensed our anger.

"We shouldn't move supplies in broad daylight. No sense in advertising how much we've got," Jeff said.

That made sense. No telling how many prying eyes we'd attract. Jeff kept a close watch on board Elysius by day while the rest of us ferried gear by night. The dinghy proved miserably unstable loaded up, lost a whole crate of gear overboard including a camera and laptop.

Nature got in the way by blowing up another southwester off the Snowy Mountains, chilling us back into winter and brought the stench of death. Rain fell that night, drumming on the corrugated roof.

I realised we lived an illusion. Our home, for maybe the last precious moments, became a warm cocoon with the fireplace glow lifting our thoughts. Faces appeared more content.

Malcolm sat near Millie, who was just back of me. Animal magnetism at work, I mused acidly. Glanced. Saw them lean, strong as gravity.

I strained to hear scraps of his raw communion.

"Had a trail bike," He said. "Ever been on one?"

Millie shook negative, bit her lip, eyes bright.

"It's a gas in tight leathers, spread across the saddle, feelin' all that power between yer legs - rippin' up a trail through bush. Makes me hungry fer more."

Malcolm whispered something in her ear. It must be dripping hot. Millie blushed. The way she leaned forward, he feasted on her smell, and the route to conquest, which lay wide open. How could she splash on that Desert Heat? It could kill a blowfly.

She saw a chance to break out of boredom. He displayed cal-

40

culation intent on breaking in, plundering her innocence.

"Not if I have anything to do with it." I seethed, eyeballing both. That's the ultimate screw-up, having a sexually aroused motorcycle freak for crew.

"Millie, dearest. Find the list of food you made, Zoë too."

She broke away from his fawning gaze, I judged, relieved to escape the pressure. Maybe she did have some common sense. Zoë ran off with her into the kitchen, but not before our eyes engaged. *Zorro* quickly picked up my vibes. She was my devoted agent, a snoop.

Ace tagged along, wouldn't go near Malcolm. He'd tried patting her and wore a set of tooth marks. She growled any time he came within arms reach. Bloody good. Double agents with a bite.

Around eleven the wind sharpened, buffeted walls, rattled windows, and bent trees. Halyards shrilled against masts far below in the cove. Surf boomed an ominous chorus in the distance, like a deep drum roll.

Restless dreams of Sascha's face and scraps of our shared experiences eddied about all night.

"I've never had a friend like you," echoed so clearly, as if she was there in the parlour.

Maybe she'd fled to West Australia where we first met. That wild possibility excited. Imagined her striding through rugged bushland.

Sascha thrived off freaky songs, much like my taste for fantasy poetry. I tried writing a few lines, but nothing happened. It's too hard etching images about depression.

Channel Two *News Express* gave no joy. Massive death tolls and reports of civil breakdown, riots, looting and atrocities globally finally drove us to selective watching rather than an endless collage of disturbing images. We tried A.B.C. radio each morning for a fresh update.

Some programs took to focusing on preventative medicine, which added to the confusing mix of trivia. Some of the remedies offered, including the most exotic herbal concoctions fresh from China, bordered on macabre.

My passing experience with the old Aborigines returned to haunt me. They'd offered a potion seemingly out of nowhere. Could ages old folk remedies have an answer to what ailed us now? How much did those two ancients have stored in their memories? Once we packed, I resolved to take a close look at the parcel now wrapped in oilskin.

Laboratory staff in many regions already suffered decimated. No promise of an antidote appeared in the offing. Authorities stated finding a solution took top priority.

❋

At last mum phoned, sharpening tensions.

"Bree, I'm still at the hospital," she said.

"Are you coming home soon? We're freaking out here." My eyes blurred, sinuses clogged.

"They won't release any of us - those still able to stand. *Martial Law* is enforced now love. Curfews. They've shot raiders on sight, shoot anything after dark."

Her voice inflections, though brave, were wooden unlike her usual sunny patter.

"I'm not well, Bree. They've dosed me up with speed- pills for so long. Can't work. I'm exhausted, dizzy."

"Those who aren't standing? Do you mean other staff have died?"

"Yes, too many. Some took their protective gear off. The heat got to them. Too few cleaners left alive now so *we* disinfect wards. Others went 'troppo', or wouldn't come in."

"Can't you escape?"

"I only got your message by accident two days ago," mum added, ignoring my plea.

"I sent a message through a guard two weeks back." I explained the trip to the hospital, and our circumstances, just the bare bones, and dads' call. News of Arie's death brought no tears. I knew she'd crack if we began sobbing. Arie was the closest of mums' friends.

"Did you, anybody, touch anything in her room - or her body?"

"No, mum. I stayed well away from her. We sprayed disinfectant at a distance. Only went in once. I used a mask. Honestly."

A chilled silence on the other end spoke volumes for my stupidity. "I feel just fine, mum. No chills, sneezing or fever." Something inside said "yet." I knew mum was demoralised now.

"All of you leave, get out. Do as your dad says. He's right. You and Jeffrey know how to sail. She's a sea-kindly boat. Get old Harry Trumble to give you a hand, check her out. He's a good mechanic. And take care of Zoë, she's vulnerable, and Millie too."

42

I pleaded, "Where are you going if we leave?"

"I'll risk driving to your aunt Maggies' in Rutherglen. I can bully a driving pass from the authorities somehow. She's running a winery with her new man. If worse comes to worse, I'll hole up in a fortified wine vat, get roaring drunk," she laughed. I couldn't help but join in.

Now, feeling a mess, her determination to carry on perplexed me. Anika Price possessed powers to recon with, even with the world sliding towards oblivion. I found it hard to measure up to her standards; couldn't match her compassion towards others.

"Bree. Bury our valuables under the garden shed. The brick flooring will lift. Use dad's big toolbox. Wrap it in plastic and hide it deep."

Zoë and Jeff vied for support from mum.

As usual Jeff rambled in stock shorthand. "Nope. Yep. The old jeep. No diesel. Maybe."

Zoë raved on, an earnest chatterbox, until Ace was mentioned. "But mumm!" she wailed, "Ace is family. We can't let her go. I'd rather stay than leave Ace behind." Her anxiety magnified the following silence. I wondered what tact mum was using to convince Zoë her devoted pal wouldn't fit on a boat. Her face crumpled in misery.

My heart ached for her. I avoided her stare, expecting my support. Ace flopped in the corner, head on paws looking an unruly patchwork. Those baleful eyes canted to one side, watched Zoë expectantly, as if to say, "what's up?"

Zoë whispered, "I'll do what I can, mum." She passed the phone as if it were hot. "This is cactus." She growled, running off, Ace scrabbling in pursuit. She joined Millie who pawed through food lists. I let them be, each stirred up, keen to do anything distractive.

Mum and I mumbled over preparations. Medical things. We phone kissed farewell. My feelings were at once, giddy, elated, but in the end, hollow. Old furies about her pushiness dissolved as I realised her real value in my life.

In the night the wind moaned, rain streamed sideways in unruly waves across windows.

Jeff and Cris, with Malcolm shadowing in tow, went in search of dads' maps buried somewhere beneath the debris in his den.

This offered a window, a chance to be alone. I needed time

to sort out some of the emotional baggage piled up over the last fortnight.

Staring into the storms' murk, I couldn't begin to imagine the dimensions of grief others faced. We'd been lucky so far.

It looked like the human race actually faced doom, a rapid extinction like the thousands of defenceless species we'd trampled underfoot. Natures' crucible would sweep through us without mercy. This Virus melted all arrogant notions about our permanency, eating away the whole teetering foundation of global community to reduce us to a few squalid remnants.

Dad said something about *Gaia*, the essence of nature. "One day it'll be the last 'over', as in cricket, and nature will 'clean bowl' us out." I'm sure he meant we were in for a hell of a drubbing. Years back I thought he was simply funny, overly pompous, evangelical. *Gaia* controlled us, both provider and taker. There was nothing else that mattered other than learning to harmonise with her. Nothing.

Dads' defence of the Amazon ecosystem through the *United Nations Environmental Council* was one that left him drained of hope. The pillaging of rare and fragile habitats continued. It was a vicious irony. Greed unlocked a Demon from some mysterious garden. Dad's efforts to slow the destruction kept him away from us then. Now he was bitter in Europe, bound for Africa.

Suffering insomnia, I prowled toying with things I'd made in crafts. What possessions do you pick for safekeeping, burial? Jewellery choice was easy, masks, a must. I would keep all of it. But the wardrobe was sheer agony. In the end I triple bagged the best in heavy plastic for burial.

My jersey outfit, the one I'd worn to the masque ball, brought packing to a halt. Peeling off, I slipped the outfit over my head, feeling its silkiness slide over my skin, the turtleneck fitting snugly, sagging just loose enough to leave the throat free.

I ran my hands slowly down, smoothing out the fabric against my hips to where it stopped, mid thigh. I'd made the buy of the century. Cut away below the breast line, it left my belly bare to the hipbone. That offered my best shape. The back was largely cut away to the base of the spine. Tanned skin glowed against its blackness. It was delicious.

A touch of 'war paint' on lips, eyebrow liner and deep green nails sharpened features. I brushed and piled my hair, letting a small, silvered tail hang behind, two honey wisps curled down each temple to the shoulder. Arabian earrings, combined with a delicate necklace of finely wrought beads of jade and gold complimented the outfit. Mum had bargained for those in her market crawling travels in Turkey. High heels and the sleek cat mask, fluoro whiskered, made me look out of a surreal fantasy. My alter personality metamorphed.

Zoë dragged herself in looking like a war orphan.

"Scrow." I rasped, making a half-hearted hiss.

She remained deadpan, watched.

"It's not fair. Ace can't be left to die. That's what'll happen," she said. Zoë's voice rose, "Nobody's going to put her down."

"We'll think of something," I said, annoyed there were no easy answers.

I attempted a seductive walk, swaying in front of the mirror, more to draw her away from worry, rather than indulging, struggling to be sensual.

"You look cool in black, Bree, like a vampire."

I fixed her with the telltale pose of Cat Woman, devourer of especially naughty brats. Her eyes lit up. Mouth pursed. Body tensed.

"Yeowl. Yer dinner." I screeched.

Pandemonium. High heels flew over the bed canopy, and the chase was on, under, over the bed. She shrieked for joy, scrambling every which way. Growling, I'd plunged onto hands and knees in pursuit. Zigzagging, we left a trail of mayhem.

"Cat needs juicy bits. Eat."

"What's this display all about, eh?" Jeff said. "A wildcat?"

"Damned if it's a tramp cat on heat," Cris chuckled.

That sarcasm stopped me dead in my tracks. Hair splayed across my face, I looked up.

"You're on some sort of binge, eh? Partying?" Jeff chided. He rasped, "If you can spare the time we've got dads' maps and a few books. It's important to plan this thing, see what we're up against. By the way, your bum is entirely on review."

I coloured, struggled to remain cool. I got up casually, and with a deep breath slowly adjusted my hair.

Zoë, quickly sensing my mood, planted her freckled grin where Cris couldn't ignore it. He gave ground.

"We've got some navigation stuff to look at," he offered, avoiding my gaze. I detected a fleeting smile. Defusing tension?

Back to abnormal? Whatever the case, my private bubble world vanished.

As Zoë and I descended to the study, the lyrics to a Neo-Gothica dirge filtered through the night's bluster. *"Main-linin' through the Pillars of Hercules, it's enough to make yer brain squeeze."* Strange as it may be, it accentuated my feelings of responsibility for the rest. Our collective efforts, decisions, right and wrong, would determine weather we survived or not. Like the sailors of the ancient world, passing through the fabled *Pillars of Hercules* between Spain and Africa, our risks were bound to be seriously scary.

"You took the high road, I took no road, never wanted load," Gothica wailed like all-knowing, cool gurus.

This whole mad situation shoved a 'reality sandwich' in our faces. We'd have to take it on, master it, no matter what the cost.

Chapter 8

Jeff prowled the pilot charts while Cris hung back, fidgeting, feigning interest. He continued sending out bad vibes about the ocean voyage.

"Suffer, baby, suffer," I whispered as I mulled over trip problems, studied dad's sketchy map of the island.

"Motu-Riva is an awfully long way," Jeff said. "Looks like maybe six thousand kilometres as the crow flies. Umm, never knew a crow to fly straight."

The wind direction arrows and the wind speed feathers located on the maps worried. There was doubt about the area just north and east of North Island, New Zealand. We'd briefly talked about using the cape as a touch point heading east. The storm frequency percentages for gales, force eight and higher, which were located in the middle of each grid square, were scary. We could reasonably expect at least one or two bad storms. We'd never survive a force nine or ten gale, twelve being the ultimate monster on the Beaufort Scale.

"Maybe go south to the 'Roaring Forties', then head east for a faster trip," Jeff said, matter of fact. "Winds mostly blow east."

"Not on your life. Don't bull me about any wind labelled Roaring," I said, knowing there were 'Howling Fifties' and 'Screamin' Sixties', icebergs and all. Southern seas were bone chilling enough for any soul, besides, my body craved heat.

"Percentages say there's a chance to miss some storms by heading roughly along the thirty degree line of latitude, eh," Jeff said, studying reactions. "The ocean current runs due east too. See the blue arrows? That would push us along."

Cris grizzled, "What's the wavy red lines across North Island?"

"Those are paths of past big storms. Big seas. Bucket time," I smiled, reading his fear.

Millie emerged wearing a struggling halter-top with the logo 'Eyes Up' across the top. She wore a soiled apron bearing a motif of a frightened Sorcerer's Apprentice hauling buckets of water.

It was clear she'd heard. She stared, mesmerised.

"It's so deep - the ocean," she said, as if discovering this fact for the first time.

"One hundred, one thousand, all the same," Jeff said, full of bravado.

"I'll puke out there," she threatened.

"What's brewing in the kitchen, dumpling?" Cris said. "May as well enjoy eating while we can."

"How timely, Crissie Pork Chops," I said.

Millie fingered Cris, "beef stroganoff."

For a moment I couldn't help visualising her eating it then spewing into the bucket.

"What's with the navigation gear, Jeff?" I said.

"We've dads' Global Position System and radio direction finder. Dad said we need a sextant for taking sun and star elevations, to tell our latitude and longitude."

"Can't you simply use the GPS?" I said.

"I'm guessing it's risky," Jeff said. "What if it fails? You know how fussy electronics are around salt water. It works now."

Malcolm arrived tagged with Zoë the ear bender.

We broke off talking navigation in favour of Millie's tucker.

She'd made a supreme effort, laying the dining table with silver, china and candlelight. Clusters of pink camellias filled a bowl in the middle.

I was stunned. Smiled. "I'm impressed, Millie."

She beamed, fingered Cris again.

We converged on the table. Zoë wedged between her and Malcolm as he made a bid for closeness.

The rich aroma of stroganoff laced with herbs filled our senses, triggering a feeding frenzy, much clattering of plates. Her hot garlic bread bettered any I'd eaten.

Zorro nattered back and forth between the two over Ace's training. Malcolm's face reflected suffering. Millie laughed and raved. It was wonderful to see my antidote working, frustrating his advances. He'd have to pull it off solo. I smirked.

※

Dawn crept; rays stealing across bed brass; bird feuds in the garden. Feathered panic. Storm clouds lay scattered northward. The wind fussed in gusts in a final display before dying. A September sun warmed by mid morning as we dug two pits.

The treasure burial finished, we spread surplus soil across the garden, disguised our digs with leaf mulch. There was comic relief in it as Zoë ceremonied the duck Boris next to my things.

That night loading supplies became a fixation. I studied marine activity as a few boats passed at a distance, running lights on, headed for who knows where.

Nobody thought anything of Jeff's tinkering with the engine, but the following morning he informed us it wouldn't turn over. Good fortune saw Old Harry, who lived a few doors over, still active and willing to help. At eighty-five his collective knowledge was prodigious. The two of them puttered over the diesel, giving Jeff the cunning rationale to delegate scrubbing the hull to us.

Marine slips were out for cleaning her. People contact. It was necessary to use goggles, flippers, gloves and scrapers and scour the bottom from waterline to keel. Cris and I jobbed as seals.

The hull presented a marine park festooned in patches of razor sharp barnacles, sea squirts and a forest of waving slime. September water was cold by my standards. We lacked wetsuits. In gasping bouts we dove and scraped amidst flashing fish keen to feed from falling morsels. Cris wallowed about before mastering the motion needed to scrape between the main keel and wing keels.

I suffered cramped toes and masses of purple-red patches all over my body. Four hours effort gave me a blinding headache and sore nipples. Even with gloves on, both of us suffered sliced knuckles and knees.

We shivered in the cockpit, hot chocolate cradled in hands, occasionally sympathising with one another's miseries.

He'd have a great body, minus the puppy fat. Pity about the roll. In shorts he was more powerful looking than I could recall. His facial lines were strong, much like a young Patrick McGoohan, the actor, only Sri Lankan dark. Cris's jet hair hung heavy with water, curly.

Such a git. Still, he wasn't being an ass today, even complimenting my agility, of all things.

Back on land we set about boarding up the houses with all manner of planking. Cris came up with the idea of screwing boards onto window frames and sealing the heads.

"That's a great idea," I said. "Mum and dad can admire your

workmanship—that's not me being sarcastic." Cris studied me, smiled.

His eyes were the deepest brown. Something arrogant and brattish lurked within, but when he managed a grin I loved their sparkle. They'd melt grannies. Terrify mothers with daughters.

The following day we spent organising storage.

Zoë and I braved swimming back to shore. We didn't say much, and fled to the shower, which we often shared. Luxuriating under the warm needle spray, and back scrubbed with a sponge, we eventually sat cross-legged on the shower floor facing one another. It was a way of opening up to share gossip. The shower cascaded, misting everything in a thick blanket.

"Are you much afraid of an ocean trip?" I said, blowing drips off my nose.

"Not if you aren't," she said abruptly, wiping shampoo off her nose. "Well, yes, a bit, Bree. No, a lot."

Silence. I waited. My love for her swelled every time she fixed me with those serious eyes.

"It's like a great hole. I imagine huge, empty spaces. That last storm made me dream of giant waves, like the old movie we saw, Super Storm, or something like that. Can't be that big, can they?"

"Those are a movie makers' freak waves. Huge storms can make some big ones," I said displaying confidence, but knowing my ignorance. Occasionally two waves could combine, catching a yacht unawares, broach it, smash cabin tops in. Rogue waves were the kind that plucked unawares rock fishermen off their perches by the dozen every year. They swallowed boats too, so I read.

"We'll try to be extra cautious. There'll always be someone on watch steering. The boat's really solid."

"How long will it take to get to Motu - whatever it is?"

"Motu-Reeva". I said, sounding it out. "Jeff says it means Sky Island. Maybe five - six weeks, Cris figures."

"Cris?" Zoë exclaimed, "he doesn't like water, so how'd he know?"

"I've known him to indulge in it," I said.

Zoë laughed.

"Yeah, he and Millie are out of their minds. They're already suffering," I said, evading the issue of storms. September blew its brains out. Weather was so cranky these days. Storm one day, frying hot the next.

"Mum says the island's dripping in food. And it's warm," I said.

Zoë fixed me with that 'oh, I've heard that one before' look. We towelled off in the bedroom.

"What're your feelings about Malcolm?" I asked, masking my malice.

"I've changed my mind ages ago. He's a slug. Imagine him kissing? Eew. Slobber. Spreading disease. Did you see his tongue? Eeew!"

"You spoke for him," I said dressing.

"So did you, umm, some." Zoë said, hands on hips. "Millie's grovelling sort of bugged me. I'm impulsive. Now he's fair game." She shrugged, screwed her face up. Smiled.

Jeff arrived carrying an aged leather case and an odd triangular shaped thing.

"What's that?" I said.

"Old Harry gave me his sextant, eh. With the correct time and logs we can tell roughly where we are."

He did a demo on how to sight a bright star for an elevation angle from the horizon, which would be taken at the same time each evening.

"And we get three different sightings from three different objects, and mark three points on the chart. That forms a triangle, or 'cocked hat'. We should be roughly in the middle of the hat, eh?"

Eh? Mumbo-jumbo. His explanation was in shorthand, as usual. "What if we aren't? What if it's cloudy?"

"Simple. We use the radio direction finder to get the loudest signal bearing and use its compass direction to draw a line on our map. It should cut through near the hat," he said. His face registered the smugness of ignorance. "Oh, and the GPS to check accuracy."

"It can't be that easy. Bobbing around in the ocean with reefs and islands near. We'd soon be shark meat." Images of a flailing hand waving for the last time, and bloody water flashed through my mind.

"I did a trade," he said cheerfully, avoiding my annoyance.

"What do you mean? Don't talk shorthand."

"Ace has a home. The Trumbles. They love Ace, spoil her rotten."

"Brilliant." I said. That took such a weight off my mind and cut one of the last strands holding us from going.

Chapter 9

We threw a send-off barbecue of bangers and mash. Two bottles of sparkling wine vanished in a flurry of toasting. Harry and Eve Trumble stood hangdog as we mumbled farewells; awkward hugs all round.

Harry wheezed, "mind you keep a close watch." He laboured for breath. "Be prepared for the unexpected out there. It'll cruel ye when yer not lookin'."

Zoë blubbered, face pink. Clutched tissues.

Ace's tail swept glasses off the coffee table. They shuffled out with her in tow. She looked back with an accusative stare, sensing things out of the ordinary. Zoe recited Ace's dislikes in food and dog washes.

Her earlier demands for a doghouse aft of the mast struck me as a portent of what she'd be like later in life. At age twelve she wore top credits for tenacity.

On board before midnight, we rummaged about making order out of chaos. Zoë and I holed up in the back quarter berths. Jeff and Malcolm clung to the settee berths midship.

Cris and Millie shoehorned into the double bunk up forward. Millie stormed about, mumbling protest. Cris hated the sight of me since I forced the arrangement on them. I'd like to be the fly on the wall as they struggled around one another.

"Like peas in a pod," I mused. And what if the marine loo next to them packed up? Imagined it plugged, slopping in rough weather.

My narrow quarter berth gave some comfort. A grey, feathered dream catcher swung by the porthole.

The lockers under and around my bunk bulged with foods and odd bits. I'd packed less clothing than desired. Super patched denim shorts, a few pullovers, and light summer gear for the most part. After all, we were for the tropics. The bookshelf held my clutter of poetry, a diary, and a few worn novels.

Elysius swung heavily on the mooring lower now by several centimetres.

Zoë and I visited home before dawn, driven by desires to cling to land. We'd frittered about losing sleep and getting little done on board. The reality of close quarter living frayed everyone's nerves.

Sascha's late night call blinked in the answering machine video. I cursed my timing. She'd called half an hour before we set foot ashore.

"*Bree, Sascha calling. Can't rave. Intend heading your way early tomorrow. Promise. I've had this place. Can't stay any longer. Much too dodgy. Bye.*" Her face bore traces of strain.

"At last. I'll kick Malcolm's butt off the boat," I said, cavorting around the room.

Zoë cackled, obviously engrossed in the possibility of making a new friend.

Attempts to contact failed, giving me a new anxiety attack.

Radio newscasters spoke of several looters shot. Vigilante patrols set up by "irate citizens", they said, failed to control many suburbs. Sydney was becoming an unliveable sinkhole.

I sensed Sascha was trapped.

At five p.m. we boarded yet again. I left a brief note in case she reached us before sailing, sketching our location in the bay. I knew Jeff was fidgety, and that meant he'd be stroppy, fired up to cut and run.

Every day the gang chewed up twelve meals. Every day chances of starvation at sea increased.

My desire to wait for Sascha went right up Jeff's nose.

"We can't hang around here. You said so!" Jeff snorted in disbelief. He pressed the point. "Weather's good. Nor-wester, eh. I don't want another southerly buster. Last one screwed things up for days. Big seas. It's time to go."

"But, if she's hung up."

"So? We're hung up six times over, eh! Either we stay like Cris and I wanted, or this mad caper gets moving."

"You're so bull-headed," I flared. "Typical male. What if it was me?"

"She's just a pal of yours, nothin' more. You only knew her for a few days, eh."

"You'll like her. Sascha's special—eh."

"Like her or not, she ain't here. Probably took off somewhere else. You know what it's like out there," he scowled.

Damn him. Jeff usually buried his feelings about personal

problems. Now he'd thrown mine back in my face. Bugger him. I wouldn't budge. Tears and reproachful looks won my demand.

Sascha never arrived.

I ripped the note off the door and re-wrote the text. How do you explain you've just taken off and won't be back for months, maybe years? It's ludicrous. I explained where we intended to go, as if that would mean much to someone stranded. I expressed my love and a hollow promise I'd find her.

My tummy growled, so I drank water and guilt fasted while we waited.

Millie freaked out. "I'll waste away on this muck." She stared at the rice and bean sludge I'd boiled up.

Cooking wasn't one of my strong points. "You mean 'waist' away? I said. "There's already enough of you."

"Aww, Bree. That's not fair."

I smiled derision. "Two meals a day keeps pudge away."

Millie pouted on the foredeck, eyes fixed on the shore. Cris brooded, tapped. Malcolm dozed, scratched.

※

We slipped our mooring eight-fifteen that evening, chattering under diesel past Scotland Island, passing close by old haunts at Currawong Beach, for this time of year packed solid with yachts. Jeff sighted the profile of lion Island dead ahead as our course set. The Northern Beaches on our right for kilometres back were silhouetted save the odd spark of light; the blackout patchy. Occasional car lights threaded like fireflies along peninsula roads.

The raunchiness of 'Living in the Wild, Wild West' rocked from a beachside pub, shot across the water. Life there defied the logic of avoiding contact. Somebody war whooped. Individual voices, shrieks of feminine laughter, carried on the wind, evaporated.

Our sails flapped as the wind played around, suggesting change. Jasmine and wisteria sweetness drifted by in waves riding on sharp sea air. Again, as in every day this fortnight, stench prevailed in invisible streams, despoiled the evening air when we moved in and out of death zones.

A macabre thought surfaced from Malcolm. "I'm doin' a body count. Got seven so far."

"Shut up," Jeff said.

Millie tittered.

The others sat silent in the shadows on the cabin top, each in their own world.

A particularly thick stink aroused my personal terror.

"You could have the virus," the voice within mocked.

Headache and sweating might not be from my period.

Jeff reached giving a poke with the boat hook. "Yer mumblin' again. Sign of madness."

"Butt out freckles."

I imagined Sascha waving frantically from the wharf as we sailed. What if someone waylaid her like those bastards tried on me?

I remembered deeper scraps of a misty day years back in England, and being lost. Words. The alleyway still loomed in my dreams. Building rubble. I'd screamed. He'd bolted. His form and voice often terrorised my dreams.

"You all right?" Jeff said, sticking his face in mine. "You've that wild look. White knuckles."

I still bore a long scar high on my thigh.

Elysius laboured past Barrenjoey lighthouse on our starboard. We entered the mouth of the Hawkesbury River Basin by ten. Heavy swell heaped up with the outgoing tide. Thickening cloud from the south promised another southerly, already hid the moon. Jeff swore.

"Probably just a weak weather front," I said.

※

There wasn't much of a jolt. We hit something solid with a crunch, ploughing it along before the object scraped past our port side. Jeff and I were in the cockpit haggling over what compass course to set.

"That looks like an old rowboat," Jeff said. "I think we've busted it open."

"There's something in it. A lump of stuff", Millie said, scrambling for a view.

The wreckage was well down in the water, wallowing in the swells and ebb tide.

"No. It isn't gear. That's a body hanging on," I said. We dropped sail, slowly turned back, motored alongside. Cris snagged the boat with a hook while Jeff shone torchlight into a face contorted with fear.

She lay clinging, iron knuckled, clad in torn briefs. I judged her to be maybe seven, but her scrawny frame made guessing pointless. The boys jumped in, struggled between swells to prise her fingers, one by one off the gunnel of the rowboat and hauled her limp frame up the boarding ladder. Zoë wrapped the girl in a blanket while Millie chased up hot chocolate.

She shook rigid, teeth clenched, spilling most of the brew before any drink went down.

"It's best we get her below under covers. She's in hyperthermia. Millie. Get your hot water bottle," I said.

Jeff carried her below. "Yer okay now little fish," he whispered. Zoe tagged along and sat holding her hand.

We'd just taken on a life otherwise doomed to drown. She was our responsibility, like it or not. Under way, we couldn't dump her, mustn't turn back, even for a day.

❧

"Ahoy, Elysius!"

A chunky looking black craft, junk rigged, slipped close by as we hoisted sail.

"Where you bound for?" Its bearded skipper called.

"East into the South Seas," Jeff shouted. " As far from people as possible."

"Good idea, matey. Sydney's a nightmare. What we've seen you don't want to know about."

"Seen enough ourselves," I replied.

"We're headin' for the Marquesas Islands," he said.

A young woman appeared on deck draped in a short lap lap. Both waved as 'Blackjack' caught the first strong darkie of wind, surged ahead and soon faded, the outline of her orange sails barely visible.

I stared after Blackjack's silhouette. That woman looked familiar. She'd pass for Sascha's sister, even her double. No. This wasn't possible. This sort of shock I could do without. "Impossible." I said.

Jeff peered quizzically at me. "You *really* all right?"

"No," I snapped. "I'm not. What's our course?"

Elysius hissed through a rising swell off the starboard quarter as the southerly strengthened.

Millie appeared stumbling, clutching a red bucket, pale faced. Her eyes spoke of the misery already spinning her head, knotting her stomach. " Oh, Bree, can you put me off? Put me down. I'll never survive."

"Try these pressure pads on your wrists. I put these out for you. Why didn't you remember?" I attached them firmly. "Keep them on. Keep your eyes and mind on the horizon. Don't focus on the motion."

"What horizon?" she moaned. "Everything's motion."

My misgivings surfaced. She'd already chundered. That unmistakable stench swilled around in the bucket.

The cabin interior stank of it even with the hatches open.

If I wanted escape from the grot of close living, my bunk, or the forward deck, offered the only escape. That tiny bow apron was hot real estate.

Jeff set a course of 080, east-nor-east. Barrenjoey beacon and Lion Island lay well astern, the lighthouse flashing its pattern of four faintly. Other than running lights, Elysius surged ahead shrouded in murk. Occasional whitecaps swished up as the southerly drove us out into the deep. The tang of clean air lifted my spirits, the smell always addictive.

After reducing the genoa sail, I tried to keep Jeff company since sleep was difficult. He wasn't happy with the cabin smell; knew his feelings for dry land. A hot chocolate offering didn't work.

My watch came at two with Cris shambling up the companionway owl-like. He sat shivering, speechless. Face fixed, he stared out to sea.

I pried, "you two get any sleep?"

"What do you think, Bree? Millie moaned the whole bloody time. She's a thrasher. I can't sleep by her. Gotta move. And she's my sister. Her nightie hides nothing. She puked up the toilet."

"There's nowhere to go," I said. "You know I don't want Malcolm near her."

"What do you mean?"

Male awareness, I sighed. "To put it bluntly, our stray wants to worm into your sister's pants. He's drooled from day one, or hadn't you noticed? She's in heat every time he moons over her." I rolled my eyes. "She wouldn't stand a chance. You watch him."

"If he does he's shark meat."

"You do that," I said, emphasising each word. Patted his hand.

I knew now he'd suffer through her tossing bouts, but it was weird. Why was he suddenly protective? "You can use Jeff's bunk sometimes, or mine when I'm topside." We sat long in silence.

"You hate my guts, don't you?" Cris said. "I accept that. I know I'm a pain, don't get things right. But that doesn't give you the right to ignore me when somethin' goes okay."

"What's that supposed to mean?"

"Bree. You're so agro. My driving rescued you from those guys. Remember? I clipped the jeep. Probably killed four thugs to save your skin. That's a lot of blood on my hands."

"You mean slime." I stared long at the compass illuminated in red. "Jeff forced you to sideswipe them. He told me. He forced the wheel over. You would've missed."

"That's not true. He did it too fast. I intended to swipe them. Jeff nearly killed us too." Cris clenched the solar panel strut.

"If I've offended you, I'm really sorry. It was hard enough surviving that scene. Manners don't count much when you're about to be smeared all over the road. My thanks are understood? Don't make it an issue. Bury it."

Cris nodded. "I just want a little recognition."

Maybe I'd been too hard on him. He was trying and had pitched in, working as hard as Jeff to prepare the boat. Still, he'd ruin it in some way for certain and arguments over who did what sure as hell wouldn't help.

Dawn crept grey around six. Jeff and Malcolm relieved us. Cris's dagger looks went to waste on Malcolm, who was fogged in.

"Steady as she goes. 075, as you said. We're still in the southern current. Need to track more north for another three days," I said forcing cheer. Jeff grunted.

Millie clattered about in the galley. This, next to the engine, was the heart of the boat. Dad had made good use of the U shape with counters and sink to each side and a stove and large fridge between. As boats went it was generous space for cooking. The finish was in peach for the counter tops and teak trim all round on white cupboard faces.

The opposite side held an equally generous chart table. The GPS, radio direction finder and radiophone ringed the table. A settee, also U shaped, lay forward of the navigation station.

"Cornflakes and coffee?" Millie forced a smile.

"Coffee. Milk." I said.

I felt sure she had no idea how much she could turn a guy on. Millie had her mum's genes for shape, but unlike Arie, was fair skinned, peaches and cream. It had to be her dad's Scottish background. He was long dead. Work accident.

"Like my bikini top? It's from Brazil. Doesn't quite fit now. Size 10."

"Very cool, Millie. A bit too much cream." I sighed.

"I'll put less in next time. Sorry," she said.

Didn't dare ask about the other half, it passing for a slingshot without the stick.

Peeking through the curtains found Zoë and Fish deep in sleep, Zoë's arm wrapped around her.

Fish was emaciated, eyes shadow rimmed, especially the right, which puffed, dark and angry. A shock of tangled, ebony hair magnified her sallow complexion. Her face was finely shaped, high cheek boned with a ski-jump nose. How she ended up drifting out to sea was a mystery we needed to unravel.

Sleep loss finally caught up with me. The last sensation was the surging motion of Elysius.

I woke in the dark to a heavier rhythm and rain sweeping the decks. Jeff was still at the helm sheathed in rain gear. He escaped as soon as I appeared.

"Plannin' to take a bath?" He smirked, going below.

I stripped to undies and soaped in the squall driven shower. Sails reefed, Elysius pounded on a starboard tack, throwing sharp spray in my face. Hair down and soap lathered, I endured a chilly half hour scrub straddling the tiller, safety harness on. It was primitive, but the need to keep clean overcame desires for warmth or modesty. A rain jacket slowly restored body heat.

I heard commotion below. "Get yer ass up there. That's yer third call," Cris snarled.

Malcolm appeared dwarfed in dads' storm gear. He looked more like a cornered rat, no doubt a touch of goblin in him.

"Ride getting rough?" I offered.

"When are we gettin' to New Zealand? This is the pits. Can't stand the company. 'Mange-brain' is in me frickin face all the time."

"Maybe if you showed more attitude, did something without being kicked."

We grabbed for support as a wave slapped hard, heaving us up before she pounded, slowed, then gaining momentum. The genoa snapped taut. Malcolm looked out as if he'd jump overboard.

"Did you ever have a job? Do anything?" I said shivering.

"Yea. Got into a scrape or two lifting cars. Dope. Spent six months in detention for assault. I'm on the run."

"A career man," I said, stunned.

Malcolm chuckled, "yea, I'd like to go straight. Get a job in a motorcycle shop. Had a good one for a while. Lost it."

I ran out of desire to question. He'd have to go.

"New Zealand's ten days away, Malcolm. Best you earn your keep."

He brooded. Nodded.

Zoë surfaced, brow furrowed. "Bree. Fishie won't come out no matter what I do. She's peed on the mattress."

"Fish is stressed, sweetie. We'll have to be patient. Show her kindness. Is she eating?"

"A little. What if she does a big number? Oh, Bree, I'll just die."

"We'll get her sorted." I said, more out of bravado. We later managed her onto the marine loo. Fish left welts on my arm where she clawed hanging on. The second time she seemed less terrified, but wouldn't make the trip herself.

The following three days saw the southerly fade and a north to nor-wester push us along briskly during daylight, but much subdued at night.

Jeff bounced into the cockpit the third evening excited. "We're almost half way to North Island. Latitude 33 degrees 15 minutes south, 162 degrees 20 minutes east longitude."

His smile was the first I could recall for several days. It soon dissolved.

"The autohelm's busted. No more self-steering. Dad said it was playing up," I said. "Leaky seals."

That was bad news for all of us. We'd be the ones worn down on the tiller.

✳

I'd just settled for a nap when the domestic row broke.

"Cris, why the lemon face? What's wrong with my stew? You try cooking with nothing. Can't find what I want," Millie said, bawling into overdrive.

"It just tastes awful, like minted clag."

"You put up and shut up." Millie cried. She threw a pot striking the bulkhead, splattering Cris with what looked like gravy. "Maggot brain! You're so damn picky. Mum spoiled you. Spoiled you rotten."

I feigned ignorance, emerging to dip some stew on rice, and sat down opposite Cris. I ate smiling approval; after all, I didn't have to cook for an ugly crew. "Good stuff, Millie. Interesting mix. Love the herbs."

"At least someone likes what I do," she sobbed from the forward berth. Zoë and Fish stared. Cris seethed.

The following few days brought finer, though fitful weather, the wind swinging every which way. Mares' tails swept high overhead signifying change.

A clean up below and some storm sail repair work seemed to improve spirits. Jeff and Malcolm worked together, stitching a tear and applying stick-on patches to frayed spots. Millie sat against the mast watching. I sensed the eye semaphore.

I thought the sail repairs ironic while mending my shorts. I nursed nine overlapping patches, like shields, each representing three of the twenty-seven stitches once in my leg.

Chapter 10

North skies darkened swallowing the sunset. Seas became foam streaked on deep jade. Clouds tumbled. Sheets of blinding light flickered. Thunder pounded again and again, rapidly approaching. The roots of my hair pulled taut. Surely we'd be hit, fried to the core.

Blasts of sleety ice struck sideways, needling my skin, making me wince.

Jeff vaulted the cabin sole to shorten sail. It jammed in the track. He swore. Elysius yawed to starboard. I fought the tiller over, took the genoa half in, thankful for roller reefing, lashed the tiller and joined him struggling to haul the mainsail down two points. What lasted three minutes seemed like ten. We clawed back into the cockpit. I banged my head against the solar panel frame and momentarily stunned, tumbled on Jeff.

"Bloody hell. Bony knees."

"Not half as hard as your head, brother."

I tasted blood. Licked a split lip. Dizzy for a moment, I saw sparks in front of my eyes.

Commotion below. Screams oddly harmonised.

"There's water coming in. Lots of it."

Millie poked her head up through the galley hatch catching a blast of water full on. She fell. The hatch slammed shut trapping her hand as she gripped the rim.

I saw her legs below flailing wildly with the motion of the boat.

She howled, "my arm, my arm!"

I battled to fit one of the drop boards in to half close the companionway door. The cockpit swilled, awash.

I saw Malcolm stagger, grabbing her around the legs, pulling her, squealing. Both collapsed in a heap. A cloud of haze, strangely white, enveloped everything in the cabin.

Zoë darted forward bouncing off Cris who came from shutting the front hatch. I caught a glimpse of her sitting in the galley sink clinging to a support post.

A sudden surge lifted Elysius heavily causing her to broach dangerously, almost broadside to the wind. Everything loose flew below clattering. Malcolm swore in combinations new to me.

Millie shrieked from the dog-pile as Jeff struggled from under my legs to turn the tiller hard over.

"Turn the spare pump on," Jeff bellowed.

I doubt anyone heard over the thunder and shouts.

Elysius still had momentum, slowly swung, putting the oncoming seas behind us and we ran, spray smothered, with the storm off our stern port quarter. Waves peaked crazily making her lurch and veer, licked into the cockpit. Jeff gripped the tiller. I threw him a safety harness. Both of us neglected to put these on from the start. We could be washed overboard, drowned by now, and everyone else doomed to follow.

The wind swung behind shifting between west and north, forcing us to gibe the main sail and genoa countless times over the next few hours. We were making speed even with sail reduced. It became a fight the whole night to keep her from slewing about in seas that now seemed to come from any direction as if intent on catching us out. Around dawn the wind eased. I dragged myself below to see the carnage.

Cris, I noted, did turn on the electric pump. The cabin sole carpet was soaked. Sticky flour and sugar clung to everything.

Millie slouched nursing her left hand. Malcolm sat close, his arm around her shoulder. Cris muttered, continued scraping up bags of sodden food burst from lockers, oblivious of anyone around him.

"None of this would happen back home. We'll drown out here," he said. "This is pukin' crazy."

"Duuh." I sneered. I was too miserable to set him right.

"Bree. I think I've broken my wrist. It really hurts. Sorry about the mess. I wanted to bake."

Examination showed swelling and raw flesh where her hand raked over the hatch rim. She could move her fingers. Pressure on her wrist brought a yelp. I bandaged the hand using a plastic spatula as a short splint to immobilise it.

"Probably a cracked bone."

Other than that, her leg welts reviewed, loss of dignity vocalised, Millie survived.

"Jeez. Glad I grabbed ye', Mil. Ye' could've busted it. Ye' landed right on me gut." He flashed a sly smile.

Malcolm fawned primitive words of rapport.

Zoë limped out of her bunk, Fish in tow. "We'll help clean the galley, Millie."

"Great idea. I see you started with the sink. Hot chocolate all round?" I said, forcing a smile.

Much of the bedding forward suffered. We'd lost cereals, flour and sugar.

Moaning in the rigging announced a rise in the wind thrashing us along. Cris helped Jeff for a few hours while I tried to sleep. I joined Cris, giving Jeff a much needed rest. The storm aged him, etching lines across his forehead and crow's feet from squinting.

"Call me ten hundred - tomorrow," he said stumbling below.

Cris held the tiller, seemed more sea aware than I'd remembered him. We took turns steering as the shift wore on. It rained in sheets like undulating curtains. None of us could properly dry as we piloted in pairs, three hours on, three off, round the clock.

A curry took flight after Millie removed the pot from the safety brackets of the gimballed stove. Zoë and Millie managed stew recovery including salvaged scraps, which we decided to eat.

"Man, that's the hairiest curry. Get ready for afterburners tomorrow," Malcolm said. "No more constipation."

The loo in its present state was the last cramped hole I wanted to frequent.

Self-examination in a cracked mirror did nothing for morale. "Bad luck", my gran used to say. "Cover it in a thunderstorm."

My lip protruded puffed and split, the tender flesh torn where I'd bashed the tiller post. A large lump throbbed under tangled masses of hair. All of my nails were ruined. A scrape along the ridge of my nose suggested I'd landed a glancing blow, probably from non-skid deck paint. I refused to count the bruises. Vanity had no chance of survival on Elysius. I eyed my sprouting armpits. Fashion dero. Dad's illusion in naming the boat Elysius was well astray; but the ancient Greeks never found it easy according to Homer's *Iliad*.

Thick cloud obscured the horizon. The satellite navigation unit read 34 degrees south by 170 east. On the ninth day we were too far south. A course correction to 070 accompanied a kindly wind from the southwest.

When not on deck Jeff brooded over the pilot charts and navigation readings. He seldom slept long.

I insisted we stay well off Cape Reinga; threading the needle between the northern tip of New Zealand and Great Island located fifty kilometres to the north. He agreed.

With the wind stiffening we slipped through confused seas within sight of North Island's cape. Its distant beacon flashes suggested we were roughly ten nautical miles off shore. Around three a.m. a set of ship's lights appeared north. These we followed until first light when the stranger disappeared in the mist. It dawned day eleven.

Jeff beamed proudly, "well, I missed the first pile of rocks."

Malcolm wasn't dumped.

"If we try to pull into Manganui on North Island It'll mean tacking. Elysius doesn't sail into the wind worth a damn. She's too heavy. We'll lose four days, maybe more. We're on a good run," Jeff piled up arguments. "Our charts are useless for that coast. On a pilot's chart it looks complicated."

"We've lost food, maybe three days worth," I said.

It was stupid to delay. We left Malcolm dozing in ignorance as land faded; His presence left me foul tempered.

The next three days saw us cover just over four hundred nautical miles or seven hundred kilometres. We spread bedding and soddened clothes across the decks lashing each item down. Jeff and Cris rigged a wind funnel to air out the interior. The sun smiled.

Zoë and Fish sat forward under the mast, Zoë earnestly reading chapters of 'Captain Popcorn Builds a Boat,' with voice impersonations.

I grumbled to Jeff. "Millie and Malcolm. What a combination. Sounds like some off colour American sit-com. He can pile the crap on."

"I'm teaching him to handle steering; can't stand a useless leech on board," Jeff said.

"More like a slug." I said.

They sat forward of the dinghy near the bow sunning; no need wondering about body language and scraps of laughter. Muffled conversation. Cris slept directly below.

Jeff spilled his worries. "I'm freaked out on navigation. My star sightings are dodgy."

"The satellite readings were cool," I said, ruffling his unruly hair. "We found the cape - good one. Keep practising." I gave a hug. Smiled. Jeff reciprocated with the usual serious smirk, a worrywart despite success.

He sighed, "We've lost the small GPS. It died. Mobile phone, too. Someone stepped on my laptop. It's stuffed. Know who did it?"

"Malcolm?" I said.

"Cris. He's so flamin' clumsy. Nearly lost a winch handle over-board yesterday."

"He's still getting his sea legs," I said. "He's much better. He doesn't carry the bucket around any more," I stressed. "What're your real thoughts on Mal as crew?"

"He's got a lot of lights on, but wherever he is isn't with us," Jeff said.

"You mean there's nobody home?" I said.

"I recon he's brain damaged, or something. What's in that bag he carries around? He sleeps on it."

"I'll find out," I said.

"Ratbag won't pay attention to what I say about steering. Keeping the main sail trim. We need an extra hand. I'm bloody tired. He's more useless than…"

"Titties on a bull?" I said.

"Dolphins." Millie cried. A dozen appeared criss-crossing our bow wave then slipping back to crest the waves alongside. Below, their squeaks punctuated the hiss of passing water. Their presence stunned us, lifting our sense of security.

Later that day a huge gull landed on the dinghy for a rest. Zoë and Fish engaged in throwing it biscuit crumbs, which the gull ignored.

All of us, except Millie, were out of clean clothing. I recon it added to the pong below, which the canvas air funnel wouldn't cure. We'd begun to recycle gear from the first few days, killing old habits of changing often. The only item I'd washed was my shorts and singlet, which was done during the tail of the storm. With warmer weather swimming wear was the answer. Malcolm wore only what he'd arrived in other than a few items grudgingly given by Jeff. None of it fit.

Up forward with Millie Mal basked in undies frayed, discoloured, and barely adequate as cover.

He came aft limping, holding Millie's hand. His dark leanness stood out, finely muscular, suggesting wiry strength, a tip rat pack-ing sexual magnetism. He fancied himself a cool dude.

"Like those sun glasses ye wear. Dead set. They really stick out," he said, wearing a fixed smile.

I coloured. Refused to bite.

Millie beamed vacant eyes, flushed sunburn pink.

"You're fried - no block-out? You fool. You'll blister."

I remembered Cris taunting her a year back. "Blisters. Where'd ye get em' from?" He tagged her with it. "Blister's off the planet."

Millie lay that night in tears. Malcolm hovered, scratching, a useless fixture.

"Piss off and do something on deck. You could've put lotion on." I grabbed the Block-out Forty. "Millie's got skin like a peach." I regret saying 'peach.'

Malcolm sulked off.

Millie radiated heat.

"Oh. Bree. I hurt every time I move. Don't want to touch anything," she moaned.

Cris arrived, took one look, grunted, and left for my berth.

I applied burn cream to her back. Every stroke made Millie moan. She was such a baby in many ways, but her misery made me sympathetic until she turned over. Without a bikini top she stood out like a beacon, raw pink from pubic line to forehead. Blisters.

"You know your game with Malcolm's dangerous?"

"No. It's not like that. Not now," Millie whined.

"You aren't thinking right about him. Don't trust the guy. You're a mess - look what you get." I eyed two purple splotches on her neck.

"He raps to me. Cris and Jeff hardly speak to me. They think I'm vacant," she cried. "So do you. He touches my feelings."

My nags and digs struck home, half in fun. These registered deeper than I imagined. Emotionally she'd become wild, unpredictable.

"You know I'm just a little bitchy sometimes. I do like you. You're a great chef."

Millie stared into me, face distorted as I applied lotion; dribbled it on; spreading; barely touching. Millie howled.

As I withdrew, I spotted it. Malcolm's bag lay under a blanket. It matched him perfectly; greasy in texture; riddled with assorted graffiti, and scuff holes. 'Mainlinin' and 'hottie hydralecs' stood out from otherwise inexplicable drivel. Wretched spelling. I took the plunge.

Inside were several small pouches. The largest reeked of marijuana. One of the others held tablets the size of sweeteners. The dag was a dope freak.

There were other odd bits. Matches, a lighter, cards, and an assortment of sci-fi and sex mags lay jumbled. An aged pack of extra long condoms held special place wrapped in a stiff hand towel alongside the dope.

"I didn't know he cared." I felt disgust.

A water pipe wedged in a side pocket alongside a long, folded knife. The last pouch held two wads of hundred notes.

※

Something cracked above. The boom must've swung, jibed too fast, too far. Thumping feet on deck, and an enraged Jeff broke the rhythmic swish of the hull.

I stuffed Mal's contents back, threw it under a blanket.

"You bleedin' drongo. I told you - keep control of the main's sheet. That boom could've knocked me overboard, killed me."

Zoë and I sandwiched up the companionway in time to see Jeff land a sharp jab to Malcolm's nose, sending him flying into the stern railing. A stream of blood splattered his chest. He lay dazed, fingering his face.

Jeff held his head and sprawled over the tiller.

I refrained from saying anything.

Zoë screeched, "Why don't you goofballs get your act together? I don't want to die out here because you spit the dummy." She burst into tears, collecting Fish and disappeared below.

Jeff and Malcolm remained stupefied. I figured she'd delivered as hard a blow to their egos as their physical traumas.

"You screw up like that once more n' I'll throw you overboard," Jeff snarled, his body hunched over, coiled.

Malcolm rubbed his jaw, staring, his stupor giving way to something darker. He sidled by crab-like expecting another blow and disappeared below.

Chapter 11

Jeff slumped in the cockpit, hand to head.

"Damn him. Nearly went over the side. Fuck, my head hurts."

The timber boom belted him a glancing blow, tearing his scalp open. Blood saturated the whole of his left shoulder, but the flow eased.

Cris arrived scowling, guessing the cause. "Trying to train the untrainable? We sure bagged a live one."

"He isn't a total write-off," I said, feeling less certain, but realised Malcolm was needed.

Below, by the concentration of chart light, I had a closer look at Jeff accompanied by Millie and Zoë, who strained to see everything. Fish disappeared. Millie frowned. I put her to work sponging blood. She uttered groans, but persisted.

"This is going to hurt me more than you," I said. "Fancy being a skinhead? I'll have to cut away some hair. Recon you need stitches. We've nothing to kill that kind of pain completely."

"Tape it together."

"No. It's spread apart. I'll stitch and tape," I said. I saw bone under blood and tissue.

"Just get it done while I'm numb and pissed off."

The operation took an hour of cutting, shaving and washing blood away. Most of his curls were gone on the left side. Once dry I used antiseptic cream, gauze and taped across both ends of the gash drawing it together as much as possible. The swelling didn't help. The only clean needle useable gleamed ten centimetres long. My first insertion of his scalp caused him to suck in air as he clenched the support post, knuckles white. I shook. Had to stop. Memories of mum sewing up a gash on Ace's flank did little to marshal courage.

Jeff growled, grinding teeth each time I drew the skin closer together. After six stitches we'd both suffered enough.

"My head aches like hell."

"You're concussed, I recon. No brains spilled."

"Thanks heaps. You've a mutant sense of humour."

"Who says I'm being funny?" I kissed his forehead.

Millie sat steeped in gloom. "Mal didn't mean to lose control."

Jeff stared in disbelief. It was impossible to tell weather he was wilder with her, or Malcolm.

Mal was topside having fled to the bow. Best he stayed there.

The wind swung around to the north early that afternoon leaving us on a long port tack with a compass bearing of 050. The seas from the south were less disturbed than they'd been for several days. A northerly swell took over giving us a rhythmic motion, casting fine sheets of spray across the deck.

As was Jeff's design, the diesel engine rattled into life for a few hours every third day, making sure the batteries remained charged and the engine was exercised. We had to know it would start when the coral reefs loomed close at hand. Navigating coral ringing the island, and threading the narrow passage into the lagoon was some five weeks down the track. Dad's rough sketch of the island from their honeymoon visit was all we had to go on. I assumed the channel would be marked.

Pungent diesel stench added to the pong and dampness penetrating everything. The engine throbbed heavily, revved up.

Last nights chilli con carne' blanketed the worst of the war of odours bedevilling us below deck.

Body pong added rankness impossible to ignore. We were thankful for sunscreen, dabbing it under armpits, subduing rank sweat. Our precious water supply didn't allow a sponge wash. We'd taken to wearing the least possible clothing on hotter days.

It was day twenty-three, the day after Jeff's blue with Malcolm, and I could sense total depression.

※

Zoë fell into the mood. "Fishie, why won't you answer me? I read heaps to you. Please read to me."

Fish stared wide-eyed.

She was sharp, could hear well and understood everything. Fish no longer cringed behind Zoë, but one could attach an umbilical chord between them.

Soon after Cris stormed by, grabbed Millie from the galley,

pushing her up into the cockpit, his hand rammed hard against her bum. "Listen to me, Cinderella."

"Get your grubby claws off me!" She screamed.

Jeff ducked down past them, fled to the chart table, and increased the engine revs. He began fiddling with the radio direction finder and short wave radio. I laboured at hair tangles, all ears.

Cris raged, "Now you're nearly crippled. Can't steer. Can hardly move. Can't cook."

Millie's footsteps thumped across the cabin, bound for the bow.

Cris slammed the companionway sliding door shut.

He persisted, ignoring open hatches; his voice muffled; clear enough above the engine. "You can't think straight. What's next? Screwing that weasel?"

"I'll do what I like. Since when did you give me any respect? I'm an outsider to you," Millie bawled. "A sister who's not a sister."

"Why can't you behave like a Ramira?"

"I could be with your mum. Arie loved me. Now she's dead. Being family is dead. You aren't a real brother so don't shove crap on me. I'd rather be an Oliver - a Price," she sobbed.

Jeff and I stared at one another dumbfounded.

"What if Malcolm overheard?" I hissed. The lump in his bunk didn't move.

"She's what?" Jeff said.

"Adopted." I said. "I never knew. Gods, this opens a can of worms. "We've got to do something, and fast."

"What? Bloody hell, my head hurts." Jeff whispered, finger tips on his temples.

"We can't play dumb," I said.

More footsteps on deck. Millie stumbled down the stairs, stormed by, face pained, puce.

"All hands on deck, Jeff. It's thrash-out time."

"Who says it's our hassle," Jeff said, waving disinterest.

"Someone's going to cop it. Thirty more days of this'll see us so strung out we'll self destruct."

"Bree. Don't confront. Wait," he pressed, "It'll work itself out."

※

We sat around the cockpit seats. Millie huddled with the girls on the port side. I held the tiller next to Jeff. Cris sat in the cabin entrance, and Malcolm perched on the stern railing. Bad vibes cut the air. It stank of heat below, and felt equally sticky crammed in the cockpit.

The sun's rays blinded the western heaven, enveloping cotton cloud in deep peach ether. Within the drift of a few thoughts, its orb sank. To the east Jupiter rose out of deepening cobalt blue. Elysius rose and plunged.

"We need a truce," I said. "If we don't get our act together we'll die out here. I don't fancy crabs picking my bones. Angry crew don't think right about their business."

"And there's an awesome shark out there," piped Zoë. "I saw it this morning."

"Why don't we all back off a bit. Say something positive to one another?" I said.

"Yeah. Some happy things," Zoë said.

A long silence followed, save the slap of a rope end on the cabin and soothing swish of sea.

"Can I say somethin'?" Malcolm said.

The rope halted thumping, as if listening.

"I owe Jeff an apology. Like, stearin' a boat is hard, man. Can't concentrate on anything for long. Never could. No ill feelin'?"

Jeff stared, face clouded. I jabbed him one.

"Uuh. I guess it's okay - as long as you get real."

"I'll do me best. Don't like gibing stuff and that tiller's real hard to steer with. That boom thing scares me shitless. And one more thing - Millie and me are cool together, see, so I don't want anyone puttin' her down. She's dead-set alright."

Cris snapped, "I'm still responsible for her."

Millie's jaw dropped.

Malcolm moaned derision, "Aw come on. In my world the rules are different. We're on our own now. We make our own rules."

"And I'm my own boss," Millie said jutting her chin out.

Cris looked toothless and miserable.

"But on a boat what's best for everyone has to be understood," I said.

"No rules were ever set about hangin' out with someone. I survive on me rules, so will Millie. What's wrong with a little fun and snoggin'?"

"I can't argue with that. It's the intimacy we worry about," I said, jabbing Jeff.

"This is our boat. We're senior, eh, but I guess relationships are a free choice as long as you keep it cool. Don't make life tough for others. Everyone needs breathing space." Jeff said, looking at Cris for response.

Cris sat mute. I knew he'd lost face; needed sympathy, a little warmth.

"Why don't we play cards tonight. Scoff some wine?" Malcolm said.

I had to admire his timing. Cunning. Zoë and Fish lit up with excitement. Millie's eyes shone. It was a great idea.

✳

"Why can't Fish talk?" Zoë simpered.

"Can she get a word in edgewise?" I said.

"You know, I asked her to read to me. She just shakes her head. She makes weird noises in her sleep."

"Maybe she's acting out something that happened to her. A bad fright?"

"She says strange things like '*mal*' and '*peste, peste*'. It sort of sounds Spanish."

I remembered her first few days. Fish mumbled from the recesses of Zoë's cave-like berth.

"What's your name, sweetie?" Where'd you come from? Where are your mum and dad?" I held her hand, which was limp. She stared past me, seldom looking directly at me. No active eye contact.

"How did you get on a boat?"

No response.

Zoë's night revelation meant she could speak, if she chose to.

This evening both joined me in my berth, which was wider than Zoë's and festooned with photos and odd bits I collected over the years. Both were busy rummaging in the tiny drawers at the foot of the bunk, hauling out anything attractive. Fish latched on to an elderly raggety-anne doll grandmother Mary-Anne, my mum's mother, gave me months before she died. I sensed an instant bonding.

"She's yours, Fish. Her name's Sabbie." I saw the spark of recognition deep in the mix of her black eyes.

73

Zoë rifled, dragging out a sheer French bra and panties propping the former across her chest.

"What's this for?"

"A rare social happening. Never know whom I'll meet in the tropics. The governor's ball?"

"And you'd entertain in these."

"Who knows? Maybe a charming Frenchman."

Zoë screeched. "It won't cover them. You won't last the distance."

"Oh, cut it out you little beast."

Zoë switched wavelengths. Frowned. "You always look preoccupied. Don't talk with me like you used to."

"Fair's fair? I'm doing shift work. It's grinding me down sweetie. Look at Jeff. He's worse off."

"Jeff's such a deadhead. He's teaching me to steer. Bet I wouldn't last," Zoë said, folding her arms. "Your eyes are hazel green, not so blue, like when you got the flu last year. You've got shadows."

"You don't look so crash hot either," I said, poking her in the ribs. Fish listened dark eyed, clutching her find.

"When we land on Motu-Riva we can go fossicking for treasures with Fish, like we did at Grassy Head."

Her face lit up in a mass of freckles and jumped channels. "I haven't been a good watchdog."

"You mean with super-stud?"

"Yea. He's sneaky. He pinched my bum. He's sick. Plays it up. He's always at it." Zoë gestured with her hands clenched, saucer eyed. "It's gross."

"He's right off. Bad family life. I'll sort him out." How could he ever be normal, whatever that is? A sensible answer eluded my imagination.

Whatever breeze we'd taken for granted died late the following afternoon. Our sails flapped about. It was stinking hot below at 35 degrees Celsius.

Jeff, after his usual deliberation, claimed, in round figures, we were 32 degrees south latitude, 169 degrees west longitude. There was much satisfaction in those numbers. Dominant wind directions on the pilot chart were favourable and would hopefully allow us to run mainly with the wind. Nature had a way of defying percentages, I mused. The ocean drift, chart marked in blue arrows, was also carrying us along in the right direction.

I had ample reason to stick my nose in Jeff's figures. Watching him muddle over his sextant readings, following on deck as he took sightings from the available stars at exactly nine p.m. was amusing. His use of the logs before marking an assumed position, his 'cocked hat', intrigued me. Slowly extracting understanding from him about the meagre equipment we used challenged my mathematical dimness. It made me appreciate the need to know where we were as exactly as possible. A string of map ex's, some smudged out and re-done, marked progress towards our targeted landfall, the tiniest of dots; the one dad swore was paradise extraordinaire.

❉

Millie and the girls decorated the table with ribbon and chains of paper loops, each fluoro coloured. An oil lantern glowed on its stand attached to the beam that supported the mast and held the folding table between the settee and opposite bunk. Six could squeeze in for a feed, a night of cards.

We agreed to take half hour watches above to be sure of weather conditions. The tiller was tied down. Elysius lazed along barely managing two knots.

"Who's into Black Jack?" Malcolm said, offering a twisted smile. In the half-light he looked the mischievous demon. "I'll be the dealer, and here we go."

Well, we went down the tube soon enough. Malcolm, alias The Shark, fleeced us inside a half hour. Millie flushed close to his side, her skin a patchwork of blister and peel; a fidgety arm draped on his thigh.

"Rags to riches," he gloated, nudging her. "I'll buy ye a mansion, Mill."

Zoë refused to bet, coveting her chips.

Cris interjected, "why not play Hearts—the Black Bitch," he stressed.

For a moment I expected Millie to flare up, but his insult didn't register.

Malcolm paused, shuffled the deck, and then continued. "That's cool, Cris. Teach me all about this Black Bitch.

"Some cold bubbles, anyone? It's getting steamy in here," I said, popping one of two bottles for the night. Blessed are those who have a solar powered fridge. The first, a magnum, lasted as long as it took to play two hands of Hearts. I stole an extra swig for 'Dutch courage'. Champaign always made me reckless.

I'd spread 'Hedonica' perfume from earlobe to armpit after defoliating them with a dull razor. A touch of lipstick and matching amber nail polish on stubby nails complimented a Lacroix string bikini, laced in abstracted frangipani patterns. Decorative Aztec bead designs linked the bottom halves.

Maybe a little friendly heat would loosen Cris up. He was dark. Silent. I resolved against saner judgement to be indiscrete, to distract him with the less prickly side of Breezie Price. I refilled my cup.

Zoë and Millie took to giggling on bubbles. Watching them, I couldn't help joining in.

Strains of *Scorpion Princess* filled the air, a kind of hypnotic bop cum rock group with Eastern undertones. Zoë lit incense to aid the odour war.

With the musical chairs of doing watch on deck, I gained a chance to wedge up against Cris.

"This sure is a tight squeeze." I stopped half way, squirming. Laughed. You've got me in some sort of leg-lock, Cris." I made a point of gyrating, finally making the inside corner of the settee. Perspiration glistened in the mellow light. Cris was drenched in sweat, beads trickling down his smooth chest darkening the band of his shorts. He smiled at me.

"I like your gear, what there is of it."

He did have nerve - and taste.

"Why, thanks Cris, I never figured you noticed."

It's a female's privilege to use sarcasm in the flirtation stakes. The sheer cheek of it was delicious. My caution crashed under the third glass of bubbles. The pit of my stomach churned, heating. I knew he was eyeing me between flinging cards down.

"That's your mum's pendant," he said. "It's somethin' else against your tan. Can I have a closer look?"

I lifted the complex linkages out, holding them close to his face, leaning a little, and dropped it into his palm.

"She'd kill me if she knew I wore it."

"No. She'd be rapt that you thought to keep it safe." His olive eyes met mine. Felt his breath on my cheek.

I knew he wanted to say more. Hoped he wouldn't. It was obvious Millie's fury hadn't vexed him too much.

"Hey you two. Play your cards or we'll be here all night," Jeff said, sniggering.

Zoë gloated, "here's a bomb for you Malcolm. Ding, dong, the wicked witch is—dead."

"Black Bitched," Malcolm laughed. "I'm done for. Yer a sharp little operator."

"Thirteen points plus seven more for the hearts you coped," she added, beating the table like a warrior elf.

Fish clapped.

I was aware of Fish sliding around behind me, half sitting on the bookshelf, her hand on my shoulder for support, the other clutching Sabbie. My flashed smile brought shy recognition. Maybe the shell was beginning to crack.

Hearts, which is an emotional game, raged on well into the night with Zoë and Cris winners. Malcolm made much on the diplomatic front, throwing in a few motorcycle jokes, and taking his beating at hearts well.

Being too restless to sleep, I relieved Jeff, who still suffered from headaches. The wound was healing, but looked angry. He needed extra sleep.

Malcolm stumbled on deck, sat opposite.

"Jeez, that was a buzzy session. Saw you shimmying up to Cris," he said, and winked. "You were right up front. Loosen yer strings n' you'll really be somethin'."

"I'm as loose as I can be in this pig-sty." Gods, he had a nerve. "You know how much you stuffed up Millie. You let her cook," I said.

"Aw, I told her to slap it on. She took her sunglasses off, not me, man."

"What's that mean?"

"Her top. I respect her. Wouldn't mess around with Mill. Cris is flamin' agro. He's a worry."

"You're the worry."

"Can't help likin' girls," he said, "like yerself."

I ignored his wormy flattery.

"Zoë's ticked off with you, says you pinched her butt. Never touch her again."

"Oh, that was nothing. I was havin' a bad dream. Think I accidentally poked her when she walked by. It was hot too. I get restless, toss."

"She's only twelve. No need to show your hardware."

"Cool. I comprehend. It wasn't my intention. My sheet must've slipped off."

The mongrel had an answer for everything.

A whiff of cooler wind caught us, coming from the west, billowing the sails. I let out the main and genoa. Elysius responded, the surge of water lifting our motion.

"Malcolm, move the tiller sooner. You can't keep her true after she yaws off course."

"Who made the tiller nob? Looks like a...

"Just steer."

"You must have neat oldies, not like mine."

"Why say that?"

"Me old man was a pisspot. Whacked mum around. Broke her nose. Bastard kicked me out. Freaked my sister out." His eyes sharpened. "Rayleen and mum ran away to Queensland. Disappeared."

"You've Family. You aren't joking?"

"Nup. The old guy got blind one night and fell asleep on the F-4. Got flattened. F flat. Get it?" he chuckled.

I knew there was bitterness underneath his front, but this. "So you became a Streetie."

"Yep. Got into dope. Lots of heat. Ran out on a dealer. Stuck one of them."

"Stuck?"

"Cut her up. A real slag. Would've killed me."

"Her?"

"Yeah, she was one tough cow. Just shived her up a bit. Didn't kill her."

I went numb, remembered his flick knife.

Chapter 12

"We've got company coming." Cris shouted.

Scrambling up on deck, still half-doped with heat, we faced a cold horizon. The first of a chain of squalls darkened the west, swept upon us, drenching salt-etched flesh.

We reduced sail area by half in case a gust came too sudden, ripping open old canvass. Every day counted with supplies dwindling. A sail rupture, main or genoa, our forward sail, would spell disaster. We knew the spares were fit only for patching.

Jeff and Cris hauled out a makeshift canvas square, which was fitted with a funnel dad stitched into the centre. With eyeleted, slightly tapered sides it served as a three by four metre rain catcher. This was lashed to each of the backstays and the stays amidships. Stretched taut, rain cascaded through the canvas tube into the cockpit.

"It's scrub time," Millie cried.

Laundry flew from below in a ragged tangle. The four drains, blocked with bathtub plugs, served as a washing basin. Millie and I lathered, taking greedy turns sousing our hair as each shower swept by.

Jeff and Cris perched on the cabin top looking like pauper emperors, exploiting the spectacle of girls slithering over swelling suds and tangled clothes. They soaped each other down while egging us on.

"Take it off. This is crook entertainment. Where's your Aussie spirit?" Cris jeered.

"Put a sock in it, *reject*." Millie huffed.

Cris persisted, "Jeff, bet you ten coconuts the small fry strip first."

"Aw, that's too much for tadpoles; how many for the big ones?"

Twenty-five each for the dumpling and weedy thing." Cris convulsed in his own cleverness.

"Weedy thing?" I said. He'd suffer in dimensions not yet imag-

79

ined. I knew Cris hated heights.

"Green or brown nuts?" I said casually, barely concealing malice.

"Take your choice, Sudsarella."

"Green, thankyou."

Millie seethed. Muttered. "That bastard called me a dumpling."

"You know what he's up for if he loses?" I winked. "Besides, you're streets ahead of these misfits."

Millie flashed a devilish grin.

We swayed, peeling our tops off slowly, twirling them on the tips of our fingers, taunting. Arm in arm Millie and I strutted, contorted with laughter, making a completely wanton spectacle by straddling the tiller.

I couldn't hack stripping completely, besides, Cris hadn't said 'all the way'. Millie, high on defiance, did.

Fish gaped, burst into laughter. Zoë shrieked with delight. She striped.

"Just like skinny dipping at Obelisk Beach," she exclaimed.

Fish followed grinning. Each threw their undies, which detoured over the side as a gust of wind hit us.

"You lose big time," Zoë taunted. "Bet you can't match that." She turned, bent over, gyrating her backside.

Jeff gaped, bursting into laughter, but Cris coloured. He realised my ploy, knew I wouldn't forget payment due, nor would the girls let him.

"Get down, help us scrub Cris," I said, offering an eyeful of cheek, pointing at my feet.

Four of us jammed the cockpit floor. Bumping and howling, we thrashed the clothing about. Cris stood on the edge, stared down, uncertain of what to do amongst four females who'd clearly lost their minds.

"Get the buckets. We need more drinking water. Move!" Jeff hollered.

Another mass, veil-like curtains, moved towards us.

The girls slipped, scrambled, heaping clothes on the cabin top to rinse and wring out. Cris and I filled buckets; suddenly we were aware it was more important to catch fresh water for cooking and drink. Clothes could always wait.

"I can compliment you on your choice of gear again," Cris teased, looking up at me. "It's not the same design." His laboured breath stirred nerve ends on my thigh.

"Can the flattery. I'm naturally suspicious, besides, never handle high voltage when there's water around." I belted his shoulder, continued feeding the funnel into each container while straddling the tiller, relishing a new sense of power.

Cris fed each precious bucket into the water tanks for the next few hours, aware of my closeness. His small talk, cheerful by his standards, revealed a Cris groping for ways to make up - or grovel. I nodded, smiled and listened, wondered how he'd cope with the wager. I surprised myself, felt genuine warmth for him.

The party over, maybe Cris was less pressurised, a threat to Millie and Malcolm. But other tensions were bubbling to the surface, as much within me as with him.

Jeff remained seated, appeared pained, his headache, no doubt. Any physical exertions, particularly bending over, were not to his liking.

Malcolm materialised ghost-like, gazing at the scene, sagged into a corner of the stern against the red and white life ring, which made his head a grinning bullseye. His mat of tangled hair hung limp over his forehead almost covering his eyes. Rain dribbled off the end of his nose.

It was as if we didn't exist. He stared through me somewhere beyond. I may as well be an apparition. He remained there soaked through for hours, on into darkness, sometimes grinning, as if sharing a joke with fantasy figures.

*

We did a stock take the following morning.

"We're low on water," Jeff said, "about two hundred and fifty litres, including maybe fifty collected in yesterday's spectacle. Less than two weeks supply if we use two litres each daily, so it'll have to be that. No washing clothes or dishes with fresh water." He cast a hard eye on us, especially Millie.

"I can cook partly with salt water," Millie declared, anxious for approval.

"You said we're about three weeks away from the island," Cris said.

"If we don't hit bad weather or a wind in our face," Jeff said.

Millie muscled in, "that's not all, the galley's in a fix. Our metho's running out. Four litres left. We're out of cereals and

81

canned meats." She waved her arms, emphasising each disaster. "Dried vegies are nearly gone. Noodles and rice, we got. Got dried fruit for another week. Half the flour and sugar went in the storm."

"What's the bad news," Cris said.

Millie's face screwed up. "Then it's cold food," she blubbered. "I've lost so much weight. My tops and shorts are loose."

Millie's face looked drawn, her eyes accusative. Jeff and I were villains pressuring them to come. Both were quick to remind me.

"I found some food under my bunk," Zoë offered.

"Well?" I said, eyeing her.

She smiled, dropped her gaze, and poked at a cornflake embedded in the carpet.

"Two sacks of food," she said.

"Yes?"

"Dog biscuits." She flashed her best impish smile.

I rolled my eyes, "Gourmet or mutt?"

"Mutt. Ace Doggie Bites," she said.

"Its gotta be a 'dog send'" Jeff punned.

We burst out laughing.

"Don't throw them overboard," he added.

"Excuse me." Millie said, "You won't catch me scoffing that muck. It's full of offal. Guts. Innards n' slime."

"You'll eat your words soon," I said.

"If Ace can eat it, I can." Zoë asserted, wrinkling her nose. Fish mimicked.

"You can cook half an hour, once a day then," Jeff said, "one burner only."

"Some of us can manage a diet," I said cheerfully, smiling at Cris's frown. I pulled at my bikini strings. "Fish and Zoë can't have their portions cut. You can play a tune on their rib cages."

The girls nodded.

I'd noticed Cris and Millie thinning out, Cris's muscular frame emerging, and Millie's infamous sun tops no longer struggling. She'd become more curvaceous as her stomach flattened out; baby face also refined. Women of any age dreamt of a figure like hers, paid thousands to go under the knife.

Malcolm sat grizzling, rummaging through his pack. I caught his anger glancing off Cris and myself while the supply crisis was mulled over.

"It's decided," I said. "Strict rations. Millie and Zoë are the food accountants. Weigh what's left."

"And drink." Zoë asserted.

"We'd better hope for more rain," Jeff said, "Wasted a great chance yesterday."

✺

Now, time weighed in heavily against us.

Life was a spark and death lay all around. Old Harry Trumble called any sea "an unforgiving mistress."

I took over from Cris on the early graveyard shift, twelve til four. There was little distinction between water and sky, no moon to cast a haloed glow on the wave crests.

Thickening cloud blotted out friendly stars I loved to gaze at. On a clear night the Milky Way's aureole made night almost dawn bright overhead, like the millions of galactic sparks Sascha and I loved staring at.

The following evening I confronted Jeff over his condition.

"You want my shift tonight?" Jeff said. "Fancy a secret rendez-vous with Cris, eh? Bit of hot pashing? Saw you sparkin' over him at cards, and the strip tease you and Madam Lilly-bum put on..."

"No. It seemed like a good strategy at the time, anyway, I'm not a prude. We needed some fun. You're worrying too much and your headaches aren't helping. Try to sleep more. Take these sleeping tablets."

"You sure about this? Six hours is too long hooked on a tiller."

"I'll be fine. After all, I've always been a night owl." I kissed his forehead, grabbed a windcheater, and slipped up on deck.

83

Chapter 13

Midnight shift was solitary think time. Cris's snores punctuated the slap and soosh of waves, and a host of burbling noises peculiar to this boat. A loose pot clattered.

Millie's seesaw voice struggled with *Wasteland's* inane 'zap' music; some of the Techno-drone craze I figured as ultra-trash, real 'Emo' stuff, like putting up with a wailing zombie in a hypnotic state, or some off-world alienoid vocalising an itch they couldn't scratch, perfect for a world falling apart.

On deck a rope end slapped in rhythm.

Over shimmering waters a platinum moon rose like an Arabian blade. The air struck crisp and clear making my nose itch. Wisps of cloud feathered eastward.

High overhead, Orion's belt and Dog Star, Sirius, played hide and seek amongst denser formations.

Nestled down in dad's old jacket, the immediate world felt less threatening.

Elysius tracked smoothly pushed by a lazy westerly. I burrowed inside the fleece, early sleep dreams fading as my eyes lost focus, became leaden, impossible to stay open. *Wasteland* lay wounded with one of its strangling end pieces. Jeff's deep-throated snore rose and fell joining Malcolm's thin wheeze.

※

Sensations of something deep and throbbing stole into my conscience. Jeff must've started the engine? The hiss and gurgle of passing seas reassured me all was right in the half world of sleep. I dozed on, my mind stupefied by the ocean's rhythm.

A sudden surge of water lifted and drove us sideways, throwing me across the cockpit, snapping me awake. Shock.

"Cripes!"

The mast and rig twanged with the jolt. A cracking report filled the air.

I scrambled, slammed my foot against the tiller, pushing hard over to port.

I stared dumfounded as a wall of flecked rust and red paint ground by. Its engine drumming, the wash from its prop already thrashed alongside.

Millie screamed from below. Footsteps clamoured. Someone tripped.

"Bloody hell." Cris raged, looking aft. "What was that?" He stared in every direction but the right one, mouth agape, dumb-struck in the darkness.

"Jee-zus frig-gin-cripes." Malcolm exclaimed in his usual inventive, and now strangely clipped tirade.

In seconds everyone except Jeff milled around peering into the night.

The craft was already a vague silhouette in the murk, a slash of grey topsides fading. A lone running light, a mere spark on the mast, was all we could make out. I'd seen no nameplate or number. No crew showed.

"Ummm - I th-think we've been si-sideswiped," I stammered in disbelief. "It looked like one of those small freighters or fishing fleet thingos."

"Why didn't you get out of its way?" Cris said.

"I must've drifted off for a moment. Stop bagging me out, Cris."

"A few? More like a whole bleedin' lot o' time." he sniped.

"You try a double shift alone, wise guy."

"Ye nearly put us in deep shit," Malcolm drawled, doing his best to look serious, but coming across as the juvenile thug, the classical Aussie 'bush lawyer' know-it-all.

"Once a smart arse, always a smart arse," I said.

My fury far outweighed guilt. "Your screw-up's the reason I'm on double shift."

Jeff slept on, sedated by a painkiller and sleeping tablet, oblivious of our brush with disaster.

"Go below. Look for leaks, thickhead. Make yourself useful. All of you," I said. "Try the port side lockers. Don't wake Jeff."

The chilling possibility we could be forced to man the pumps added a horrible dimension to our situation. If the leak was bad, then what? We were 1700 nautical miles west southwest of Motu-Riva. Suddenly it felt a world away. What if a storm hit us? We could go down in minutes if the hull rupture was big enough.

Lights flashed below.

"There's some water under the galley sink," Millie cried.

"Yea. Under the quarter berth too," Malcolm said.

Cris arrived minutes later frowning with the post-mortem news.

"Found a crack, more a seam, and not very long from what I can tell. It's along the waterline. How strong is this tub?"

"It's extremely strong, and it's a yacht. Best you treat her with respect."

Cris snorted, "didn't want to go on this..."

"You two would be rotting back there. Here, you live. Be bloody thankful. Stop whingeing like a brat."

His face darkened. "Can you blame me for being crapped off? We came *that close!*" He waved his closed thumb and forefinger in front of my nose. I wanted to bite it off.

Sleep was impossible. I felt wired in the wake of our night visitor. Bilge pumping every hour proved the leak small.

On a port tack, we exposed enough of the surface to see below the waterline and note the abrasion along the hull. There was little to see. We made up a mix of fast setting concrete dad kept for patching breaks in the hull's tough shell. It would fuse into any cracks.

I hung upside down, held by Cris and Zoë. Application took several minutes, and with a fine, plastic tape sealed over it, the patch set.

Malcolm appeared before watch change looking lost in Cris's manged, shag sweater, but suitably at home.

"What ails you?" I said, barely keeping a lid on contempt.

"Bet that scared the crap outa ye," he chided.

"You could say that. Won't help hair colour." I half smiled.

"I figured your frillies needed changing." He shifted closer, face on. "Did you find what ye wanted in me pack?"

"Umm. More than I expected." I blushed.

"The pills?" I said, keeping eye contact.

"That's me 'stash'. It's mescalin, like that peyote jazz the Mexicans get from cactus. Real buzzy head-trip. Makes snoggin' hot," he leered, "makes yer tips tingle all over. Want some? It's free."

"Keep it to yourself. That muck's better overboard. The dirty money in the role, how much?"

"Maybe seven thousand."

"You sliced up a girl to get it?"

"Naw. Girl? Chisel-faced bitch. Remember? I told you. She's alive and a lot wiser."

"Don't you dare push stuff on Millie. Ever. I'll see Cris and Jeff give you a permanent bath. Get me?"

"Millie's high naturally. We lift off."

He rolled his eyes, flickering his tongue out. Reptilian.

Images of it licking over Millie, slithering snake-like - I shook my head.

As if by cue, Millie slipped into the cockpit, slid up against Malcolm, both wrapping in a practiced embrace. Her skin formed a patchwork of mottled white and brown. Newly broken blisters wept.

"Golly, Bree. Cris is swearing mad. Says you're a piranha, or something."

"Pariah," I said. "Piranhas will bite your little butty to the bone. Cris is toothless."

"What? Whatever," She said staring. She wore that stunned look like the time Jeff scorned her out over writing 'vergina' rather than vagina in her health exam.

"So. You figure Cris wants a snipe at me?" I said.

Millie laughed. "He's still afraid of you."

"He wants you on tap," Malcolm grinned. "You really put the software in his face."

Millie giggled, slapped his hand.

I regretted giving him the chance to twist my words to his own end.

"Lancelot's got great stayin' power."

"Didn't he get skewered in a battle? Chopped." I said, retreating below, wedging Cris hard against the companionway wall.

"What's the storm front for?" he said.

"You'll see soon enough."

"Yer just sore cause you aren't gettin' any. You know you've got the itch," Malcolm called, his voice trailing off. "Why not get it scratched?"

"What's grease-ball talking about, Bree?" Zoë said. "What itch?"

"It's nothing. Hot air. He's primitive."

"Oh. *The* itch."

She waved a card from the pack they were using.

"He's this guy for sure. The joker."

Moments later Millie flounced down into the galley; attacking grubby cups with the salt water we used to save fresh water. Cris's raving penetrated the cabin, low and intense. The clatter of dishes blotted out the drift of his words. I knew who was on the receiving end.

"My brother's such a spoiled sport. He needs a life. He's not bossing me or Malcolm around."

She flung a mug up the stairway.

"Ow! What the hell are you on about? Quit your bitchin'," Cris said.

Millie sobbed, slumped over the sink.

Let gnashing dogs lie, I figured.

Jeff poked his head dreamily through the curtains.

Zoë jumped in through the front hatch. "We've got a fish trapped on deck," She said, amazed. "Shiny. Blue. So cool—and a blue squid."

"Go away. I won't cook it." Millie groaned.

"Japanese eat raw fish. It's sliced thin. Delicious. Protein." I declared.

"Raw? Ewe," she shook.

Jeff butted in. "Pardon me. What's the commotion about? Had the screwiest dream. Millie threw a saucepan at me."

"Well. It was a huge one—a domestic blue," I said, "an ocean-going soapie."

Jeff gaped at us, lost for words.

Chapter 14

Time dragged as we nosed towards Motu-Riva.
Miserable rations, stingy drinks, raised the spectre of starvation, demoralising and dangerous far from land.

My stomach tightened, ribs became easily countable. "I'm supposed to be filling out, getting curves. Look. My arms are like, well, like..."

"Rubbish," Jeff said, "you're naturally lean. There's real muscle somewhere. You look great."

"Fibber. Thanks heaps."

"You've put Cris in a tail spin, aye," he mocked.

"Drivel." I gave him a cold stare.

"Hey, cut the ice. He's agitated. But, I can't figure you out. Juice him up one sec, and then wag your assets. Now he's a deadhead."

"It's a female's prerogative," I raised a brow, "besides, I've an ulterior motive."

Not being into scheming, Jeff registered confusion.

Zoë and Fish pattered down the stairs, wedged into the settee.

"We netted four flying fish. One got away."

"Then everyone gets half a fish. Lightly cooked. A minute a side. On 'couscous'," I said, smiling, giving both a hug. Fish clung hard, showing surprising strength.

"We've two litres of metho left," Millie sighed.

"We'll soak rice and grind it with a pestle. With a dissolved stock cube it'll make gruel, like porridge." I said, "With sliced fish?"

The boys rigged netting under the boom to snare flying fish that at night skimmed out of the sea onto our cabin top. They'd lay trapped, mouths gulping, trying to spread quivering fins, powerless to flip over the high gunwale running the length of the boat. One turned up in the neatest place.

"Jeez. You guys sure dig a cruel prank. Root a crow." Malcolm said, huffing.

"What's that?" Jeff inquired, grinning, continuing to tinker with the engine.

"Me bleedin' bed, mate. It's under me pillow. Still alive."

"Sounds bleedin' fishy to me," Cris added, peering down the stairs.

"A red herring?" I asked.

Groans. Malcolm cracked up.

"Eew, that's scaly," Zoë cackled.

That was enough. We howled with laughter.

"The smell won't be noticeable, Mal. Anything's an improvement," I said.

He at least could laugh at his own expense, craved attention, took a prank well. My sympathy lasted long enough to like the sleaze bag.

Malcolm's face distorted, mouth gaped as he slid half the fish onto his tongue.

"Beauty or the beast," I sighed, "you're such a goof."

"Thanksh ever," he gagged, accepting compliment.

※

A string of ex's marked the calendar Jeff kept over the chart table. He recorded each reading he took by the stars and the GPS, side by side. The only Pacific chart we owned was kept under a sheet of plastic. On it he'd marked an X for each of three star sightings and dated it. A line was drawn to join these.

We were about seven hundred nautical miles from the island, roughly on the same latitude as Rapa Island far to the east, the most southerly island in the Austral volcanic chain. Our course had changed little over the last few weeks, averaging around 040, a northeast set. The ocean's current still carried us about a dozen extra kilometres a day towards our destination, and the winds remained kindly, perhaps too easy, making me edgy.

Occasional stiff squalls and patchy rain from the south interrupted good weather. A quick wash and a few litres of water collected for drink made these an exciting break in the monotony. A monster storm, like the dreadful ones created for films, lurked somewhere on the ocean ready to swallow intruders. Chart information we'd mauled over again and again suggested this was a time when conditions were not likely to be severe. Nobody told the ocean that.

Fine days brought a great albatross skimming by, giving us the once over.

A black fin edged with white and missing a chunk from the back edge suddenly appeared one morning. It tagged along for a few days, wandered back and forth in our wake. We guessed its length at four metres. As swiftly as the shark became curious, it vanished. No enticing food scraps were ever left to throw overboard. I didn't think it approved of offerings via the marine toilet.

Fear of violent weather dominated my late evening worry time. The last storm left immovable residue, a collective stench. The old diesel stank. All we'd need was an ocean turned topsy-turvy to renew the nightmare of seasickness and dampen everything down.

How I longed to stand on something that didn't sway. I woke tired, went to bed grimy. Toothpaste and salt water don't mix well. I cannot live with furry teeth.

"Dog biscuits on mashed rice. Ugh," Jeff said. "Now I know why Ace chased his tail."

"That happened before dinner," I said. "Got the urge?"

"Ace liked her food, and so will I," Zoë insisted.

Millie wrinkled her nose. Watched. I knew she savoured a beef curry, or sweet peanut sauce. Her mouth set tight. I couldn't help salivate.

"You're not going to? Bree?"

I licked cracked lips. "It looks okay. Sort of."

Zoë stared at hers as if mesmerised.

Malcolm doted over sliced fish smeared with a pinch of spices. "Jeez, It ain't much, but if Millie done it up, I'm game." He began to munch with his mouth open.

Jeff poked at five mashed biscuits, eyeing strands of suspected sinew and oozing tissue topping a tiny portion of rice. "Bloody hell, I need sunglasses for this," he muttered.

Cris gnawed on a dry piece he'd broken up. Jaws ground. Teeth crunched. Faces laboured.

"Cris sounds just like Ace," Zoë said, "only not as pretty."

"Growf!" Jeff bellowed.

Zoë and Fish cringed. Giggled.

I swallowed as much as I could with minimal chewing, washing it down with a sip of precious water. "It's not bad."

Nothing remained uneaten. Dessert was a stale cube of cooking chocolate found under the sink, one each.

The following night Jeff toyed with our cranky short wave radio searching for news. My stomach rumbled under the treble of radio static and snatches of babble from who knows where. Reception improved around midnight.

Any news in English was thick with updates on plague, now totally out of control. Appeals to people to return home were issued.

A news commentator spoke bitterly, "Again today, scenes of tragedy unfold as desperate mobs loot anything of use in coastal towns. Livestock has been decimated and market gardens stripped."

"Police warn that any looters will be shot on sight. Anarchy and murder will be severely dealt with."

"A fat lot of good that'll do," I said.

"Too true," Jeff mumbled.

Another station, from Queensland, interviewed a doctor with a neatly clipped Indian accent, who was at the end of her tether. "What the Spanish are calling 'The Devil's Claw' or Plagarras, is scouring the human race. We don't yet know what to do. Humanity is on its knees. Best we pray to God for a solution."

This was followed by a litany of do's and don'ts.

Other stations rattled out commentary in French, Spanish, Indonesian and a host of languages I didn't recognise. All bore the sound of urgency. Desperation.

Reports of Taliban insurgents in Afghanistan being wiped out in heavy air strikes made scant news.

Waves of boat people continued to flee, breaking onto the shores of Australia, and swarming east into the Pacific. Fiji's tiny army was beset by thousands of landings.

"Your friend's somewhere in Sydney," Jeff said.

I nodded. "Don't talk about it."

Jeff shifted topics. "There's fish and fruit on the island. Not many people. Only a handful now, so dad said. A 'Tsunami in 07 wiped out the villages. Survivors went north to Tahiti."

"No," I said, "I didn't know that."

"He told me last year in one of his reveries. I'd forgotten it."

That really miffed me. I thought dad told me everything important when he phoned. I knew of tidal waves, but didn't connect.

"Getting there won't be a minute too soon. I'm scared for Millie," I said.

"What Airhead Millie and Dunderhead do isn't our concern.

As long as they perform their watches."

"Jeff. She's fourteen."

"More sixteen. I know it's the legal age. Tell hormones that. If they've got the hots we can't just pry them apart. The worlds changed."

"And if she gets pregnant? Cris'll kill him if I don't first," I said.

"Cris has no control over her."

"You dislike her that much?" I locked eyes with Jeff.

"No. Sometimes I like her, but she's mostly up my nose." He shook his head. "Bloody rules aren't the same any more."

"I watched her eyeing you off last week. She wants your attention. Talk to her, share a few thoughts."

"I hadn't noticed. Mal can have her," he said. "He'll soon get tired."

"She deserves better, dopey." Jeff's stubborn streak was as gnarly as his hair. His indifference burned me, but then, my own feelings about independence blurred the issue.

Radio Pacific drifted across the airways. Strains of a Polynesian choir filled the air, rich and sensual, then the set crackled and cut out. Jeff swore.

In my books now no news was good news.

For breakfast I helped Millie and our two midgets grind the rice we'd soaked overnight. Seven hundred grams wasn't much ground into a coarse paste. We ate twice a day, portioning out remaining scraps of dried beans and fruit. We were now in blue waters. No flying fish appeared.

The most dreadful thing of all was running out of stove fuel. No mug of coffee to spark the day. No cooked meals.

Jeff seemed undisturbed, tinkering with the engine, whistling scraps of 'Bananas in Pyjamas'. He stopped. Sucked in air.

"There's oil in the bilge. The plug must've corroded, fallen out. Damn. Can't use the engine. It'll overheat and cut out."

"Can you fix it?" I said.

"Can't get at it. Tight as a drum. No room to work. No spare plug. Umm. No oil.

"Then we're powerless when we go through the break in the reef. The south entry looks narrow."

"There's water damage to the map. Can't tell if there's a passage through the north reefs," Jeff said. "Maybe we'll get enough out of the old thing before it dies," he speculated, brows furrowed.

I saw him finger the healing scar on his head. A fuzz of hair softened the redness.

The tiny map dad stashed in his log book ages back, the one I thought of as a hopeless scrap, now became a treasure, our lifeline. It lay before us, sketchy and badly faded, but looked drawn to scale. The south passage showed clearly enough.

"It's a kilometre wide," I said. "If the wind's from the south we can sail straight in."

"Think again. Try half that distance if we have to tack against a northerly. Bloody awkward, The boat's slow," Jeff said.

"Fancy doing a three kilometre swim to the island? Sharks," I said.

Jeff's brow rose.

I imagined us smashing into the reef, thrown into the breakers, fins slicing closer. There were big ones in the deeps. Tigers. White pointers. "If we can't see the passage?" I said.

"Zoë can go up in the bosun's chair. She's half monkey anyway or Banoba. She sticks her nose into everything," Jeff chuckled.

"Be thankful she's a climber," I said, resenting my body didn't share some sort of dangling gene.

❋

Keeping an eye on the hungers of Millie and Mal continued. They were usually split up on shifts at the helm. Zoë and Fish acted as interveners, largely out of loving Millie's interest in fashion, music and verbal diarrhoea. The tiny galley was the focal point. They often sat cross-legged, face-to-face on the floor.

Why Millie accepted her red and purple bruises under the earlobes and elsewhere bugged me. Necking? Whoever coined that had little understanding of anatomy.

Tonight I couldn't sleep, longed for a landfall. Jeff and Cris clamoured around on deck drawing in sail. The wind freshened. The cabin lay deep in shadow.

It's strange how a whole collection of familiar sounds won't disturb you. Toss in one bedevilling extra, and the mind strains to account for it, like a scritch, scritch of something outside on a windy night while you lie snug under warm covers.

Forward, something at first muffled, deep throated and laboured rose as Elysius plunged. Each successive wave magnified it.

Utensils clattered in the sink.

Wind moaned through rigging.

Shallow breathing quickened, soft and rhythmic, becoming more insistent.

On deck the working of the winch jarred my senses as the genoa was taken in.

"Damn them." I muttered. My ears flexed. Strained. I held my breath, unable to move.

"Not so -" she rasped, "let me."

She whimpered. Pounding, rhythmic, like kneading and slapping of bread dough.

My temples hammered. Sweat beads joined, flowed down my face, stomach tingling. I smelled their heat.

I lay angry in the ruins of a useless hope. He'd struck. Furious in my revulsion, I craved for what I'd never found the nerve to do.

The seas quickened. We were healed over, plunging into building waves. She lifted, slamming tons of concrete into tons of water.

Her groans rose with the pounding of the waves.

Millie laughed. She muttered love words.

I fought with images. Emotions.

A sudden blast of wind set the rig humming, the sail peaks snapping. Cris scrambled below, soaked, snatched rain gear.

"You've seen a ghost?" I said, peering up into his face, desperate to distract.

He leaned into my berth. "Join us." he said, "I don't like what I see."

I spotted Malcolm slithering into his bunk; naked and flushed, he made as if he'd just woke. Mal struggled, an underworld pantomime with a blanket over his head, hopping into shorts, one arm hooking the compression post.

"I think Mill's sick again," he said, "heard her moaning, Cris."

Cris was oblivious, intent on bracing for the night. He scrambled up the stairs.

I struggled into rain gear.

Chapter 15

Cris gaped at the seas, mouth open, looked angrily at me. "We're stuffed. It'll friggin' drown us, Bree."

I shook my head, emphasising the exact opposite, but felt the bottom drop out of my stomach.

The storm boiled, rushed with dense downpours of rain, needling flesh.

Jeff already battened down the mail sail, reduced the genoa, leaving just enough sail surface to give Elysius headway. Even with so little canvas exposed, I wondered. Why didn't these rip apart? They were so old and frayed.

"It's impossible. Which way are we going?" I shouted to Jeff.

"Forward. Not much. Maybe two knots."

"The waves." I pointed senselessly. Jeff's pug nose rammed into my ear as we lurched.

"Big, and getting bigger. I lashed the sea anchor forward with plenty of rope. Might need to ride it out."

"Better do it soon?" I shrieked, but the wall of wind stripped words, warped them, blowing endings away.

Cris clung to the tiller as if frozen.

"I'll take it a while," I mouthed, pointing.

"No." His head shook, eyes remaining focused on each mass of spew-streaked sea.

Cris the control freak? Craving to prove his worthiness? Such was his growing romance with water. But this Cris I admired.

Elysius rose to meet each wave. Her generous clipper bow and beam helped to lift us, rather than ploughing into each mass.

Sheets of spray peeled off the wave tops, created a grey mist, melding with the rain, making it impossible to see more than a few metres ahead.

If a King-hit wave came we'd never know it. A double massif of water could tower, crash tons of water on us.

The sky remained a deep charcoal-like murk, no distinction possible between sky and the madness mauling us about. I felt detached from anything solid, as if we'd be sucked up sky-bound in a cyclonic spiral.

Plunging into the trough made my stomach clench. Each time she rose, splitting the wave peaks, sending jets of water back slapping our faces, the sea spoke of its mastery. The waves were at least six metres from peak to trough, some bigger.

Safety harnesses were essential. If anyone had to move it was vital to be hooked to something solid. Our slackness weeks back taught us a cheap lesson.

Anyone swept overboard now wouldn't live long enough to be plucked from the waves, besides; trying to turn around as rescuers would be suicidal. Being too slow, coming about to retrieve someone would see us broached by a wave, hammered side on. We'd turn turtle.

Elysius could behave badly in foul weather if not closely steered, like saying a 'mantra', watch - always watch.

"Go below. You and Dunghead do the next shift," Jeff gestured.

"He's looking after Millie. She's seasick," I said. What a fib. Better to contain the facts for now.

"To hell with Millie. You need a second on deck. We do two hour shifts until the storm breaks."

"Thanks heaps."

Even with oilskins I'd iced through, shivering. My skin rubbed against the worn oilskin lining, neck and breasts stinging with any sudden movement.

※

"Boofhead! Mal, shift it, you're on," I grimaced, leaned on the chart table support post for relief.

"Gee-zus. It's real bad." Malcolm declared.

At least he'd wrapped his lean mind around one fact; this was a nasty storm, appeared accepting. Maybe with his constant scrapes in life, he was better equipped to handle this voyage than Cris.

The following days redefined hell as wet and bloody cold. The only good omen was an easing wind shift from the west. We plunged and shook ourselves into exhaustion. The waves became tossed. Confused. Dancing seas with cross-chop are the kind that grind away energy, make you not care any more. These harboured killer waves. And there was hyperthermia. Oh, for a mug of java. Savoury stew.

The girls managed to feed us our quota of biscuits minus the rice. Cold Bonox in water.

"Six a day," Zoë said. She'd decked out in pink and blue tights and a wool pullover, her face taut, eyes big and anxious.

Millie moaned, crawling on hands and knees pushing her red bucket like a crutch. A puddle of murky bile swilled in the bottom.

There's no pleasure without pain, I thought, patting her back. "It'll soon be over, Millie."

She clutched my leg, eyes vacant. "I'm scared."

"Me too," I said.

"You don't look it. Why aren't you sick?"

Fish plonked herself next to Millie. Grasped her hand.

What a curious little thing. Disturbing. Silent. Now intensely expressive. Her eyes captured attention, like a war orphans, deep socketed, accusing, sympathetic.

Fish's smile was all the more captivating. Nothing we tried unlocked her thoughts. I sensed volumes pressured inside. So near. So far.

Day three saw the storm ease. Elysius heaved, quaking to a stop, regaining momentum. Repeated.

Malcolm lay strapped into his bunk self-satisfied, as if lost in another world. His pupils were large in the chart table's half-light.

"Are you stoned?" I demanded.

He grinned like the goon he was. "On love and an 'upper'," he said.

"Meaning? You doped her then took advantage."

Malcolm barely acknowledged I knew his conquest.

"It was just a tranquilliser. She wanted it."

I eyed the bag he kept under his pillow. "We're due up top. Get your head together," I said.

He made for the stairs like a drunk in a trance. I snatched the tote bag, pushed him up the companionway into the cockpit, and in full sight of Jeff and Cris, with all my strength, heaved the bag over the side.

Malcolm gaped after it, shook his head.

"Aw! What'd ye do that for, ye moll."

I glared at him.

If looks killed I'd be dead now. So would he. First.

The boys looked at one another, grim, but grinning.

※

Early the fourth morning broken cloud and an easing wind gave us an alarming view of the seas. Somehow, I thought they were smaller. Maybe I'd gotten used to them.

Jeff grabbed a pan, began bashing it with a ladle. Motu-Riva's just over the horizon."

"You're not serious?" Cris said.

"Get me off this thing." Millie's muffled cries came from up forward.

"How far?" I said, seriously doubting.

"About one hundred thirty, if the GPS isn't lying. I've marked it and double checked." He pointed to an X only millimetres from the island dot on the pilot chart.

"Storm must've pushed us nearly two hundred east."

We ate two extra biscuits each that evening.

※

"I see something. Clouds and a mountain." Jeff shouted. "Land, real land!" His eyes remained glued to the binoculars. It was two days later, six fifty-five a.m. on a testy, cobalt blue sea. October sixteen.

"Brekkie time," I proclaimed. Bit my lip too hard. Zoë gave me a kick.

Within the hour we made out two peaks. Ragged cloud masked whatever else lay ahead. A shroud of mist enveloped the rim of the reef adding obscurity to the final barrier we longed to see.

Each took turns peering through the glasses, trying to confirm the obvious, but still gaped in disbelief. Despite foggy minds, the idea we'd land grew, fired a dizzy kind of elation.

But four days of battering with nothing left dry took its toll; time and misery are aeons long when you're trapped and emotionally brittle.

Jeff and Cris were exhausted, sapped of colour. Malcolm momentarily ceased being Mr. Cool. He brooded; sulked since his precious goodie bag lay with Davy Jones's deep.

I felt sorry for myself, lost interest in mirror studies. Matted hair. Bruises. Split lips. Unwanted shadow. I'd never recover.

Wouldn't pass as a sea hag.

Millie remained below in misery unable to take anything down. Death grey isn't a pretty colour except on a ghoul at a masquerade.

"Are you sure it's the island?" she whispered, staring up, imploring me to make it real.

"Quaff this." I measured out a shot of overproof rum into cold coffee. "Down it."

Millie swallowed. Choked.

"Bree. Shivers. My gut. It's on fire."

"It's what we all need. Everyone gets a shot."

"Rum? You hid it." Jeff accused.

"The secret medicine chest," I said.

Millie wretched. Heaved up.

❋

"The gap in the south of the reef," Jeff said, his face set grim. "It looks passable."

"The sooner the friggin' better," Cris growled.

"Rushing in could be a disaster," I said.

Jeff and I looked at Zoë. "You've been up the bosun's chair before. It's fun," Jeff forced a smile.

Zoë stared at the mast spreaders swaying high above. She nodded, "Sure thing."

For a child of twelve she ignored fear at any height. Ever since able to walk Zoë climbed anything. Book cases. Tree house. Dragging her out of a tree was common until we realised her agility far surpassed ours, said going up the mast was like going on the 'Slingshot' at Surfers Paradise. She called it the 'chunder bucket.' Wore platform shoes to pass for height, false ID for age, wormed her way in.

High in the spreaders Zoë could see the southern passage and telltale foam where deadly coral lay.

"This is the slot we've got to find," I said, fingering dad's faded map, "It's about a kilometre wide."

"Those splotchy marks. Are they reefs?" Zoë said.

"Looks like it. You're our eyes, Zorro sweetie. Warn us." We clung together fierce in love and determination.

By mid morning Elysius lay a respectful half kilometre out, running parallel to raging froth and rebounding waves. Zoë perched,

100

giving a reedy commentary of anything unusual.

"There's little pancake islands on the reef. Palm trees. Dolphins!"

A pod of these suddenly knifed gracefully by, making a game of the bow wave and chop, racing ahead as if impatient for action.

Zoë screeched, "I see a break."

It was difficult to spot from the cockpit. Jeff fired up the diesel as we closed, scraping by the western rim of the reef. With a sick engine we needed to use sail to keep speed up for any sudden manoeuvre.

"That's shaving it," Cris censored, mouth working, wanting to say much more.

It looked like we'd need a double tack, a zigzag course to get us through. The wind remained stiff from the northwest.

With shallow ridges of jagged coral on either side, Elysius plunged ahead hard into a strong tidal flow. Within moments we seemed almost stopped dead in our track, the engine throbbing at half speed, sails full on, vibrating. The sea about was sudsed where waves met exiting waters in a wild boil.

Zoë screamed, "coral! Hundred metres."

Jeff hollered, "Tell us when to tack."

It took ages before we closed the distance to the coral heads on the eastern side.

"Come about." Zoë and Jeff cried almost in unison, Jeff snapping the tiller over to starboard while Cris winched the sheets in on the port side, his arms flailing. The sails, thrashing and chaffing, cracked into tight curves on the new course. Elysius struggled, gained headway.

"Two hundred metres to the west rim," Zoë howled, barely heard, as we prepared to tack again.

"Shit." Jeff snarled, "We're trapped in an eddy."

"We'll get driven onto coral." I said.

I saw what confronted us. As we approached the west side of the reef gap the seas pushed us forward, but to our right there was a strong outflow judging from a broken palm frond whisking by.

We tacked once more gaining slightly until mid- stream, but lost all gain on the following tack.

"I've gotta flog the diesel," Jeff said.

We jumped ahead when the old Yanmar began pounding her heart out below. The stench of diesel smoke and oil soon began curling up from inside.

Once more on a port tack, we were able to gain distance, putting us half way through the passage. At that moment the diesel died, the acrid stink of smoke driving Millie on deck, hacking her lungs out, eyes watering.

"It's now or -" Jeff cried, coming about on a starboard tack with the wind filling the sails in a sudden gust.

Cris swore under his breath.

Ahead lay a maze of coral outcroppings like ribs across the eastern side of the entrance.

"Keep her high. The tides dragging us out," I said.

Jeff nodded, his eyes glued to every movement.

"There's a hole in the coral," Zoë's voice barely registered.

Suddenly we were funnelling in a back-eddy, wedged between two ridges of coral, so close the boat hook could touch them either side.

A shudder and grating ripped through Elysius. We lurched heavily, but kept going as we reached the end of an outcrop on our left.

Cris panicked, "we've hit something."

"We're sinking!" Millie shrieked.

"It's just the keels, dummy." Jeff yelled. "We've got three of 'em. Come about." Jeff commanded.

With a flurry of hands and arms we changed direction, and on a port tack slipped by another lump of coral and into the lagoon.

You'd think scraping through the coral's eye would raise a cheer. We sat mesmerised. Against a backdrop of reef breakers, we feasted on tranquillity and colour.

"It's awesome, like the Barrier Reef," I said. A school of fish flashed by swirling silver, slashes of electric yellow.

Motu-Riva lay beyond, imposing, rugged. A series of five jagged peaks, rearing from the ocean depths, lay strung out in a line from east to west.

Dense patches of trees, palms and scrub clothed the slopes from the shoreline to the near-vertical escarpments in a riot of rich greens. Above a myriad of ravines the peaks soared, raked with tumbling cloud.

Primeval majesty. The valleys loomed dark and brooding, suggesting a mysterious past.

I recalled scraps of mum and dad's tales. Dad said the Motu-Riva natives were a strangely staid lot, except for the young who hungered for contact. Mum introduced them to some Latin

102

American dances.

I suspected I'd been conceived in one of their yeowling matches on that stay. At home, late at night I woke to mating sounds, at first using my Walkman to blot it out. Agitated, soon imagination demanded I listen.

Now I felt the island's magnetism coursing through me. I shivered as much from cold as anticipation.

Fish tugged at Cris's arm, pointing to the spreaders, her face etched with fear.

"Where's Zoë?" Cris said. "She's not up the mast."

We leaped to the sides of the boat, peering back into the breakers.

"She's fallen overboard when we hit the reef." Jeff said, panicking. All we saw was a maelstrom of roaring foam behind us.

"I can hear her squealing somewhere," Millie said.

"She's out there," Cris insisted.

"Not so fast," I said, heading for the bow, peering down to the chain holding the bowsprit.

"Zoë, dearest, what possessed you to hang out on the chain?" I shouted, feigning anger.

"Just testing the water, Bree. Its real cool, Whale Beach cool." She glowed joy in her newest find.

"You wanted off first?" I chided.

"How'd she pull that stunt off?" Cris said.

"Spider monkey," I said.

Jeff sighed, "throwback. Suffered it for years."

"Where do we anchor?" Cris said.

We scanned the coast and made for a flatter stretch of land halfway to the western point.

"That's a boat of some kind. On the reef," Cris pointed, "maybe five kilometres?"

I peered at the smudged shape, angled oddly against the inner edge of the reef encircling the island. Its hull stood out darker than surly rain clouds obscuring horizon to the west.

Glasses made out the hull as black, her two masts angled. At a distance I knew this boat, but from where?

Chapter 16

By late afternoon we dropped anchor close to a shallow inner reef aproning the shore. Land loomed close, drawing us. I smelled the richness of vegetation, the power of flowers and things pungent, earthy.

Rainsqualls drove us below to spend a fitful evening picking through soggy bedding and sorry clothing. Over-tired and high on adrenalin, I couldn't sleep. Images of bananas and succulent melons, a plate of savoury chicken cacciatore, excited.

The boys lay zonked out except for Malcolm, who sat stroking Millie's face and hair. She sprawled against him, a tangled wreck, mouth open, deep in sleep. I watched from the rim of my vision, reflexing away as his hand played.

"Lets make a tent on deck," I said.

"Just like old times," Zoë laughed. She hissed at Malcolm, sticking her tongue out. His, long and pointing, mocked her.

We spread the water gathering tarp over the solar panels to make a crude tent shielding us from showers. We drank water from the tarp funnel. Fish slurped.

Wrapped in blankets, it was bliss to huddle together in the cockpit gazing at clouds scudding over the island. Patchy silhouettes of the peaks emerged and dissolved. A family of tall palms swayed by the beach.

"There's a light way off. I saw it flicker." Zoë said jumping to the cabin top.

We stared for several minutes. Nothing. There must be a village close by the lagoon. The very thought of touching land and speaking to someone, an islander, thrilled me.

"I imagine a party of bronzed natives decked in flowers, glistening, umm, muscled, bearing coconuts and fruits to lay before us tomorrow," I said.

"Are you all right, Bree?"

"No, but I'll have to do." I ruffled her salty curls.

Fear of contact with islanders brought back reality.

Fish's face contorted, wormed in tighter, whimpered as if confronting another ghost from her hidden past.

"Why's Millie pashing with Malcolm? She's got no taste." Zoë griped. "He's such a pox head. Bet she's hooked on his hydraulics." She thrust a fist upward.

I laughed. "Where did you cook up such a notion?"

"I saw it. Remember? It's gross.

"Can't see any way around it."

Zoë giggled, "for sure."

"I mean they've meshed. You know. 'Madly mated'. Nothing we can do about it, except wait. She'll see through him."

I didn't believe my explanation.

"There it is." She pointed. I saw the glimmer of light. Faint sounds like drums rose and fell. The storm remnants booming on the reef rendered it indistinct.

I wondered what it would be like, snug in some island hut, sitting on woven mats under a palm leaved roof.

"We'll get ashore early tomorrow. Get some fruit. Coconuts."

"Do you think anyone will come see us?" Zoë said.

"I don't want to mix with anyone. We've come all this way to escape people."

"What if the plague's here?" Zoë said solemnly, her eyes watery.

"There's no place left to run. We're here for the duration. Months. Maybe years. Besides, there aren't many people left on this island. It's really isolated."

"What happened to them?"

"Jeff says dad mentioned a massive tsunami, a tidal wave, several years back, two thousand seven, I think. Most of the villages and people were wiped out. That's partly why he picked the island."

"That's awful."

"Don't expect a great social life. Just solid land and safety. We can swim and fossick like we used to."

"Awesome," Zoë sighed.

Far up on the most distant peak a second light flickered, much brighter. I wished for the binoculars, but couldn't find energy to move.

A jagged peak appeared to be a strange place for a light.

Slipping into deep sleep, there was comfort in wind and rain, canvas flapping, the gentle heave of lagoon water. A rope slapped, familiar, in concert.

※

Daybreak rushed. Dawn light slashed the eastern edges of the volcanic ridges in rayed gold and rich greens of every hue. Shadowed slopes revealed deep ravines running irregularly, mainly south to north, etching their way between jagged, bare peaks. Thick groves of trees clothed the slopes almost to the top, forming dense canopies. Some patches echoed regularity like in stepped terraces.

Morning wind wafted from the north, bringing a confusion of smells off the island.

"Lets hit the beach, find some food," Jeff said.

Before anyone moved Zoë and Fish dove in, thrashing their way to shore. Zoë was a natural in water, while Fish was less a fish, more a splasher. They let out cries of delight, rolling over and over on white sand, throwing their clothes in the air.

Cris and I endured the trip in the dinghy stone silent, unfinished issues brewing. Millie and Mal dawdled, eyeing Cris, as if unsure what to do. I saw Cris's exhaustion; face set hard, eyes cast down.

He sat on the shoreline waiting for Millie to land.

I cringed watching him reach out to help her from the dinghy. I assumed he'd taken pity on her. She was so sickly looking.

"I don't want your kind of help," she said. Millie clung under Malcolm's arm. I realised in the freshness of the morning how ill she'd become, and the growing reliance on lover boy. I'd devoted my energies so much helping Jeff keep the boat going, not exactly ignoring Millie, but not interfacing much. Exhaustion doesn't help social chatter.

Cris made things tougher. He'd be reasonable one moment, followed by a plunge into dismal brooding, I assumed must be entirely over Millie. I couldn't read the signs leading to his mood swings. It could become intolerably ugly if he knew everything.

"What's wrong with you two, eh?" Jeff said, bushy brows rising. "You look doped or drunk - the way you're walking."

"Put a sock in it," Millie mumbled.

I scowled at Jeff. He could show zero sensitivity, said the dumbest things, especially baiting Millie.

Sailor's legs. It was true. Every time I moved I braced myself

106

for the motion of the boat and swayed as if drunk, our minds still programmed by the sea. The girls staggered about in fits of laughter, falling over one another in exaggerated play.

Once on the beach we lay strung out near a dense clump of palms, regularly gulping water from a nearby stream, basking in the warmth.

The grouping reflected the politics of our voyage.

"I'm setting up camp. Don't know about you lot," Jeff prodded.

"Yeah, do that." I said. "We've got to scrub up. I'm sick of pong. I'm starved. I nominate you guys scrounge up some fruit. Coconuts," I gestured, ribbing Cris. "We'll sort out a camp site, get a fire going, and move our bedding and clothes. We can't live on Elysius another day. It's rank as a dead roo's bum."

The boys left to explore, heading up the slope towards a shallow valley a few hundred metres away, disappearing amongst a dense thicket of broadleaf and trees.

The island was bigger than I expected, considering the sketchy map dad had drawn, and at least eight kilometres long if the scale was right. Smudging made it difficult to tell width or shape on the northern side. The lights we saw were far to the east.

I felt edgy about meeting islanders.

The morning passed ferrying everything essential to shore. Zoë and Fish, babbled, spread clothing and bedding over bushes. They ran off to find fruit.

I brought the treasured rum and coffee to shore, started a fire and boiled a billy for Millie. She lay pallid, obviously in distress.

"You've had a hard go, what with the storm."

"I'm seriously crook." She whispered. Sweat beaded her face. "I haven't had a period. Overdue a week. Look at my stomach. I chucked everything."

A single tear rolled down, hung on the tip of her nose, fell on the sand.

"We've all lost too much. My belly's just as empty as yours." Slapping it made a hollow sound.

"When was the first time?"

"What?"

"Mal had you."

"How'd you know?"

I raised an eyebrow, smiled, and sighed. "I heard the whole damn show. Let me?" I made a face.

"Don't tell Cris. He'll kill me. Please?"

"It's just between you and me."

I squeezed her hand, towelled her face.

"I love Pookie. He's strong and sweet. He turns me inside out."

"Poo What? How'd you cook up a dag name like that?"

"It's personal."

"Best you keep it quiet. Love's made you silly.

Lets hope your overdue is sea sickness - stress."

She slowly sipped the spiked coffee, overproof, and sank into sleep, the cup half finished. I finished it, felt the fire course from stomach to brain, instantly tipsy. We rigged towels over sticks and left her shaded. Zoë and Fish played in the shallows, each clutching a banana, engrossed in collecting shells.

A narrow, inner reef ran parallel to shore. It was almost exposed lagoon side, but deepened towards the beach, making a safe haven.

I left the beach, intended a short trip, hoping to find a fresh water pool. A crude road ran parallel to the shoreline. It was thickly overgrown with saplings and bush. Beyond lay a series of narrowing valleys divided by sharp ridges. The farthest valley immediately right was widest, and most inviting. Clusters of mangoes drooped, thickening the air with sweetness, making my mouth water. Several pawpaw trees stood heavy with fruit.

Birds chattered, bickered in high canopies.

A stream bubbled through dense groves and clumps of dwarfed coconut palms. Further up a stream chuckled over worn slabs of burnt-red volcanic rock, tumbling from pool to pool through broken dams that must've irrigated terraced crops. A riot of greenery and thick ferns crowded in the higher I went, making an overlapping roof. Hibiscus displayed generous sprays of flowers, pinks and deep reds.

Footprints grooved an ages old trail, which wended its way upward, inviting. Rivulets dripping off rock outcroppings added lightness to the stream's base notes, forming a myriad of subtle sounds.

A shallow dam appeared on my right. Flashes of sunlight dappled the water.

I pulled off my singlet, peeling it away from flesh made raw and swollen by the storm, and gingerly slipped into the coolness. Salt and grime dissolved. Lying back immersed up to my neck, slapping water, my body stung everywhere.

❈

Birds shrilling in the thickets shocked me awake. Still dazed, I groped for my gear and found it was gone.

Who'd steal clothing? What if a stranger - an islander - came by? I panicked. No. It had to be the boys.

Telltale footprints in mud confirmed my suspicions. Jeffie's big, pudgy feet, size ten cleated thongs. Cris's elongated foot, minus the right little toe, spelled mischief.

Along the rim of the vale lay clumps of shattered stone, some large pieces poking out of the earth, as if trying to surface. With a small chip I cut fine vines, made a three strand plaited belt, and shredded long palm leaves to loop over the weaving, covering front and back. This made a crude, somewhat scratchy mini skirt. I added small yellow flowers pushed through the weaving. Tiny hibiscus made a gorgeous lae, which hung softly around my neck. It made an imperfect cover, enough to stuff up their fun, yet avoid abrasion. I slipped a red flower over my right ear.

❈

Whistles and catcalls.

"Jeez. Look. A native hottie," Malcolm said, " hey, babe, you speak English?"

"You giving favours? Shake yer little tooshie," Cris jeered.

At least he was happy.

"*Parlez vous Anglaise?*" I mocked. Boy, could I kill French. "The boy who gets me coconuts may win my favours." Pouting my lips, eyelash batting, I mocked Cris. He held his smirk, then turned away, head shaking. Laughed.

Zoë and Fish scurried to gather vines and palms, returning to make a cheeky mini version of my native gear looking like something out of a child's pineapple ad. They dumped some by Millie, who now sat up. She'd gained colour. A coconut shell and mango remains lay by her side.

Zoë nimbly wove a belt for her and a fishnet bra from finer vine, which she laced full of daisy-like flowers.

That evening we sat around the fireglow, creating grotesque shadows in the thicket of stunted palms. Our fire created an am-

109

phitheatre of light. Jeff and Cris sat back-chatting, eyeing us occasionally, offering crude suggestions. Malcolm sat apart plucking a limp clot of chicken feathers.

Zoë, Fish and I clowned in a circle, palm skirts swishing. Gyrating about, we egged one another on.

I felt giddy with freedom. Unleashed on an island, social norms fading away.

I eyed the scrawny chicken dangling on a spit. Malcolm's find. He'd returned with a mesh sack of items, including a knife, hatchet and lump of what looked like bread, a squashed damper. Hunger cancelled curiosity as to where he found it. We knew he'd gone farther than anyone else. Obviously street wisdom brought home the bacon.

We hold the Guinness record for the quickest scoffing of chicken.

"Where'd you get the chook?" Jeff pressed.

"There's a bunch of huts way over. I did a raid on their food supply. Knocked the bird off while it slept. Snitched the bread from a cookhouse. These dudes cook in a shed. Piece of cake," Malcolm said. He exaggerated astonishment at his own success.

"So. It's not wild. You thieved," I pointed.

"Millie needed real food."

I couldn't argue with that, but angering the islanders would work against us.

"What if they attacked us?" I said. "Maybe there isn't much for them to eat either. At least you could front and ask for some food. You're such a sleaze."

"They got barriers up. Skull signs. There was a guard along the trail sportin' a gun," Malcolm said.

"We should try to make proper contact soon," I said, "make a peace offering, like a gift? Stuff your sticky fingers. Screw-up, ever consider they'll shoot first?"

"Aw. It ain't that bad."

"I'm prepared to hand you over as a gift. You need a damn good roasting."

We didn't have long to wait.

※

Three islanders, one waving a feeble torch, approached by canoe. It was very late. They stood off a hundred metres from shore, clothed in darkness. Flashes of firelight bronzed their faces. They watched.

Jeff waded out to waist level. "Hello."

"*Voule vous francais?*" The chief said.

"The guy's French," Jeff said.

"Duuh, that figures, Jeff, we're near French Polynesia. *Parlez vous anglaise?*" I shouted.

"*We, mamselle.* Little bit."

"Who are you?" I said.

His voice boomed across the water, "I chief. Where you from? *Muri?*"

"Australia," Jeff said, "you play cricket?"

"Austreeah? What is creekit?"

"Well, that worked just fine." I said.

"Oh, shut up, you do better," Jeff griped.

"*Poulet!* You have." The chief said.

"We had *poulet*," I said. "Girl. *Mamselle.* Sick."

I dragged Millie forward, rubbed her tummy, hand to forehead, swaying. "Eat chicken. Eat *poulet.*"

There was a short silence broken by heated words in dialect.

"Rat man thief. You like others. Thief food. Thief *vahine.* Go away. *Vahine,* she have big sick." The speaker thrust his torch, obviously aimed at Millie and Malcolm.

In a fit of humbleness, Malcolm produced the axe, offered its return.

That did it, royally.

"*Tupapau. Tupapau. Aita.* No!"

The three began shouting rapid fire Polynesian, none of it complimentary in tone. They paddled off into the dark.

"That fouls everything up, smart arse," I said, "you did the deed, now undo it."

"I didn't know it was stolen," Millie pleaded.

"If it's such a piece o' cake, you find something to offer them, like fish," Cris snarled.

"How do ye catch a fish?" Mal said.

"Con the bloody thing. Dope it," Cris said.

"Make a fish spear. Simple," I said.

For the next two days Malcolm swore, splintered and whittled wood while Zoë force-fed instructions how to tie the triple, serrated heads to the shaft. She dished out far more criticism than she got.

"Now make it hard over the fire." She taunted.

Jeff and I sniggered.

Malcolm, Zoë and Fish spent the whole afternoon on the reef edge nearby sussing out prey. The girls swam, peering through goggles into the turquoise shallows. Malcolm clung, hunched to the edge of the dinghy, looking every bit the rat. By dark they returned with six sizeable fish, each weighing roughly two kilos.

"I'll go with you to make peace offerings," I said. "We keep two, offer four. And the axe."

That evening we sat around the fire eating savoury fish soaked in coconut milk and limejuice.

"What did the chief mean? He said others." Jeff mused.

"He called them thieves," Cris added, showing rare interest. "What's a *vahine?*"

I said, slowly, "that's Polynesian for girl, or woman. So the chief has a bone to pick with someone, not an islander."

"Sounds like kidnapping. Maybe the chiefs daughter got nicked, eh," Jeff said. "Maybe there's more trouble than we want to know about."

Chapter 17

Our fourth morning came fresh on a southerly breeze.
Malcolm shambled along decked out in mended shorts as stylish as he was weedy. Our route took us through thriving scrub that enveloped the path. I'd decided keeping to the tree line was safer than exposure on the beach.

We crossed several dilapidated pole bridges, which spanned streams still gushing from the storm.

Near our pathway to the left were several rectangular pits dug out of raised limestone shelves, like the sea level had once been several metres higher, or the island somehow rose. Maybe the ancient volcano wasn't extinct after all, just snoozing.

All appeared charred around the upper rim and full of stagnant water, swarms of insects.

"You think those pits were some kind of cookin' oven?" Malcolm said.

I could tell he was concerned. "I've read where they used to truss up the enemy they'd captured, and slow cook them under heated rocks and palm leaves."

"You mean whole?"

"No," I said seriously, keeping eye contact, "the women slit open any still alive. The chiefs ate the, you know -" I screwed my face up. "It was for their *mana*. Spirit power. Women quite enjoyed the leftovers."

"What? Jeeze, you read some weird stuff."

"Use your imagination, Malcolm."

As we continued walking he cast glances at me.

Mosquitoes clouded, adding to bites suffered from beach gnats.

Fifteen minutes into our walk the first barrier appeared at a narrow pass where a ridge crowded the beach. It consisted of freshly chopped saplings woven into a wide frame.

Scrawled on a scrap of plywood were the words, 'NES PAS' and 'NO PAST'. A crudely drawn face, splashed in red paint, looking like an ancient god of some kind, stared blankly past us.

"*Tiki* Man," I said.

Malcolm stared, unable to comprehend.

"The tribe's spirit," I pointed out. "So, this is all your fault, Malcolm. You've mucked up big time."

"Yer bein' bitchy, Bree. Butt out. Watch me win these guys over."

"And pigs can fly," I said. "You're not peddling scab to gutter mates." I added, "Oh, the women stretched and cured the scrotum. Made pouches and wrapped charms in them to hang around their necks."

"Yer kiddin' me."

"Do I look it?"

Mal carried the fish strung together. The stolen axe hung on his belt. Jeff made sure the axe returned sharpened. The damper was wrapped in broadleaves, tied with vine. I carried a once brightly patterned crocheted cover as an extra offering.

We skirted the barrier, but soon another much larger blockade closed the path, forcing us to halt.

Somewhere in the maze of brush stacked against the frame I sensed more than one islander lurking. Silence told us we were unwelcome.

"Lay the goods out. Stand back."

Malcolm made to speak. I jabbed his ribs. "Now."

"Ow! Bleedin' hell," he grimaced.

"Let them speak." I gestured with my hands, palms up, arms extended. Several minutes passed. The murmur of conversation from beyond the barrier barely registered.

"They aren't real hostile," Malcolm said.

Twigs snapped. Bushes suddenly parted in a flurry.

An enormous explosion ripped the air, crashing between the hillsides, rebounding.

I jumped. Shrieked. A hibiscus bush burst apart centimetres to my right, shredded.

"Jeezus. Run for it," Malcolm cried. He bolted.

I landed on all fours. Froze. Surely they couldn't fear us? They did.

"Rat man. Missie." one of them bellowed.

I fled, dodging, branches slapping my face. Within seconds I overtook Malcolm. He was hobbling like an old man. Mal stumbled and fell in the creek.

I grabbed his arm. We scrambled up the bank, slithering on red muck, clawing our way.

"That was flamin' close," I gasped, drawing a splinter from my hair. "My ear's nicked."

"They meant to wipe me," Malcolm panted, oily hair splayed out. "Can't aim a shotgun." He laughed.

"Suit yourself," I pursed my lips. Wanted to belt him where it'd hurt most.

Jeff and Cris appeared on the run.

※

"This is the pits," I said, fingering the puncture at the top of my ear. "We should make another peace offer."

"No. It's wait n' see time," Jeff said, hand on chin, brooding.

"Lets find out more about this place," Cris said. "I recon we leave the islanders alone for now. Where are these other people? Like, if they hassled the natives, aren't we in danger?"

"A cool point," I said, "so you do some climbing. Monkey business. Have a look around from the peaks."

"Not before all the gears off the boat, eh." Jeff cautioned, placing his hands on his hips.

Jeff in power mode, I thought.

"Maybe we should move. Find a hole to hide in," Malcolm said, wearing seriousness badly. "I don't like the idea of gettin' bagged on the beach. Worse than bein' caught starkers, eh, Bree?"

※

Everything useable, except the filthiest clothing, came off the boat including flares, rope, and old sails. The crossbow, shotgun, a slingshot and recurve bow added some sense of security. All ended piled out of sight in a thicket of ferns.

For the first time since we landed Cris wasn't sulking. I watched him nimbly weave fine rope into mesh carry nets. His hands were beautiful, so supple.

Zoë and Fish helped pack these with cooking items and bedding. He whistled, mimicking local birdcalls.

"Take that, beast."

"Ow. You kicked my butt," Zoë pouted.

"Just watch it," he said, not looking up.

115

Zoë continued fussing about, being sure to present a target. Fish, wearing a demon smile, joined in for similar attention. Zoë expertly taunted him as she'd done many times.

The oldest sail served as a square for roofing, the remainder to be made as an extra rain catcher.

Early the following morning over fruit, fish fillets and coconut milk, the days' efforts were aired.

"We should explore in two groups," Jeff said. "Meet at sunset top of the path where we, uh, explored the first day." He looked down. Smiled.

Cris smirked, "there's a nice bath up there."

I refused to bite.

"Sussing won't take long. All the valleys look short and narrow," I said. "Should we go higher, near the top?"

"I'm for checking the whole area as far as the middle peaks," Jeff said.

Malcolm nodded, "the higher the better."

Millie tittered.

By midday the whole camp was stashed at the top of the same pocket valley I'd found.

Passing my bath site I spotted a fresh set of splayed footprints deep in the reddish mud. They weren't ours. I kept it to myself.

"We've got to go further, maybe to the right. It's not so steep," I said. I felt a sudden twinge of fear, an urgency to know what threatened us and to find safety.

We split up, Jeff and Malcolm, grizzling with one another, heading over the western ridges.

I latched on to Cris, our probe going eastwards towards the highest peaks. By following a narrow valley running northeast it might be possible to explore several other ravines. The most prominent summit was only a few kilometres away, so lofty, yet I imagined reaching out to touch it.

Thickets of banana, coconut, papaya and orange trees dominated the valley rim. I inhaled a cocktail of scented air, ether-like and layered with sandalwood, which filled the vale. My senses spun bringing on a bout of sneezing.

Telltale signs of ancient cultivation, and recent efforts, showed in shallow dams, most of which were collapsed. Everywhere growth invaded once cleared spaces.

Cris's bare chest heaved, glistened sweat. We were unfit from being couped up for weeks and starved. He examined the rings of a sapling.

"It's about six or seven years old," he said.

"That fits with the big tidal wave thing," I said, "nobody came back to plant crops."

We picked our way slowly through massed vegetation. The red soils' richness made everything riot for space and sunlight.

Worming up crevices laced with tree ferns and vine, we rested on a narrow ridge overlooking the next valley, which appeared an intimidating mass of greenery.

"You aren't doing very well. Why not patch it up with Millie."

"Yeah? She's always been a thorn. Way back."

"The tinsel and fantasy stuff. Her fashion mania?" I said.

"More. She always got at me. Played up to mum and dad. I coped heaps of blame, some right, lots wrong."

"You've been known to torment children and little dogs - and me." I caught a flash of mischief in his smirk.

Cris wiped his chest with the singlet looped around his shorts. He'd turned nut brown, much darker than me. I sensed his heavy odour, not unpleasant, hinting of musk. He peeled another sugar banana, dropped the skin on an inquisitive beetle.

"She's so up herself. Mirror, mirror on the wall- you know," he made a face. "I bugged her royal highness. Glue in her cosmetics. Turps in shampoo."

I hooted, "you diabolical bastard. Glad you're not my brother."

"Thanks," he said, "I'd be dead by now."

"You two are so unalike. Fair skin and hair. Dark skin and dark hair. Sure she wasn't the milkman's special?"

"I'm half Sri Lankan, half Scottish from dad's side. I'm a mongrel."

We laughed.

"Haven't a clue what she is. Millie was adopted when I was four. She's foster."

I put on an air of complete surprise. Didn't Cris realise they'd spilled the news back on board weeks ago? I spluttered for words.

"Wow! That's a bomb. You've blown me away. Does she know?" I played dumb.

"Damn rights, she does," he studied me. "I still feel responsible for her. Malcolm's a blood sucking disgrace."

117

"She's wild on him," I cautioned, resting my hand on his arm. "No sense in riling her. Let it go its own way. She'll dump him."

"If he's getting in to her, I'll kill him. Seriously. She's not humiliating my family."

"No you're not. Wake up. Millie's declared she's on her own, besides; maybe she's the one cracking on him. Millie needs affection like you do," I patted him, "we all do." I felt a twinge of arousal.

"Don't tell anyone she's..."

"Promise," I said, crossing my fingers.

"You sided with him, voted him in," he said.

"Yes and no. I couldn't stomach knowing he'd die left behind. I admit being a bit soft in the head."

We sat melting in sweat, island ether, and the drone of insects.

"Who'd look at me?" Cris said, switching wavelengths, catching me by surprise.

"You're A-okay when you're not being a total nong." I squeezed his arm, tweaked his nose. "Let's move."

As we descended deep shadows hid details immediately beyond us. Anybody an arm's length couldn't be seen.

A short distance beyond, we reached a stream junction. One spurred off to the right, babbling into the undergrowth, its origins in scores of rivulets fingering off the shoulders of the twin peaks hidden above. Earth dampness hung sweet-and-sour, sucked into our nostrils, filling our lungs as we laboured upward.

Light cut the canopy web. We reached a clearing. Someone once lived here. Several raised platforms of mouldering stone peeked from under rotting leaf and layers of vine. Some dark red slabs still stood, enclosing one terrace with a wall two metres high. Strange line forms in relief created patterns obscured by mosses and gnarled fingers of root breaking the slabs asunder.

"This looks like a religious place," I said cheerily, "ghosts from ancient times."

"You shouldn't joke about it," Cris said, shivering, "I don't like it."

At the head of the valley lay another broad, stepped platform, the edges of which were collapsed in a jumble of once neatly cut stone.

"This is terrific. There's a gap above between the cliffs. An escape route," I said.

Cris remained sullen. "As long as we don't mess with those figures. I'm spooked just lookin' at them."

It was then I spotted the shattered remains of three statues, the largest staring skyward from the far side of the platform. A clump of ferns grew out of one eye socket. The other cavity and arched brow looked expectantly as if trying to address the peaks.

Cris oozed sweat, fidgeted with the machete.

"Don't touch any of them," he said.

"I'll do what I wish. Don't you want to find out things?"

"This place freaks me, like there's something watching us."

"You're just unused to wide open spaces. It *is* kind of spooky."

"It smells - off."

"Sickly sweet. Like banana and caramel custard gone rank. The place is full of fruits. We can live with it," I said.

I poked around. Cris made quick time crashing through, leaving me far behind. He hated the site, but wouldn't wear having me regard him as a wimp.

I stopped at a small brook and soaked in the coolness, examined the latest scrapes and the faded scars now accentuated against tan, rinsed shorts. Several patches were frayed. My singlet, once a designer statement, hung in shreds at the back where I'd snagged branches. At this rate the jungle would rob me of everything worth wearing, and some of my gear was missing. Grass skirts weren't a bad idea after all, offering lots of ventilation and freedom of movement.

✻

"What's it like? How far?"

Zoë bugged us for detail. Millie sat camouflage pink and brown in her bikini near the fire. She'd obviously spent the morning sunning, as if it would do her any good. Vanity made Millie a slow learner.

Cris wandered off to bathe. I felt like sneaking his clothes away, but decided more golden opportunities lay in the future. Best to toy with the victim.

I hummed, absently singing, "*put the rum in the coconut n' shake it all up, put the rum in the coconut, n' sip it all up…*"

"What are you up to, Bree?" Zoë demanded, planting her freckles in my face.

Oh, just a debt I want to collect soon, Zorro," I winked, wrapping my arms around her, squeezing hard. Her wiry response was reassuring. Zoë thrived in this wonderland.

"What would you like?" She beamed. "Fruit and fish or bread-fruit and fish?" Zoë uncovered their catch, a very large groper.

"Me and Fish speared it." Fish joined, wrapping her pencil arms around Zoë.

I ruffled her tight curls, and extended the hug, a long hungry one.

I imagined the two of them thrashing, their bodies turning aqua as they dove, poking around the crevices and holes where octopus and other denizens loved to lurk. How they managed to land and carry this big-eyed monster was a mystery. It had to weigh at least fifteen kilos. A partial answer lay by the fire. A mesh pallet woven from saplings, and fine vines, with two heavier branches running the length, making the handles at each end, allowed them to share the load. Zoë and Fish were seriously going native.

Well after sunset Jeff slid and swung down the ridge above us. Somewhere beyond branches snapped, crashed.

"Jeezus." Malcolm's raving continued, punctuated with moments of thrashing and muttering as he drew near.

Jeff jumped the last few metres, landing with a thump, out of breath.

You've gotta see the north side. There's a ship anchored. Real close."

Malcolm plunged through the overhanging trees, upside down, legs tangled in vines that had a mind of their own. Millie rushed to help, grappling, holding his head up.

"You drongos are warped. Get me down," he grunted.

Cris arrived. "Let 'em hang a while," he leered.

I laughed. "Bugger needs some colour. Looks like something out of a..."

"Sewer," Cris said.

Millie flushed. Bit her lip.

Jeff slashed the vines with the machete, sending both sprawling.

"Anything for a pash," Zoë scorned.

"So. What's the ship thing?" I said.

Chapter 18

Huddled around the fire, we watched mesmerised while the groper sizzled. Baking on embers was an ancient ritual, something ingrained in all of us, surely genetic. Millie squeezed lemon over the carcass when Malcolm didn't have his paws glomming her. That impulse was just as genetic, and older. Both were bolder in their passion for one another, yet I sensed Millie wasn't at ease in its chemistry. Little things.

Dancing firelight made caricatures of us.

I figured Malcolm truly appeared the skinned rat. His sideburns faded to a weedy patch of whiskers he'd cultivated before we first encountered him. They were longer now, promising to look like wisps of hair Chinese gentlemen wore.

Jeff's stocky frame loomed bent, elfish in shadow, his curly hair and knitted brow distorted.

Fish and Zoë's faces melded together, like two comic caricatures in a Greek play.

"A two headed demi-monster," I said, pointing, making a face. Both beamed, feeling they'd somehow accomplished something of importance.

Millie baked, hothouse beautiful, nursed broken nails.

Cris thrashed through growth beyond camp, intent on relieving himself. Too much mangoed banana shot through. Digestive shockwaves. Never knew he could really run. At least we didn't have to squat for long, attracting ravenous mosquitoes. 'Dunnieville' became 'Ranksville' when the wind did a turn, bringing essence of latrine back on us.

"The ship's an old rust bucket. Big," Jeff said, pausing as Cris swore. "One of those ocean fishing vessels. Couldn't see anyone."

"The one that nearly ran us under?" I said.

"No. This thing's a different shape from what you described, eh. Huge stern. Cream colour. Half rusted. Couldn't see anyone. And there's more. Looks like all the villages coped it on the north side." He shook his head. "Heavily overgrown. There's an airport too. It's a tangle of wreckage, everything's piled up against the slopes."

The wind sharpened from the south filling the dark with an orchestra of hisses from the canopy, the jungle alive in gossip. A baleful three-quarter moon eyed us over the hills before snuffed out in thickening cloud.

Far to the east drum-like sounds echoed, each beat diffusing, rebounding amongst the peaks.

I suddenly felt my hackles rise like I'd entered a time warp, a space of dark mysteries.

Rain pelted in jumbo drops, shattered on the canopy. We gathered under a makeshift awning, stuffing fish down and slices of breadfruit wrapped in leaves baked directly on the coals. The fall became a torrent. Our cone of warmth smoked, spluttered and died.

The drumming high to the east stopped.

Night chill descended. Droplets spent their time finding my neck no matter how I shifted. Two soaked shocks of hair wormed their way under my arms. The demes managed to find the best cover. Sabbie grinned under Fish's arm.

*

Retracing Jeff's route, an hour's hike brought us to a jagged ridgeline made raw by a chilled river of wind over-spilling its edge. Recent slides exposed tuff from ancient eruptions. We held a commanding view of the coastal strip, and the whole northern half of the island's lagoon and ringing reef.

To our immediate right a great escarpment rose crowned by four high peaks, the greater two dad's map scrawl indicated were Big Shark, Little Shark.

Below lay two gorges that funnelling towards us. Along a narrow flatland banding the lagoon, lay scraps of shattered settlements, stacked against the lower ridges.

With the glasses, I scanned the foreshore. "The tidal wave - all those people," I whispered.

I swung the glasses across the lagoon, which glowed in shimmering turquoise, forming a great arc rimmed with a white tiara of coral. Jade ribbons of tiny islets perched on the coral as if remnant beads on a broken necklace.

"Hey. Am I seeing things? Look. There's a bleedin' volcano

122

way to the east. It's smoking," Jeff said.

I swung the glasses around. A trail of haze wisped northward from three ragged cones that pierced the lagoon's symmetry adding a shock of raw earth to the perfect blue-green of the lagoon. Beyond the northern reef lay a broad underwater ridge, suggesting the island shoulder might one day heave out of the ocean from disturbances deep in the earth.

To the west, a kilometre from shore, and just beyond a finger of land pointing directly towards it, the intruder lay anchored.

"There's someone on deck near the pilothouse. Looks Asian. He's huge. Imagine being snogged by him. No. Blubbered to death," I said, adjusting the binoculars.

The ship's size was hard to guess, maybe seventy, eighty metres. Rust obscured the *S-331* emblazoning the side amid ship.

There was a raised foredeck at the bow, followed by a low mid section, piled with what looked like netting and a flotsam of crates. Behind this lay the wheelhouse high on the second level. A series of cabins ran aft on the two tiers of deck. Towards the stern was another open, low deck cluttered with large crates. A squared off stern rose two stories, the top level being a cluster of cabins.

A narrow walkway ringed the second level of the main structure. Three sets of stairs, front, middle and rear served the pilothouse and all aft cabins.

I watched the Asian, who was soon joined by four equally weedy types. They were in animated conversation, pointing shoreward.

S-331 wallowed in the remnant swells licking over the reef's shoulder and through a great gap in the coral.

I suspected this lot were escapees from the chaos of Asia. I remembered a scrap of script collected from my poetry studies by a Russian guy named Bely.

'*We sense the apocalyptic rhythm of the time.*

Towards the beginning we strive through the end.' Scary thinking. The beginning of what? I could imagine us soon festering in a state of savagery.

What lay below expressed a pinch of that nightmare?

"I smell trouble with that bunch," I said. "Wonder where they're going. Can't see any women. Kids."

"They might leave soon," Cris said.

"Where would anyone go from here?" Jeff said.

"Antarctica," I joked. "Chances are they don't have much fuel."

"One thing's for sure. They've riled the islanders. The guy in the canoe was agro over something they did," Jeff said.

"He grizzled something about *vahines*? Maybe, like you said, they abducted someone." I said.

The hulk Asian wedged into the wheelhouse sideways. His pals disappeared in a cabin several doors back of the pilothouse.

A thin trail of smoke drifted from a single stack amidships.

We lay in silence buffeted by wind rattling through branches of long dead trees. Scraps of cloud scudded overhead raking the peaks with showers, drenching us. My stomach growled. Too much fruit, I thought. Nipples puckered, ached.

"I'm a freakin' mess," I mumbled.

"Umm. Err. Your bun's falling down," Cris chuckled.

"There's nothing wrong with my..."

"The bun on your pointed head," Cris said.

"Oh." I flushed, realising my coiled hair hung loose.

I turned to spy on the craft we'd spotted on the west end of the reef the day we arrived. She lay at a slight angle to starboard, her black hull mainly in the water, the nameplate barely readable, but I knew her.

"That's Blackjack."

"What?" Jeff said.

"She passed us leaving the Hawkesbury."

"Shivers." Jeff exclaimed. "Unbelievable. Weren't they going to the Marquesas Islands? That's a hell of a distance from here."

"Yeah. We need a closer look at her." I said, longing to find out who the girl in the lap lap was.

"Blackjack's in full view of the ship." Jeff said.

"Then we take a snoop after dark," I said, doing my best to be positive, matter-of-fact.

"Why bother? We're supposed to be hiding," Cris said.

I scorned. "What's happened to the guy and woman on board? Remember? We've reason to know." Her dark curls and shape haunted me.

"First, we check out things below," Jeff said.

Our route followed the south side of the meandering ridge, bearing westward, descended into a patchwork of abandoned cultivations and dense bushes festooned with flowers.

"Hey, coffee beans," Cris said, shaking a bush laden with dark red berries.

I knew his hunger for good coffee.

"All you think about is feeding your habit," I said.

Cris wrinkled his nose.

We picked up the shoreline path on the western tip. Scraps of corrugated roofing and splintered timbers lay strewn about. Masses of sand and shattered coral attested to the waves' ferocity.

I toed a broken vase marked in green and blue spirals. Poking a pantry door caked in sand, a hinge squeaked in protest, clung to its frame. On the door remnants of an illustrated recipe for fish Mornay, printed in French, made the carnage immediate, too close to my stomach's needs.

Beyond, a patch laid cleared, small crosses marked the resting places of fifteen victims. Five were tiny with single names engraved. Jacque, Marie, Teio and Dominique were inscribed on white picket fencing. The fifth was unreadable.

To our immediate right lay the tail assembly of a twin-engine craft rammed against a hangar, contorted like some mad modern sculpture.

"Someone lit a fire down here," Jeff said, toeing a pit close to the shoreline.

"It's still warm," Cris added, feeling the remains.

"That's from yesterday, maybe last night. The ash is caked on top," I said. There were bare footprints.

"We'd better stay under cover."

Cris poked the embers, deep in thought. Fidgeted. Looked around. " Nothin' goin' on round here."

S-331 loomed about a kilometre away. If anyone watched the shore, we'd be spotted soon enough.

I studied Blackjack again. She was much closer. No life signs.

Our route skirted a series of stumps in a line, once a jetty. Sections of decking lay strewn amongst building foundations. A large church spire rested upside down, leaning against a clump of palms, its broken cross embedded in soil.

Beyond the jetty, to the left, the peninsula we'd spotted from above thrust north into the lagoon like a fishhook, curving towards the ship.

Jeff nudged. "Lets have a closer look, eh."

"I'm seriously curious," I said.

Cris shrugged. Mumbled. "It's hot. This place stinks of death."

"Come on Crissie. I'm a stickybeak." Gods, he could whine.

But it did have a peculiar smell.

By mid afternoon we wormed a route through stands of new palms and broken scrub made skeletal by the wave.

I was disappointed. No crew to be seen. Each of us hogged the glasses in turn, scanning every nook of the ship for life.

S-331 was obviously one of those clapped out oceanic fishers, drift netters that scoured huge areas into near lifeless deserts. Despite being festooned with aerials and electronic gizmos, she was well past her 'use by' date. I studied her chaos. Who could tell what might be useful information tomorrow.

"It's a pigsty," I said.

"This is stupid. Crawling around in this mess. Nothing's happening," Cris said.

"Just keep your big arse down, ham head. Better to know the enemy than wave your flag," I said.

Without warning, Cris got up as bold as you like and descended from our hideout to the beach in plain view of the ship.

I half growled, shouted. "What the hell are you doing? Get under cover."

"Cris—ye dumb bugger, don't." Jeff said, turning red, sucking breath in.

"Get lost. There's nobody around. I'm going back to camp."

Sudden commotion. Shouting in what I took to be Chinese. A piercing crack of automatic fire came in two sharp bursts, crashing against the northern cliffs, echoing.

Leaves above us rained. A chunk of palm flew.

Cris dove into the underbrush, clawing over the ridge. He tumbled headlong. Disappeared.

Jeff and I bolted down the sheltered side of the point. Scrambling over a rise, Jeff snagged a foot, fell spreadeagle on top of Cris. Both grunted, swore.

"You silly, stupid goon." I snapped. "Now we're known."

"Where's yer frickin' brains," Jeff said, gritting his teeth, gathering himself up, his knee wedged in the small of Cris's back. He spat sand.

Cris lay clutching his right side.

"We know for sure what they think of us," Cris said scrambling to his feet.

Harsh laughter, high pitched, carried across the lagoon, suggesting the assailant intended to enjoy finishing the job.

"Pirates," Jeff said, "probably armed to the teeth."

"Is this a debating club?" I kicked Jeff's shin. Kicked Cris harder.

"Ow! Jesus. That smarts."

"Let's move. Dunghead."

"You're bleeding," Jeff said.

Cris grimaced. Said nothing.

Another round of fire snapped through bushes nearby, probing to flush us out.

Momentarily exposed, I caught sight of a tender being swung over the side. A moment later we gained cover from a knoll of rock, leapfrogging down. Branches whipped my face. I landed on all fours, gasping.

Towering over us stood a massive statue, a *Tiki*, chiselled from dark, granulated tuff. Its grinning mouth and squinting eyes faced inland, seeking adoration from long dead worshippers. The body, like the other I'd seen, was squat, its legs bent as if about to give birth to some embryonic deity.

Jeff leaned against its backside, legs apart, gulping air. For a moment I imagined him squeezed out of the idol, fresh, dripping afterbirth from the spirit world.

This platform had been cleared of debris. A paved corridor ran dagger-like towards the heart of the island.

"Run for it," Jeff shouted. "They're after us."

We sprinted along the pathway, leaped the edging stones, and ran zigzagging through the debris towards a dense stand of palms. Rasping for oxygen, Jeff and I dove into thickets leading into a shallow valley immediately below the ridge we'd used to survey the northern rim. We burrowed into the undergrowth.

Shouting. Curses from nearby as their motor cut out.

"I think they snagged the shore reef," I gasped.

"Where's Cris? He was just behind us," Jeff panted.

We listened, but no footsteps marked his arrival.

"He's hurt," I said. "Must've taken a tree splinter. Bloody fool."

"Last I saw Cris, he was hunched over, running to my right towards the church steeple," Jeff said.

"He's not fast," I said.

"In more than one way, eh. We'll have to wait until dark. They're too close."

For once in my life I feared for Cris. What a git. Predictably unpredictable, defiant.

It's terrible hearing your pursuer, but can't see where he is. We lay perfectly still. My breathing compressed to bursting, muscles screaming for supply.

One was close enough to hear my breathing, so I feared. What noise I made felt magnified to the world. My temples pounded. I saw sparks in my sweat-blurred vision.

Jeff gritted his teeth, hands clenched, white.

I heard the guy kick tin roofing. Pulled it up to look. Further over another chatted to a third. Laughed. I smelled cigarette smoke. The thug nearest farted, sighing satisfaction.

They moved away towards the end of the island, prying and kicking likely hiding spots.

We scrambled over the remnants of a terrace wall, and crawled upward over each elevated level; arrived at the vantage point used that morning, and collapsed.

Below one crewman sat by the launch scanning the hillsides. The others continued hunting. Behind bushes I focused the glasses on him.

"He's a scrawny bastard. Bandana. Batik, I think. Black board shorts. Got tattoos all over his chest. Pot belly. He's smoking. Face out of a torture chamber. Bastard's peeing."

"How stupid were we, eh?" Jeff said. "No weapons."

"A gun? Useless. A popgun against what?" I said.

"Military stuff, the kind that stitch big holes," Jeff chided.

"Let's hope the girls and Mal moved our stuff to the new location," Jeff sighed.

More shouting from below signatured gangster angst.

"Suck rotten eggs, you bastards," Jeff said, lacking conviction.

The launch pulled away. We lay, aware of our exhaustion. My heart still pounded.

The first stars glinted eastward. We lay, faces skyward, as darkness enveloped.

"I wonder what stars Sascha's under now."

"It's still daylight in Sydney. Same stars. You've got a big thing about her?" Jeff probed.

"Yeah. She's the best person I've ever met. Remember? I once said you'd go for her."

"Like her." Jeff cautioned.

"She's got fire in her veins. Nobody can ignore it. I'd die if she met a bad end."

"You make it sound like a romance," Jeff teased.

"In a way, I guess it is. I love Sascha. Mind. Soul. Body."

Jeff coughed. "What's love? You aren't..."

"No, silly. I'm hetero. It's something you can't put your finger on. Words kill it," I mused. "Believe it or not, Jeffie, I think Millie has her saucer blue eyes on you. Better not look too deep."

"Oh, cut it out. She's trashy. Let's find Cris."

"She watches you. Wishes. Mal's too pushy. Too hungry. There's a cool girl under the props department."

Far to the left bushes swayed. Twigs snapped. We ducked behind a slab of broken rock.

Out of the dusk Cris staggered. Caked blood covered his side, soaking his shorts, and splattered his leg.

"I've been shot. The bugger got me." He looked astonished, as if seeking explanation from us.

Chapter 19

Cris insisted on walking, salving his dislocated ego. It was a short but difficult distance to camp. Darkness made walking a nightmare until a three-quarter-moon rose from the ocean's black abyss. Its light reflected into shimmering filigree as waves rolled endlessly in. Without luminosity we'd be paralysed until dawn.

My eyes watered. I sighed. Snuffled.

"What's eating you?" Cris grated.

"Not a damn thing a few years ago wouldn't cure."

Some patches of the ridge, though overgrown, proved unusually flat and passable, certainly shaped by human hands. Descent was another matter. Irregular rills cut deep into the ridge's shoulder creating cones of abrasive stone. On the south side masses of clinging foliage made every twist and turn an ordeal. For much of the descent we struggled, stumbling over roots and vines that constantly snared us.

"It hurts like hell. Can't bend much. Can't twist at all." Cris said.

"You'll feel it stiffen soon. The bloods caked."

Jeff hacked a crooked trail to meet us just above the camp. I guessed it to be near midnight when we made the final descent.

"There's no sign of Millie or Malcolm. They've gone walkabout," Jeff said.

Zoë poked her pug nose in. "They carried our cooking gear to the new camp. Followed your markers. Won't be back til morning." She handed me the medical kit.

Jeff vanished, looking for firewood. Fish bolted at the first sight of blood. Cris looked miserable, more from embarrassment than pain.

"I don't understand. You may as well have stuck your big bum in their face - with a bullseye painted," I said.

He sighed, shook his head. "It seemed like a good idea at the time. Didn't think anyone would be crazy enough to shoot."

"These guys are whackos," I said. "Smarten up. You could be dead."

"Didn't think you cared."

"I don't, dopey - well, I do. Hey, all of us stand a better chance of survival if nobody's shot."

With water and torn strips of shirt, I daubed blood away, soon found the problem. "Amazing."

"What?"

"No bullet," I said, frowning.

"Aw, what's that mean? There's something there. I feel it. Aw, not that damn needle."

"Hey, Jeff's still got brains. You've attacked a tree. Biggest thing I've ever seen."

"It's needle nosed pliers Cris."

His face fell as I gripped the jagged edges and slowly pulled a massive wedge shaped splinter out. Cris's face distorted, but he wouldn't cry out. I judged the wood as clean, probably from a shattered tree, sun and salt bleached.

"Lots of blood. Good quality," I said, smiling. "Big bandaid. No stitches." Iodine and an antibiotic tablet finished the job.

"Eew. That's a mega splinter, five centimetres at least. What's that stringy stuff?" Zoë said, failing at diplomacy.

"Butt out gnat. Your mouth needs sewing," Cris growled, giving her the dirtiest look.

"I owe you and Jeff an apology," Cris said. "Thanks for the patch-up."

"No problem, as long as you don't make a habit of it." I leaned over and kissed his forehead, decided not to bag him out; couldn't see where humiliating would help us, or any chance of warmer relations with him.

Cris drifted into sleep. I catnapped til sunrise.

Rat and Millie arrived arm-in-arm, looking content.

"A hot night on the town?" I said.

Malcolm drawled, "Just a wrong turn, Bree."

"That's for sure," I said.

"We found a hut," Millie said, dreamy-eyed. "We slept there."

Both caught sight of Cris bandaged up.

"Did he stick his neck out again?" Millie sniped.

"That's an unkind thing to say," I said. "He made a mistake." I don't know why I apologised for Cris's actions.

Neither offered a kind word after explanations of what he'd done.

Moving the camp gear spanned the next two days. Cris developed a fever the second evening, but otherwise appeared well enough to move.

"I'm sick of fruit," He said to himself.

I was relieved he didn't answer himself. "Fancy some barbecued rat? There are heaps of them around, big ones."

"I know of a large one," he said.

"You owe me twice," I said, struggling to keep my eyes open, but mischievous enough to goad him. He'd never collect.

"Sorry you're so ticked off," Cris said.

"I mean, the other debt."

Cris gazed, his brain running in low gear, "What bloody debt?" He spat at the fire.

"Coconuts. Green ones. Twenty-five."

"Aw. Yer bleedin' joking."

"As soon as you are able. Up the tree, like the ape you are. Use some climbing genes."

"You've blowfly in yours," Cris said.

"A bet's a bet," I said.

"You know, you and Millie were a pretty crook show for a bet. I expected you'd go all the way."

"Not on your life. Why the saucer eyes then Crissie? You looked like a cat after a canary. And don't get picky. I'm mostly modest."

A log hissing a see saw tune collapsed in a flash of blue-green flame. Sparks flared. Smoke eddied, acrid with traces of sweetness. I thought it like our relationship, laughed.

"Private joke?"

I didn't answer.

"You've inflated since I bombed you. Nice..."

"Oh, shut up!"

"Like your mum's," Cris said.

"Do you mind? They're mine. And you wish, brass-ass." I said, cuffing his head. "Must be fever giving you big notions." I made a face, knowing Cris wanted to bug me. His fear of heights was worse than mine, and I'd cornered his oversized ego.

I banked the fire with the remaining deadwood, and bedded down on a carpet of fern fronds. Exhaustion came in an irresistible wave. Rain punctuated the drone of night life. I drifted, half asleep, studied the soft lines of his face as he lay on his back wheezing. The fire clinked, died.

※

We'd avoided slashing a trail from camp in case the "ratbags", as Jeff coined them, nosed around. Jeff and I fussed for hours erasing signs of our presence by burying food scraps and the fireplace. It's amazing how much trash was strewn about. Fish bones. Fruit skins. Zoë, as instructed, made cuts in a branch to keep track of the days since we landed, a small but important task, even though we had watches. Her tally stick lay scorched. Flattened ferns were uprooted. The pit used for a dunny, was filled. I left that charmer to Jeff.

A mass of ferns, elephant ear and hibiscus created a barrier a stone's throw to the east of camp. Our route up the first ridge followed an overgrown path. By stepping on chunks of stone where possible we'd leave little disturbance.

Several days raced by as we cleared the best platform. The site featured slabs of volcanic pumice head high placed around most of the perimeter. Several pieces lay toppled, covered in growth. It took all our strength to lever them up using long poles and chunks of wedging wood. Cris sat brooding, upset with the site. We ignored his bleating about disturbed spirits.

Millie pitched in, grunting, straining her petite frame as if to prove her worth. Alongside her, I smelled her sweat mingled with Jewel of India musk, a heady and suggestive brew she guarded well, but needlessly.

Malcolm exhibited his prowess by hanging from his timber lever like a hairless sloth. His pair of grey daks, newly torn, couldn't last much longer. He was strong, but lacked weight even with Zoë contributing. She scorned him out, jumped to the pole above him.

Rat Man reminded me of an Indian beggar. Millie poked at him and simpered.

Jeff and I cut boughs to create a network of struts like spokes on a wheel. This produced a shallow, curved roof with a framed smoke hole at the centre. Millie lashed vines and finer branches into a network running at right angles to the poles. This kept the sail canvas roofing from sagging. Where the pieces met we stitched up every metre, and overlaid strips of bark from one of

133

the bigger trees. These were anchored with flat slabs of rock to counter the afternoon winds, which often blustered up the valley from the southeast. Even blood sucking mossies went to ground then.

October twenty-seventh. The weather was shifting dramatically towards warm and wet. I suspected we'd settled in the soggiest, steamiest glade on the island. The high peaks towered directly above us. We felt safer.

In the eleven days since our arrival, the afternoon temperature never went below twenty-seven sticky degrees. The island valleys created giant saunas.

Bugs buzzed everywhere. Mossies, big hairy ones here, we loathed. They came in swarms to torment as the sun dipped over the western ridges and the wind dropped. In defence, three smudge fires were set in a wide triangle. These were worth the security risk. Better to suffer smarting eyes than dozens of itchy welts. And mossies could bring diseases. Fever. The mosquito net, which we cut up, wasn't big enough to cover all the holes.

Our presence brought another worry. Steroid rats. Several scurried around the perimeter of our camp, their beady eyes bright in fire light. Cris spent part of his cranky evenings shooting arrows at any bold enough to show. He grunted with the jolt from each shot, his face flushed with sweat. Fish acted as arrow retriever.

Zoë whinged, "I'm a steamed duck. Why are we stuck here? It's neater at the beach."

"Too dangerous." Jeff said. "We'll go down to fish soon. Night's safer."

Cris was still bothered with fever. I'd dressed the puncture each morning. There were no bandages left, so I used torn strips of Jeff's old plaid shirt. At nightfall the skin around the bandage flared up angry pink, which worried him, but the wound was healing. I made a point of chatting up his practical skills framing the tent, gave him leeway to explain his projects. He tied my mind up completely with his knowledge of knots and lashings.

I pressed the point of visiting Blackjack that evening.

"I'm visiting the yacht tomorrow. Anyone coming?"

"If you insist," Jeff sighed. "We need to fish. Have a look then after dark. There's no moon tonight. Good cover. No point in getting yourself trapped, eh."

"We take the shotgun," I said. "Rat and Millie have to come. No point in creating a scenario for murder."

Millie hesitated by Cris, placed water and fruit by him. Cris managed a thankyou. I knew she was the lesser of two evils, but hated to be alone if Cris's tongue took a turn for the worse.

Zoë and Fish joined, eager to fossick and swim.

⁕

Inventing a route to the beach over unknown ground became a madcap party. All, except Jeff, babbled and teased one another. The dense undergrowth muffled our words. I felt a nagging uneasiness as we approached the beach, following a network of tiny streams, but there was no human presence. We clowned our way onto the sand minutes before sunset. The wind smelled salty sweet.

Sitting on bleached sand, soothed by a warm breeze, our existence mutated to positive.

The sweeping curvature of beach took on peach and amber hues as the sun sank. The darkening sea boomed against the islands outer defences. A kaleidoscope of colours laced through thin bands of cloud low on the western ocean.

The girls swam, fish spears poised, Zoë shrieking with delight as they stabbed at darting schools. Waves radiated, turning the lagoon around them into a light show. Both emerged, each with struggling fish, their slim bodies glowing golden, clothed in water beads.

"Bet you guys can't do it." Zoë swung her backside around, did a handstand and raced into a double somersault. There was no stopping her precocious moods. Her brazenness long ceased to surprise me. I love her all the more for it.

"Yer nothin' but a pair of tarts, eh," Jeff jested, with mock indignity.

"Queen of hearts," Zoë sniped. "Guys. You'd better watch the turtles."

"Wadaya mean?" Malcolm drawled.

"Turtles chomp off dangling things. It'd choke on yours," she cackled.

Malcolm looked stunned, as if experiencing it. We cracked up. Fish rolled in the sand. Millie looked horrified, then burst out laughing.

"Jeeze. Yer joking."

I squeezed Malcolm's shoulder. "You might be street smart, but

Zorro's nature smart. Keep the snake coiled."

We left Malcolm and Millie on the beach to entertain one another.

The hour row along the foreshore and out to Blackjack gave me time to gain nerve. What little I'd remembered of our encounter with this boat on the Hawkesbury estuary failed to calm my unease.

Rounding the western point of the island, *S-331* loomed dark, except for a lone pinpoint of light. I guessed the rust bucket to be at least two kilometres away. Darkness never felt so reassuring.

The wind dropped, magnifying the squeak of the rowlocks across the water, but the din of waves battering the outer shell of the reef gave me confidence they wouldn't hear us. A residual mist mellowed the ships profile.

As we approached Blackjack her size impressed. Much longer and beamier than Elysius, her black hull swept upward at both ends, her stern a tapered square with a large overhang. The cabin was twice the size of Elysius's. Jeff hoisted us up into the cockpit, lifting my tensions as if a palpable danger was just around the corner waiting to pounce.

Zoë and Fish sat arm-in-arm opposite, staring, keen to fossick. She always read my nervier moments.

Jeff went below, lighting the candles, which were our only remaining source of night light. Dad's habit of storing emergency supplies was a boon to us now. I imagined soon making rush torches soaked in dieseline and pitch as we began shrinking into a stone age existence.

"You'd better come look at this," Jeff said.

We descended the companionway into a vast cave, opulently appointed, but in total disarray.

Drawers lay dumped, contents strewn across the floor. An ornamental teak liquor cabinet lay open, emptied.

The navigation cabin, once well appointed with electronic gear was stripped, wires protruding everywhere. I delved into a side locker. Ocean charts. Scores of them. Jeff leaned over the chart table as if looking at paradise lost, trying to imagine all the latest equipment, now pirated.

In the half-light the interior forward was a carnival of pungent ruin. On the settee, a plate of food lay scattered, mouldering. Salad and chicken. An overturned coffee mug and sunglasses lay on the opposite side. All the lockers lay open, gutted of contents.

The food lockers were empty, as was the freezer and fridge.

Jeff went into the bow cabins. "Same mess up here."

I heard a prolonged trickle of water. Flushing.

"Toilet works."

Zoë picked up clothing. "This is a ladies stuff. Batik." She held a floral sarong in one hand and a delicately laced mauve bra in the other. Thirty-eight-D, I guessed. Sasha's build. All of it top fashion labels.

"Whoever raided this boat really did it over," Jeff shook his head, his face screwed up in disgust. "Bastards. Rotten swine." His fury filled the cabin.

"They've sprayed stuff all over the ceiling," I said indignantly.

Jeff raised his candle to match mine.

"That's not food or drink. It's blood."

I felt nauseous as we traced the splatter back to its source. Zoë stood, mouth opened, eyes transfixed.

Fish sat on the companionway step, whimpering, shaking in spasms.

Jeff whispered, "There. On the galley counter."

A clot of coagulated blood caked a white plate, emblazoned with a blue anchor. Jeff fingered a tuft of long, dark hair wedged in a crack in the bulkhead joinery directly over it. A single rivulet of life ran down the tan laminex. The more we looked the more blood appeared. A curved smear of it streaked the entrance wall.

Something squishy and soft rolled underfoot. Lifting my foot, I stared at the decomposed, bloodied remains of a finger, a man's, judging from its thickness.

The most mournful howl erupted. Inhuman. Heart tearing. As if from a banshee. We froze in the sheer force of its penetration.

Fish stood, every sinew in her tiny body distended, like bunched wires. Urine flooded down her legs. She bolted upwards, slipped, cracker her jaw on the brass edged stairwell, and with legs flailing like pistons, launched into the cockpit and over the stern.

Zoë raced up the companionway on all fours.

Fish and Zoë hit the water in unison. As I reached the stern, Fish emerged spluttering, choking.

By the time Jeff reached the stern Zoë had Fish's body gripped tightly from behind, a hand firmly clamped on her mouth.

Hauled into the dinghy, Fish curled up in the bottom, moaning.

"*Mama, mama, despírtate. Háblame por favor. Despírtate ahora.*"
Her voice dropped into incomprehensible jabbering.

"What the hell?" Jeff said.

"Fish is Spanish—I'm sure. *Por favor* means please. Don't know much more, but *mama* means mum, and that means something horrible has happened, I recon." I cursed my lack of anything more than crude French and scraps of Spanish.

I shooed Zoë into the bow and gathered Fish up, rocking her. I remembered a simple lullaby mum used on us when nights were cranky.

"Hushabye, hushabye, sandman's coming to take you,

Throwing love dust in your eyes,

Bring happiness and a new day."

I repeated. It worked then, but didn't now as Jeff stroked our way back to the beach. She continued to moan.

Fish possessed a life and a name. I was in awe of what might spill from her tormented psyche.

Chapter 20

Malcolm displayed a cluster of silver-blue fish strung on a branch fashioned as a loop. A fire burned close to the water's edge.

Mal crowed, "We lit a fire on the beach, sucked them in, big time." He did a shuffle, legs bowed, waving the spear. Millie smiled as he cavorted, but cast nervous glances at us.

"Great stuff. Did you ever consider who's watched you?" I stabbed my index finger against his nose.

"They won't scalp us," Malcolm whinged, ducking, swiping me away.

"Wouldn't mind if they did, wise guy." I ignored his catch, which was enough for everyone. "Count me out for eating it."

Malcolm shrugged. "No need gettin' agers."

We headed for camp, stumbling in the dark, looking for white marker arrows laid out on the path, and cloth strips hung on branches. Jeff wandered off to our right, rather than left, and found markers.

"I'd swear the strips weren't set this way." He stepped beyond a stand of bushes.

"What the hell."

Jeff vanished, amidst a flurry of snapping branches ending with a dull *SPLOOT*, like bellyflopping in a vat of porridge.

"What the blue blazes." Jeff spat, and spat, thrashing about. He emerged wearing a crown of slime.

"Who the flamin' hell'd dig a damned, stinkin' pit there?" He limped, swiping at gobs of muck.

"That's what you get for ignoring my suggestion, Jeff, dear. It was a left turn." I said nothing else to upset his ego. We sat while he regained composure. I collared him, making sure to keep distance from the others, who babbled on about where we should go next.

"If you insist on using the wrong shampoo you'll be bald by thirty."

"Bree, anyone tell you you're a pain?"

"Yes. Even related to a blowfly."

"But a touch thornier, eh?" Jeff said, ducking.

"It's good to know my assets are appreciated. Seriously. Somebody's done dirt on us. Those markers were changed," I said.

"Naww. We've done so many twists and turns getting to the beach."

"If you insist; No. I feel it. We're being watched."

"Did you see what was on the galley floor?" I said.

Jeff stared stone faced, annoyed with my vagueness.

"A finger." I hissed. "A man's finger. Felt it squish under my foot, saw it just as Fish screamed."

"So that was it. Figured it was blood. Cripes, can she scream. Scared me silly. Nearly did my pants," Jeff said. He paused. "Bet he had a ring. That's what they do, just hack it off if it won't come away. He's dead for sure."

"The girl's taken. Their captive," I said.

"I recon they'd use her, then - " He ran a finger across his throat.

I commonly suffered runaway nightmares. Graphic scenes from newscasts of human victims tortured and killed, flashed daily on television months ago. These and my secret fears haunted me. Civil wars and piracy had released the worst of depravity humans were capable of.

Jeff was blunt, and right. Well, he was mostly correct, but my emotions dictated she must be alive on the ship.

We traced our route, Millie squealing, Rat limped cursing at the rear. Stumbling over roots, we felt our way into camp, hand-in-hand. I figured the blind led the damned.

Cris eyed us from a separate campfire, "That's a sorry spectacle."

"Pot calls the kettle?" I said.

"This dumps no better than the last. Gives me the creeps. I saw shadows. Heard footsteps," Cris said.

"Rats." I said. "More than one variety around."

The night turned miserable. My mind wouldn't slow down. What little sleep I got teemed with dreams and suggestive images of what the girl from Blackjack suffered. It must be many days since she was taken. Her clothing lay strewn around the cabin. The batik wrap-around she'd worn on deck the night Blackjack passed us laid amongst the ruins. I couldn't bear to touch any of her things without feeling I violated her person, like a vulture feasting off the dead.

Of all nights Cris picked this one to snore full throttle, sawing the night, as if celebrating loss of fever. He murdered my sleep. I sensed his mood swing after being alone, knew a nearby broken *Tiki* fired secret fears and self doubts. Heaven knows what other complexes lay between his oafish ears. I knew more than ever he craved approval. Love, and part of him was undeniably appealing, sensual. I flushed, imagined, felt heat.

The demi-monsters lay huddled together close to Jeff. Fish muttered in patches, as if in a debate, the language clearly Spanish. She certainly looked South American with dark skin and black eyes. Her face was strongly Mediterranean, just a trace of something extra in the high cheekbones.

Rat and Millie burrowed, entwined in the far corner, a small partition of woven branches declaring their status. "Things needed to morph there. It has to change," I whispered. There were no minder parents to make guidelines, pass judgement. I didn't fancy having two rutting lovers, and Millie sure to self-destruct. Rat would walk away.

※

"I don't see why the islanders wanted to write you off, eh." Jeff said, munching a fifth pygmy banana, clutched a blanket against the morning chill.

"If the shot was an accident - maybe he snagged the trigger. Stumbled?" I said gingerly fingering the healing hole punched clean through the top of my ear. I re-inserted a conical seashell for decoration.

" Bree. The guy in the canoe made it clear. They don't want us around. Umm, maybe..."

"It's not cool having an enemy on either side of us. Just improving relations with the islanders would help heaps. Something really nasty happened to them before our arrival. Even if they don't want anything to do with us I recon a patch-up's needed."

Jeff mused, "Then the solution dear sister is an all girl delegation. Turn out your charms, you and Moonie."

I agreed.

Millie pouted, voice muffled inside the hut. "It's Millie to you, poxhead."

Jeff coloured. "Sorry. Humble apologies." He made a face, pleased with the dig.

"Why not Zoë and Fish along?" I probed, trying not to smirk, but burst out laughing. "Sorry, I just love Days In Our Lives drama."

"Traitor," Millie said.

"Fish is fragile. Needs time to open up. She doesn't need stress."

That made sense. No telling when she'd let rip an earful.

Both girls joined, huddling by the fire, mooching over leftover fish. My stomach growled.

Jeff punctured coconuts on a sharp stake, offering each of them one. "Sorry. No straws." Fish cast a shy smile at Jeff.

I tried to break ice with her. "Love, can you tell us your name?"

"Feesh." Again flashed a grin at Jeff.

"Your old name."

"Estrellita Rodriguez. I'm called Estie. Feesh es better."

Her voice carried a distinct accent, strung metallically high, a Spanish pixie. The name rang familiar, something stellar, maybe a star.

Jeff said softly, "Can you tell us where you came from?"

"Glenorie."

"That's not far from Berowra Waters. Did you find a boat there?" I said. "Did you row down into the Hawkesbury?"

She nodded.

From the upper reaches of the Hawkesbury River it would be easy for anyone to paddle, following any one of its meandering branches. Fish picked a derelict boat, leaky and unmanageable, would've ended up sucked out to sea on the strong tide.

"Your family, Fish. Where are they?"

Her jaw set hard, face darkening, staring into the fire.

"It's okay," Jeff soothed, wrapping an arm around her. "We're your family now. You can tell us what you wish, when you wish." He gave her a kiss on the temple.

I melted, never saw him show much affection, other than the odd compulsory peck. I smiled, catching his eye.

Cris joined trying to be civil, a good sign - and about time. He sat beside me, whistling a tune, a bit like 'if you go out in the woods today'. Zoë poked a stick between his fingers, trying to ruin his musical reverie. She ducked a cuffing.

142

"Sorry about my bad vibes. Thanks for patching me up. The scar's healing." He traced its still angry edges.

"If we find the hospitable side of the islanders, maybe one of them could hide it with a real tattoo. Match it on the other side. Maybe a set of handles."

"And who's going to use them?" he sniped.

"Some junior tart," I said.

"Wouldn't you like one of those sexy flower wedges the girls go for?"

I frowned. "Don't fancy being stamped for life. Most of that stuff's corny. Remember Nola Doyle? That year eleven frump. She got three, one on each cheek, and the other, well, you know. She paraded them at the swimming carnival."

"She was hot," Cris said.

"Peasant. Maybe something small, out of sight," I said. "Celtic. Like abstracted animals entwined. Those are beautiful. The islanders use tattooing as a sign of sexual maturity. You might try a bullseye, Cris. You're obviously fair game, and in season."

The girls rolled about with laughter.

I rose, escaping his reprisal, which left him flustered, but smiling and brewing new fantasies. I dragged Millie away from curling her locks. She rubbed a mottled purple patch on her neck.

"You and I are going for a hike to the top." Trying to be resolute, I pointed to the highest snag of rock towering to the Northeast. "The boys have fishing to do and a hut to build. Cris refuses to sleep on the platform. Jeff says we check out the north-east side."

"Cris is so superstitious, Bree. Mum always loved charms. He wasn't rapt in it. I went along with the fun parts, but really -" Her voice trailed off. "It's silly, like what you said, your granny covering mirrors in electrical storms."

The day we found our first campsite, I remembered Cris eyeing the mouldering shapes, thick in moss. He was full of fearful imaginings. Kept looking behind.

"All her potions didn't help. What a horrid way to die," Millie's lip quivered, eyes watering, spilling tears into her cosmetic box. She snuffled.

I did remember the bronze statue of Celestial Girl, the one Arie adored. Arie said she was a fertility goddess; also protectress, something we needed now.

"Lets hope 'El Punio', what the Spanish call The Devil's Claw, doesn't reach the South Seas. If rats here pick it up from anyone reaching this far south, we'll cop it," I said. "We'll need more than a bag of charms." Thinking about it put a wet blanket on my mood.

Climbing the ridges proved easier now our bodies were toned. Dense fingers of vegetation splayed upwards, becoming scrub on the barren upper reaches. These gave us plenty of stubby branches to cling to. Millie, who was least fit, puffed pink, and insisted on stopping every few minutes. We worked our way across the sharp ridges, following a network of rutted trails.

Trying to keep as far away from the sheer escarpment on the north side proved nerve wracking. The worst patches of trail were no wider than a half metre, making my knees knock. Much of the soil crumbled, the rocks rotten. Whole chunks frequently gave way, gathering scree, mini sliding, rattling away into thin air. Animal droppings clustered everywhere, and when careless these morning offerings squished between our toes.

We stood on the remnants of a once massive rim, most of which had subsided, eroded into the ocean.

A blast swept up the escarpment from the south, hissing through tufts of wiry grass and stunted bushes, buffeting us, giving me goose bumps. Vertigo sensations made me queasy. Millie's clammy hand clung to mine.

"It must be four thousand metres down to the sea floor," I said.

Millie sighed, "Thanks. God, you're morbid." She added, "I don't ever want to go out there again. I'd rather die here. You know, several times I wanted to jump overboard. End it. But I was too weak to get up. I'm not like you, Bree. You're strong."

"No. Just stubborn."

She pointed. "Look. Goats."

"Fresh meat, Millie. Take a look through the glasses." Beyond the peaks to our right, a rolling plateau spread. Further east thick mist shrouded the volcanic vent fuming in slow epic birth.

We sat mesmerised by crags and meadows, surreal under searing sun, saw ponies grazing in a sea of flowers by the far rim, wondered why they were there.

The cliffs on our left, the ones we'd studied the intruders from the day Cris wiggled his bum, looked far more forbidding from our present perch. These made wonderful homes for sea birds. Flights of plumed parrots squawked, eddying upward, landing on flower-tipped trees clinging from crevices. Their red and white feathers

144

blended with the red and gold tipped blooms. It was easy to imagine the trees giving birth to parrots, the reds blended so well.

"Look to the west. There's the ship," I said.

Millie, wrinkling her nose, giving scant regard, instead, shifted to peer into our vale and eastward.

"I can see a thatched house. Smoke."

"That's one reason I wanted you along. Jeff thinks we should contact them."

"But, you nearly got filled with buckshot. Malcolm told me - and laughed. That really sucked."

"If it wasn't an accident, I recon the guy wanted Mal's hide, not mine, and was a rotten shot." I raised an eyebrow.

She frowned, uncertain what to say.

"Anyway, what possible threat could two sexy girls be? Better than lover-boy. He really made them hopping mad."

"But he got chicken for me; the best meal ever."

I knew as an opener my line of persuasion was full of holes.

Millie persisted, "Didn't Jeff say all the rules have changed? We were starving, too."

"Not quite—most sensible rules hold, otherwise we risk making enemies. If we spin out - go wild - like listening to our hormones."

"I know. I've turned on. It's so strong." She blushed.

I shifted direction. "You've got more love marks than mozzie bites. I saw you sulking a few days back. What's eating you?"

Millie bit her lip, cupped a buttercup. "He's sweet to me mostly. You see that. When it's good the whole world explodes, disappears." Her eyes saddened. " But sometimes Pookie's so aggressive. He's, well, strange. All I can do is hang on. He's a spider." She fingered her bruised arm. "Aren't the females supposed to eat the males?" She said half-heartedly.

"Sweetie, don't tell me the details."

I lied. Why can a dag like him make my skin crawl with goose bumps, stomach turn queasy?

"He slapped me really hard on my side, too." Unabashed, she pulled her shorts down, revealing bright pink finger marks bruising. "I cried. He tried to make it up after. Why would he want to hurt me?"

"His family life was the pits. I don't think Malcolm can love. He gets his rocks off by conquest, so belting you around is raw pleasure. Bet you don't know about his wretched parents. So - you're deep in dung now. Try to shift to neutral ground. Cool out."

Millie sighed, shrugged, tears streaming, the buttercup filled. I knew she was listening, craved my opinion.

"Find some excuse. Sleep separately, you know, women's problems. Guys can't hack that. Remember what I said about Jeff? He actually likes you, so sit by him. Teach him how to weave. Use your finger magic. Nobody weaves like you. Admire something he's done."

Millie glanced, wanted to believe; traces of doubt.

"Whatever you do, get yourself away. You don't deserve sadistic lovemaking—unless you're a bit kinky?"

"Not *that* way." Millie whispered.

"What if you are really pregnant? There's no doctor."

A flash of dread replaced her thoughts. I sensed Millie wouldn't have nerve enough alone to shut him out. Fear might be the mother of invention.

"I'll back you up. Spend more time with Zoë. He gets real edgy around her."

She smiled meekly. "What's with the rubbing, Bree? Sometimes you really attack that scar."

"It's my way of de-stressing, like when Cris taps." I knew Millie hadn't bought my explanation.

"It's time we prepared a peace offering to the tribe. Better dress up," I said.

"What on earth with? My best stuff's ruined, or lost overboard."

The afternoon we invested in cleaning what survived as wardrobe. In the heat of late afternoon, we escaped to a falls I'd discovered nestled deep in a narrow ravine. It was no wider than two arms spread, just enough to have elbow room if we sat on the ledges each side of the pool cavity scoured out by endless storms. Millie soaped up humming and swaying to an old Reggae tune Arie used to sing. I stood amused as she slathered in suds.

She stopped, looking up.

"What is it? Do I look freaky or something?"

"Uh. No."

"Well? Get it off. You can't wear those mangy shorts forever," Millie said.

"We're so different. Breasts. Build. You know."

She cupped them. "They're super sensitive."

"Not surprising", I said. "Mine are ineffectual, like they sprout-

146

ed half way then stopped growing, except the nipples got bigger. It's such a hang-up on cold days."

"They're sexy, like they're saying come and get me," Millie teased.

"Well, the whole world's deaf," I said, laughing, hiding old fears.

Millie ran the sponge down my back. She lathered and hummed. I relished her openness.

"There's nothing better than sharing a back scrub," She bubbled, blowing suds off her lip.

"It's great for gossip," I said.

In the middle of lathering I fed her more ideas about what made Jeff tick - all three.

"You're a real friend, Bree." Millie burst into giddy laughter, gave me a hug. "Do you, umm, have any feelings for Cris?"

"Feelings? Well, I love his eyes when he laughs, which isn't a lot. He's insecure."

Millie giggled. "Called you an Ice Castle."

"Oh, yeah, I remember."

"Hey, your not like Zoë?"

"What?"

"She always collects strays." Millie giggled.

"Eat soap," I laughed. We rinsed, wind dried in the updraft.

I still felt guilty just standing by early in the voyage, far more neutral than I should've been. Millie and Mal's relationship grew damn fast. My only rational excuse was an intense dislike for anyone pegging out rules on my own relationships, not that I managed many, so it wasn't cool dictating to her.

How long was it since I knew a guy I liked enough to try being close? Two years. Ages. A certain party-pooper plagued the one and only nervy relationship I dared. That being stuffed up royally, Jasper split for another flirty femme less complicated, more adoring. He probably wasn't worth the emotional angst.

＊

Preparation the following morning was festive, tense. Malcolm sensed something different in the air, since Millie played hearts with the girls the previous night, slept with them, and ignored much of his attention seeking.

She wore a loose, white crocheted tank top with yellow

147

shorts. Dark eyeliner magnified her blue eyes. The tacky innocence I'd known months ago no longer existed. On my insistence she stuck a yellow lily with curled ends over her left ear, symbolic of freedom.

I resorted to my best, and only, patched denim with the Snoopy singlet. A touch of Millie's violet lipstick and eyebrow liner gave my face a lift. Too much makeup was such a turn-off. Jeff called it 'war paint'. With my hair brushed loose, a disgusting mess of split ends, I tied it back. A tiny red hibiscus perched above my left ear. We shared a touch of Ambrosios perfume, Arie's favourite.

The girls offered their latest garlands of tiny flowers.

Our route, as Jeff insisted, was over the upper ridges we'd viewed the day before, and to drop down into the valley most likely leading to their village. This would help avoid manned defence barriers. He argued, that the beach approach would give them too much time to react. We wanted, above all, to avoid openly hostile contact. The women would surely be more placid, and not armed.

By noon we'd made miserable progress, an up and down scramble that grew hot and sweltering each time we wrestled around heavily treed slopes. The final descent following animal trails took us into a broader valley. Pausing to renew wilted flowers, we criss-crossed a brook several times, picking our way parallel to a well used path.

Faint notes from a guitar filtered through dense growth, its origin confused in the tangle of vines. Chords haphazardly played. Another would-be musician battered a drum. The village dogs quarrelled. A plover, and its mate, high on the grasslands above, shrilled its call, as if warning intruders away.

Close by girlish voices rose and fell, babbling. Water gurgled. Rounding a boulder massif, we spotted four of them, bodies glistening brown, busy making faces at one another, giggling in their inventiveness. The eldest two were no more than thirteen, judging from their budding willowy frames. Both were mirror images of one another. The others were Fish's age.

We ducked.

Millie whispered, "What do we do, expose ourselves?"

"Oh. Millie." I sniggered, "Not if you don't want them freaking out. Take your laurel apart." I began plucking, throwing flowers into the stream a few at a time, watching them drift and bob around stones as the current quickened.

At first the smallest girl cried with delight, cupping up several blooms. One by one they turned, looking in our direction, faces wide eyed.

We stood up slowly, parting the bushes, and waved.

" Hello! *Parles vous Anglaise?* Friends."

All stood statue-like. Time warped in the hot rays.

The tiniest girl, Fish size, waved back. The eldest two screamed. That figured. Age breeds suspicion. They bolted, shouting in their native tongue as they vanished, "*Piti vahine. Piti vahine!*"

"I bet that means monster girls," I said.

Other voices joined in down the valley, including the deeper shouts of men. The din of excitement raised the hackles on my neck.

Millie spoke slowly, glancing back up the trail. "I'm not so sure we should push our luck."

I grasped her arm. "What's the worst they could do? The girls will blab about the flowers and my horrid French, and your fairy hair. We sit and wait."

Perching on a slab of worn stone gave us a clear view of the trail. The shouting subsided, but it wasn't long before a growing fever of voices announced their intention to confront us. My heart and temples pulsed. Sweat beads joined, trickling, irritating.

The delegation, glowing gold and brown in stippled sunlight, streamed towards us, elderly men in front, women back several paces, and tailing, a cluster of near naked children, who provided most of the noise. I saw the twin girls looking sheepish as I smiled.

Their leader, a tall craggily built fellow, blustered back and forth, waving a black staff carved in intricate wedge shapes. He wore a tan, fibre-woven cape finished in black and orange geometric forms, much like some I'd seen in native weaving. His face was stubbled and heavily pocked, cheeks and eyes sunken under an ancient baseball cap crowned with a New York Yankees logo. A yellow and orange shirt, blue board shorts and thongs completed his regalia.

We stood. I shoved Millie off the rock, seeking a lower point. It was sensible for foreigners, especially girls, to avoid standing equal height to a chief. I slumped.

I hissed, "Smile, Millie. Smile."

She bared her teeth in a fixed grin, thrusting the fish offering forward.

His eyes lit up in surprise, which he quickly concealed. He ignored the fish with a wave of his hand.

An old woman, bent, but not frail, wedged in between the chief and a stocky fellow I recognised as the paddler from the evening visit weeks before. His massive arms, folded in front over a huge paunch, glistened, bearing a maze of intricate tattoos. He eyed us, devoid of emotion.

Before I could fracture more scraps of French, The chief rasped, thickly accented, "I see you decide to stay. No?"

"Yes!" I blurted.

The audience fell silent. My mind raced.

"*Aita*. No! You must leave *Motu-Riva*. We no want devilish plague," he growled.

"No plague. We can't anyway, our boat's unseaworthy. We are stuck."

He stepped forward onto the rock, accentuating his tallness. "You have stepped on sacred home of our old gods. *Tupapau'* know you there. You leave or you be cursed. Die."

Live gods? Not possible. I thought missionaries wiped out the ancient gods. Dad once said they were still deeply superstitious, like they lived in two worlds. Maybe the old ways lived on despite evangelical freaks hammering away at their ancient customs. Mum thought it a pity the islanders she met were so subdued, and figured the hellfire sermons made them fearful, but this lot didn't look entirely crushed.

And obviously, they'd been snooping around us all along. I made a note to sheath the outhouse in banana leaves, not that it would keep a god out.

"We don't have the death." I slapped at a mosquito sucking blood from my neck, and another threatening my legs. "We love your beautiful island," I waved, gesturing to the elders.

Several children burst into fits of giggles until the chief whacked his staff on stone.

In the pregnant silence Millie stepped forward again, holding the fish, her eyes cast down. In doing so she entered a shaft of light, igniting her hair, silver-gold. Her body turned neon, palest pink, as if internally lit.

The islanders uttered a strange sigh, ecstatic, awed.

She cast blue eyes upward into his dark sunken eyes, peach face contrasting with his weathered, pitted lava, imploring. It was a theatrical moment. "We've nowhere to go in the whole wide world," Millie said.

A ripple of mixed French and island dialect passed between the clusters of elders milling about behind the chief. Some were clearly hostile. One sported a double-barrelled shotgun.

The elderly woman, who stood only half the height of the chief, shuffled towards Millie, ran her bony hands up her arms and stroked Millie's cheeks. She nosed against Millie's nose, sniffed and inhaled. "*Nehe. Nehe.* Beautiful." She crowed, taking the fish and backed off smiling, exposing a set of tooth stumps.

I'd give a lot to have a snap of Millie's face, the Cheshire smile plastered on, as if permanent.

The chief stood rigid, eyes fixed, unable to respond. His power game was coming apart.

"You from across *mooree*." She rolled the 'r'. "Australeeah," She croaked, "I Mareva." She stepped closer. "You healer. Like your mother." She reached up.

I instinctively bowed expecting the greeting nose rub, and tried to match her actions. Mareva reeked of old smoke and fish.

"Mother. Father. Here long ago from *mooree*, West." She pointed.

I remained stooped, stupefied, caught in a peculiar numbness, unable to fully understand. "How do you know that?"

She cackled, face lighting up. "You have Anika's face and eyes. She have green eyes, like sea," she rasped, waving her frail arm, more a bag of parchment draping bone than live flesh. "You too. I have picture of her. You taller." She suddenly became solemn, nodded. "God *Iaha* of *Moana*, the Great Ocean, bring you here."

Mareva turned to the others, firing off a barrage of words in native dialect. Some smiled, but most of the men remained stone faced.

The chief spoke. "You leave sacred place. *Tupapu* is angry. You go." His face contorted as he jabbed the staff head into Millie's navel, then mine.

"Strangers come to Motu-Riva, sacred island of sky. Steal food. Kill people. Take *vahine*. Bad spirits." His presence filled the glade. He turned, sweeping his arms towards everyone.

All except the old woman retreated. Her brassy voice rang out. "You move hut from sacred temple. Come back when it is done. We talk." She hobbled away clutching the fish.

Millie moved for the first time in minutes, staring at me. "Healer? I can't believe it."

"Well. I am hot with a needle."

Millie shrieked with nervous laughter. I hoped the chief didn't hear her over the receding clamour of voices.

" We'd better move our butts back to camp," I said. "We've located on hot property. We're in for another move."

Chapter 21

"Will you listen? We've simply got no choice. Move *now*." I said.

"Their chief's chucking a number? Some ancient taboo? Why'd we pick this frickin spot in the first place?" Cris said. "Maybe that's why I've weird dreams."

"Cut the spook stuff, boofhead. Nothing'll bite you unless you believe in sorcery. The chief hasn't any horns," I said.

Jeff and Malcolm cast sour looks at Cris. I couldn't express sympathy with him being chicken-shit scared. Jeff mumbled in shorthand. Malcolm and Cris seldom spoke to one another about anything meaningful.

Jeff wouldn't be in panic about spirits, rather, he'd sit up for the show. As for Malcolm, sheer sloth ruled. He was somewhere round the bend. He'd taken to disappearing for hours at a time.

Millie cooked on a wire grill Jeff devised for her efforts. She'd marinated breadfruit slices and taro, soaked in coconut milk and limejuice, sprinkled with sea salt we'd distilled on a plastic sheet. An elongated, filleted fish, Zoë referred to as 'Stretch', cooked slowly in its juice. By boat standards our meals were a feast. We tried eating one meal a day together.

Fish fussed over an exotic fruit salad. Displaying sugar bananas, arranged like flower petals, she recited each fruit like a ritual. "Platannas. Mangos. Papaya. Bread fruit." She smiled a new confidence.

"I know this place sort of grows on you," I said. We've put in hard work making it home, but -" I shrugged.

"I don't like sleeping where humans were sacrificed," Zoë said. "Fish, too."

I sensed Zoë revving up.

"They ate their enemies," Zoë said. "Chopped them up." Her impish face screwed up in delight. Cris and Malcolm bagged her out.

"Aw, can it. Bleedin' carnivore. Bet you file your teeth if we

153

stay here much longer," Cris said.

Fish thrust her face into the circle. "Better to bite you. You tough meat. *Muy loco gringo*." With each word she poked Cris's stomach. He, in turn, annoyed by ruffling her hair.

Malcolm became nervy, "Do ye think there are spirit things here, kinda?" Nobody answered. He fell into rat thoughts.

Cris said, "There's something weird about this place, like I said. Noises. Things around camp."

"You're afraid of your own farts," I said. "Those are nocturnal animals. Rats."

"I know that." Cris said. "There's something else."

"Yeh. I get a feeling I'm watched, sometimes, like at the waterfall, eh." Jeff said.

I eyed Jeff, wondering if he toyed with our fears.

Cris and Malcolm, in a weird fit of communication, continued to niggle about their special gripes until both realised they'd actually shared thoughts, and promptly shut up.

The girls argued over cards with Millie. Jeff tinkered with the boat's dead radio and dead pocket computer. I sat up, rebuilt the fire, keen to catch up on my diary, and pondered what might lie ahead of us.

Mareva's sharpness of mind disturbed me. How could a stooped bag of bones strike on a memory of my mum across twenty years? Uncanny. She'd made my skin tingle. Still, there was power and importance in her old frame. I knew I'd see her again. I drifted into unanswerable questions. Maybe she was a priestess of some kind. She'd walked all over the chief. He may as well not have been there.

There were other things I didn't relate to. Why no teenagers, so many teenies, some of them dressed in rags, or nothing at all, and just a few older people about. Surely they'd be taken to the big islands. Surely many wanted to come back after the tidal wave.

Me, a healer? That was wacky. She must have a closet of answers, or bones. I held a closet full of questions, and bones of my own.

※

Moving. This one took the cake for brutality. Jeff decided we needed a higher spot for the radio, so he dictated moving to a

154

pint-sized valley hard against the highest peak. Well, it was more a poor excuse for a valley; rather, a long curved ledge broken into three segments flanked a gully, forming the high side. Two levels lay split in jagged steps below the main slab, which was elevated perhaps ten meters above the ravine. We found enough room to build lean-tos against a vertical backdrop of volcanic rock. The valley floor was obscured under a mass of vines and trees in an advanced state of strangulation.

"I need height for the radio. I'm goin' nuts trying to make the damned thing work, find out what's going on." Jeff said. "It's cooler up there."

We complained without conviction. Sealed off from the rest of the world for weeks, hunger for news grew in importance with each day, though we seldom badgered him about it. We had to face realities no matter how crappy.

Despite improved fitness, shifting high-rise drained our strength, consuming several days. Swarms of famished mosquitoes harassed us. Bathed in our own juices, we turned into beacons. Jeff called our route "the bitch n' bite track."

The ledges became cramped for space once the ridgepoles for three lean-to huts were anchored. It did give us a narrow view through the canopy below. Any intruder would be seen before they spotted us.

Jeff set to work with two scavenged truck batteries used for on-board domestic needs, four solar panels for charging them, and an assortment of wire, fittings, and the gammy shortwave radio out of Elysius.

In problem solving mode, brow creased, he grumbled through steps foreign to everyone. The machine, which could be capable of connecting us to the outside world, lay exposed on a sheet of plastic. Jeff cursed it for cutting out on us on the boat, now re-named it Grettle.

Millie sat close by wrapped in a blanket, shaking in spasms. Malcolm perched on a ledge like a brooding vulture; unable to interface with Millie. I noted he couldn't handle being near sickness. Kept muttering about fevers.

"How do you know what goes together?" She said awed by the dozens of wires and circuit board. "What's this piece?" She pointed to a riddle of circuitry.

"A capacitor." Jeff continued mulling through wires totally absorbed, ignoring Millie's blank look.

"Your hands are twice mine," She said, offering hers, slender and white.

"Umm," Jeff said.

She continued. "I guess it's like cooking a fancy d-dish," she stammered, body shaking, "m-miss something and it flops."

Jeff barely grunted, but looked closely at her. "This thing's old as my grandad, eh, as cranky and twice as corroded," he said.

Millie laughed. She burrowed deeper in covers.

From across the shelf I watched her edge closer. Jeff shifted, turned, leaning forward. He mumbled; exchanging words I assumed explained the function of a radio part he pointed to for her inspection. She nodded. Laughed. Said something pleasing. He smiled.

I'd have to get details out of her. Mysteries, even minor ones were intolerable, especially between those two.

He felt her forehead. "Mill's got a fever," Jeff said, raising his voice. "Lucky you didn't get skewered by Chief Pickle's club. Sounds like the old girl's a great contact, eh."

"Sour pickle. You should've seen Millie bat her eyelashes," I said, "stood right up to him. He was gob-stopped, like his pants were suddenly round his ankles."

Millie laughed, lapping up praise.

"Mareva's pretty cluey," I said.

The late morning air took on a pressure cooker density, pungent and steamy. Millie flopped back lethargic, her face dripping, clothing saturated.

"I feel like I'm made of lead. Can't move," she moaned. "Can't stop drinking. Why's it so damn hot?"

I made sure Jeff stayed close to her with a sponge and bucket of water. He needed to be responsible for Millie's well being until I returned.

Malcolm again vanished.

The girls whined for a swim. Apart from cooling off, I wanted time to unlock a few of Fish's secrets, at least, that's what Zoë told me I wanted to do. Striking up conversation would be easier between the three of us.

The usual stiff winds from southeast failed to materialise, turning lagoon water into a glassy, opaque green.

Halogen sunlight glazed everything, hazing the white coral sands. It permeated the jungle reaches, enveloping the canopy. Leaves sagged. Both shark-toothed peaks thrust like a mirage,

156

shimmering, detached.

I plunged, skimming along the bottom, strands of fantastic seaweeds brushing my body. Anemones swayed, tentacles endlessly undulating, collecting particles of food. Tiny shoals of fish of every colour darted away. Secreted under a coral shelf, a huge black and white striped eel grinned, its body rippling, slipped sideways into a crevice.

Zoë and Fish dove ahead sleuth-like with their spears poised for action. A poisonous stonefish darted off, disturbed by their probing, disappearing as quickly as it appeared out of sand. Stepping on their spines spelled disaster for any of us, even a death sentence.

I lay back in the shallows. The girls splashed about, nut brown demi-sirens, each an epicentre as they fanned water in sweeping arcs. Both wore strands of delicate seashells, which Jeff hand drilled and strung on nylon line.

Elysius swung on her anchor, a forlorn hulk, devoid of life. I cringed at the thought of telling dad how his dream boat ended - if we ever saw him again.

"You're going one better than the natives," I said.

"You should talk," Zoë gyrated, hands on hips. Fish copied. Both shrieked.

"What if the islanders drop in? You'll ruin what reputation we've got."

"We're cursed already," Zoë strutted, eyes shining.

"Me no care," Fish said. Both disappeared, gliding along the bottom.

Against the muted rhythm of ocean swells on the reef, an engine throbbed, bursting around the western point. It revved suddenly.

Zoë and Fish broke the surface waving a speared crayfish for my pleasure. "Look at this beauty," Zoë crowed.

"Get out of the water. Fast! We've got bad company." I waved. Pointed.

They stared dumb as I crab crawled up the beach, trying to hide behind a slab of rock.

Both bolted, thrashing water, racing for the tree line, arms and legs flailing. They dissolved into dense ferns and reeds.

I grabbed the binoculars, tore at my singlet, which ripped on a branch, hooked my shorts, did a hip hop putting them on, and plunged into an adjacent patch of palms, swore. I crawled into a patch of pandanus leaves higher up. This gave a good vantage point.

"Little girls. We sorry. Come here. We flends," one rasped, as the craft approached. Laughter.

I heard their launch crunch coral on the shallow inner reef. I cursed my decision to be so far towards the western point. They'd taken less than three minutes reaching us.

I parted fronds, trained binoculars on the intruders.

Three Asians stood clad in shorts, yellow-brown torsos glistening. Two wore bandanas, one chequered red, the other a faded blue batik design.

A third guy, bandy legged, sporting a wispy moustache, stood sinewy arms folded. His broad face bore a scar running across his forehead. A machete gleamed, hanging from a leather strap across his tattooed back.

Red turned, lifting a massive weapon out of the launch, resting it on his rotund belly. The damn thing looked powerful enough to vaporise rather than just rip a body in two. Its nozzle glinted gunmetal blue.

War always fuelled additional feuds, and there were scores of pirates following the civil upheavals in East Indonesia. Drug triads thrived too, carving their empires out of misery and blood.

I guessed several attachments must be heat sensors or night vision like American high tech stuff.

Red paused to pee.

How revolting - in plain view. That's the second time he's done that. Bladder problem. I slipped away, doubled over, worming through thickets of elephant ear and tree fern, pausing on a higher ridge to watch their game.

"We come. Get you." He waved the girl's clothes in the air. Bluey stuck Zoë's pokadot shorts on his head, laughing. How I longed for a gun.

Red crooned, "We flends. No hurt."

The girls materialised from a thicket of tree ferns to my right. "He's got my favourite pants," Zoë said.

"Never mind your wardrobe. We've gotta steer them away from camp and the dinghy hideout. The day they shot at us, we were at the western end of the island, so maybe they'll think we live over this way," I paused, catching my breath. "It's best we lead them in that direction."

"Then double back," Zoë beamed matter of fact.

158

"They'll see us for a few secs on that ridge." I pointed to a raw scar flanking the nearest peak.

Within a half hour we reached the exposed face. The beach lay far below. Two motored out to Elysius, were already picking over her for valuables. Before long they gathered empty handed in the cockpit. Red waved his displeasure, and went below. He emerged moments later, a wisp of smoke rising from the companionway. It subsided for a moment, surged, billowing, curling into the void.

"Look. Bree. The bastards are burning our boat. Dad'll kill 'em." Zoë burst into tears, clutched my arm. Fish joined in uttering an eerie howl.

I stood dumfounded. Bit my lip. Elysius carried us through some of the ocean's worst, but no boat could defy fire.

Within minutes flames licked, engulfed the cabin, popping, snapping in curling sheets. Her death cloud spired as high as the peaks.

"Why'd they do it?" Zoë said.

Red and his mate were back on the beach, scanning the slopes. The third vanished. We stood, featherless ducks in a shooting gallery.

"Let's move. They want sport," I said, prising Zoë's claw off my arm, "no sense encouraging them."

"What if Jeff sees smoke? Won't he come and run into these guys?" Zoë said.

"That's your job." I said, spotting the missing dreg with the blue bandana. He'd already made alarming progress, being half way up the slope to our right.

Red also began pursuit, heading straight for us.

"First we give them the run-around. Don't talk. Run your butts off."

Most of the slopes offered dense cover, between scarred patches. Thickets slowed me to a crawl. I knew from their shouting, each aimed to cut us off, hallooing to create panic. Scar face worked the launch along the shoreline, shouting, using glasses to guide his pals towards us. Bluey's see saw voice pierced the heat.

The girls were well ahead, worming their way through thickets I found impossible to penetrate.

Branches and tendrils reached out, raking my skin, slapping my face. My eyes stung.

I darted left glimpsing the girls as they bobbed and weaved, disappearing amongst towering fern trees. The goat trail I was on skirted a steep ridge leading to the summit Jeff, Cris and I crossed a fortnight earlier.

I strained for a look at our pursuers. In that instant my left foot shot down as the ledge gave way. I did an agonizing split, arms flailing for anything to grab, twisted to the right, and rolled over the edge into a clumsy backwards somersault.

Upside down, my instinct made me flatten out to create drag. Clawing a bush with my left hand, I spun around, faced up, legs pivoting ahead of me.

My momentum slowed, but not enough to stop. There was nothing more to grab. Both feet struck a rocky ridge. I flipped, landing winded, spreadeagle and slammed into a stunted tree. It gave way, roots and all. I rode on like a witch on a ragged broomstick; legs splayed wide, becoming airborne, crashing through a maze of giant tree ferns and branches, and landed hard, knocking the wind out of me.

Masses of debris cascaded. I lay, spitting dirt, gasping, afraid to move. My whole body screamed insults. I clutched a mass of foliage and roots in both hands.

Close by water trickled into a pool.

I stared, dazed for several minutes, began to focus to my immediate right where a slash in the hillside revealed tunnel-like cavities, some appearing deep, others, more narrow rills glistening with seepage. Panic stricken, I struggling to collect my wits.

Somewhere close, stones tumbled. Feet probed.

Chapter 22

Rolling over, I winced; nerve ends screaming protest. I slid into the pool, immersing my legs. The coolness sent shockwaves. I stifled a cry. Clouds of grit eddied, flowing outwards towards a gaping crack in the hillside several meters away. Open sky indicated a sheer drop lay beyond.

Opaque light filtered through tree ferns leaning fan-like, overlapping. I studied the ragged hole marking where I'd plunged.

Laboured breathing. Footsteps inching along, above and to my right, announced the approach of one of the pursuers.

Pain. Surely, I'd broken something. I moved, felt gingerly, not wanting to splash and give away my location.

Of the three tunnels I'd sighted two appeared as ancient subsidences worn away by water. The third proved to be an exposed volcanic vent. These might offer some hope of refuge. The first came to an end a few metres up. The second looked better, but was too wide and steep to grip onto.

The narrowed vent offered only worming room. It twisted upward into unknown cavities and darkness.

He spat, sending a spray through the ferns. Droplets fell on my shoulder. His voice rasped, "hey, woman. Come out. Ming treat you number one okay."

I bit my lip. Breathing constricted. My heart pulsed ready to burst. I realised he knew exactly where I was. "Over my dead body, slime-bag."

He sniggered, coughed, convulsed with laughter.

Fired by fear I wedged up into the tunnel, clawing, using every means of leverage to crawl higher, coarse gravel against broken skin. The tunnel tightened as I squirmed around a diabolical twist, shaped like the neck of a toilet drain and littered with chunks of pumice stone.

Even Houdini would wish he hadn't tangled with this one. Contorting, my back arched and one arm ahead, I wormed upward as the tunnel twisted left. Being skinned alive and unable to protect extremities is horrible. At this rate I wouldn't have skin or curves left.

Gulping air, I cursed for being careless in the first place, calling on my truest mentor, mum.

"What can I do now? I'm stuffed," I muttered.

Water bubbled below, the sounds magnified by the cavities' acoustics, me the stopper. My lips were parched, mouth stale. For some weird reason my right cheek began twitching. Screwing my face up didn't help.

"Aw, damn. Just move it," I said, and began wriggling, fumbling for leverage.

A wisp of acrid smoke drifted upward.

"He's lit a cigar. Cat and mouse bastard," I griped. Ming intended hanging around.

If smoke was rising, maybe the passage widened out like a funnel to draw it upward, sensed a whiff of air on the back of my hand.

Which one was Ming? The scrawniest weed would be able to crawl up here and drag me out screaming. Judging from the grating voice, I suspected it was Red with his paunch. He'd have to wait, and a waiting game gave me a slim advantage. How long was it til dark?

I figured the girls would be back at camp. Zorro could out fox any of these clowns. As for myself, I felt stupid and useless, flayed like an Aztec victim.

Faint crackling sounds rose from the lagoon. Vapours of acrid smoke found their way into the cavity.

My sense of time warped.

"You not be fraid, missie. Come out. Ming not beat you," he crooned. He slurped water, exaggerating his pleasure.

"Come now. Have nice, cool drink with me."

I wormed further. Shadow gave way to subdued light. The walls released their grip, levelling out into a chamber, which allowed me to role over. A fragment of sky appeared at the cave's end a few metres away, clearly a dead end.

The day lay beyond darkened with cloud. Freshets of breeze hissed chilly, caking sweat, dirt and blood.

A sudden blinding flash, rolling thunder, bounced between the valleys. Incandescent fingers snapped in quick succession. The sky pounded, each report deeper, more menacing. The ground shook. Bits fell from the ceiling in a fine film, catching my eyes.

As I twisted to the side, illumination highlighted an eye socket, curve of skull. My heart jumped. It stared balefully as if questioning my presence, the jaws matching my gaping mouth. Much of it lay protruding from debris piled against the wall. Scattered ribs poked upward. I realised, several of these ridged into my back, one wedging hard into my tailbone.

I extracted the offending piece. "You waited a long time to do that," I grizzled.

Lightning flashes rippled casting light into the cave. I spotted a stone spearhead wedged between two ribs, saw the deep, killing gash.

"Who were you in the flesh?" I whispered. "Did you hide here from battle? Bleed to death?" I fingered the brow edge, brushing away dirt. A smooth brow. Female? Males had a brow ridge. This skull was too delicate to be a male. Maybe she fled here during some horrific tribal war, escaped wounded while others of her tribe were butchered. I'd read of losers submissively being clubbed to death, and prepared for eating by the victors. "Better than chicken," some castaway European once wrote, obviously in ill concealed approval. Probably joined in.

Food. Even beans would taste as good as chicken. Hunger made my stomach growl and burble, like it was my bodies' roll of thunder, pathetic protest.

I pulled the skull clear, examined the shape in flickering light. A slash of pale yellow protruded from the debris revealing a circular carving consisting of sharp, geometric lines, some kind of abstracted amulet. I pocketed the spearhead and charm.

Sheets of rain lashed, sending torrents crashing into the gully. An acetylene-like flash left sparks in front of my eyes, my hackles standing on end. The report exploded immediately overhead, as if unzipping the sky. I shivered, cringed, and closed my eyes.

Through the din, the rattle of the launch's engine fluctuated, faded. Mouse was safe.

I waited as the storm peaked, illuminating the rain, freezing its motion. The wind, clawing branches and whole trees, sent them cascading below amidst torrents of water and loosened rock.

As quickly as it had come, the skies transformed, glowed iridescent pink westward. Like an enraged beast, ragged clouds muscled southward.

Backing out of the tunnel aggravated every source of pain and insult I'd inflicted. Stopping to rest every few minutes, I worked my way across the face of the hill, finding a diagonal route towards the ridge I'd fallen from.

Dusk settled as I felt my way down into thickets of trees, pungent, fresh from rain. Shredded foliage lay in a carpet. Cascades of droplets from branches chilled my skin. I made for the beach.

"Halloo! Jeff, you out there?" I cried into the night.

Insects frenzied, filling the night sky. Far to the south ribbons of electricity marched without sound.

Swimming at night scared me half to death. I didn't give a damn now, despite the waters seething with all sorts of sounds. Salt water beckoned, nature's healer, and my whole miserable body ached for heaps of that. I dreaded morning. Who'd want to look at a walking scab?

Half moon rise bathed the island, making travel through the jungle possible.

Jeff and Cris spilled out onto the beach several hundred metres away, their silhouettes glowing ghostly grey. Fish, looking more drowned than alive, struggled ahead, arriving wild eyed.

"Bree, you look awful, like skinned tamale," Fish whined.

"Where the hell did you get to?" I said, as Jeff arrived.

"Stow the agro," Jeff said. "Our camp's nearly blown off the ledge. Zoë's nursing Millie."

I nodded.

"You saw the smoke?" I said.

"Yeah. Figured something was up. Just got going and the girls literally flew into camp. Took ages to get the story out of them. That's when the sky went berserk. Never seen a storm like that."

Cris stared. "I hate to mention it."

"Bloody don't." I said.

"Looks like you made an all points landing."

"Don't mention a bloody thing—if you want a life," I said, fighting tears, lip trembling.

"You're amazing—I mean, surviving the fall," he said. "Sorry, didn't mean to be a flip. You really look in pain."

"Oh, that's for sure, eh." Jeff said.

"Crap. For once, both of you *get real*." I said. "I *am* fuckin' wrecked, so skip the comedy act." I threw a fistful of sand, tears welling up with the shock of movement.

As if calling our attention, flames burst near the stern of Elysius, casting ripples of amber light across the waves, then subsided.

The boat smouldered, her rig a skeleton, hull paint peeled,

164

and blackened. She remained afloat, the chain and anchor holding firm, her last grip on life.

They sat in silence with me until dawn. I refused to move and soaked to help cut spasms of pain.

"I don't understand how anyone can be so miserable to us," Jeff said.

"We cleaned out anything useful from the boat didn't we? It's just plain spite. These mongrels hate being denied," I said, crawling out of the shallows.

"They didn't burn Blackjack," Cris said.

"Maybe because it's a junk someone sees a use for." Jeff said. "Umm, some of our clothing was still on board the boat."

Venus hung glowing in the west. I felt like Mars after battle.

Chapter 23

Zoë calmed once sure I didn't need a "blood transfusion," began removing bits of cinder embedded in my back.

Fish sat cross-legged, dabbing at my shoulder.

Zoë whispered, "You look just awful, but I'm worried more about Millie. She's real sick."

"You a lot like hamburger, Bree," Fish said, snuffling.

"Thanks Fish, darling." I ruffed her curls, realised she could make an emotion distinction between accidental scrapes and blood from serious wounds.

"Millie's fever's bad. Tummy's sore, too," Zoë said.

It's weird how someone else's misery can lift you out of self-pity; after the trauma, a gravel finish only wrecked my vanity.

Malcolm sat across the camp scratching in thought. "Jeezus, what's eatin' her?"

"I'd guess, fever. Some bug this island has. Maybe you shagged once too often," I said.

"You mean Millie's got a kid?" He said, face clouding over. He fingered reeds Zoë nagged him to weave.

"Could be. Only takes once," I said, eyebrow rising. Rat wheels turned slowly. He couldn't begin to imagine the traumas ahead if she'd scored one. Never mind his feeble notions, my mind freaked at the implications.

"If she is, you can't have your way any more. She's too fragile," I said, matter of fact.

"Millie ain't comin' across anyway. How'd you stuff things up?"

"Tough beans Malcolm. Maybe she's changed her mind." I shrugged. Pain cut across my shoulders. "Girls have that right. Didn't you know?"

I sent my gravel pickers off to refill the bucket.

"Yer a nosey little bitch."

"Big bitch. Remember that, dearest Rat. You're here because I took pity on you. My mistake. Anyway, thanks for the compliment."

166

He drawled, knowing I hated it, "whoever worked you over must've been a real goer. I'd do better."

I imagined Rat's anatomy rearranged. I studied Millie's breathing, struggling to ignore his dig, sponged her forehead.

"What's your game, skulking away from camp?" I said.

"Aw, just growin' dope. Made my own little garden."

"You bastard. You kept seeds?"

"My bag you threw away? I stuffed it with clothes. Yours." He smiled. "What's mine is mine, Bree."

I seethed. So that's where my best undies went.

"You should light up, have a toke. Loosen it. Lettin' go is hot on a high," he said, eyes rolling.

"But, you were agro when I threw the bag overboard. How come?"

"You brown nosed in me bag. That's reason enough, besides, you've thought all along my stash was gone."

"The last thing we need's your crappy games. You're either with us or you're out," I said.

His face contorted in mock pain.

"Leave Millie alone." I said.

"She gets her rocks off. Millie's me girl."

"So you keep saying," I taunted. "Your chicken's flown the coup." Millie's eyes fluttered, her breathing laboured. "Don't count on her. No self respecting guy belts a girl up."

"She likes it, well, rough. That's love play. What about you? The way you're strung out you'd go off like a rocket."

"Pig's arse! Pull your head in. Better still - get lost. Permanently."

Jeff passed by whistling. He paused to study Millie. Our eyes met.

He turned on Malcolm. "You're really the lowest life form. She's got something seriously bad. Bree can't do much more for Millie."

"Yeah. Wonder Bitch hasn't got all the answers," Malcolm said.

Jeff paused, clenching his fists; "she's worked you out long ago. Lay off bagging Bree, or she'll..."

"It's okay. Mal's about to find basket weaving therapeutic," I said, sticking my middle finger up.

Jeff grinned, changing channels. "Maybe the islanders know what to do. They'd get the same sort of sickness."

Malcolm nodded, remained impudent, studying me.

"I'll take the girls with me if they're presentable," I said, motioning as they returned.

"Zoë told me to take a hike. Wants to wear what she pleases," Jeff said. "She's a cheeky little beast and you're encouraging her."

"You sound just like dad," I said.

Zoë smiled, stuck out her tongue.

"She's independently expressive - and quite mad," I said, laughing. "Seriously, Jeff. Give us a break."

The girls took up scraping growth from a stone carving. I suspected we'd blundered onto another religious site; knew the symbol they started on was phallic; something Malcolm would relate to. The less said, the better.

I hobbled over to Jeff's radio project, each step an ordeal, stiff tendons protesting. I was sure I'd cracked my pelvis. Ramming the tree slowed my plunge; a mule may as well have kicked me. Better humiliation than a broken neck.

I remember the aftermath of a day ride I'd once endured on a wilful horse, aptly named Pepper.

Jeff motioned me close. "I'm checking Blackjack over tonight. We didn't sort her out properly. Our ratbag friends could've missed stuff."

"Zoë, Fish and I'll see the islanders. Wait for you in the palm grove where we hide the dinghy. It's a full moon," I said, poking my point home.

"They won't be about at night," Jeff said.

"Oh, really? Don't count on it," I said. "Take Rat with you. You'll need shifty eyes."

We dressed in remnants of finery, a patchwork, uncoordinated colours, and all of it shabby. The girls went mad layering on shell necklaces.

They danced along well ahead chattering, their regalia subtly chinking as they ducked and weaved through the brush. Once on the beach, they sprinted off, Zoë doing cartwheels and Fish crying in her pixie voice, "*Yeriba, yeriba.*"

It wasn't long before both returned with several giggling children in tow. They encircled us. Two were the youngest girls Millie and I spied in our first encounter at the water hole.

"*Aloha*," I said, waving. Their round faces shone, eyes rolling, bursting into gales of laughter. Like a giddy squall, hair and sand flying, the mob disappeared heading for the village. Dogs soon joined in, likely the most exciting event in their fly biting life. I hobbled, walking with short, ungainly steps.

Moments later the elders appeared aligned behind the two chiefs in order of rival cliques. Waves of laughter swelled beyond in the village, mocking the severity of their faces.

"You not leave," The tallest, our earlier adversary said. "*Tupapau* make spell on you. You die. Spirit fever coming for you." He waved the staff in an arc over my head.

I stood my ground, eyes fixed on his, jaw set. "Our boat is burned." I pointed.

He nodded, "Jehovah burn boat."

"Pirates. Evil men did it. We are staying." I placed my hands on my hips. "I must see Mareva." I rubbed my stomach and forehead. "Silver girl. She's sick." I mimicked fever, feeling totally silly.

He stared, perplexed, as if confronting someone bewitched. "You have Great Sickness?" His nose flared. "More strangers come with sickness soon."

His breath engulfed me in a smoky halitosis. I shifted up wind.

"Just fever." I gesticulated, trying to fold my lacerated arms as a statement of confidence. The pain wasn't worth enduring. We remained awkwardly poised, deadlocked. What nerve. He wanted to play it both ways with the old gods and Christian fear. Either way, we weren't going to budge.

Mareva shuffled onto the beach, a dark apparition against stark white sand, and more in keeping with storm driven seaweeds lapping the beach rim. She grinned, and fired a volley of commands, again not stopping to acknowledge either chief.

Pock face and his beefy companion, who displayed an impressive mass of delicate, black tattoos, remained unmoved, while the others withdrew a few steps. I guessed these two couldn't afford losing face to a mere girl.

"This is Niau, our elected chief, and Hiva. He is also a chief," Mareva said, waving in recognition.

I offered a hand. Hiva hesitated, but accepted, enveloping mine in a bone-crunching grip. I smiled, tears welling as he released. Niau, alias Sour Pickle, remained aloof, eyes clouded. He fingered a cross.

Mareva pushed the deadlock aside.

"You have very bad fall. Need skin ointment. Get boy friend rub all over body. Then special juices - coconut oil I give you," she wheezed, looking up, her head canted to one side.

I accepted, kneading my aching hand. "Millie. Silver girl. She's sick."

"Maybe it is *Moki* working black magic. Many strangers come to island in past, get fever. Some die. I make medicine, come see you when moon up."

We settled under a palm-leafed lean-to, leaving the chiefs in conference with the elders. The discussion was intense, and in dialect, impossible to interpret. I sensed two heads were poles apart.

We shared coconut milk in chipped daisy cups.

Two girls, the pair we surprised in the stream, fawned nearby, but were too shy to speak. Both were slender, shapely in budding. I upgraded their age to no more than fourteen. Both wore orange and yellow floral skirts and white cotton tops, one logoed 'Save a Whale.'

"I once train to be nurse. Work on American hospital ship in big war," Mareva said, grinning.

"You must be very old, and wise," I added gravely.

"Oldest. My clan will die when Gods take me across water. In great past we were strong. Thousands." Her arms swept wide. "My great grandfather, many generations back, Teimua, our high priest, have magic powers. He talk to Gods. Bring good *mana* to people until white man's pox came. Our people die, taken like fish swept from sea. Skin rot. Bodies poisoned. Boils all over. Great, great mother tell me these things." She lapsed into thought, began to whisper a chant from deep in her conscience.

> "Oh Great Ancestors, seed of our seed
> Creator of our blood,
> Oh Spirit Goddess of the veiled world
> Deep beneath Motu-Riva.
> Your seed fades in this realm of light
> As the sun's orb sinks beneath the
> Great Ocean.
> Will thou draw us away, oh spirit
> As your rays die, to be never more?

"That's beautiful. Sad. Why so few of you now?" I said. "Surely lots want to return. The island's wonderful."

"After Great Wave, nobody left on other side. All drowned. Most left on this side go far away. Find work. Christian God al-

170

ways tell us how we should live, but not protect us. The Great Wave swallowed our sacred land." She waved her arms erratically. "All my people die in church." Her eyes watered. "Yes. Some come back after Wave. Start to clear. They give up. A trading boat came each month. Not come now. French leave. This Great Death make us so alone."

"The chief?" I said.

"Niau. He angry over his own sorrows. Not my clan. Good Christian. Niau is rude, but has good heart."

"He said something about a *vahine*. Girl?" I said.

"She is his adopted daughter, Kalani. The foreign demons take her away. They have other." She fell silent.

"Other girl?"

"You very nosey," she croaked, running her sinewy hands across my cheeks, tracing my upper lip. Her parchment face canted up into mine. Mareva radiated a musty ancientness. Her eyes gleamed. "Strong eyes, Bree. Green like deep lagoon. You woman soon. Good man find you. In my culture you too old to be virgin. Need fire in your belly. *Navenave*." Mareva chuckled, nodded.

"How did you come to that conclusion?" I said, annoyed. Laughed disbelief.

"Mareva knows your power, we call *mana*, knows your fear, and your hunger," she said. Her blackened forefinger traced the length of my scar. "You will see."

My back prickled the way it used to when I watched spook movies. "Are you a sorcerer, a sort of shaman?"

Mareva laughed, rocking back and forth. "My Gods speak through me when they have a bone to pick."

"Is that why Niau is afraid of you?" I said.

She coughed, laughing in short fits. "You see very good! Hiva is different. He is of the *Old Way*."

Mareva motioned to the girls, who promptly sat by us, legs crossed, their hair hanging in black rivulets over glowing amber skin. "This is Fau and Alili. They grow up. Make good lovers soon. Good wives."

I rubbed noses, brushed their silken cheeks. Each bore a fresh, geometric tattoo on their right hand.

Mareva said, "Your brother, he is strong boy. Good for them. Maybe make them woman soon. They can cook."

I stared dumfounded at Mareva, and then at the girls, who giggled, their faces bashful, wanting to share her delight. I sensed they were not at all ignorant of Mareva's meaning. I wondered how long they'd been learning. "How do you know about Jeff, my brother?"

"I have many eyes on island, yes." She gazed through and beyond me.

A compression of children ran through the shallows kicking fans of spray, squealing. I rose, aided by the girls who were aware of my decrepit state. I couldn't sit for long without seizing up.

I nodded respect to the chiefs and elders, who were still standing in a knot in less earnest conversation. Stalemate, I thought. Refusing to leave the stage.

Mareva waved as I departed. "I bring girls with me. They see your brother."

I rolled my eyes, planting a smile of reassurance. This, I would have to see. Jeff under the gaze of maidens? These two obviously sized him up, but how?

The old girl was a mover, again posed more questions than she provided answers to.

Several children tagged along the beach until we reached the bend where we'd first landed.

The girls ran ahead keen to explore beyond our usual fishing spot. This brought us close to the western end of the island. We were all ears for any sign of approaching craft.

To our right Fish spotted a dwelling, someone's cottage, derelict and overgrown with vegetation. Its exterior sagged, mouldering, splotches of discoloured yellow finish suggesting a once charming home.

The door lay open, its wooden frame eaten away. There was little left in the single room other than a collapsed card table and a bamboo mat sprouting reeds, once a bed for family. Part of the rusted corrugated roof hung over the side, wedged in a stand of banana trees. A single hand of bananas hung inside below where the roofline should've been.

Droppings littered the floor amongst an assortment of debris. An old bell crowned alarm clock lay mute amongst newspapers stacked in a ruined cabinet.

I wondered why anyone on this island needed to watch time. All of us were adjusting to the rhythm of nature, especially with a heavy fruit diet, our habits much less programmed than in Sydney life.

An English newspaper, *Pacific Times*, dated *August 9, 2007,* bore headlines, '*Civil War Spreads*' in faded print; Weathered pictures of human misery. The rest was too bleached by sun to read.

The devastation visited on Motu-Riva came months before this date. Jeff intimated dad said a Sunday in May.

"There's a graveyard out back," Zoë said. "It's fresh."

Beyond a tiny thatched cookhouse, a cluster of mounds lay in a line against weathered red stone. Bleached timber crosses leaned, the names faintly scratched on. I read one. Maree.

A recent burial stood apart, the soil still free of growth. On its crown stood a crudely carved Tiki, defiantly gaping, as if challenging intrusion.

"Someone's changed heart about beliefs," I said.

"You mean they're Animists?" Zoë said. "Remember? You told me Arie believed in nature worship."

"It's Pagan of some sort. I get the impression a few have gone back to some of the old beliefs." I continued taking in the sad contents of someone's life.

We poked along the shoreline, just short of the point. As usual, the girls ranged ahead, dashing from one find to another.

I saw Zoë freeze. Fish ran past her. She let out a nerve-tearing scream, snagged her foot, sprawled in the water, and lay transfixed.

"Bree!" Zoë cried, her voice rising shrill.

I managed a lame sprint as Fish scrambled to her feet. She bolted by me, ears back, wild eyed.

From a distance I thought it was a mutilated sea creature, long decayed. My mind struggled to focus.

It was the near skeletal vestige of a human, a male. The cadaver lay wedged between slabs of coral. Its remaining clumps of clinging hair swayed with the surge of current and wave. His face was eaten away, raw sockets fixed on the sky, the teeth grimacing. A school of fingerlings darted from the ribcage.

Zoë's fingers locked onto my arm. "Who is he?" she whispered. She stepped back, but remained fixed in horror.

"Uh. Wouldn't have a clue," I lied. "Poor wretch." I saw the neat entry hole in his right temple with a jagged exit hole on the opposite side, much bigger.

"Go. Get away from here," I said. "Find Fish."

Zoë suddenly spewed breakfast, the stench of bile and banana assaulting the air. She ran.

Fighting nausea, I steadied, focusing on his ruins, imagining him alive, laughing, sharing a joke with friends.

Here a wonderful intelligence died horribly, all the potentials of life snuffed.

In a flash, I saw the severed stump of his ring finger.

Chapter 24

"The poor guy needs a decent burial," I said.

"That's terrific. You find - we do the dirty work," Malcolm grizzled.

"I couldn't cope with a corpse. It freaked the girls out. Do the right thing by them. Make yourself useful?" I said, hurling a coconut husk.

"We'll do something. Maybe tow it out near the south entry, let the tide take him away," Jeff said.

Malcolm groaned, "aww, leave it alone. He might fall apart if we try to pick it..."

"Shut up, Malcolm," I said.

Jeff ignored him. "We'll do it. We'll leave at dusk, be back by midnight."

"Don't shine any light outside. Block the portholes. Remember it's a full moon after ten," I said, ruffling his hair. "Remember the charts."

I cuffed Malcolm. "Be brave, and useful."

"Why not make a shopping list?" Malcolm said.

"Oh. By the way, Jeffie, two young maidens are hot to size you up," I said, barely able to suppress glee.

Jeff coloured. He whispered out of Mal's hearing, "can't cope with the one you've dumped on me, let alone three." His brow wrinkled.

"They're awfully cute and friendly," I gave him a suggestive hug.

Jeff frowned, "later, much later for that."

"Remember. Diplomacy. Put yourself out," I said.

✳

Mareva arrived by late afternoon, with Fau and Alili demurely in tow, each wearing floral mini-skirts slung low on their hips. A mass of frangipani flowers lay in loops from their necks, their

175

pink, yellow and white petals framed by long, jet hair. Jeff kept busy, coiling rope and fiddling in his toolkit.

The scent of fish, smoke, a hint of musk drifted by.

The girls latched onto Zoë and Fish who sprawled on matting observing Jeff. Fish slumped into misery since stumbling over the body. Zoë hardly spoke at all, which was some kind of record.

Fau and Alili managed to position themselves in line of sight with Jeff. Each smiled when he looked up, their gaze dropping, but dark, inquisitive eyes never failed to return.

He hastily cinched up the rope, prepared to escape, managing a fleeting grin edged with annoyance.

Jeff stumbled, hesitated, before managing a bow to Mareva. She beamed back.

I wondered if he realised her intentions. A bit of wild life lurking around would do him good. I imagined a throng of tiny children swarming around his ankles. I burst out laughing; covered my mouth.

Jeff squinted at me, which made him a caricature in the light, and all the funnier. He hastened to escape.

Millie sat up against the rock face overhanging our lean-to. She nibbled on coconut flesh he'd left her.

Mareva exchanged greetings, eyeing her over, searching for symptoms. She wasn't long in offering opinion.

"Your Millie has island fever. After our ancestors dammed the water, fevers came. This one maybe not kill Millie."

Millie whispered, "Maybe not? What the hell do you mean? I'm so damn weak. Always thirsty. Can't eat in the morning without chucking up." She cast an empty smile.

"I know other way you are sick. You not have woman's monthly?"

Millie blushed. "No, not since before we landed."

She stared at me, eyes filled with remorse.

"Mareva know if you have baby." She hooked a finger over Millie's sun top, pulling it down. Millie's face fell, flushing red, but she was too ill and stunned to object.

"These are tender to touch?" Her weathered finger probed each breast.

"Yes!" Millie winced; her mouth opened to protest, but remained mute. She stared at her breasts, mesmerised, as if they'd become strangers.

The girls stood statue-like either side of me, shocked by

Mareva's actions.

"What are you gawking at? I'm not a freak show." Millie said, pursing her lips.

The girls shied away seeking distraction.

"We'll help you if you're pregnant," I said, trying a smile to overpower my frown.

"I don't want a kid," she pleaded.

Mareva stood grinning over Millie. "You make good mother. I will help when time comes. Oh, yes." She patted Millie's upturned face. "I deliver many babies."

Millie's face distorted, etched in raw fear, her eyes locked on mine.

I remained lost in panic mode.

Millie turned away curling up on her bed sobbing, her body convulsing.

Moments later Cris crashed into camp, dishevelled, a crossbow slung over his shoulder. Great White Hunter returned empty handed once again. I'd tried to suggest he develop some stealth skills if he hoped to kill any game. It's amazing how unsolicited advice sours relations, not that ours was so hot. I smiled in mock sympathy; still, I admired his determination. He'd come a long way. Loved those shoulders, pity about the vacant spaces.

Cris moved to the far end of the camp, evaluating the mood mix. He stared hard at Millie's shaking form.

I knew he wanted to cut her with some snide remark.

I shifted the subject. "Why are some of your people hyped up about *Tikis* like they're taboo?"

Mareva sat lost in thought, the silence protracted.

"Chief Niau. You know, bossy scar face. His clan fears *Tikis*, oh yes. The big one you saw was uncovered by the Great Wave." She swung her hand to the north, as if executing a regal gesture.

"You saw us there?"

Mareva grinned tooth pegs. "My eyes tell me everything. Other chief, Hiva, make us put it back on the temple platform. He say *Iaha*, our Supreme God, say we must drive away intruders. He and many islanders think the Gods are angry with us. *Oro*, God of War, must be respected, now evil strangers come," she rasped. "It is our deepest hunger that *Oro* help destroy them. She shook her head slowly, "It is hopeless, foolish. We haven't many men or guns to attack them with," she sighed.

Much smoke. No fire. I thought. Well, they had spark and

spirit. This explained the drums we heard, especially at night. They wanted the intruders to fear them, like frilled lizards puff up, hiss, to intimidate a much stronger enemy.

"We must stay away from them," I said, knowing it was only a matter of time before they confronted us.

I untangled the ivory charm from my hair, which covered a few of the worst scrapes. "I found this. What does it mean?"

Mareva drew breath. "Where you get that from?" Her eyes widened. "Oooh."

I saw her reach, then draw back; sensed her reverence; a glimmer of a darker disturbance.

The charm held a peculiar ambience, being slightly elliptical, and divided into finely dotted lines radiating from the centre. Some ran diagonally, cutting across adjacent lines. Each tiny hole had been notched into the surface, forming an intricate geometric pattern. Some points were more deeply cut. The edges held weathered markings made by generations of wearers, marring its completeness. The polished ivory surface, aged yellow, glowed with a tinge of green as light slashed through swaying broadleaves.

"I found it in a cave by a skeleton."

"That charm. Our people used long ago when they travelled the Great Ocean. Women wore one like this to protect them in time of dangers."

She continued, "Before white men came with diseases, our people were many. Fighting was a clan's way of life. You see many flat places high on hilltops? They used them for protection if fighting went bad."

I produced the finely fluted spearhead. "Whoever wore this didn't do so well." Now I knew the victim had caught its bite in some terrible tribal war.

Mareva's gnarled hands stroked my hair. "Your hair is like waves in the ocean we sailed endless moons ago. This charm is for your *mana*."

She rasped softly, drifting into a trance-like state.

"Hold her in your loving shield
O' Great Waters flowing under white clouds.
Young women know the rhythm of your embrace,
Stirring now towards rebirth
As the ancients did, ages past.
You are the fragrant flower born of fire

178

Uplifting, unfolding from bud to blossom
From whence new seed springs."

Everyone sat dumb, awkward in silence. It was strange. I remembered a similar sensation by the meteor crater in the Kimberelys, and that felt so long ago now, a different world altogether.

Mareva smiled a thousand wrinkles. "I have potion cream to sooth your skin and special drink for Millie."

From a mesh bag she produced an old mayonnaise jar and a smaller one once used for lobster and ham spread. The latter bore a black paste she indicated was for my scrapes. The other, I imagined, a mutation of iodine, chilli and vinegar, was for Millie. A dab on my tongue cured my curiosity.

Zoë came to life, her voice sad. "Who's buried near the end of the island by that old house?"

Mareva's eyes lost their lustre. "That is where Kalani, the chief's daughter, lost her lover. They killed him. He suffered many wounds." She gestured all over her body. "I not tell you before—all things in right time."

Another victim, I brooded, realising our peril.

She raved on, filling us with mind boggling family lore, a dizzying confusion of names. I guessed Mareva rambled through a dozen generations before abruptly stopping. She regarded us as great listeners.

Cris sat by his own fire. He whittled at a new crossbow stock, the wooden shaft pressed into his groin. His strokes, muscles flexing, firm and measured, struck me as urgent, sensual.

Cris cast furtive glances at Mareva. I smiled at him. Winked.

Using an oil torch, Mareva and the girls, whose faces betrayed disappointment, left. In their wake, muted rays flickered ghostly amongst the palms. The girls began singing an old Simon and Garfunkle rock song, Bye, Bye Love, in French.

> "Au revoir l'amour,
> Au revoir le bonheur,
> Bonjour la solitude,
> Je pense que je vais pleurer."

"Now that the old spook's gone could you help me haul a pig?" Cris said.

"You're weak as marshmallow. She's very kind," I said. "What's this wonder pig? Can't you get enough grunt out of those hunky muscles?"

"I've got it trussed way up the hill. Needs a bit of stick." His eyes flashed, locked on mine. This was vintage Cris on the loose, brazen, taunting.

"What's that supposed to mean? I'm overdue for Submission?" I feigned anger. Fisted. "I'll belt you first."

"You frosting up?" Cris said.

"Like an - ice castle?" I taunted.

Cris flinched, looked down.

"If you dumped the emotional baggage, we could be closer, maybe," I said, turning my nose up. I saw my barb stung; that he knew I remembered what he'd blabbed within earshot of Zoë.

"Baggage?"

"The way you pick on Millie. Your shitty mood swings."

Cris fell silent for some time.

"How close?" he said.

Zoë eavesdropped, enraptured.

"Silly. At least not poles apart. There's something cool about you - just stop crapping on. A real friendship means loyalty, like caring for others who depend on you, and who you depend on for survival. Acceptance." I pelted him with husks.

"I'm at your service," Cris bowed, became lost for words.

Zoë interjected, "that's tragic. She wants more than stick, stupid. No thorns."

I smirked, "butt out, Zorro. At any length, I'll decide the measurement."

Zoë laughed. She ran off, dodged well-aimed firewood.

We worked our way along a trail worn by daily forays. Ribbon markers defined sharp drop-offs where a wrong turn at night invited disaster. Puffing, our breathing fell into a rough rhythm.

A half kilometre on the humped mass of a large boar lay rammed against a tree.

"Didn't want to look like the Hunchback of Notre Dame, and break my neck," Cris crowed. "Might scare the girls. Shot it right through the heart."

"What's the arrow in its skull for then? That's gruesome. Take it out."

"It tried to gore me. Look at the tusks."

"They're huge. Wear them around your neck. Anything for improvement, you know, virility," I said.

The boar appeared bigger in the solid shadow cast.

I was impressed, but not keen to let his ego inflate any further.

We battled to haul the damn thing down the switchback path. I slipped and fell on my bum too many times. If nature had given me a tail, it'd be fractured right off. The boar's weight swayed under the pole, as if contriving to topple us over the edge. The timber's roughness dug tomorrow's bruises deep into my aching shoulders.

Just short of the camp, Cris untied it, and by sticking his head under its belly, heaved the animal over his shoulder. He staggered down the last steps, and thrust the beast off his back, forcing Zoë to scramble away. "At last we eat real meat."

I mocked, clapping in slow motion.

Zoe gaped at the stiff bristled hog, disgusted at first by its distorted expression, but she soon babbled about a monster barbecue.

Fish panicked, began frantically attacking the blood on Cris's shoulders with a rag, as if possessed. "No! No more."

Flashes of Shakespeare's Lady Macbeth crossed my mind. It was she who couldn't wash away the blood from her murderous hands. Out of the dark recesses of Fish's past, I wondered whose blood haunted her.

"At least some females appreciate me," Cris jeered.

"That's not it, dung head. She's terrified of blood," I said more harsh than intended. I pulled Fish away, wrapping her in my arms. She began rocking back and forth, as she'd done many weeks ago.

"Hey. You won't believe this," Cris said. "There's a boat in the north lagoon. Packed with people. It sailed in just about noon. Looks like one of those Indonesian fishing things. Big."

"That's great. Thanks for being up front with your priorities. Don't you see? It means heaps of trouble. You should've warned us."

"There's no panic," Cris said. "Hell, you're so one-eyed."

"Don't you understand? Jeff and Mal could've been warned off going to Blackjack if you got your act together."

Reproachful, he sat by me. "These Asians won't be interested in us, besides, they're newies like the rest of us, Bree. Refugees."

"Have you got a short memory or what? Hey, they might have the plague," I said.

"The virus couldn't last so many weeks. It's a long trip," Cris said.

"Why didn't this lot stop at a main island like Tahiti?" I said. "Who says the virus can't survive a month before symptoms show?"

Cris shrugged, "maybe they weren't made welcome elsewhere for good reasons?"

"Hurray." I whacked his arm with a stick. He grinned, radiating heat and perspiration. Part of me wanted to kick him. Something inexplicable moved inside, longed to touch, be touched. The notion shocked me.

Fish squirmed on my lap.

"I saw you working on another crossbow. It's gorgeous. Beautiful shape. You're a real craftsman."

His eyes reflected embarrassment and pleasure. "We may need Maggot Maker one day."

"What?" I said.

"It's a better name than Heart Breaker," he said.

Cris surprised, especially good with hands-on things. I wondered what he'd be like up close and personal. That was hoping for far too much.

I said, "If some were dying on board they've probably brought rats. We've got lots of rats. They'll eat anything dead. The islander's dogs will dig up corpses."

"In a few months it could be our turn then," Cris said. His expression struck me as fatalistic.

"What would you do if one of us had it?" I said.

Cris slumped, poked at the fire and kicked the carcass. "Throw them overboard?"

"Yes. You would, and so would I." I said, my skin chilling with images of flesh erupting in pustules. Complete ruin. "If I had it, I'd kill myself. Jump overboard."

"If you knew you had it, wouldn't it be too late for the rest of us?"

"Yes. Remember your mum? Your fear saved you. The fact she went to bed on coming home, before you both came home, before you shared her breathing space. She had the cough of death. Things she touched."

"I don't want to think," he brooded. "I never thanked you properly for what you tried to do for mum. I didn't have the guts to try saving her. Hadn't a clue."

"It's all right. Like I said, nobody else has a clue about it either.

Remember? I really admit it. Might have even tried to save your miserable hide too," I kissed his forehead. He tensed, flinched in surprise.

"Jeff's going to freak out about the boat," Cris said, nudging the hog.

I remained silent, sensing his anxiety, stroked Fish's tight curls. Her hair spring-coiled in the island's warmth and humidity.

Cris suddenly slashed the boar open, entrails erupting, slipping down, pink and blue, tumbling onto the fire's edge, hissing. The stench made me retch. I refrained from saying anything. Knew he was angry with himself.

Fish burrowed as if trying for rebirth, her thumb rammed in her mouth. She sucked, her breathing shallow and wheezy.

Zoë, depleted of excitement, lay entwined in Millie's arms, as if she'd become her child.

Cris, shifted, sat dark against the firelight, lost in thoughts, but kept sneaking glances.

I drifted into a half sleep sitting up. Desired rational thought. Instead emotions surfaced heating the pit of my stomach blinding reality.

The warmth of breath on my cheek and fingers enmeshed in my hair startled me. I felt lips tease against mine. Through the web of sleep I half kissed back, confused by the surprise of it.

Suddenly awake, I dug my fingers into Cris's hair. I bit his lip, raking it as he pulled back. Pushed.

"Ow," he hissed.

"Not sorry I bit," I whispered, cuffing his ear.

His warm breath sent adrenalin pumping. Fingertips traced up my back. Dark memories welled up, said resist. He fumbled, tugged. Ties knotted. He teased with his nose, the ache and anxiety unbearable. Smudge smoke made my eyes water.

Branches snapped close by. Malcolm cursed.

"Stop. Stop. We've got double company," I said, snuffling, catching my breath, and pointing to Fish. She still slept, wedged between my legs. I pushed him away gently, then shoved, but he wouldn't let go.

"Hey. You've gone too far. Fair's fair."

Cris sighed, "What're you on about?"

"Zoë's my—*your* reminder, dopey. You know..."

"Aw, Bree, that's mean, you know I hate heights." His eyes, black against the firelight, pleaded, sought weakness, fingers still fumbling for the key.

The ties gave way. Cris's fingers trembled. He may as well be an octopus in spasm. I slapped a venturing hand.

"Ow. Hey."

"I still ache all over. Don't push me or your luck."

Footsteps closer.

Chapter 25

"Don't ask about the burial," Jeff said.
"Bloody awful. Dude did fall apart," Malcolm said, watching me on the sly. "Bree's had a turn-on."

Cris again fiddled with the strings I found too painful to reach.

"Get on with it," I hissed, face flushed.

"Here are the maps," Jeff said. "Umm. Your riggings still loose, Bree. Spinnakers won't set, eh." He grinned.

Cris smiled, savouring my annoyance.

Payback due. Angry, I avoided eye contact, poked the fire, aware my skin hummed with heat.

Malcolm leered, flicking his tongue.

Fish woke, dazed. I settled her in with Zoë.

Malcolm clutched a thick role of nautical charts. "These are crap. What's the use if we ain't got a boat?"

Jeff presented a black carry case, an aged pocket computer and other salvaged bits. He motioned to us, revealed a black pistol.

"It's a Glock-B, long barrel, like the police use." Jeff said. Forty cal. "Fifteen shot clip. And there's two boxes of ammo," he said, sliding the chamber open. "Belonged to a guy - Jess Walters. Found it under the stern locker."

"It's scary looking," I said, fingering the engraved initials on the stock.

Malcolm stuck his nose in. "My uncle Damon had one of those. Nicked it. It'll blow a hole in a cat. Leave the ears and tail."

"That rhymes with rat. So, what happened to dear Uncle Damon?" I sniggered.

"Oh. Uh. He sort of disappeared."

"That figures. Maybe he was on the receiving end?"

Jeff lifted the pistol, considered its weight. "At least we've got a real weapon and a hundred rounds."

Cris produced a piece of bronze pipe salvaged from Elysius. He held up a half dozen lethal looking darts. He'd carved the tiny shafts from hardwood, and tipped each one using metal cut from old coat hangers. Sanded and polished, the shafts fit precisely, sliding down the tube.

"With poison on the tips, this'll do more than brown their pants."

"Didn't know you were a jungle romantic," I teased. "Got enough hot air?"

"Poison?" Malcolm scoffed. Ye packed a little chemistry set?"

"The islanders. Mareva. She'd know how to find poison, maybe from a blue ring octopus. A stone fish?" I said.

"At least a blow gun's quiet. So's a crossbow," Cris said, patting the original model.

I realised he was far more resourceful than I'd imagined, his visions set on our worst danger.

"We've got new company," I said, drawing a deep breath. "Cris spotted boat people." I refrained from saying when the craft arrived.

Jeff looked unruffled by this news. "Didn't see them. Guess it's just a matter of time before more reach here. The worse the plague gets, the farther they'll go. I expected more."

We rehashed the plague danger, refugees and how to spit the pig until well beyond midnight.

The new arrivals forced us onto a defensive war footing. I remembered the vintage Dad's Army shows, and the enemy, who never quite showed up. The war was usually between personalities. In a nutshell, that was the situation for the lot of us.

One fact remained obvious. We needed to avoid contact. Be watchful. Despite all our petty differences, nobody disagreed.

The girls slept. Millie snored. I sensed the need to stick closer to her.

"We'd better watch the newies from the bluff. We'll do it in shifts starting from mid day," Jeff said.

All, except Cris, grabbed a few hours sleep.

He made a huge mess cleaning the boar, insisting on throwing more guts into the fire. We copped the stench, too tired to protest. He succeeded in rudely ramming a pole through its body length-wise, lashed its legs together, and set it on timber struts at each end. The beast hung over the fire, hissing and spitting on fire fed fat. By morning waves of irresistible smell filled the campsite, disrupting dreams, overpowered sleep.

Dawn broke cloudless as rays laced the top of our vale. Parrots, cuckoos and plovers revelled in the freshness, each shrilled as if competing, yet together, hundreds melded in harmony. It was the best time of day. Cool. Sweet.

Jeff was on a high. With a plate of charred meat, he turned to the radio gear lying mute in the shelter. I remembered his fits of anger on the boat when the rig cut out. It was the only way we could tune into the world. I'm sure he figured the rig was feminine with a mind of its own.

I sat back half asleep as Jeff chewed. He absently whistled Three Blind Mice, a few bars at a time, between mouthfuls. Most of the notes were out of tune, yet warming, comical and reassuring. He settled in by the fire, easing the components out of their casing, feeling gingerly for a weak connection amongst the maze of old circuitry.

Great White Hunter came bearing a slab of charcoaled meat. "*Cordon bleu* for you."

"You've rings under your eyes. Been up all night?" I said.

"Shootin' rats." He pointed to three large, mangled specimens strung up by their tails well away from camp. Cris revelled in picking them off with crossbow bolts.

He embarrassed us by eating with care, meticulously sliced portions and chewed, not making a mess. I watched as I licked juices running down my fingers. Cris gave me a disparaging look, as if to say, "I wouldn't take you anywhere looking like that."

I bagged Rat as partner for first watch on the northern lagoon, feared encouraging Cris's flammable passions or my own.

I insisted Malcolm lead. Didn't fancy enduring his lechery. The climb proved painful. Tendons ached. My pelvis hurt, especially with long, jolting strides.

We picked the mid peak of the island chain, which gave a parrot's view of *S-331*, lying about three kilometres to the west. The boat people, who were half that distance, anchored our side of the promontory where Cris committed his master stupidity.

Binoculars, fifteen powered with zoom, offered a detailed view of the newcomers.

The boat was lean, rakishly built, and sharp at the bow. The rest consisting of a high, ramshackle coach house running almost to the stern. Weathered timber, patchy blue sides and cream topsides made the craft plain, except for colourful washing, which festooned lines forward. Brilliant batik prints gave her a madcap carnival air. A woman appeared stripped to the waist. Some were ashore along the beach.

No name or number marked the newcomer's hull.

"That's what they call a 'dhow'." I said.

"Never mind the duh-how," Rat said. "There's plenty happening on that Asian bucket."

I handed him the binoculars. "How many, umm, rats can you see?"

"Maybe six or seven. Ye know, I don't mind bein' called Rat. Rats survive. They're cool buggers."

I refrained from answering. He was right, judging from the night eyes around our camp, his own track record.

"I figure these Asian dudes are up to somethin'. Like you said, they've got guns. I see a bazooka, or rocket launcher on deck," Malcolm said.

"That figures. One of them sported a big thing when they chased us."

He grunted. Nudged, chuckled, "didn't get to use it on you?"

I gave him a foul look.

We placed scrub bushes in front of us for camouflage. Noon heat made me drowsy, tired of watching. My strength sapped away.

"We're in time for some fireworks, just like the movies," Mal said, with relish.

Despite his protest I prised the glasses off him and scanned quickly. The ships launch held three men. Another three were on the pilothouse deck, toying with an object I couldn't see clearly. The big guy, the one built in a sausage extruder, wasn't there. Ming's red bandana and rotund belly stood out in the launch, which was motoring towards the point.

"He's as keen as ever," I whispered.

"What's that supposed to mean?"

"The bald guy on the launch. He's the one who chased us. Me."

Judging from gestures, there was strong vocal exchange in progress between Ming and a few men who gathered on the dhow's forward deck. This continued as Ming and the others jumped ashore, hauling the boat onto the sand.

The women, sensing their isolation, clustered in animated conversation, their body language semaphoring fear. Several children splashed about unconcerned.

As Ming strutted across the beach, a flash erupted from S-331, followed by a puff of smoke. The sound rolled up the slopes, impacting like thunder, filling my body, and jarring my nerves. My hackles rose. Secondary reports blasted from behind. Masses of birds seethed in a cacophony of squawks as they spiralled into the heavens, eddying in confusion.

A projectile struck the refugee's craft amidships, sending a jet of flame and smoke boiling in an arc, landward.

Bits of cabin and bodies spiralled end over end, splattering the lagoon. Screams rose from the stricken. It listed, already sinking stern first in the shallows.

Several figures staggered from the ruptured cabin. A male, alight, plunged. Another opened fire on S-331 then turned his fury on the launch. Two of the Asians ducked behind it and responded. Automatic fire crackled and crashed over the peaks.

Malcolm tore the binoculars away, snapping the aged leather strap around my neck.

"Tell me this isn't happening!" I shouted.

"That guys got guts. He's nailed one on the launch," Mal said. "They aren't finished yet. Your pal on the beach." Mal was ecstatic.

I watched, numb, as Ming opened fire on one of the women, who'd bolted into the water. She flew forward with the impact.

Ming turned on the remaining women, who were transfixed with shock. Their screams rose through the din, arms raised in submission. One by one Ming fired. One by one they slumped, falling back, like rag dolls.

Each report brought pitiful shrieks from the children. Two gathered by the first victim, trying to lift her face.

I saw two figures scurry along the beach. Both disappeared into scrub.

Ming paused to reload, and turned on the children.

I jumped up, screaming, "I want to kill you!" I shook my fists. Bit into my knuckles.

"Jeeze, yer a mad bitch. Ease up. You'll remind them we're here."

Malcolm's fingers dug into my neck, pulling me down. I clung to his arm, staring, unable to tear away from the carnage below.

The chaos climaxed as Ming and his pal pushed the launch out and began probing, cutting down survivors. Dark patches spread where the children floated close to one another. One of the women crawled towards the water, collapsed.

I slumped, drained of all resolve. "Why would anyone slaughter innocent people? Children." I pleaded, eyes streaming.

Malcolm wrapped his wiry arm around my shoulder. I wanted to vomit, could only dry retch.

"They're scared stupid of everyone else carryin' plague. Chicken shits." Mal sneered.

Ming and his sidekick boarded the dhow, which lay smoking, half submerged, the shock wave having snuffed flames. Both probed its ruins.

"The buggers are lootin'. Bet he gets a bit." Malcolm said.

"What? All they've wanted is hope. You'd join in if given the chance. Wouldn't you?" I glared.

"Cool it. I'm not a ghoul. I prefer clean dirt."

"Really," I scoffed.

"It's a scummy world, but this guy's got standards, Bree." Malcolm pointed to himself, as if I might miss his gem of truth.

"I'm judging you too much?" I said. Something snapped inside. Bile etched my throat. I choked.

"Yeh. Tell me about it."

I felt the suppleness of his hairless skin as his arm slipped around my waist.

I cringed. "I won't scream. Let go of me." Adrenalin pumped, my stomach knotted.

"You're goin' all twitchy. Calm down," Malcolm smiled. "Ye sure feel..."

"That's awful. How can you toy around with all this happening? You have a go at me because you think Cris got a bit. Well, he didn't."

"Danger's a turn-on."

"So you keep bragging."

His shorts, as thread bare as his beard, bulged.

"Ye know, it's the first time we've really touched," he said.

Before I could wrench free, he swung me onto my back, knocking the wind from me. I turned my head away and clenched my teeth. Swore to bite.

He fingered across my stomach tracing around my navel. His finger clawed at the stud of my shorts. I punched grazing his cheek and stiffened ready to knee hard.

"What's happening?" Zoë's voice pierced the tension.

"The others. They've got to know," I blurted, rolling away, prying his forefinger from my shorts. I sat up. Blood trickled down

190

my shoulder.

Fish arrived, gasping her asthma-like wheeze. "What ees that big noise? Fireworks?"

Jeff and Cris followed, taking in the carnage below.

"Get down," Malcolm said, making dramatic gestures.

The refugee's boat listed further, settling on the bottom, its bow breaking the water.

Zoë wedged in, stomping on Malcolm's gammy foot. Our eyes locked.

"Look to Fish. She'll go crazy. I'm okay." We moved on Fish, sweeping her before us.

"Let's get out of here. Millie's alone," I said.

As we picked our way towards camp, I heard the boys in excited conversation, Malcolm's voice bragging his version of the events.

In camp, Millie sensed my anger.

"Don't ask," I said, slumping by the fire. I slashed a chunk of meat and chewed. "The boys are doing boy things. I don't give a pig's fart about the human race."

Chapter 26

For days we vented anger. The nature of the Ship's crew made our previous ideas about defence ridiculous. Nobody could face rockets.

Cris and Jeff re-speculated the killers must be a *triad* gang involved in racketeering weapons and drugs.

I realised why the islanders had no stomach for facing this lot. The pro-action faction was toothless, too few to put up any resistance. Their Christian opposites were equally paralysed, and there were more than twenty children to protect, some obviously orphaned.

Jeff earlier proposed we wait it out until *S-331* pushed on elsewhere. I felt less optimistic, arguing they'd been anchored there at least three months.

I felt particularly bitchy, sniping at Malcolm and cold-shouldering Cris's hunger for attention.

Jeff read the war clouds well enough. He kept to the radio problem, toiling for hours, explaining to Millie how it worked. She pitched in passing any tools he wanted, and items sometimes not wanted. She displayed a remarkable nimbleness in handling the solder gun in tiny spaces. Displayed a keenness for detail.

Millie grew clever in talking with Jeff. She tried asking about important things, and left him room for thinking, rather than chattering over trivia. His usually irritable reactions to her gave way to odd bits of personal conversation and the occasional furtive smile.

My fixation was on tidying up the camp. Cris tried coming to my assistance, but I refused help. He was most annoyed when I re-lashed the ladder used to climb to our nest, his ego rebuffed. Each lashing cinched tight was a substitute for Malcolm's neck.

I craved to escape, find total isolation.

Zoë, sensing my wrath, longed to worm her way into my thoughts. Cunning made her wait.

King Rat shadowed about darker than usual. I knew he studied me. Unrequited lust must do strange things to a guy who equated sex with violence and conquest.

There's nothing wrong with lust as long as both involved happily burn together. Thinking this out was easy enough, after all, sex was supposed to be 'no holds barred', as my mum quaintly put it. But, the idea of emotions rampaging with the wrong guy made my nerves stand on end. Love was a minefield. Commitment fragile. Still, I hungered for experience, feared letting go. A 'shrink' would have a field day picking me apart.

Rat rattled the depths of my feelings, showing not the slightest care while helpless people died. It mortified me that I'd made such a horrific mistake bending, accepting him in the group.

I reminded myself over and over through the nights. Dreams, the usual dead end variety, fractured in endless scenarios of argument and none meant a damn thing.

By firelight I tried to mend torn patches, and a gaping rip in the seat suffered during my fall. I gave it away.

The girls joined me for a cautious day on the beach. A slab of coral nearer the village offered the only barrier to prying eyes from anyone rounding the western point. We could hear well enough over booming surf. The villagers were conspicuous by their absence. I figured it must be Sunday worship, or they knew what happened. Hid.

Zoë and Fish set up a fish blind woven of stripped bark from a hibiscus tree. They'd taken several days to weave it, making a simple funnel some five meters long consisting of a double fence; very broad at one end and narrowing to a dead end near the beach at the other. Sharpened poles were driven into the bottom and acted as support for their trap. With gutted shellfish thrown in close to shore as bait, they circled the outer end of the trap hoping their prey would enter the funnel. Small fish escaped, but lowering a mesh gate trapped anything desirable.

They spent hours coaxing shoals of bream toward the trap, all to no avail. They did disturb another poisonous stonefish, which was speared, quite the most ugly, menacing creature I'd ever seen.

I studied them the whole morning, waving sympathy when told of a near miss and clapped at each fish they speared. I felt detached, light-headed.

All of my scrapes healed quickly in salt water, bar one, thanks to Rat.

Zoë sidled closer, out of earshot of Millie and Fish, who wandered collecting shells.

"What's with Cris yesterday? He called Millie a lazy slag," Zoë said.

"Not now," I groaned. "How can anyone figure him?"

She nodded. "He's sort of cool, Bree. Love his eyes."

"You can't live with eyes and brawn. He's an emotional minefield."

Zoë cackled, "He's got an interesting body. Muscles." She flexed.

"No. Don't start. He's all smoke and no fire." I lied realising Zoë missed the performance.

"Well, maybe it's because you're a wet blanket. You spook him," Zoë prodded.

"I'm holding him to the bet. He isn't game enough. I want twenty-five palm nuts from the top. You, Zoë dear, are my witness."

"Uh," Zoë's face twisted, "he tried recruiting me to climb for him."

"Since when?"

"The day before the refugees got wiped. You should've seen him try, like a great hairless sloth. Hanging there." She spidered up a nearby palm, dangled from the underside, her backside swaying. "He fell off." She dropped, wiry legs kicking into a backward somersault. "Ask how his tailbone is."

"I'm stunned. Why didn't you tell me?"

"He tried 'mojoing' you with the pig. I figured you'd scorn him out. What's the deal with Rat? I recon he jumped you." Zoë's eyes narrowed.

I held my temper. "He caught me by surprise. I was a blubbering mess. Bugger pushed me down."

Zoë nodded solemnly. Her eyes lit up. "Why don't you pounce on Cris before I do? He's hot."

"You little beast. You're too young to think of that."

"Wanna make a bet? Why not give him a go?"

"Brat." I swiped at her. She ran, knifing into the lagoon.

Puberty hormones ran rampant in a hothouse. Zoë was stretching fast. She'd proudly confided me of her first period. We'd missed her thirteenth birthday a week ago, November fifth, much to her Scorpio annoyance, but then, I'd forgotten about my seventeenth during the last great storm, October twelfth.

I marvelled at her resilience. She'd managed to isolate her emotions from the killings. By the time she arrived it looked like a distant movie set, but I knew she saw the bodies. Maybe Arie's death and the corpse in the lagoon jaded her feelings.

❉

I raised the issue of the ship's mob once again, much to everyone's annoyance. "What if they can't leave, and set up living on shore? There's plenty of material to make huts."

"If they do, expect them to explore the island. Native drums won't scare them for long, eh." Jeff stroked the fuzz on his chin.

"If they start snooping, we'll drive them off," Cris said.

"And kick up a hornet's nest," I said. "They're trigger-happy."

"Gotta spot the bastards early," Cris said. "Maybe some booby traps."

Groans all round.

"And every feral creature prowling at night? We'll all need to change our underwear," Jeff said.

"Those who wear any," I said, thinking *déjà vu*.

Zoë giggled.

"If any dudes come, we kill 'em," Malcolm drawled.

"Oh. Just like that," I said.

"We've got two crossbows," Cris said. "They're silent. At fifty meters, I can't miss. A bolt from Maggot Maker - they'd never hear it coming."

"Pity it can't detour for two," Jeff said.

"It's easy to reload. Seven seconds," Cris said. He cranked the lever, pulling the heavy nylon string back into a slot linked to the trigger mechanism. It caught precariously. Placing a stubby arrow in the track, he swung around. Malcolm ducked. Cris fired at a tree several meters away, smashed through the trunk in a shower of splinters.

"If that was a guy," Zoë said, wide eyed.

"Was, is the word," Cris said. "Ninety kilos of punch at a hundred meters a second. More wham, mam, than a magnum."

"The glock pistol?" I said.

"Only as a last resort," Jeff said. We gazed at its menacing lines.

"Remember? It's not so accurate beyond forty or fifty meters." Malcolm said. "You'll be shootin' down, through leaves and branches n' crap. At moving targets? They won't be marked for our convenience."

"Let's hope. Best to avoid them," I said, hostile to Rat's feral intelligence. "We keep a watch up top."

❋

After much frustration and fiddling, Jeff switched the radio on. Nothing. "Damned if I know what's wrong with the bloody thing."

"You've got a way with mechanical things. First the engine, now this," I said.

Jeff swore. He belted the casing. It came to life, squawking in protest, rife with interference.

Millie squealed with delight, "you're so clever." She beamed.

Jeff scanned the bands slowly. Stations came and drifted away, most very weak. "It'll get better after sunset."

We sat, rapt as he toyed into the evening. He picked up Radio Moscow, which boomed with its English broadcast in full swing. Their newscast focused on new peace proposals with Chechnya rebels, and a civil protest in Georgia and Kosovo over oil, before summing up news of the capital. The announcer was blunt and measured.

Figures for the capital suggested Russia was in serious trouble with a massive crime wave in drugs and white slavery. Young blondes disappearing made me twitch.

Plague figures were "low." No more than a quarter million in the city to date. "Medical authorities are confident of controlling its spread. Russian people stand together in this great crisis of the Motherland." He said.

The rest of his comments dwelt on the weather as unusually cold for November at thirty-five below, Celsius. The national anthem blared.

I knew little news out of Russia was ever bright.

Radio Tahiti came up in excited French. I picked out scraps, but couldn't piece it together. My French terminated in year eight. Ms Planchette drove me batty with her drill routines. No free spirit room.

Tone of voice in newscasts told us humanity was in trouble in the Pacific, but an island group managed to belt out a lively tune. Ukuleles strummed, and vocal harmonies rose in eternal celebration, defying the downward spiral of people everywhere.

Asia was seething with news, most of it in regional languages, none of it sounding positive.

Radio KBAY, San Francisco, caught our attention, giving our first detailed picture of that part of the world. A battery of commentators shared the airway, like it was an election madhouse. At least eight of them expressed the virtues of speaking through surgical masks.

The ad breaks avidly promoted 'Braithwaite's super gauze masks'. Jerry, an in-to-it announcer, emphasised the "denser, thicker protective layers, for your security. Only thirty-nine, ninety-five at your local drugstore, in arctic pine, each antiseptic, oh, and in six other exciting odours."

"Wonder if they mail order," Cris said.

Jerry returned to Congressman Wilks. "Now, Congressman Wilkes, the rioting in Los Angeles is unabated, as of this morning. Is there any hope of National Guard units penetrating the Watts Precinct, and surrounding areas?"

"No. We've withdrawn surviving units to protect key business areas, communications and strategic food supplies," Wilks drawled, "Governor Crebb has extended Martial Law restrictions from four pm til ten am."

"Then rebel forces—err - bands have much of the city," Jerry said.

A General Fox interjected. "They'll be starved out, those the plague doesn't kill. Anyone, *anything*, trying to move out of the cordoned region is shot on sight."

I imagined him chewing on a cigar.

A California State Health official, Dwight Salanger, introduced plague figures from across the nation. "Some areas appear less affected than others, but these figures are unprecedented in human history. New York has topped a million and a half known deaths." He went on and on with talleys, state by state. Not all were listed.

"That's pushin' thirty million. Jeff said. "Just the known cases and deaths. Shivers."

"Somethin' sure pulled the plug on us," Malcolm said.

News from elsewhere wasn't covered until late, almost as an afterthought.

A female health authority advised families to bury their own dead in the back yard or at neighbourhood burial sites, emphasising the need to use the heavy body bags issued in each area.

Jerry announced the importance of body pick-up. "We are all responsible for isolating the deceased and the dignity of their passing. God be with us." He updated the deaths of prominent staff and family members.

"Dignity. That's a nice, safe word," I said.

"Yeah. A sanitised funeral with flowers," Jeff said.

An official, Johannes Spits, a *United Nations* spokesman, came on briefly, claiming there were virtually no victims recorded from desert areas.

"Well, hell. There's nobody there," Jeff snorted. "Imagine a stampede to Death Valley."

"The Gibson Desert," Zoë said.

"Dad worked with that guy," I said. "He's a quarantine expert—so called."

A spot ad came up for Super C vitamin pills.

Over the following days we learned there was no breakthrough in any laboratories struggling with the *Jetoba Virus*, named after the Amazon tributary area of suspected origin.

This pathogen proved elusive, suspected to have mutated, possibly a relative of the *Sabia Virus* outbreak in Brazil during 1994. The *Sabia* type had been haemorrhagic with wild fever, rashes and internal bleeding, much like the dreaded *Ebola Virus*, which regularly ravaged in Central-West Africa. "*El Punio*," more commonly *The Devil's Claw*, now terrorised the world, an emerging super pathogen.

Japan declared its surviving researchers as 'National Treasures'. They worked in isolation, linking to other institutes through a network of computers.

The following day, we picked up an A.B.C. broadcast after Jeff extended the stainless steel rigging cable with a spool of wire for an aerial. Malcolm held the cable end on his tree perch, making reception much better.

"Don't move, Mal. Hang on right there," Jeff said.

"You've found a vocation," I said. "A bit to the right, Rat, dear. Stick your leg out north. Arm south."

"Which leg?" Zoë giggled.

"Oh, for a lightning strike," Cris said. "Orgasmic."

"Aw, shut up guys. This is the pits."

"And the rest of the world is just that, deep in it," I murmured, fingering the charm.

Chapter 27

"Rat really got under your skin," Zoë said, munching ground coconut and fish on toasted breadfruit.

"It's much more. Feel like I'm losing it," I sighed. "Living in paradise isn't all it's supposed to be."

"It's the best. I could live here forever," Zoë said.

Fish nodded. "Me too. I have 'familee'. You are like a mamma, but not fat like my real mamma."

We laughed. Hugged. I blew both a raspberry. Fish gave affection freely, but we dreaded her hidden traumas.

"You've become a pair of hedonists."

"What is that?" Fish said.

"Lazy. Fun loving. A pair of lushes," I said.

"What ees lush?"

"Flashy."

"Oh. What ees flashy?"

"Seriously Zoë, what about mum and dad?"

"I'll visit. They can come visit, too," Zoë laughed. "Sometimes I'm really homesick. Miss my showers with you. Lavender bath soap. My bed." She rolled her eyes. "I do worry about mum, but I know she's alive. I just know. Dad's smart enough to keep out of trouble. Maybe when this is all over he'll come home and be with us more. He's always away." She paused. "If we have a home."

I studied both, so well on the way to adapting, much like the native children. Since the beginning of the year Zoë bloomed, a wonder of fine muscle, coltish, acrobatic lines. Tomboy sensual.

"Jeff says stay off the western beaches," Zoë said. "He expects trouble, says they'll come for food."

"I'll go see Mareva. Maybe poke around the eastern end. We've never been there before. It's safe enough," I said.

Rather than travel directly to the beach, I re-traced our route to the first staging camp, and stopped at the shallow dam first used to bathe. It was the coolest, most comfortable space to wallow in, one that must've been used long ago by a tribe. Soft ferns, maidenhair and delicate flowers, gave it a feminine aura.

The pathway skirting it bore a young porker's hoof prints and worm squiggles, but no human had stepped here since the last rain. Unable to relax I moved on.

❈

Stiff gusts from the southeast lashed the reef, ruffling the lagoon into tiny whitecaps. Fishing was lousy, offering up two tiny bream. I arrived at the village outskirts by using the trail. Fingering the seashell wedged in my right ear, I remembered Malcolm hobbling in retreat. Pity he wasn't shot.

A few islanders were far out along the eastern rim of the lagoon, their spears regularly plunging. A pair dove amongst coral ridges further west.

The yellows, oranges and reds of their clothing contrasted the dense patches of greenery fringed with white-laced edges. From our mountain observation each lillypad islet stood out against cobalt depths beyond. Several of these lay in a patchwork chain surrounding Sky Island.

After the salutary nose rub, we sat under Mareva's sagging lean-to she watched her world from.

"The chiefs aren't here?" I said.

"They hold war council about Kalani. Much talk. Do little." She pinched her fingers together. "They are equal, so each blocks the other out."

"You know about the boat people?"

She nodded. "Chief Hiva watched from Little Ma'yo Mountain, what we call Little Shark Tooth. The Gods have put a curse on those devils. The chief saw you and Rat Man." She said, slowly.

I felt my face burn with embarrassment.

She laughed, dismissively. "Soon, evil men leave or die. *Tupapa'u* make black magic we call *Moki*. Let them be dragged across the altar of *Moki*, disembowelled, thrown into waters of death."

I could see little that would bring such a gory prediction about, black or white witchcraft.

We talked some about the villager's problems with supplies and the withdrawal of assistance from Tahiti.

Mareva seemed resigned. "The French, they will come back some time. They are too busy now to bother with us. We could

200

have left by boat, but didn't," she grinned. "You take Fau and Alili back to see Jeff? They talk about him," she said.

"They need to go by the mountain trails. Cris booby trapped the valley."

Mareva shrieked with laughter. I smiled, confused. Couldn't see the joke.

"Why are they so keen on him?"

"Oh, yes. They see him under waterfall."

"I'm sure he'll be thrilled." I raised an eyebrow. I laughed. Jeff was right about being watched.

※

I borrowed a small shell of an outrigger canoe. With each stroke it darted across the lagoon. Fish flashed by. A great disk shaped shadow skimmed the bottom, crossing my path, heading east. I trailed its massive bulk, marvelling at its grace. Passing inside the fishermen, I waved, hoping they wouldn't see the giant turtle. Cooking one for soup went against everything I loved, and turtles were a favourite. On the eastern edge at a reef gap it slipped out into deep water.

I paddled slowly, studying the rising ridges, one behind the other, peaking with the jagged tooth Mareva called Mount *Riva Ma'yo*, Big Shark Tooth.

It was easy to conjure a slumbering monster with its scaly plates tapering off either side, its tail curled, lying in the deeps far to the west. Ribs, some scar patches like bloodied bones, radiated down its verdant flanks. Smoking nostrils brooding.

"You're a shambles of a beast. Nothing but a puff of smoke," I said, softly. I wondered if Motu-Riva's daughter, 'The Sleeper', would wake one day, and the whole island erupt with it.

Three tiny islet peaks reared immediately ahead, side by side. Landing on an apron of black sand beach, I climbed the highest cone. The wind whipped my hair loose in tangled strands. My skin drew taut, rashed in Goosebumps.

Mareva had called these rounded islets, *Toru Vahines*, The Three Sisters. "They are big, like pregnant woman's breasts," she cackled, revelling in her earthiness.

I wondered why three.

Her story went that there was a race between the women and men to see who would be first to catch a great sea turtle. The males lost, having stopped to take a nap. From that day the islands were seen as female. It was much like the hare and the tortoise story.

Motu-Riva shone beautifully for the islanders, though it could turn savage. They saw things in nature, moved with its dictates. Life rich in so many ways city people couldn't comprehend. Small happenings. Simple delights. Apart from the menace of Ming and his ilk, here were also many dangers we hadn't been there long enough to be fully acquainted with. Strange fevers. Poisonous creatures. I studied the fume-shrouded slopes of 'The Sleeper' to the immediate north.

Despite its wonders, not all the pieces in my life fit here. There would come a time to leave. Surely the plague would die out soon.

I saw Mareva and the girls, heading for camp by the mountain route. Jeff would just have to hang in there, dig up his reserves of charm.

I beached the canoe on the largest outer islet to the south opposite where we'd first landed, only a few kilometres away. From there the island's razor ridges braced proud, its valley greenery sensual. Latrec rich in hues, Sky Island beckoned dark, ever embracing.

Most of the islet Mareva called Motu-Tapa was flat, littered with shredded material from pandanus leaves, banana groves and shattered husks from palms. A hut's skeleton lay in a heap.

The beach rim dazzled white from crushed coral shattered to trillions of grains. A large bank of it spread well into the lagoon. Thundering waves reminded me of destruction and the way life defied it here. The palms were much bigger than those on the main island.

Creatures scurried about in the undergrowth. "Rats. As big as alley cats," I said. Granddad used to rasp out a song with those words, something about a 'quarter master store'. One advanced, standing up, checking out my presence.

❋

A squabble of gulls plunging on fish woke me. The tide slapped my feet. The sun lay far down, not more than a few hours to sunset.

I skimmed towards the island, driven by a bracing wind, as much as by paddling. The wind scoured, and sun glare made it impossible to see without squinting.

Passing Elysius sobered my mood. Her hull lay further down. Now it was nothing more than a memory time capsule of our struggles at sea. Dead.

After running the boat up under cover, I sat under the three palms grove. I listened and watched, now our constant custom. A millipede probed, hesitated, then crawled across my thigh on millipede business, and was gone. Nothing else moved except the tufts of grasses, and swaying, hissing palms.

❋

In the darkest shadows of the trail, I almost walked straight into him. His bulk filled the path. Startled, he took a step backward, releasing a net full of fruit from his back.

"What you do here?" He said.

I stared, struck dumb. It was scar face, the one with bandy legs.

He lunged forward, swearing, as a strand of mesh snagged on his sheathed knife, throwing his momentum sideways.

I dropped and dodged to my right into a family of tree ferns. I slid, fell on one knee and sprawled. His breathing closed.

"Wu have you now, bitch."

His hand raked my ankle. Slipped. I glimpsed his face, eyes bulging with effort. I jabbed his nose with my heel. He snarled. Swore.

Regaining the path, I ran. Adrenalin pumping, my stomach and bowels turned queasy. My head spun, as if detached from my body.

Exhilaration. Legs wobbling, I made for thick growth on my left beyond a narrow defile where the path steepened abruptly.

Something whizzed by from above on my immediate right, crashing into bushes.

I glanced. My head exploded, darkening in a confusion of sparks, falling away.

Chapter 28

Nightmare. Real and nauseous. Metal rattled against my ribs. Hanging upside down, the right side of my head throbbed. I strained to move my hands. They were bound behind my back.

I'd been dumped over a seat. My mouth pressed against the metal ribbing of the hull. Through blurred vision, I saw a massive foot wedged into a rubber thong, black toenails curled and broken.

Seawater sloshed pink as the craft howled a metallic staccato across the water, jarring my cheek.

I tried squirming to lift my head; received a sharp kick.

"Wu got little bitch. I teach you big lesson." A hand grabbed my hair, wrenching my face upward.

Leering over me was a guy of gigantic proportions. He grinned lopsided from a pitted face.

Greasy coveralls draped his massive girth, and equally huge chest hanging, bags of waxen lard. He squinted, eyes narrowing above grizzled jowls, as if debating whether to squash me or not.

"You're hurting me," I said, choking. I tried to show anger, but knew it was useless.

His breath stank of stale tobacco, the most repulsive stench.

"Who are you?" I said.

He stared, unconcerned. His fist knotted tight. My scalp screamed.

"Where are you taking me?" My lips cracked, mouth tasting of bilge.

"Why are you doing this to me?" I said, tears welling up. Again my anger fell flat.

"You make good galley girl on ship," he said, his words thick, and heavy.

Behind, Wu's hands dug hard into my waist.

"No," Chun said, "she Chun's girl now. You got island woman."

Wu said something sharp in dialect. It sounded like Cantonese, similar inflections, the way Martha Wong, a school pal, spoke to her mates. He was angry, but fell silent under Chun's implacable gaze.

Chun let my hair go. He wasn't much on conversation. It was obvious I'd become a possession. The full implications of this grew, and with it, panic. Desperation said escape, in the most immediate sense. Something inside made me hold off thinking crazy things. I mustn't go to pieces.

Wearing island fare made me cringe, feel vulnerable.

The launch swung left. I took a mouthful of salt water. Spat. We scraped and battered against the ship's hull. My head ached to the core. Chun bellowed orders. Shouts. Ropes were lowered and attached. Wu threw me over his shoulder like a limp doll, and began climbing a rope ladder. He swung over the railing, dumped me on a clump of netting.

Chun remained seated as the launch rose on davits into its cradle amid ship. He reminded me of a huge Buddha, or the corpulent Craver from the film Zero Gravity. Craver was a cannibal.

Wu stood over me. He wore the same blue pokadot headband I saw the day they chased us. His hair swept back, knotted in a ponytail. He hocked and spat.

"Thanks heaps. Ratbag." I said, staring tight mouthed. Nothing else came to mind, and speaking made my headache worse.

I peered towards the island, glowing in the last evening light. There was no chance of escape with my arms trussed up behind. If my hands were free and I swam they'd catch me, or shoot me before I reached the peninsula. It was so near, so remote.

S-331 was close to deep water at the northern entrance of the island and protected on the north side by a hooked ridge of coral. Rubbish this mob threw overboard during their stay would regularly attracted sharks by now. I didn't fancy being ripped to pieces and fought over. I remembered the big one that followed us for days.

I knew Jeff and the others wouldn't look for me yet. They'd likely realise trouble, start hunting the following morning.

My prospects began to seriously impact. Panic made my stomach knot. I had only my self to blame. There was little sense in weeping and protesting. I'd got myself into this stupid situation and would have to find a way out.

I scowled at Chun, twisting, presenting my hands. "These hurt. Cut me loose."

He remained indifferent.

Wu and the crew gathered around me in the dusky light, making snide remarks in dialect. Laughing. Ming, balding and pot-bellied, squeezed my shoulder. I cringed, drawing my knees up for cover. He reeked of stale sweat.

Chun's gravel voice sent them to unload the fruit and one trussed up pig, still alive, squealing in terror. I couldn't fail to see our mutual dilemma.

"You wash. Cook." Chun waved a blade in front of my nose.

"What makes you think I'll do that?"

His voice dropped, his speech a gravelled singsong, "bitchy bitch have no choice. Be good girl. You no good, I sell you to Wu. Maybe Hak. He like beat his women." Chun gestured to a wire-muscled guy sporting a mangy goatee. He was a crossbreed, part Asian, and part southern European, having a darker skin than the others, European features. His back crawled with dragon tattoos.

"Over my dead -" I bit my lip, mouth trembling. "You miserable bastard. Put me on shore. I've never done anything to you."

Chun snorted, "Blondie please Chun. First, you make food. Cook. Later I tell what you do."

Any fight I'd tried to display evaporated. His demands sickened me, but there was no point in angering him. My life at that moment wasn't worth much. They would get as much pleasure out of killing me as they did the boat people. The odds of having to endure the unthinkable threatened to melt me down. It was impossible to withdraw emotionally. I measured my breathing to keep control. I must do something positive.

"I'll cook and clean for you. Please cut these ropes," I blubbered, tears welling. "Honestly. I'll do what you say. Can I have a shirt to wear?"

"You work hard. Maybe you live."

I nodded, dropping my eyes submissively. Sobbed.

He cut the ropes.

Men hated to see a female cry, even rejects like these.

He pointed to the metal stairs leading to a second level behind the raised wheelhouse and motioned I should carry the fruit and screeching pig. Chun followed, wheezing.

❋

The galley laid two doors aft of the wheelhouse. Through filtered light from a single globe, the wreckage of a once organised kitchen emerged. A pair of deep sinks lined the left wall. A long work counter dominated the middle. Everything lay impossibly cluttered with dishes and filthy pots.

Cockroaches scurried across an equally putrid floor. One raced in my direction, stopped, waved its feelers. Monstrous. Twice the size of any I'd seen.

To the right I saw two storage rooms, their doors open. A sack of flour lay burst amongst a clutter of tins, boxes and refuse. Everything wore a sour stench.

"My god. Those bloody things are on steroids." I turned. "How can I clean this mess?"

"You fix."

"Fix? With what?" I stood next to the pig, which was grunting its despair. I stroked its head, which made it squeal in a frenzy, thrashed its bound legs.

Chun waddled around the galley, collecting large knives and a huge meat cleaver. He stood eye level with me, his mouth twisting into a grin. With a savage stroke, Chun stabbed the pig through the neck. It shrilled, legs flailing in spasms as blood shot out. I doubled over, heaving what little my stomach held, and sank to the floor, clutching my throat as if he'd slashed me open. Splotches of blood streamed down my stomach.

I screamed. Grabbed a pot. Threw it as he left. Cockroaches scurried everywhere before continuing grazing.

Hak arrived. I put the workbench between us. He dumped old dishtowels on the counter.

"Thanks heaps."

"No. Hak my name."

"Creep."

"What that mean?"

"If you want to eat get out of the kitchen." I clutched a dish-towel for cover.

Hak sniggered, "I win bitch at poker. Hak like blondie." He laughed, hocked heavily, spat.

"I'd rather die."

"Oh, Hak help you. Make dying fun. Special." He dodged around the counter.

I jumped to keep opposite, grabbing a small iron fry pan. He left shrieking pleasure. Sometimes learning to shut up came hard. My wits needed sharpening, not my tongue.

Escape was possible only if I knew the layout of the ship, which was a clutter of gear and packing crates on deck.

My arms worked leaden, mechanically shoving at the mass of filth. A pot containing gruel, nondescript meat, crawled with maggots.

Bucketing galley scum down to the railing where we'd boarded gave me a chance to look around. The weed sporting a blue bandana sat smoking on the hatch. I saw he was stoned. An automatic weapon lay on his lap, his finger caressing the trigger. They obviously kept a watch during the day and probably at night.

I laboured at emptying the contents while straining to see, but it was too dark, the shoreline indistinct.

Hunting for food, especially protein, became an obsession. I ransacked the cupboards and examined the back rooms. There was an assortment of tinned goods, most of which didn't fit in with Asian cooking. A can of beans and tiny sausages called 'little boys', tasted better than I remembered roast chicken. I licked and scraped out sauce until my tongue ached.

Remnants of a medical chest lay open. With a rusty needle and thread, I stitched two dishtowels into a crude boob tube, the sides remaining open. It barely fit, but tailoring rank dishtowels was a hopeless cause. Both were frayed and well aired with holes.

It's crazy. I'd look perfect strutting around Kings Cross in Sydney, or at a party. The daggiest cutaways were the *in* thing, the saucier the holes, the better.

I dabbed some iodine on the lump raised on my forehead. A red welt had spread from my right shoulder, down my chest, already darkening. Strands of coconut fibres came away as I gingerly tidied my hair.

I swore to seek revenge as I stood in front of a cracked mirror, but fury was as wasted as my miserable image.

Slumped on the counter, the pig stared back as if surprised by my presence.

Chun's hulk filled the door. "What you cook. Crew hungry. Cook now or I beat you." He raised a tattooed arm.

"Can't cook in this filth. I'll cook when I've cleaned. Understand?" I began slicing chunks of flesh from the pig's hindquarter using a bread knife. "Sorry porky. Better you than me."

A closer rummage through the back storage rooms uncovered an odd mix of supplies, none of which would combine to make any meal I'd ever prepared.

"Beggars can't be choosers," I whispered.

This band had left in a hurry. Several tins of dog food indicated someone once owned a pooch.

"Bet they ate the poor thing," I said.

There were several sacks of rice. Some of the tinned stuff had lost labels, having suffered water damage. A line of jars held sinister looking goods, from dull greens to angry reds. Curries. Maybe hot chilli mixes. One sniff set my sinuses off.

Some of the tins appeared flecked with rust. One appeared swollen on top. The thought of using poison played on my mind. Rummaged cupboards for chemicals. Even the mad notion of killing the lot of them struck me as wonderfully horrible. What if they suspected? If I failed? I'd surely have my throat slit, much worse if they played around.

Clearing the clutter proved impossible, so I heaved the worst cases into the left storeroom. I kept enough cutlery and plates, guessing there were no more than eight crew.

※

Ming stuck his nose in as pots resounded against broken dishes. I glared at him, hands on hips. He eyed the rice boiling and the crude strips of pork sizzling in a pan. He smiled. His rotund belly glistened like his bald patch. His eyes sparkled, could pass for kindly. Papa Ming? Children on his knee - children in the sea—dead.

"You get away from Ming once," He frowned. "I promise treat you good. Only beat you sometimes." Ming chuckled. "Chun mean man with girls. Now you are his toy - he kill last girl." Ming stepped closer, ran a finger under my chin, down my stomach, reeking of scented oil and dope.

I gripped the pan. Stepped back.

"He kill Wu Fu Sheng with bare hands. Wu play with his woman," Ming said, his voice soothing, eyes wide and earnest.

"Where's that leave you?" I said, rallying what little energy I possessed.

"Ming sharp gambler. Number one. Chun owes me much. I feel lucky. Win you soon."

I sighed. "Hak has the same bloody idea. I'm not for sale."

Ming's eyes narrowed. He scoffed.

Bullseye. I smiled.

209

An old clock registered eleven-thirty. I guessed it was more like three in the middle of the night. A potpourri of rice, pork strips, beans and artichoke hearts simmered in spices and a generous serving of hot chilli sauce, its power unknown. I was drunk with tiredness. I curled up against the bulkhead, too exhausted to care about cockroaches. Something Chun said in the launch about a woman drifted through my thoughts, but eluded me.

I woke to hammering somewhere in the ship's interior. Light splashed into the galley, blinding me. My ankles were chained and padlocked hard against the counter leg. Who'd dare do this? I stared at the linkages, and felt the venom inside swell, the need to risk at any price.

Chapter 29

The new arrival paused to scoop up dregs from the cooking pot. This character appeared neater than the rest. His pants were clean and pressed. His facial features hinted he was of Philippino descent with something else in the mix. Despite facial pitting, the guy was attractive. *Aura* designer glasses protruded from a shock of black hair, suggesting a hunger for fashion and wealth. A wonderfully intricate tattoo of a dragon in greens, blues and dark red, swarmed across his back. I couldn't help wondering where the tail went. Grinning, he unlocked my chains and departed without saying a word.

I spent early morning tidying and cleaning, found my friend porky crammed in the fridge. One eye stared balefully at me. Cutting meat from his flank still made my stomach turn, but I had to eat protein, gain strength.

Someone had been in the kitchen before me. Several bowls were stacked clean. The dishtowels were folded. Was Ming going all out to please me? That would be some kind of joke. No. None of this mob could change their stripes. There must be a female on board. Chun had said something to Wu in the launch.

"You've got other girl," I said, mocking his up and down way of speaking. That's what Chun rammed down Wu's throat. Which one was she?

Another round of clatter came from deep in the ship. A hammer struck rhythmically with force, punctuated by high-pitched voices.

By mid morning the galley was a pressure cooker of heat and pong. Scrubbing floors wasn't my forte', but this level of filth made it a must, besides, I needed time to think and keep Chun impressed. They might become careless as I busied cleaning and made trips to dump dirty water over the side. Gaining greater freedom of movement was a do or die situation.

Hauling two pails of scum, I struggled to the lower deck. Wu sat stupefied, his eyes heavy from heat and boredom. He sighted me, swept the machine rifle in an arc, aiming across my stomach. It was one of those stubby types with a large shell clip. He dropped it between his legs. I felt his watchfulness as he drew on a rollie.

I studied the shoreline. Poured slowly. Beyond the peninsula, the refugee's boat lay submerged, its shattered cabin and bow visible. Unless the islanders had buried the dead, the bodies must still be exposed, but then, sharks would have sensed the blood. Feasted.

A flurry of birds rose from below Little Shark peak. Maybe Jeff was already training glasses on the ship. He'd usually taken the morning shift watching.

They'd visit Mareva. Find the canoe. Footprints might tell them I'd met unwanted company. Jeff would be furious. He always figured me wilful. A "bleedin' loner."

I noticed the rope ladder still hung over the side.

"Why you throw water over side? Use sink. Use head. No need you come down here."

"Chun clogged the toilet up," I said, pointing to my bum.

Wu scowled, wheezed with laughter. Hacked a smoker's cough. He hocked, spat and lit another rollie. Nicotine tar lay thick on his index finger.

"Which girl is yours?" I said, trying to sound casual.

"Native girl. She not much good. She not work, not play. Bad in bed, Wu get rid of her."

Hak appeared to relieve Wu, whose face in an instant turned deadpan. I could sense mutual animosity, worried about what he meant by "get rid of her."

I retreated to the galley. At least Kalani was alive. That was fantastic news. It sounded like she was getting up Wu's nose.

I felt better for this revelation, but taking stock of old and new wounds was sobering enough. Bathing my goose egg in warm water stung like a bull ant's nip. The shoulder abrasion darkened; bruised blue-grey, tinged green. My pelvis must be cracked. Being knocked out in full flight surely aggravated it. All together, I'd surely win a place in a Rocky Horror pageant.

Master Chun shambled in mid-day. Ming lurked nearby.

"You not good cook. Do better."

"There's hardly anything worth using. No ingredients," I shouted, waving a tin of sauerkraut in his face, hoping he'd understand better.

Chun looked surprised, his mass lurching backward. His face

turned stone-like.

"Girl hungry. She need food."

"If you keep this up I'll need a dictionary," I said. "Girl? Who?"

"Ming take you to girl." He departed, ambling off awkwardly, rubbing between his legs in obvious distress.

I shuddered. Wu was a deviate. Hak was vile. Chun simply overwhelmed. Ming was something else with his sweet, sly smile. At least he talked more than the others. Maybe he'd give a little if I buttered him up, but power freaks always set too high a price for favours.

I used mango and banana and cooked more of poor porky. The mess looked okay on a bed of rice. Ming sat on a stool by the door, drawing on a cigarillo. He was stewing over something I suspected involved me.

My back to him, with a pencil stub, I printed a message on a scrap of paper.

'Kalani. I will try to help you escape—Bree - Yours and Mareva's friend.'

I wrapped the message in foil before covering it with rice. I hoped she'd be sharp enough to notice, know enough English to understand.

Ming spoke, hesitating between words. "Wu owe Hak money. Hak take Wu's woman for gambling debt. Hak is hungry guy. Not nice man." He shook his head.

I stared icicles, brushing smoke aside.

"I soon win you. Chun lose big at poker last night." He grinned. "You give me down payment now. I treat you real good. Not chain you to galley. Not beat you. Ming promise."

"Take me to the girl. Now."

Ming coloured.

"Now!" I held the iron skillet.

Ming did his best to smile, bowing.

Heavy steps padded along the deck.

Chun shuffled in, eyeing me, beginning an animated conversation in dialect. He advanced, wrenched the pan from my hand. His great ham gripped my throat. My feet left the floor. "You come my room night, then you Ming's. You pay gamble debt. Do as Ming say." He sat me on the counter. Both departed in heated discussion.

My insides flip-flopped.

213

"I come back," Ming said over his shoulder.

What could anyone feel or do? There wasn't enough time to sort out anything clever. I had to think something drastic. If I went down, somehow I'd make it a damn good fight.

Ming led me along the upper deck promenade past the room the crew were using for night activities. The reek of stale air and tobacco radiated from the open doorway, confirming this was their gambling den. We turned left into a narrow passageway. He keyed a door open. I noted the key used. He carried several on a ring attached to his shorts by a nylon line.

The room was shabby. A girl lay face down on a bunk. Her dark hair swirled, dishevelled. The sheets were heavily soiled. She wore a short skirt of pale orange. Tiny black dolphin motifs rimmed its lower edge.

Ming shook her. She moved, swinging her legs over the edge of the bed and began fumbling with her skirt. Her black eyes remained fixed on the wall.

I knew it was Kalani. She had the chief's fine cheekbones, and was as beautiful as he wasn't.

"I've brought you some food and drink," I said, pushing Ming aside, kneeling beside her. She stared at me as if in a dream trying to understand the inexplicable. I stopped her undressing.

"I'm Bree. A friend. You are Kalani?"

"You not talk much," Ming said.

"What harm can that do?"

"Chun say no talk with girl."

"I will if I wish. She looks terrible. Who's using her?"

Ming frowned. "Some—not Ming." He put his hands up. "She not good. Just like 'vegeble'."

"You lot make me sick." I put the spoon to her lips, fed her and made her drink the chilled water I'd doctored with lemon juice and sugar.

I turned on Ming. "You ought to be strung up for this. How can any *real* man treat a girl so badly? Women have rights, don't you know! She's starved. Look at her ribs."

"Wu not feed her for many days. He own her, now Hak own. She not cook." He gestured, hands opened defensively.

"Own, own, own! You bastards are bloody mad."

"They not nice like Ming. You see. I had wife and children in Manilla. See." From his wallet, he produced a soiled picture of a diminutive young woman, slender and malnourished. Four grinning urchins hung about her shoulders.

"These mine." He said, subdued.

"Well, this isn't a meat market. I'm not for sale."

He ignored me. "Wife die in riots. All my children gone."

"The plague?" I said, feigning sympathy.

Ming nodded. "We take ship. Take what we want. There no future in Asia. We leave here when engine fixed." "Leave?"

"Maybe five day," he said. "You will come."

"No. I've a sister. A brother. And friends. Haven't you any heart? I'm not going, and that's final."

He ignored me. "There is nothing, just this ship. I am cousin of Chun. We run brothel in Manilla. Guns in Indonesia. Opium. He is very powerful. Chinese people call him *Fu Kee Lang*.

"Which means?"

"He is *The Fearless One*. Chun want to go America. Maybe north, maybe south. Who knows? You stay alive with me. I protect, like other woman."

"But you said Chun killed her."

"That one Philippino bitch. He threw her overboard in Sunda Strait. Bad temper."

"You mean there's another girl on board?"

Ming baulked, but his eyes confirmed it.

"Where is she? Can I see her? Does she have black, curly hair?"

He shook his head vehemently, "She hellish, wild woman. She all tied up. Get good beating. Chun chop off..."

"At least tell me where she is. He won't chop anything off for that." I touched his arm. Flashed a smile.

Ming stared long and hard. "She is in storage room, back of ship." His eyes registered regret.

"Let me take her food," I smiled.

"You be good to me," he said, moving closer. I felt his hand on my back. Rank breath. My heart raced.

"The girl. You do me that favour first then I'll think about it." My lip quivered.

"We go at night time. I tell you when." He kissed my forehead.

I winced, shoved his groping hands away.

Kalani devoured everything. Her eyes were searching mine for answers. I smiled. Kissed her cheek. Hugged. She ponged of stale sweat. "I'll see you soon."

Back in the galley I sat shaken by my luck in meeting her. The down side was worse; game playing with Ming made me feel cheap and dirty.

Now that there were two girls alive, there was no easy way to escape. My conscience wouldn't allow me to gain for myself what I might be able to give to them.

The rest of the day was horribly hot and frustrating. Scrounging for what food was edible verified this bunch couldn't make it to the Americas. They would stay for sure, and the island was far too small to share with this lot.

Chun shuffled in, beaming hard approval.

"Silly bugger," I mouthed, my back to him. "He thinks I'm cleaning house." I turned, smiled, and made a face.

The sum of my food scrounging unearthed a canister of Drano, soap flakes and a jar of Exlax. As much as I wanted to, Drano laced in food wouldn't work. Too easily detected. Vile stuff, caustic, and it smoked. Besides, if they made me sample I'd be violently ill, desperate for a quick end.

I toyed with the idea of making them so sick they could barely crawl between bed and toilet. It might be possible to grab the keys, release the girls, and swim for it, or make a crude raft.

Soap flakes would work best. I remember being puking sick after sampling soap as a five year old, thinking it was cream co-loured chocolate. Mum always said I loved to stick things in my mouth. Snails. Mud.

Flakes would blend with rice, and a mix of hot mango chilli would disguise it long enough. They'd be mad as death adders when it took effect.

"The mother of all diarrhoeas," I said.

I'd have to make a separate dish for myself.

They might react differently if some ate just a little, which would mean big trouble for me. If Chun came after me, could I argue that the pork was off? Pretend to be sick too?

What if they bound me up before it took effect, and before I could make myself scarce? There were a lot of 'Ifs'.

I fingered the cracked mirror. A large piece came away, and with it the seed of another idea.

Using morning light, its reflection must be easily seen from the high bluff. Jeff would be scheming some rescue plan, unaware there were two girl's on board, and equally ignorant of my intention to free them. He'd take his time planning, but exactly how he'd pull it off was hard to imagine. It must happen late at night, and that spelled danger, confusion.

As for Cris as rescuer, he was too clumsy and compulsive, likely to do anything harebrained. Malcolm was a shadow, self-centred, and wouldn't care a damn about me. Zoë was all heart, but too small for this sort of venture. If she, or Jeff died trying to rescue my skin, life wouldn't be worth living.

In the gathering dark, my depression deepened. I was alone in whatever I decided to do. Jeff must be warned off any rescue attempt for the time being. If I knew his nature, flashing a light would make him react early. Jeff needed time to think things through. And what if Cris went off on his own bat? He could muck any plans up. Zoë was impulsive. What if she goaded Cris into action?

Chapter 30

Ming dragged a bunk mattress and tired navy blanket into the galley.

"You sleep on this better," he grinned, proud of his thoughtfulness. He unchained me.

Tired and dazed, I hobbled to the sink. Began scrubbing. No sense pandering to displays of kindness. He'd get off on the flash of a smile.

At this rate, I'd make a great washerwoman. I hand washed towels and a pile of malodorous clothing the crew dumped on the galley floor. Chun's shorts bagged out, big enough to fit four of me. I moved it with a broom handle.

Scrubbing clothes gave me a chance to wander the deck in search of hanging space and to note the layout of the upper deck walkway. The only potential route to a hiding place, other than several pokey staterooms, was the top of the wheelhouse, the highest point on the ship. The boxy stern structure stood almost as tall. Simply hiding was just a dead end option. They'd soon find me.

Jeff and the others weighed on my mind. Rescue must wait at least until I could sort out how to release the girls. The only way to warn was by leaving a written message, something simple, large, even a dunderhead would see from land.

I scissored the blanket Ming offered into three equal strips. By hanging two vertically from the cabin wall, and attaching the third piece diagonally, a 'N' could be made big enough for anyone to see with binoculars from shore, that is provided the wind remained from the southeast. Any north wind would swing the ship completely around and hide my message. An old life ring, already hanging on a bracket just aft of the galley, made the 'O' needed for 'No'. It was primitive, but anyone watching, especially Zoë, would know something was up. Hopefully, Jeff would be suspicious enough to wait and see. He'd know charging in was suicidal. Time. How much? If there was any chance my scheme might work, I needed breathing space.

The more I thought about it, the more it struck me as mad. Anything could happen to screw my plans up big time.

Hak studied me as I spread out washing. He took particular interest in the wall hanging, which still lacked the diagonal piece. "What you cut sheet for?"

"Cleaning rags. To make a new top." I hugged the remaining material, and did my best busying, hanging underwear.

"Come," he scowled, "you help. Bring rags."

Trailing behind, I hoped he would forget about me. Detouring to the galley, I fussed about all to no avail. Hak, tight mouthed, shoved me out. We made for the lower deck and down into the darkness of the engine room. If Hak aimed to isolate me there'd be no defence. He was much too powerful.

A dim extension light swung with the ocean swell. Through half-light the rust stained bulk of a huge engine emerged. Pieces of machinery lay on the floor. Tools lay everywhere. A massive head plate from the top of the engine lay encased in chains, and propped against a bulkhead wall. Even to a mechanical dummy like me, it was clear they weren't going anywhere soon. The ship appeared crippled.

Engine room air stank of oil, a scent I found strangely pleasing on its own, but S-331's bilge was something else, like fermented pee and other unmentionables.

We were alone.

Perspiration poured, blinding me. Wiping didn't help. The itches from accumulated grime returned, spreading with sweat beads seeping down my back.

Hak's naked torso highlighted under the globe accentuated his wiry muscle. Dragonesque tattoos, whose three heads were etched in black and blue, grinned from his chest. He paused, dipped a sponge in a bucket of water, and squeezed it over his head. Rivulets splattered on the rust ribbed floor. He turned, offering the sponge, his face a shadowed smirk.

"You like wet." He slopped it over me. I backed.

"I didn't come here to shower with you. What am I supposed to do?" I waved at the engine.

"I teach you how to please." He advanced.

"Chun is my boss. I his girl." Cripes. I was talking shorthand like...

"You very attractive, Blondie." He crooned.

The stairway was narrow. Light rayed down, mocking my longing to escape. He shifted to block the exit.

"He'll kill you," I said. I lifted a huge wrench. It may as well weigh a ton. Swinging it would be a joke; rather, it would swing me.

"He not care. Chun owe much money. He is my cousin."

"Listen, dipstick. He'll know if I say you..."

My teeth rattled as he pushed me against the wall. His hand wedged my jaw upward. His lips pressed, bruising mine, making it impossible to breath properly. Everything inside cried, knee him. I remained frozen.

Footsteps rang on the stairs. Wu and two others arrived. The guy who had unlocked my chains was one. He wore pressed coveralls. His frame was almost delicate, sinewy. He stared indifferently from fine-rimmed glasses.

The other was gnome-like and stocky, his expression, a card player's facing a difficult decision. He was the youngest. A third I'd never seen before, much older and arthritic, shuffled in, obviously in pain.

Wu sneered at Hak. He glowered at me. Wu struck up a conversation with the others about the engine. I dropped the wrench, which rang, cutting the air, chopping Wu's words short. He tensed, as if to strike. I dropped to my hands and knees, just out of range, intent on cleaning.

The rest of the day was horrible. I rubbed furiously, as punishment for being caught. Didn't someone say bad fortune comes in threes? Maybe my run was on number two. Didn't the Chinese think three was a lucky number? There was some weird irony in it.

Turpentine rioted in my sinuses, and my stomach turned queasy. Kneeling amongst the filth and parts, I dripped until there was nothing left to drip. Cleaning became unbearable. The whole chemical ether made my headache return with a vengeance, enveloping the top of my head in a tight band.

After what seemed hours, I made a break for the stairs, unhindered by my captors, who were busy installing parts. I ran for the galley and a cold drink, which sickened my stomach.

The heavens lay darkening in a foul haze. I attached the diagonal strip of sheet, now filthy with grease, and completed the 'N'. It'd be my luck to need a pointer to broadcast the message. Arms waving, I gestured, shook my head. For all my efforts, they'd probably think I'd gone mad, or taken up dancing. I stared at the bluff and shoreline until my eyes hurt.

※

Chun appeared, as I lay exhausted on the mattress.

"You not sleep tonight. You and native girl entertain us. Cook good stir-fry. Ming have birthday celebration. He forty-thlee. You say life begin at forty." He laughed, delighted at his cleverness.

The entertain idea put me in knots. If it were a birthday, maybe the lot of them would fall down drunk, or dope themselves into oblivion before we had to put out for them. I sure as hell wasn't going to be the icing on any cake.

They were all pisspots. Sake', a slippery rice wine, lay in cases in the galley corner. Their den reeked of opium and marijuana. I knew the pungent smell of the latter from some deadhead's freak-out party I'd secretly gone to on a dare. I'd smelled opium that night, heavy, almost sweet smelling.

I knew now their habitual nervousness meant one crewman always stayed on watch. What if he ate later than the rest? Would Ming have the keys? The whole messy question suddenly closed in making me numb.

Exhausted and rat haired, like a new age witch, I hovered over the wok. The grated flakes of soap blended well with the rice. I'd added pork strips, mango and banana slices on the rim. A generous portion of hot curry added colour and disguised the soap. My nose ran with its sharpness. Everything was carefully arranged in bowls on two trays, and stacked for a single delivery. One part on each bowl rim nearest me was free of soap in case they made me eat some. I could spoon what was safe. That was the theory. They must eat at the same time, and take down plenty of it.

I froze, straining to hear. Someone padded the deck close by. A shadow. How easy it was to be found out.

In a fit of nerves, I dithered over each bowl for colour and appearance. It was a mad guess how long it'd take before they knew the food was spiked. I'd have to hide well away until they were clenching their guts.

It was close to eleven when I arrived at the gambling den, from which dense smoke eddied, curling upward like a malignant spirit. An antiquated fan buzzed and jerked, as if confused from many beatings.

Specs lay in a corner nursing an ornate hookah, a giant water pipe. He was paralytic, wearing a silly grin; he was well into other worlds.

I stood in the doorway, as if fixed to the deck, my arm aching with the tray's weight. Kalani lay curled fetally on a bunk in the far right corner.

A card table dominated the room. Chun, Wu, Hak and Ming loomed larger than life over the poker game, which was well under way. Judging from the pile of chips in front of Ming, my future looked clear. Wu possessed an equally large pile and a slip of paper. A promissory note? For what? For whom? The tension was palpable.

Tattooed and gleaming with sweat, Hak sat squinting, coveting a small pile of chips, which indicated his inferior place in the lust for power. Looks are deceptive.

"Come in, Blondie," Chun said, waving a massive arm. He removed a bottle of rice wine from the corner of the table.

I dropped the tray awkwardly and backed off, but not before he grabbed my wrist.

"You have some food. You too skinny." He made an obviously crude remark in dialect. Hak and Wu brayed with laughter. Ming frowned as if to appease me.

"You good looker. Worth much," Chun said.

I couldn't move, couldn't think. His pudge fingers wedged into the back of my shorts and wrenched them down tearing the seam apart. I stood naked except for the dishrag top. My knees knocked.

"Take top off."

I stared disbelief, caught in terror and his iron grip. He released my arm. I removed it.

"Let hair down." I untied my hair. It fell in a rat's nest of tangles. Their eyes crawled all over me. My stomach quaked.

"She worth lot more. She a virgin," Chun sang, drawing pleasure from the notion. His hand clamped around my leg, slid inside my thighs. I wanted to plunge over the side, couldn't.

"You eat now."

"I-I've already eaten. Can't eat chilli. I g-get sick." My teeth chattered. I screwed my face up, eyeing the bowls through tears, no longer sure of which parts were safe to eat.

Chun scooped a spoonful.

In desperation, I quickly scooped some I guessed was safe,

stuffed it in, not wanting to swallow. The chilli set my taste buds on fire, spreading into my throat, knifing into my sinuses. I choked. My eyes streamed. Sweat poured. "Shee? It'sh okay."

"You not like what you cook?" Hak said, bemused. Suspicious. He stroked my hair.

"It'sh too hot for me. Jusht right for you." Forced a meek smile, face twitching in spasms.

"You try more." Chun forced a spoonful in my mouth.

A commotion erupted on deck. Shouting. Feet drummed on the upper companionway. An enormous crash of automatic fire enveloped the ship. I spewed and shrieked. The whole table jumped as my knee rammed the tray, sending the contents onto Chun's legs.

He swore, cuffing me a glancing blow across the face. Ming cursed. All raced on deck, The Gnome bowled me flat as he followed. Specs remained glassy-eyed.

Kalani sat up, her eyes darting. At least she wasn't doped.

More shouting. Another burst of fire. I grabbed her hand and my clothes. We slipped doubled over along the companionway, and ducked into the galley. I left her there while I gathered enough nerve to have a peek over the railing up by the wheelhouse. The shakes wouldn't go away. I clenched the railing.

Up forward they were leaning over both sides. Lights flashed. Voices hot in dialect, swearing. I heard "I kill bitch." Knew he'd blow me apart.

I motioned Kalani into one of several vented clothing lockers located in the back room, the same one used as a rubbish tip. "You stay." Pointed. "Wait. Hide." She panicked as I tried closing the metal door. "We'll go back to Motu-Riva soon," I smiled, patted her arm wedged hard against the door. She nodded, her eyes wild, darting. I pressed the door closed and piled tins and boxes against it, did the same to a few other lockers. With luck she'd be safe until escape was possible. How that would happen eluded me.

I grabbed a large iron skillet and threw it over the side of the ship as far as possible. It splashed loud enough to be heard over the verbal racket they were making.

They continued to search along the sides of the ship upward. A light flashed in an arc where I'd thrown the pan, then shifted forward. Slashes of light struck out towards shore illuminating palms.

Slipping back to their den, I stopped in the doorway, saw specs grinning. Further aft a dark form silhouetted in the gloom, and sidled around the stern cabins. It happened in the blink of an eye. The cabin light was enough to mar my vision, but someone was there. It had to be one of the crew, probably the old guy.

Footsteps rang metallic.

With a bucket, I frantically scraped up the still steaming remains of the dinner while fuming over the whole dumb scheme. I'd never felt so depressed in my relief.

Chun barged in, eyes bulging in rage, "where girl go?"

"She ran off," I pointed, looking clueless. I may as well defy a tornado.

"You lie. Where she hide?"

"She's probably over the side. Swimming. Haven't you terrified her enough?"

"Lie!"

"Not lie."

Hak entered, his hair as feral as his look. "Someone cut ropes on davit. No can use launch. It too heavy. Who your flend?" He snapped. "Skinny guy." His fist smashed on the table. Chips flew.

"Nobody I know," I said.

"I shoot him. He die." Hak stuck his face in mine. "Shark food." He smiled gold-capped teeth.

I shrugged, kept a poker face. Maybe he did hit someone. Skinny? That couldn't be Malcolm.

Fantastic. Ridiculous. He would never risk his scrawny neck. An islander? No.

The davit ropes used to swing the launch over the side could be fixed. There wasn't much sense in cutting them. Yet, he was cunning, a wild card. No telling what might inspire him other than food, dope and sex.

Jeff and Cris must have cooked up something, but what? Who was stirring the hornet's nest up forward?

Ming stormed in, his mouth set, Papa Ming nowhere in sight.

"Find girl." Chun snarled. "You come."

I jumped. He gripped my forearm. I stumbled along in his wake like a petulant child. The rest scattered, their ears back, hungry for a victim.

Chun propelled me into the storage room where Kalani hid.

"I come later. Fix you good. Ming have you. Birthday present." He leered. "Maybe he sell you piece by piece." The door slammed.

Keys rattled.

I lay exhausted for a long time wired on the verge of hysteria, dreading his return. Outside, shouting announced the hunt for Kalani as they ferreted through the ship. Judging from the doors slamming, they'd descended to the lower levels. Voices rose and fell, muffled ghost-like.

Someone entered the galley, scrounging about, throwing things, and bashing cupboards. He tried the door. His nicotine wheeze told me it was Ming. He departed.

The room luminesced a sickly grey-green, like the horrid paint used in our school toilets. It stank with stuffiness and heat. I figured it was the middle of the night. Knees up, I rubbed my arm, nodding into sleep. A door slamming jarred me awake.

Furious, I kicked a box, dislodging a cockroach traversing its rim. I wondered if it was the same brute that greeted me at the galley door. I screamed, lashing out as one crawled across my back.

Chapter 31

Subliminal alarm. I woke uneasy. The air hung heavy, stale.

"Kalani?" I cleared rubbish from the locker. She'd fallen asleep, knees wedged. She woke wild eyed, and then her eyes softened. They were dark pools in the half-light, big.

"Chun's coming for me. He'll have no reason to re-lock the door. You swim to shore?" I gestured using a swimming motion. "Go to your father. Find Mareva."

"I speak English okay. How do you know my name?"

"Mareva told me."

Kalani's face lit up. "She my other mother. Teacher."

"Like she's Fau's and Elili's mother?"

Kalani beamed, her white teeth stark against silky, cinnamon skin. Her joy was infectious.

"They are my cousins. Orphans. Their mother and father die in Great Wave."

"These men. They hurt you?"

Her face dropped, jaw set. "Yes. Many times they abuse me. They not very good. Clumsy. Smelly." Her eyes moistened. "They beat me up. I not cook. Not wash for pigs."

"Listen. I'll try to get away. You stay in the locker. Sneak away late tonight." I showed her how to jamb the inside mechanism so it couldn't be opened from the outside. "When it's quiet swim from the back of the ship."

"You come with me? Please?" She said, shaking her head.

"No. There's another girl on the ship."

"Oh." Kalani's eyes dilated. "She crazy. Demon girl. She hit big man. Scratch like cat. Her name is Angelina." She laughed at the name then frowned. "I see her once."

Kalani's face darkened.

"Sharks near ship. I see them," she said.

My heart sank. Of course, we had no way ashore other than swimming. Sharks are scavengers. After the massacre, any late arrivals would keep a sharp interest in the lagoon. Instinct driven,

226

they'd cruise for days, hungry for whatever else might turn up.

I couldn't think of a way out other than swimming to the outer reef, which the ship was much closer to. Struggling barefoot, its coral would slice us to ribbons. The nearest islet was a kilometre southwest, a miserable outpost of battered palms atop the reef, and no bigger than a football field.

"You don't want to stay here past tonight. Find a hideout at the back of the ship. I'll find you there." I shrugged, smiled, unable to offer anything better. "I'm sorry to leave you."

S-331 heaved uneasily.

"It's so hot. A storm coming?" I said mutely, unable to conjure even a bandaid solution.

Kalani nodded, "storms sweep my island in December. January bad month." She paused. "Your friends come? Guns shoot. So much noise. My heart leap from my mouth."

"Yes. Maybe one of them upset these mongrels."

"Mongrels?"

"Dogs." I made a face, barked.

She giggled. "They eat dog. Not like each other. Maybe eat each other."

We cast wry smiles, longing for the unimaginable.

First light filtered through the door vents. Kalani unhappily wedged into the locker.

We were thirsty and tired. She'd have to endure being cramped and hot for the whole day without food or drink.

I felt super edgy, knowing Chun would be in a black mood. Once in his grip, I'd pay. I rubbed my arm.

It wasn't long before I heard the heavy pad of his feet. I stood weak as adrenalin rushed and nerves tightened.

I switched the light off, which gave me some advantage. His eyes would be unused to the darkness.

My school self-defence instructor once drilled the stuffing out of me, like a mantra. "If you can't escape, get in close. Use your knee. Hit hard. Hit his privates. Snap it in two. Ram the palm of your hand up into his nose. Hard. You'll only get one go. Make it count." He made it sound so matter of fact.

The door grated open. I stood centrally, allowing as much uncluttered room as possible. Chun filled the entrance, the background light haloed, magnifying his mass, turning him into a supernatural demon.

He advanced. A thin blade glinted from his ham hand; his

small eyes frowned from dark sockets. For an instant I panicked.

I hung my head, offering submission. The knife flashed its hunger, long and lean. I watched his free hand.

"What you put in food? Hak sick. Bad. Wu puke guts out. He throw up bubbles."

I smelled alcohol on his breath.

"The pork. The pig. It *must* be bad," I pleaded, looking wide-eyed and pathetic.

"Lie." Kicking crockery aside, he lurched forward.

I realised ramming a knee into a mass of flab wouldn't work.

I lunged in close and struck, driving the bony palm of my hand into his pug nose with frantic strength, taking his upper lip as well. Bone crunched.

He bellowed, his left hand clutching his face.

I dropped, twisting to the right, and sprang past, slipping on broken plates. His blade swept in a crazy arc, snagging hair. He spun, sliding, arms flailing, and crashed on his back; ejecting an air-ripping fart. The bellow became a roar, like nothing I'd ever imagined a human could utter. My bowels turned queasy.

I bolted through the galley, snatching the fry pan, and dodged around the front of the wheelhouse, heading aft on the starboard side.

Using the life ring hung on the cabin wall as a gripping point, I tried to scramble up onto the roof. My fingers clawed, but couldn't grasp the upper edge. I slipped, landing hard on my butt.

Chun raged orders. Hak's clipped anger joined in. He wasn't sick enough, hunter on the loose.

Being caught by either meant a payback death. Knew of atrocities carried out on women in war areas, terrifying things—the thought of mutilation. I wasn't good at coping with pain.

I flew down the aft stairs, several steps at a time to the lower deck, U-turned into a central companionway, which descended, ran forward through the middle of the ship. It provided access to storage rooms. Hurriedly I checked three out. These were cave-like, largely empty and appeared to be directly behind the engine room.

Feet thumped along the upper deck, heading aft suggesting three pursuers.

The rooms were dinghy under yellowed bulbs, which were located over each doorway. I plunged into a closet-like alcove at the far side of the third storage area, the most distant from the entrance, and furthest aft.

I sat shaking, angry I'd peed my pants, and freaked out. My skin crawled, chilled, forehead hot.

I still gripped the pan, needed to prise cramped fingers off.

In the dim light there were lockers and racks of aged, yellow, weather gear hanging limp. An assortment of boxes lined the far wall. A cluster of lethal looking gaff hooks lay rusting on a shelf, mute testimony to the over-fishing of the oceans. I grabbed one.

The entrance door above opened. Slammed. I shifted behind the door, backing into something soft. Alive.

I leaped away, turned and struck off balance, raking the door handle.

"Jeez. Go easy, ye mad bitch."

"What? How'd *you* get here?" I rasped.

"Can't ye guess? How do rats do it?"

"Anchor chain?" I said dumbly, unable to think of anything else to say. I strained to see his face.

"Nix. There's rope hanging over the arse end of this scow. These lads watch from the bow."

"How do you know that?"

"We've watched, man. They're el slacko." He leaned to whisper; "Looked for you in the kitchen last night round three or four. Figured they had you on your back somewhere."

I jabbed him hard in the gut.

Footsteps rang hollow on the stairs. Someone entered the adjacent room. I heard low-pitched moaning, breathing laboured. A light flashed in disjointed movements.

"Blondie not here," Hak's voice grated. "*Owoom,*" he muttered gutturally, chain-swore, left on the run, but before making the upper deck cried anguish. I heard his bowels emptying, cascading down the stairwell. A vile stench, unmistakably diarrhoea, seeped into our hole.

More voices above, muffled and urgent. Hak stumbled on deck overwhelmed in misery.

"Is that your doin'?"

I nodded. "He tried some food I prepared. It's, umm, doctored up."

"No love loss for sure."

"Shut up. Get serious. Why didn't Jeff or Cris come? Why you? Didn't any of you see my sign?"

"Well..."

229

"What's the point of making sense with you?" I knew he wore that damned, supercilious grin. I longed to wipe it from his face.

"Zoë saw it. Jeff knew you were up to somethin'. They flogged ideas to find you. Sort out what we could do. Thought I owed you." Malcolm paused to scratch. "Cris can't climb worth shit. Says he's keen. Jeff got the bug from my Millie. Serves him right for havin' her heat on his lap."

Chalk up seven points for Jeff, three more to go. "How'd you get out here?"

"That canoe thing. It's tied under the stern overhang."

"At least you're good for something," I said, immediately regretting my nastiness.

"Didn't you think I cared enough to rescue you?"

I remained mute. Whatever the reasoning in that warped mind, his presence just scored him a brownie badge.

"The guy in the water Hak said he shot. I half figured it was you."

"Aw, thanks. You're real sweet. Yeah. It was. See, Jeff wanted me to sabotage their motor rig. I fixed the engine. Peed in the fuel tank. Ripped wires. Cut ropes. Silly bugger missed me. Sprayed the water. Made a great fluorescent show."

"How original. I still can't believe you're here."

Malcolm took my hand and squeezed it. "Breezy, neither can I."

I laughed, gave him a hug, his hands instant grappling hooks.

"Now I gotta get your bod off this damn tub. How you managed to get an invite, I'll never figure."

"Not yet you don't."

Malcolm sucked in air. "What the stuff you on about?"

"Two girls. One's locked away somewhere. The other's the chief's daughter, Kalani. She's hiding. Should make it to shore tonight, but she's petrified of sharks."

"I comprehend. Sure ain't gettin' my arse bitten off for anyone. One out of two girls ain't bad," he said glibly.

"The other one's off the yacht. She comes too. I can't leave her."

"They been feedin' you dope? You owe her nothing. Don't even know her. You're dead meat if you get caught, Bree. They'll stretch you on the operatin' table, slit you wide open." He motioned from throat to crotch.

"I know that. Don't you think I'm scared?"

"You keep gettin' yourself into weird situations," Malcolm lectured.

"Ming. He's got the keys. He feeds her," I said.

"Sure thing. Just blow the guy some kisses," Malcolm sing-songed. "Oh, Ming, sweetheart, lend me your keys. I'll bend over backwards for you," Malcolm sniggered. "He'll sure as hell open both your locks for you."

"You're hopeless. You've got no..."

"Guts?"

"Heart!" I jabbed him angrily. "If I could get Ming alone, I could bait him. He's got a *thing* for me. You could hit him from behind with this." I held the fry pan. "Knock him silly."

"The way things are, you'd better bend your bare arse for him, and point the way to paradise. He'll just as likely drill you full of holes. Yer right up there with the faeries."

I knew he was right.

"Kill, is more like it." He reverently held up the switch knife I thought I'd thrown overboard. It flicked open. "Slit his throat. It's faster. Neat. Most he can do is gurgle. Scream blood bubbles."

"She's in a cabin somewhere in the stern," I said.

It was hard to accept. I'd become as murderous as they were, but the idea of shoving a blade into someone chilled me to the core. Could I ever do such a thing? Malcolm was so blasé about it. Easy come; easy go; like all of his appetites. I sensed his tension. Closeness.

"We need to know when this Ming weirdo sees her. We're in the dark here, and useless," he said. "No tellin' when they'll turn up here again. Risky."

"Then, you'll help me?"

"Do I have a choice?"

"Yes. No!"

"If it goes wrong, I'm over the side and you're on your own."

I couldn't blame Malcolm for saying that. I'd blown a great chance to cripple the whole crew. Now we might escape using the outrigger canoe, but the ship was a hornet's nest. They'd be on the prowl.

In the back of my mind there was something out of the wreckage of my scheme, a spark of observation overlooked. No matter what I did to retrace my activities, it wouldn't come to the surface. My thoughts wouldn't focus. Malcolm's breathing suggested he was dozing off.

I nudged. "I put grated soap flakes in their curried rice."

"Jeezus. Braggin' already. Glad ye don't cook for me," he yawned.

I laughed, felt bitter, foolish. "Wish I could've wiped the lot. Arsenic. Botulism. Poisoning. Anything."

"What's this botchew jazz? Do ye bite them first?"

"Mum told me. Bacteria gets into tinned stuff if the seal's broken, or rusted through, and can really make you sick. It'll kill."

"You mean if you had the chance you'd poison the lot of 'em?"

"I. Yes. Well, they murdered all those poor people. Children."

"Wow. And you figured I was scummy for slicing a chick up. I'm humbled in your presence."

"Stop the holier than thou crap." They're such a pack of - that's it. The tin. The tin!"

"What're yeh on about now?"

There's a bad tin of food in the galley. The lid's swollen."

"Aw, Yer troppoed out. They've fired you as cook."

"I'm going back. Watch out for Ming. He's bald, has a paunch. Hak's got tattoos. Wu's the one with the little ponytail."

"Hey. I'm Little Red Ridin' Hood. Don't ask me to take on all of 'em."

"Get real. I'll sneak into the galley late tonight. It'll take an hour to do some rice and mix the stuff in. I'll leave it in the fridge."

"Dummy. They won't fall for that," he sniggered.

"They're hungry and lazy," I said.

"Sounds like me."

"You can say that again, bozo."

"You know Bree, they'll come after us on the island if we steal their women, so don't count all your chickens..."

"I know."

"Getting off this tub ain't easy with extra baggage, Bree. This rat travels light."

"Where's Zoë and Fish?"

"Your little sis is all steamed up, a regular little terrier. Needs a leash."

"So do you." I sensed he liked my jibe. I waited for a response. He played dumb.

"Wouldn't surprise me if miss nose-it-all sticks her beak round the corner. She's making time with Cris out on the point."

We sat the hours out dozing in an ether of tension as much as foul air. Malcolm ponged. I reeked of everything revolting. Animal. My monthly threatened.

How to sneak into the galley posed problems. They'd be prowling the decks. The roof of the cabins presented the only possible route not regularly observed by the crew. It was festooned with housing for electronic gear, which made it easier to find cover.

My skin was dark enough for night stealth, but my ability to spider over the top of the cabins was another matter. I hurt in too many places. Lying in hiding for hours made muscles stiff, movements clumsy. The crew would go off at the slightest disturbance.

Entering the kitchen was an enormous gamble. I'd have to find everything, and cook in the dark.

Movement filtered through from forward. Tools rattled. Voices. An *Abba* song, '*Ring, Ring*', belted through the steel bulkheads.

"That's Specs and the Dwarf. They're working on the engine."

Malcolm snored in spasms. I catnapped.

❉

We hung out at the back door once it was close to dark. The sky brooded blue-grey, wind fitful from the southeast.

From our position, it was possible to see anyone approaching the aft cabins, which were located on two levels, about a dozen meters away. Noise of their descent on the stairways either side of us leading to the after deck would warn us to vacate. We'd have a few seconds to spare. We kept the door open a crack.

Ming showed up about mid evening with some fruit and drink. He made his way to the second level cabin, furthest left. He paused, scrutinising the decks, then entered.

Wu showed up shortly after looking the worse for wear. Both were soon hard at it in dialect. Wu was wildly angry. Ming sounded evasive. It was impossible to know what the issue was. I put it down to bad eating, gambling debt, and lost pleasures. Both departed in separate directions. I spotted a pistol on Wu's hip.

"We've been down here too long," Malcolm said. "We go up on the cabin roof."

I nodded. Malcolm swung easily onto the roof. He hoisted me up, as if his arms were hydraulic. I couldn't be that skinny, surely.

"You're on your own. Hope there's some rat in you. See you

back here in an hour."

"Two." I squatted; joints knotted up, and crab-crawled towards the galley. The crew's cabins were soon directly under me. It was like walking on ice. Temperature change, or just the pressure of my weight might make a plate buckle ever so slightly. I tread where the plates joined.

Heavy cloud veiled the peaks, spilling over the escarpment, their undersides swirling end over end, threatening rain.

I reached the galley, lay on my back to rest and wait, and closed my eyes. Scraps of muted conversation drifted through the steady boom of surf. Someone clattered cutlery in the kitchen. He whistled strains of the same *Abba* tune. It was Specs. He left.

Imaginings welled up. Sipping a tall glass of iced tea with a slice of lemon made me resentful of stale shipboard water. How I longed for a bathtub soak with scented bubbles. Lavender. And a manicurist, hairdresser, and a masseuse, male. An overhaul.

Drops splattered. I licked parched lips, split with dryness. Tasted salt. My stomach rumbled. More drops. Huge. Splooshing. Several giants pelted my face, went up my nose.

In an instant, the skies opened up, deafening. Ecstatic, I rubbed my skin, shedding layers of filth. I lay, eyes closed. The roof drummed and danced. *S-331* smothered under the staccato of rain and dark.

The torrent blasted, relentless and cold, but now it was impossible to be sure there wasn't anyone in the galley. I wouldn't hear feet approaching once I entered.

Chapter 32

As a child, darkness freaked me. Now it was a friend. With luck the rain would continue driving in torrents making it doubly hard for anyone to see or hear. The crew were unlikely to wander the decks.

That's what I thought until someone else arrived, throwing a pot on the stove. He whistled. It must be Specks or the Gnome.

Hak's abrasive voice silenced the musical reverie. It depressed me knowing he was directly below. For a heart-stopping moment I imagined he felt my presence. I strained to trace his actions.

A fresh torrent of rain needled the length of the ship. She heaved slowly, swinging on the anchor. I felt vibration course deep in her hull. Moments later both left the galley on the run. I leaned over, studied the darkness, my eyes half closed, water dribbling off the end of my nose.

Voices babbled from the stern. Something was wrong.

No lights shone from the gambling den. With Hak and Wu nursing their plumbing, and Chun undoubtedly keen to kill me, they'd lost interest in gambling.

I wondered about Ming. He'd be secretly enjoying his winnings. I sensed Ming's fixation on me. My flirtation and promise meant a heavy debt he'd crave to collect in full with interest.

Slipping over the cabin side, legs swinging, I dropped, landing on all fours, and skulked into the galley, making for the back room. I turned the light on long enough to survey the ruins.

Patches of blood splattered the floor and shattered crockery. The amount of blood was scary. Had he found Kalani and killed her? The locker she'd hid in was closed. With the worst fear, I opened it. No Kalani.

In the adjacent storage room, shelves lay in ruins, ransacked by a heavy hand. All manner of tins, marked and unlabelled, were strewn about. I risked using the light. With such a feeble glow, it took far too long to find the tin. Odd noises grew in my imagination. The howl of the wind made it worse.

Cooking in the dark was the pits. Just finding a pot without waking the dead spooked me. They'd shifted things about from where I put them. Men always dropped things where they feel like. No bloody sense of order.

I made enough rice for several servings, keeping a bag for us to eat, and mixed the contaminated ingredients in the rest. Again, I added some chilli to disguise any odd smell, and left it in the fridge. The porker grinned.

"It's for them. Hope I don't end up like you."

With the twine used to secure my boob tube, I tied a length to the stool, which allowed me to step up, reach the cabin top and retrieve it.

Before I could hoist the stool clear it took off in the wind, slamming twice into the cabin side before I yanked it onto the roof.

A light flashed aft. A door opened. Closed.

Lying there, hugging the stool and bag of rice, I waited. Time dragged on. One of them must be outside listening. Having any airhead notions about them being lax would be fatal, so I closed my eyes and tried to be still, but shivered, my teeth rattling. How long is enough? Twenty minutes? An hour? My jaws set so badly I finally made a move. Hunger and tiredness would bring on hyperthermia quickly.

※

Malcolm was gone. I stared stupidly at the storage box trying to gauge the length of time I'd been away. My sense of time was hopeless. Insisting on two hours to do what must be done - did he actually listen? Finally, my addled senses suggested my scheme took closer to three hours.

"The bastard's left me." It slowly sank in. I sat fuming, remembering his smart-ass philosophy. "This rat travels light."

The truth finally dawned with the realisation I was sitting in the very reason he'd want to move. The storm was blasting wet and ever colder. I plunged down the stairs below deck, leaped over splotches of Hak's faeces, cursed him, and entered our hideout. Rat wasn't there.

"If you ran off with Kalani and left me, I'll kill you." My angry words dissolved in the tempest. I holed up in the back storage room, shoved in clots of rice, and fighting sleep, fell into it.

The heavy staccato of tools working on metal woke me. Specs and company were at it, this time with much energy. Would they have eaten my offering? All I needed was a little luck. My hopes lifted.

Outside the moan and whine of aerials in the wind blended in shrill, harmonic discord. How I longed to plunge over the side and swim for it.

I groped for the rice bag; found the precious rice spread across the floor. A huge rat stared glassy eyed a mere arms length from my foot. He continued eating greedily. Grabbing a gaff hook I smashed into the animal, but the beast was quick and though startled stood off as if to challenge me for the remains. I backed away and left it to eat as a second monster joined in. Rats and cockroaches were great candidates to replace humans.

S-331 heaved, yawing from side-to-side. The storm entered a new intensity. I opened the aft hall door into a maelstrom of swirling wind and rain. It must be daylight, but there was no way of telling.

The lagoon danced murky froth and greycaps, the peaks lifting, streaking in utter confusion.

Heavy grinding sounds enveloped the ship from deep in the stern. She must be dragging her anchor. Finally reality sunk in. They were frantically trying to finish repairing the engine. Without power the ship would back into the reef. Her prop and rudder damaged.

Worse still, S-331 was close enough to the northern entrance to be driven into deep water. If she ruptured her hull on coral we could be swept away and this rusted derelict would take all of us with her to the bottom of the ocean.

The "tub," as Malcolm so poetically put it, might not leave the island—ever.

Regardless of the storm, finding him was a must. I crabbed across the deck. A crate grated ominously on my right and slid down the deck, ramming into another. I skirted them.

The stern superstructure rose two levels. A narrow stairway linked to the second level. This was bisected by a short passage to the stern. There were three tiny staterooms each side. I was sure Angelina's prison lay in the farthest left.

I found all the doors on that side locked. Nobody responded.

I spied Malcolm curled up on a tarpaulin in one of the storage alcoves within the narrow passage ending at the stern. He woke.

"Sure one of them ain't yer lover? You've been gone a bleedin' long time."

"Wretch. I thought you'd left me."

"You can thank that native chook. She buzzed off in me canoe."

"She didn't know you used it, besides, it's theirs."

"Now we're stuck like two turkeys in a shootin' gallery," he said.

"You realise she left before this storm. I recon she knew it'd be a bad one."

"Aw, I'm encouraged for her."

A bucket skittered across the deck, slammed into the aft bulkhead. The ship heaved uneasily, grinding bottom. Something metallic cracked. *S-331* groaned to her keel.

"Jeezus. We can't swim."

"You can't - double points, brain-thrust. She'll be back. I know she will," I shouted.

"Okay, Miss hotshot, what next?"

"Simple. We get Angelina out."

"You've got magic keys?"

"No. You could pick the lock. Force the door open."

"No chance. You've watched too much American crap, besides, got nothin' to muck around with."

"So. You mean we wait til one of them comes?" I said.

"Spot on. We jump the bastard," he smirked. "You whack that scummy hook into his neck, or skull."

"You're sadistic. I can't do it."

"If you have to you will." He gripped my arm. "I'd kill to save your scrawny ass."

"That's - nice to know." How dumb. Couldn't think of anything else to say.

"Look. It's curved. Right? And heavy. Sink it in his vocal thingos," he said, sensing my resistance.

We fell silent.

"Look," he said, cupping his hands to be heard, "whatever happens we need a boat."

"Oh, sure. One stroke forward, four back in this storm. The wind might swing around. It does, you know." I knew that was grasping for a thin straw, and a short one too.

"Might? Fat chance. This friggin' storm could last days."

"We just wait? I'm so hungry," I said, feeling a pang of guilt.

"Don't start raving about beef stroganoff. I'm bloody starvin'. You could've grabbed something from the kitchen."

"I uh - did. Rats got at it. Wanted it more."

"Jeez-us!"

※

Wu struggled up the stairwell, swore at the storm. He hugged a bowl of food against his stomach.

I stared, horrified. He carried the same container of contaminated food I'd made up. I nudged Malcolm.

"She mustn't eat it," I hissed in his ear. "*That!*" I pointed. "It's poisonous enough to kill someone." There was no choice. I'd unwittingly forced our move. I stared. My mind seized up.

I saw Malcolm flick the switchblade open, its mean steel shining wet.

Wu slammed the cabin door. We crawled out into the tempest. I followed, fish hook in hand. The roots of my hair strained, stretched. I felt sick.

Malcolm peered at me, his eyes wild. Deranged. His whole person streamed sideways, shorts snapping with each gust.

The ship convulsed, its stern swinging more westerly, and collided with coral. The wind dropped, as if gathering energy for another onslaught.

Malcolm waved the blade across my stomach. "You bang on the door. I'll wait for the guy to come out."

"You mean I'm bait?"

"Yeah. Show some skin. Get rid of that damned top."

"You're jokin'."

In one swift stroke he grabbed the material and slashed the stitching, ripping it off. "Look like you're injured. Cry. Scream for help. You need some blood on you."

"Whose?"

"Yours."

"You're mad!"

"He'll be distracted just long enough if yer bleedin'. Hurry."

I shook. Crossed my arms.

Malcolm bunched the material, exposed his backside and jabbed the knife in twice. He caught the first spurts of red, sponging it up.

I stood gaping as he bled. Some splattered on the deck and

my legs. Something inside me wanted to scream everything away. This was totally cracked.

He wiped it over my chest, pressed the bloodied mess in my hand, and grabbed the hook from me. "Clutch your stomach. Double over when he comes out. Squeeze it. Moan. Have kittens. Quick. Before the rain..."

He rapped hard on the door and stood flat against the wall. The hook hung from his left hand, blade gleamed, poised to strike.

"Oh, help. Please help me." I leaned against the wall. The door opened suddenly, slamming against my hand.

"Ow! Oh, I'm hurt bad, Wu," I wailed, squeezing the blood down my front, and fell to my knees moaning.

Wu stepped out. He wrenched my hair. I stared horrified into the muzzle of a pistol. He grinned, shoving it hard into my mouth making me choke.

The fishhook cracked on Wu's skull, the shaft head and hook following through, slamming into his pistol hand. Wu screamed.

I felt his fingers tense on the trigger. For a split second my brain went blinding white. Wu swung around off balance, grappling with the pistol. He slipped, falling against me.

Malcolm leaped on him. His blade arm plunged. It sliced into Wu's hand between the thumb and index finger. The gun rattled across the deck.

Both rolled over me in a death struggle. Wu grasped Malcolm's throat. Blood sprayed across my face, blinding me. Wu's head struck my forehead. I saw sparks. Went blank.

.The next conscious feeling was sitting up. Someone was choking, rasping for breath. I saw Wu lunge for the gun, his left hand still gouging Mal's throat.

Mal bit Wu's nose, broke his grip. Both grabbed the weapon. The gun detonated, ricocheting off the bulkhead.

"Get the hook. The knife - Do him. I can't - hold the bugger."

I snatched the hook shaft, which was split in two, and leaped on Wu, wrenching his head back by the ponytail. He lashed upwards with something hard, slamming my chest, winding me. I gouged the hook deep into his neck, pulling up on it.

Yowling like a demon, Wu erupted from under me, and leaped over the railing head first in a crazy somersault. He crashed onto the crates below, and lay still.

We gasped, sucking gulps of air. Fell back on the deck. My

body shook uncontrollably.

"You okay?" Malcolm said.

"I'm not d-dead. That's about all," I chattered. Laughed hysterically.

"You did real good."

I screamed. "You could've hit him sooner. He nearly blew my brains out."

"Yeah. We were lucky. He forgot the safety catch."

"We?" I said. "We?"

"Yer here, ain't ye?"

"Thanks a heap." I took a swing at him.

"Uh, oh, thanks for wipin' him." Malcolm said, ducking.

"We've got to move fast. Get her out," I said.

We cringed, locked together as ice-tipped rain stung, rattling against the bulkhead.

Chapter 33

"Angelina. We're getting you out," I said. "I'm Bree. This is Mal."

"Cripes. She's chained to the bed frame. Can't take that too," Malcolm said.

Angelina stared, wild eyes deep and dark, stunned.

"Where on earth did you come from?"

"It's a long story. Later," I said.

"Thank God you've come."

"You didn't touch the rice?"

"Shivers no. It's scabby. Muck."

I decided to remain the anonymous cook.

She wore a soiled batik lap lap and singlet. Despite her ordeal, Angelina's massive shock of curls managed to look elegant, framing her fine, though now emaciated, features. She appeared to have a touch of Aborigine or African in her makeup.

Malcolm fidgeted by the door, watching. "They probably heard the shot."

"How do we get this rig off her?" I said.

They'd padlocked a chain tightly around her neck and attached both ends to the bunk frame. She could barely sit up.

"I got this jewellery after I kicked the blob in his privates. Punched him too," Angelina said.

Suddenly it was clear why he'd delayed doing me over, remembered his awkward gait. "I'm on his most wanted list. Busted his nose."

"That's wild." Her eyes flashed. "Your still alive."

"I could ask the same of you," I said. "More about that later. We've gotta get off this thing."

"Cut the gossip. Take the bed apart. Make it fast," Malcolm said.

The side frames of the bunk lifted out of slots easily, but the bed head was fixed with the chain and locked around its base.

Malcolm took one look, slammed the door, and blasted the

lock. We shrieked in unison. Jumped. My ears rang.

"Can't do the other one on your neck," he said.

"But I'll sink," Angelina pleaded. Her face fell.

"We can't swim. The storm's insane," I said.

"Bree's got it all worked out. We hang onto your chains and walk along the bottom."

"Thanks a heap poxhead. Shit. Get real. They'll look for Wu," I said.

On deck we glanced to where Wu had plunged, and froze.

"The scab's gone," I said. "Gone." A patch of discolouration showed where he'd landed.

"That's one miserable bastard," Malcolm shook his head. "They'll be on us real soon."

We bolted for the central corridor at the very end of the ship. A hatch in the huge transom offered the only point of escape. This craft was originally wide open at the lower level of the transom, but someone did renovations on her and enclosed the entire stern. A huge roller once fed a massive net, some of which still lay on the lower decks up forward. The length of rope Malcolm mentioned hung, swinging, secured on the roof of the cabins. Davits for a lifeboat hung empty. The heavy line swayed just short of the sea, making an easy drop into the water, but now, without a boat, and the ship heaving, it would be suicidal.

From where we stood there was a clear view of the stairway and the walkway around the ship's main cabin block. There was little protection for us now. We raced to build a makeshift barricade from cabin furniture and drums of fluids found in the storage area where I found Rat cat napping. Several heavy tarpaulins, which were folded and thick, served to give some extra protection. It took all our combined strength, which wasn't much, to heave each into position.

We struggled, the rain and wind bullying our efforts to shift a mattress and cabinet.

Malcolm found some aged life jackets. In my scrounging for materials I uncovered a set of emergency flares, dated 'use by Jan. 2008', five years out of date. The flare gun looked okay.

I fired one off at a high angle to starboard, away from the side of the ship the crew most frequented. It streaked in a long trajectory, bent by the gale, its fluorescent red dimming in the haze. I shot a second higher before the first faded. I kept three cartridges.

"A fat lotta good that'll do us," Malcolm said.

"It might make them hurry, whatever they're planning," I said. "Jeff must be doing something."

"Don't know where you get that kinda faith."

"Don't you ever trust anyone? We have to."

"They're comin'," Malcolm said, pushing my head down. He sighted along Wu's pistol. "There. On the second level."

I peeked; saw Hak's dim profile skulking along the deck. My heart sickened. He was armed. It seemed ages before he made a move.

Bits of leaf and shredded palm flew by. That was peculiar. It must mean the wind was shifting, coming more from the east. Winds sweeping across the peaks would carry debris a long distance. There was little visible to indicate we were anywhere other than in the middle of a mass of seething murk. The rest of the world may as well not exist.

His shot cracked, thwacking into layers of heavy tarp. A ragged hole marked its exit close to Angelina's head. We huddled at the thickest point behind the barrels.

"This pistol's got eight shots left. I'm not wasting em'," Malcolm said.

"Think they'll have a real go at us soon?" I said.

"Naw - unless one tries to climb the roof. Get above us."

"That leaves the fat one out," Angelina said. We shrieked, much more from tension than humour.

"The rocket thing they used on that boat. We'll be torn apart if they use it here," I said.

"If worse comes to worse, you two jump. The reef's about three hundred metres thataway, maybe less." Mal pointed beyond the stern.

"Dill. She's got chains," I said.

Malcolm's face darkened. "Try two life jackets, and swim damned hard," he said.

Hak's words carried, mutated by the wind. "You give up now. We not kill you. Wu not dead."

"He's cracked," Malcolm said. "Thinks we're dummies. What's he want us for, dancin' lessons?"

"It's humiliation. They can dish it out. Can't take it. Don't reply. Silence is a good weapon," I said.

Angelina squirmed into the jacket, which accentuated her bust making her look like an oversized red-breasted parrot. Her black hair spiralled in loose loops, recoiling with the wind. We

244

wrapped the second jacket around her waist, leaving arms free. The chain ends hung to her knees. She'd tied the lap lap high around her waist to give more freedom.

"Inflate those n' you'll deflate yourself." Malcolm said, touching the tip of his nose with his tongue.

"Is he always clowning like this?" Angelina said, screwing her face up in wonder.

I raised a brow. Grimaced. "Danger makes him horny. Can you believe that?"

"If he's a pal of yours, guess he'll do. He's sort of cool. Looks like a..."

"Just watch for the groping." I said.

Shots, in quick succession. One struck the barrel. Another pinged sharply immediately behind. I figured it nearly parted Malcolm's hair.

"Must be near dawn. Wouldn't know it," I said. "If we don't get help there's no real choice. Hold out or swim."

"Cripes, I'm hungry," Mal said.

"Don't think about it."

"Heard some religious dudes tried livin' on air and water," he said.

"They're all dead. Heaven bound," I said. "Stop talking about food."

"I didn't."

"They starved me," Angelina said. "Did me a favour for a while. Lost a lot of padding."

Somewhere forward the crew were busy. A dim light from beyond the pilothouse spelled trouble. Faint shouts.

The Gnome joined Hak carrying a large object. Moments later a light exploded into life, casting an incandescent shaft through saturated air.

"Shoot it out. It'll blind us," I said.

"It's too far away."

"Try."

Malcolm stuck his head up and took aim. Another shot ricocheted behind us. They were shooting high. Malcolm didn't flinch.

His first shot was lost in the din of storm and shrieking aerials. The second struck the floodlight frame sending its beam to starboard onto the raging sea.

In the flicker of a blink I saw a scrap of line distended, illuminated like a strand of spider's web above the waves. It was perhaps forty metres from the ship. As suddenly as it appeared the silvered thread dipped beneath the waves. Gnome bolted for cover.

The lamp swung back, teetered, flickered, and died.

"Jeeze. That leaves six shots."

I crawled to the access hole and stared into the maelstrom below. Vertigo set in.

The ship munched coral.

"I saw a rope. A line." I pointed to the narrow patch of sea we could view on our right.

Malcolm looked hard at me. Shook his head. "Yer seein' things. Hallucinating."

"No. I know it was there above the waves," I shouted, furious he had the nerve to challenge me. I couldn't believe my eyes fooled me.

A whole palm branch struck the top of the cabin.

"You'd see almost anything flying in that mess," Mal said.

The air exploded in automatic fire. A flurry of bullets ripped through canvas on our left, whining off the wall. I picked up something hot resting against my leg - a warped bullet head. Another salvo smashed through the barrels in front of us, embedding in the mattress, which was doubled over. A single missile zipped by my ear followed by a tuft of packing.

The smell of kerosene filled our senses.

A third volley shredded canvas and splintered the cabinet.

"They're probing for a weak spot," I said.

"That's just about everywhere," Malcolm said.

We huddled together, wet and chill penetrating to the bone. Malcolm bobbed up for a look almost as if he enjoyed a rat verses cat stand-off. It was strangely reassuring. He was Rat, and for all his sleaze, an amazing apparition.

The shooting stopped.

"This situation smells," Mal said. "We make a move soon."

"One rocket thing and we're gone," I reminded.

"Jeeze. Yer smart for a blonde." He edged over to the far right, took aim through a small gap and fired.

Shouting suggested he'd upset them.

"I heard the rockets that day. The screams. Horrible," Angelina said.

I'd lost track of time and that was something precious we'd just about run out of. "There's nowhere to go except the exposed

246

reef," I said. "We might make it to an islet."

"Better there than here. I'll do anything," Angelina said.

"Better minced feet than minced meat," Mal said.

"You won't have to do that, guys."

We turned as one.

Zoë stood legs apart, hands on hips, a demi-water nymph, bare and beaming.

"Aw, jeezus. It's the pest."

"Get down." I cried.

Zoë ducked, but no shots followed.

We scrambled for the hatch and hesitated, staring down the rope. Chief Hiva sat in an outrigger canoe. One moment he was rising, grinning within a few metres of us, the next he'd drop into a wave trough. Another craft bobbed madly nearby attached to a line.

I turned to see where Malcolm was. He'd disappeared.

"We're going. Hurry. Where are you?" I cried.

His voice came from the storage room. "I've got things to do. Get movin'."

Chapter 34

We clung hard to the line. The seething froth below made distance warp out of focus; Self-preservation is stronger than fear.

Hiva gripped the rope end below. Each of us swung down in a crazy ellipse, legs swinging over the canoes, which wallowed heavy with water and slid from under us. Waves swelled up, threatening to crush us against the stern overhang.

A shot cracked above.

Malcolm didn't appear. Seconds felt like minutes; my imagination playing havoc with my nerves.

"We go now!" Hiva bellowed.

An enormous detonation flashed, jetting smoke and debris onto us. Angelina shrieked. She slipped off the canoe, scrabbling for a grip. I grabbed her hair.

"Ow! My hair - don't let go."

Masses of smoke streamed in a boil from the stern and through the escape hatch. Seconds later Mal plummeted, his face blackened, mounted on a lifejacket. Singed, arms flailing, clutching the pistol, he disappeared.

Moments passed. His head popped up, an arm waving. Mal thrashed well beyond reach; there wasn't rope to throw to him. We watched as he swam his peculiar stroke, head held high like a beginner, intent on reaching us; he faded away, a shadowy form in the boiling froth.

"The current. It's too strong. He hasn't a chance." I shouted.

"Malcolm. Malcolm!" Zoë howled, waving her arms.

The might of the storm surge reversed the usual drift of tidal flow, driving the waters like a river towards the coral shoals and sea beyond. Malcolm struggled perilously close to the north entrance. The madness of ocean pounding the reef would quickly swallow him, merciful in its cruelty.

His arm rose again, as if effort was useless. Within a minute he'd vanished. We stared, straining to regain visual contact, stunned.

"Mal's gone," Zoë sobbed. "That's cactus."

Above, a massive *HISS* and *CA-RUMPH* vibrated hull plate, illuminating the stern.

"He might make the reef," I said.

"Let's move or we're wasted," Angelina said.

"All pull on rope," Hiva said. "All pull. Paddle no good. Maybe we live we all pull."

He gave a fierce yank on the line, which suddenly lifted, whipping the water, dragging us. They must be pulling from shore side. Hiva's powerful arms added momentum, hauling us along despite swamped canoes. The outriggers still gave us buoyancy, the pontoons kept us upright.

We pitched in, pulling hand over hand, moving close to the hull, desperate to clear the ship and blend into the soup beyond. They'd be looking for our charred corpses by now. If any one of them bothered to look over the side we'd be dead.

We breathed in gulps and gasps, matching one another stroke for stroke. I counted each. "Fifty-five, fifty-six, fifty-seven." My back and arms ached, muscles screaming for relief. Angelina began crying, venting her anger at being so weak. Beyond the ship's bow we ceased pulling, clinging in the face of the driving wind. I feared loss of grip would undo Hiva's massive effort. A loop of rope trailed behind us, a testament to his effort more than ours. He continued pulling, his sinewy muscles standing out, vertebrae distended. We slowly, in rhythmic surges, distanced ourselves from our prison.

This enormous lifeline of rope must be Jeff's doing. Amongst his many frustrating qualities, he hoarded almost everything off Elysius including the anchor rope and masses of spare line, new and old. He presented the other kind of rat, a packrat.

"I'm a wreck. No strength," Angelina gasped. "Buggers nearly broke me."

"I don't think that's possible," I said.

"It was close. Sorry about your friend Malcolm. He's a cool guy."

He's? Angelina voiced as if Malcolm was alive. It struck me strange. I suddenly felt guilty.

Zoë sat behind me, her face set in anger. She whined, her mutterings surfacing over the storm.

Bits of debris swept by. Coconuts and shredded branches bumped and scraped us. The smell of wet, raw earth and cooking smoke touched my senses, exotic perfume in the midst of bone chilling spray.

An exhausted reef heron struggled by dipping and weaving heading for the ship. I stared after the bird, hoping it might find refuge and avoid the cooking pot.

Could Malcolm make the reef? With enormous seas rolling over the coral barrier, it couldn't give him any chance to reach an islet, unless he was driven towards a long band of coral that lay two kilometres north and east of the entrance. This islet, clothed in bushes and palms, stood in the lee side of the island out of the worst of the ocean swells. To my addled mind it presented a glimmer of hope. Deep inside I knew differently. Malcolm lived a land rat, and he was gone, swept under the ocean's gargantuan power. I imagined him saying "jee-sus" as each wave broke over him, wearing down resistance.

S-331 barely registered as a silhouette. Shrouded in spray haze and smoke, she must be doomed to pile up on jagged corals. I wished it so. Why couldn't the damn ship be swallowed whole?

✳

Directly ahead, Jeff, Cris, Kalani and Niau, the other chief, strained. Behind, Millie and a dozen elderly islanders grunted with short, stiff tug-of-war strokes. Fish and several children hung on in the middle, lifting off the ground each time the rope became taut. The last few metres brought us ashore on the edge of the point. I clutched a handful of sand.

Angelina and I rolled off the canoe. There were voices all around. I felt hands, and being lifted, carried in a dream-like world, along the apron of beach to the platform where the scowling *Tiki* stood.

Nearby under a lean-to sheltered fire Zoë rattled off scraps of the venture, describing Malcolm's plunge. Millie walked away. She collapsed in shock, refusing to accept he'd gone.

"He's the bloody father of this child. Now what do I do? Who'd have me now?" She sat apart, staring out to sea as if expecting him to materialise.

Jeff joined me, his back to Millie, and examined the lump on my forehead. He offered warmed coconut milk with a hug, and refrained from asking. His eyes, stressed and shadowed, evaded me.

Fau and Alili rushed in for a snuggle and nose rub. "Fish and smoke," I laughed, too weak to say more. They looked at me and giggled, not wanting to miss a joke.

"We so pleased to meet you gain, eh?" they said in unison, tittering. Jeff ruffled their hair. I sensed his shorthand English lessons were popular.

Kalani approached, two battered hibiscus flowers cupped in her hand. She slipped a yellow one with a wine centre over my right ear. The other, a deep crimson, she offered Angelina. We hugged, leaning against one another in silence.

"We look for you long time, Breezie." Fau called. "Cris very 'upseat', eh. Not sleep."

I watched Cris coiling great lengths of rope. He glanced, gave a terse smile and half bowed. I waved, felt pleased; flattered he'd lost sleep.

The *Tiki* towered over us as if we were an offering to the island's Primal Godhead. Its squint eyes stared expectantly. In the dawn's race, a shaft of silver touched the ridges beyond, slashing the treetops. The *Tiki* glowed in the illuminated backdrop and faded as cloud swept the ridges. Great Shark Tooth's peak thrust out of the murk and vanished.

I fingered the charm and touched the base of the statue. "Thanks for seeing us through," I said, looking up.

Hiva nodded, grinned. Niau stood aloof, obviously disturbed by such heathen reverence, but managed a curt nod.

Zoë and Fish wedged in on the sheltered side of the *Tiki*, wrapped in one another, sharing a hot drink. The chiefs and islanders formed a semi-circle and to our astonishment bared their buttocks to the ship delivering scathing comments in Polynesian.

We clapped, ecstatic with their gesture of defiance.

Cris squatted behind Jeff. I felt his eyes. Sensed he'd stored yearnings I wasn't sure I could give answers to. But in the wild morning light he was awesome.

The wind died and rain lessened to short bursts as each broken cloud dumped. Beyond, the waves shook the foundations of the reef, their explosive impacts magnified as the wind eased.

Numbness gave way to leaden exhaustion. The idea of sleeping without fear rose seductively. Losing Malcolm and the hatred I held for my tormentors wouldn't tip me over the edge. Adrenalin still screwed my emotions.

I managed to re-enact sinking the hook into Wu's neck, thrilling in the wonder of how I did such a thing. I couldn't remember exactly where it caught his flesh. His demonic shriek still echoed in my mind, raising my hackles. There was a fire I didn't realise existed in me. I'd learned I could kill someone. That frightened me. It wasn't altogether the doing that disturbed, rather, the pleasure I felt.

Angelina bunched her chains while Jeff examined the lock. "I owe you and Malcolm a frickin' lot," Angelina said. "All of you." She looked around, flashed a smile.

"*Manava. Manava.*" Several islanders said, bursting into laughter.

"They mean, welcome," Hiva said. "You have given a daughter back to us. Now you are our daughters."

"I am honoured and in your debt." I said.

The islanders broke into new levels of animated dialect.

"Angie. They killed your man?" I said.

"Uncle. Jess Walters." Angelina's face clouded. "Poor bugger. Two of them came to pay a polite visit; at least that's what we thought. The guy with the tattoos, and that Ming character. We made them coffee and sat down for a bit of gossip. Even baked a cake."

"Weren't you afraid, what with the plague?" I said.

"They looked okay, besides Ming was so charming and concerned. A real sweetheart. He asked if we needed anything. Said they had lots of goods and food. I became suspicious when the other one began snooping around looking at everything we had. Jess was edgy too. We only had a pistol, and that was hidden away."

"Yeah. Jeff, my brother, found it. So you came unstuck."

"Yup. Ming's pal went back to their launch to get some Saki drink, he said. He returned with a bloody cannon. Jess just turned with some glasses at the sink and the bastard shot him point blank in the face. I collapsed."

"Hak's pure evil. And Ming. Two-faced," I said.

"Yeah, him and that nutcase Wu." She bit her lip. 'Wu was the worst. I went screaming mad on the ship."

Angelina's voice rose shrill. "In the end I tried to provoke them into killing me. Being raped and starved, beyond hope. It's sickening to be so powerless. Who'd have thought such a brilliant place would be so foul?" Her face screwed up.

"Giving up hope? I know," I said.

❋

Making for home, the spectre of the coiled rope reminded me of an obese caterpillar. The boys and four islanders draped it over their shoulders, swaying and twisting around obstacles.

My legs felt leaden, but my emotions bordered on elation as we followed the foreshore around the point and back to our original landing base. Hugs and *au revoirs* given, and much hand shaking, we struggled up the trail.

On the periphery of vision I saw Jeff lingering, holding Fau's hand, her fingers trailing off his. He gave a squeeze, turned, and embraced Alili. He blushed as I caught his eye. Millie remained lost in her own thoughts.

The storm eased by mid morning, sweeping northward, powered by a chilling sou-westerly. A glory of rays broke through shredded canopy. Patches stood skeletal, stripped of leaf. Palms on the rim of the beach lay bedraggled or flattened. Some leaned at crazy angles, crossing one another. The beach was strewn with palm branches and hundreds of coconuts driven across the lagoon from the outer islets lying to the south.

Our valley fared better. Small stands of bananas drooped, their great broad leaves shredded. Everything sagged, sopping wet.

Swollen streams roared red, burbling and crashing over crags, gouging gullies. Several waterfalls splattered across the camp platform.

Bedding lay soaked under canvas awnings flattened by the buffeting. We passed the morning propping up timbers and hanging sheets over branches to dry, turning the camp into a teepee village. Steam rose, sauna-like.

I sat against the rock shelf basking. Closing my eyes, Malcolm's form appeared, vanishing in haze. Dreams, opaque and mellow swept me into deep sleep.

❋

"Wake up Bree," Zoë said, prodding. "You've been dead two days."

Fish smiled. "You big mess. Sticks in hair." She plucked a twig out. "You have humongous lump."

I lay on a bed of rushes under a tarpaulin. Everything felt sticky. My head throbbed from oversleeping, but through caked eyes the world looked wonderful.

Cris loomed into view. "You must've stirred them right agro. Jeff's kept watch on them. Their launch is in the water. There's a lifeboat, too."

"So what? I've had it with that lot," I yawned and pulled the coat over my head.

"They mean to land and not for a social visit," Cris said. He lifted the coat, waved a cup of mocha Motu-Riva coffee he'd baked and ground up from local beans. It was black and bitter, and good.

"You should've been on board for Ming's birthday," I said.

"Yer goin' warpy again," Cris said.

"Hey. I missed my thirteenth," Zoë said; keen to remind us birthdays were important.

"How's that for luck, pest?" Cris said.

I caught up with reality. "They'll land. You're dead right, Cris. These guys want revenge. Triads have a code of sorts. They hate losing face - especially to females. Reckon I got up their noses."

"What is Triad?" Fish said.

"A gang. Thieves. They steal and flog drugs," Cris said.

"My father's brudder run drugs een Columbia," Fish said, looking pleased she could offer something important.

We stared. Cris choked on his coffee.

"These characters are family, except for two," I said. "The one with glasses and the stubby guy aren't Triad. Specs has some European in him."

"The family that kills together thrills together," Cris said.

"Or vice versa," Jeff said, descending the path.

"You're sick." Zoë said. She poked Cris's ribs. Threw sticks at Jeff.

"They're worse than crims," Angie said. Her fury rose to the point of angering me, but ensured none of us would waver, try to make peace with them.

I hobbled off into the bushes to scratch and think. Both offered little satisfaction. Constipation is a strain, but a period is just vexatious. Bites announced the birth of a new generation of creepies, things that fly, buzz, find ways into your clothing, nip and sting, all inspired to a frenetic din by the saturated jungle and heat. Again we lit smudge pots, fought being on the menu of more than one kind of predator.

Chapter 35

Our impromptu service for Malcolm was brief and heart-felt. The girls set a wreath of flowers afloat on the lagoon as we gathered by the beach.

"Whatever any of us thought about Mal, he was one peculiar character. A sloth. Obnoxious," I said. "But he managed to get on the ship. He didn't have to do that. I probably owe my life to him. Have to admit he was a pretty neat rat, so I'll miss him." I felt awkwardly sad, tinged with guilt, but couldn't find tears.

"Me too," Angie said. "He had guts." Her lip twisted. "He must've been some cool guy."

Millie tried to cope with the history of their relationship, but ended by blubbering about the baby. "I hope it looks like him - if it's a boy," she said as if startled by the possibility it would be a girl and look like him.

Angelina glared as if she'd been bitten. "A what? You mean..."

"Say something, Jeff," I said, ribbing him.

"Well, umm, I guess he turned out a winner. Got a shock when he insisted on going to the ship. Umm, he had lots of angst and paid a hell of a price. Made a good aerial too, eh." Jeff scratched his chin.

Cris remained mute. Nodded, his head hanging.

I noticed him sizing up Angie. Male thing.

"He's not really dead," Zoë said. "Rat's too hard to kill. He's sort o' still with us."

Rat's wreath drifted, eddied with the tide.

We broke away to escape the emotional low by eating, each of us brooding over what to do next. Chomping into stringy goat's meat isn't a fun fair. Memories of farm goats eating undies and used tissues didn't dampen my appetite.

"If we don't stop them there's no place to hide except the hill tops," Jeff said, chewing gristle.

"There's no water there. No food," Millie bleated. "I couldn't bear going hungry." She rubbed her stomach, made me wonder if her body was simply freaked out from the voyage, or from being banged and she wasn't pregnant.

⁂

"If. When they come we've gotta deal with them somehow. Chances are we can't kill all of them," I said.

"This Hak guy and Chun. If they go down will the others run?" Cris said.

"Specs and The Gnome. They're mechanics, not killers," I said. "They never looked part of it. Leave them alone unless they actually shoot at us."

"I'm glad you can make that distinction. Why not ambush?" Cris said. "I've worked out all the distances for the approaches to camp, and the best strong points." He held up the new crossbow, complete with recurve arms.

"Says you. Simpleton," Millie said.

"Macho words. Against what they've got? One rocket and we're dog food," I said. Cris's romantic notions of fight ticked me off; still, he was the only one who'd thought ahead about confronting them and shown guts about it. His cleverness impressed.

"How's it supposed to happen, brainwave?" Millie said.

"Simple, airhead. We know these valleys. They don't. They don't know we're armed, so it'll be a big surprise. Draw them into the narrowest gully. Maybe a decoy to lure them."

"And who's the victim?" I said.

"No need to pick. I'm the bait," Angie said. She leaned over the ledge above us. She'd taken to showering several times daily, as if trying to scrape off filth they'd heaped on her.

I sensed her morbid desire for action.

"Me too. I'm with Angie," Zoë said.

"Not on your life, flea," Jeff said. "You're too head-strong. You stuck your nose out. I told you not to go to the ship, eh."

"I counted for something, eh. I found them, eh!" Zorro's jaw set. She fumed. "Didn't I? I'm faster than any of you sloths."

Jeff was beaten.

Despite Jeff's grizzling, the plan took shape. Angie and Zoë would keep watch on the beach. Of the three valleys that led in our general direction, the first we explored after landing was the most obvious choice for ambush. It was narrower. The flanks rose sharply, thick with vegetation. By barricading the top of the trail where the valley floor narrowed to a few metres, the only escape would be back the way they came, but not before the trap was sprung.

We spent the morning cutting timbers for a log barrier. Cris and Jeff gathered rock, which we stacked as reinforcement at each end. Every timber was pegged and bound with rope and vine. Branches were rammed into the ground in front to slow them and act as camouflage. From the sharp turn in the trail below they'd only see greenery from less than a hundred metres and be in full view well before reaching it.

Hiva, in a state of agitation, arrived with an equally vexed Niau. Both offered islander support by blocking the common trails. They had few shells for their shotgun. Niau frowned, paced about deep in thought, obviously seriously disturbed. I judged his Christian beliefs gnawed at his conscience. Striking the odd angry drum offered a way out of his dilemma.

Hiva was blunt about their ability to resist. "Our people can make much noise. Beat drums. Make hell of good war chant. Maybe keep men away, make pit traps." He waved massive arms.

Solemnly, we nodded, knowing their defensive attitude. It remained for us to sort out strategy and confront Chun and his gang.

Hiva, frowning, gestured me aside while the others tried softening up Niau, who as an oddity wasn't much of a talker. "We have big problem. Two from refugee boat escape. They hide on north side. They look sick, run from me. We are much afraid."

My jaw dropped, heart sank. "I saw someone running away the day Ming killed the refugees. Damn, I'd forgotten," I said, dreading the implications. "It was a crap of a day. So, why tell me now?"

"Mareva call you Healer of many things."

"Oh, that's my mum. I just patch up holes."

Hiva grimaced. "Niau is what you say, a wild card. He is hunting, wants them dead. Now. Burn bodies."

"Ridiculous, that's murder, he's Christian."

"Make no difference. Mareva say he very bitter. His family all die in Wave. You find these people. Plague must not come to Motu-Riva."

I realised Hiva had dumped a load on me and not offered a clue how I'd deal with it, and right in the middle of our present danger. Resentment welled, but I held my tongue, resolved to keep their presence secret from the others, to face one catastrophe at a time.

The chiefs left as suddenly as they came, keen to make preparations. Kalani remained.

She explained they'd made drums from old World War Two oil containers. Pigskins stretched taut made a deep sound that carried high in the hills, into every valley.

Kalani rose to leave. She smiled and we hugged, but she'd become strangely awkward and shy. I suspected her hormones on the loose, which made me feel hot, giddy.

As her form faded I remembered how disturbing the drums were the evening Zoë and I bunked down in the cockpit. They'd materialised, ghostly vibrations from the island's ancient past when wars raged and feasts celebrated the sheer joy of surviving.

Zoë and Fish joined me to slap coarse mud between logs. I brooded over prospects of plague, remembered my fever from the outback and Arie's gruesome death.

"I'm petrified, Bree. Rat's dead. Nothing's right any more."

"Si. Senior Rat was a very funee one," Fish said.

"Yeah. I can't believe he went like that. He was brave. No, mad, reckless," I said, feeling depressed.

"I liked him - mostly. He was hot," Zoë said.

"He was that alright. Too hot."

"What's life without passion? Lots of it." Zoë said matter-of-fact.

"So. You've got it all worked out?"

"Chilli hot," Fish giggled.

We cracked up laughing.

"He was a tainted talent," I sighed.

"You really hated him," Zoë said. Her eyes narrowed.

"Sometimes. I could've strangled. He was always dodgy. You know about old dogs? New tricks. Poor Rat did try to fit in."

"Yeah." Zoë rolled her eyes.

"That's crude." I flung mud at her. Mud, rendered a thickened soup, gushed in every direction. I dragged both squealing into the mix. We wallowed in its rich redness until, weak from laughter, we lay panting, lobster skinned.

"Jeezus. I'm a corpse and this is all you slags can do?"

"Malcolm. Rat!" We cried, struggling to stand, spitting mud.

He sat on the top of the ridge a pauper king holding audience over low life.

"You're supposed to be dead," Zoë accused. "You made me miserable. Angry." She burst into tears.

"How'd you do it?" I said. "The current..."

"You were cactus," Zoë blubbered.

Malcolm slid down, limped to join us. His face was pallid. Cheeks sunken, shorts hanging frayed; gaping tears exposed a lacerated thigh. The pistol grip stuck out, hung low inside the waistband.

"You guys left me," he mimicked hurt.

"There was nothing..."

"No friggin' worries," he said. "I was swearin' mad. Called you a chicken-shit bitch, Bree." He winked. "It was weird, man. Next thing I knew I'm movin', like on a river." He waved his arms. "Next thing, I'm headin' for that black scow."

"Blackjack?" Zoë said.

"Wow. You caught a back eddy," I said. "The reefs like a hook. It forced the water around, so you got a ride south. Shivers. How many lives have you got?"

We mauled him with muddy hugs.

"Eddy. Freddy. Whatever. Got sliced up. Bloody coral. Otta be a law against it. Didn't get to the boat. I landed on some miserable island, waves washin' over it the whole damn time. Slept on some coconut palms heaped up. Met me rels. Shared it with a bunch of the hairiest bleedin' rats. Showed me respect. How cool is that?" He nodded. "Oh, buy the way; I heard the whole damn wake. Not bad."

Voices. Hurried footsteps. Cris and Angie burst into the clearing.

"What? I can't believe it's you," Cris said. "You're unreal, man. It's good to see you," Cris fumbled for Malcolm's hand. They pumped, uncertain of the novelty of friendship; ghosts of old animosities.

Angie wrapped herself around him and kissed him full on the mouth. "You poor, poor maggot. You're a wreck. Look at you." She swept him off towards camp, arm around shoulder.

Malcolm's limp appeared worse; his hand crept high around her waist, then we saw his lacerated feet, a mass of shredded skin, bloodied.

"You really need to look after yourself. You've gotta eat more," she said, as they faded from view.

I stared open mouthed at Cris.

He shrugged. "Beats me. He's down then up for the count. Some bastards get all the luck."

"Some bastards make it. I'm famished," I said.

"I won't take you anywhere looking like that."

"I am what I am, besides, my blemishes are my own."

"Still, there's enough sauce to look at," Cris said, raising a brow, grinning cheek.

"Try this on," I said, winking at Zoë and Fish.

"Hey. I don't need your bloody beauty treatment. Hey!"

Chapter 36

I watched Jeff tapping and fiddling with the radio, prodding it to life. Dampness had found its way through the oilskins he'd used as protection. It whined and moaned, full of mid-morning static. Stations welled up out of the noise soup and faded. By nightfall Radio Moscow's English station joined the noise, playing a hollow martial tune, as stark as their winter desolation.

"Why so down? You're looking better. The lump's gone," Jeff said.

"Damn thing's growing inside. My head's splitting."

"Maybe some food, eh? Bodies like it, Breezy. I could play a tune on your ribs."

I chewed the last of the goat's meat Cris bagged. He swore up and down it was a pig in the brush. Macho hunter needed glasses.

"Fau. She's casting moon eyes?" I said.

"She's a fast learner. Alili too."

"Learning what?"

"English, nosey. They're easily distracted. Laugh at anything." Jeff said, trying to be unconcerned.

"It's your quiet charm, Jeffie. Irresistible. There's more than fish and smoke? Fire? Maybe?"

Jeff grinned. "Fau's special, eh."

"I don't envy you. I mean, making a choice."

"No need to. Anyway, they're inseparable. I'll keep em' guessing, eh." Jeff's grin broadened. "They're teaching me about the island."

"Oh yeah, Spin another one."

Jeff switched channels. "The demons are up to something. They take off with food every day, head for the escarpment. They usually hit the beach. Something's up."

"Maybe they're just exploring. I've never known Zoë to walk in a straight line." I felt uneasy, remembering Hiva's warning.

"Millie. What about her? She's really stressed. Angelina's

much too strong for her; besides, she's still twitchy about Malcolm. You'd think she's missed the race."

"She slept by me, umm, she was cold last night. I kept her warm. Hey, that's all." Jeff shut off.

"I saw. Give a little more attention? Keep making her feel needed. Little things."

"She's pregnant," Jeff frowned. Flicked the dial. "It's Malcolm's. I'm not cut out for proxy fathering."

"Millie's sensitive. She's afraid. Maybe she's not pregnant. Females have false pregnancies. Anyway, if she is, the child's part of all of us, like Millie? Rat could only be a floating father. A child needs constants. Real role models."

Jeff brooded. "Yeah. She's not so painful now. A bit sugary. She sure can cook, eh."

Jeff would think of food.

"The launch is still alongside," Cris said.

"They'll come even if the ship's engine's fixed, do us, then leave," I said. "Lets hope the prop and rudder aren't stuffed. Can't imagine co-existing with deadshits."

"We aim to kill. Just like old times, Bree?" Malcolm nudged.

I couldn't find the words to tell him where to stuff his 'old times'.

"What about any wounded?" Cris said.

"Put the bastards out of their misery." Angie said. "If any of you can't do it, I will."

"Wow," Malcolm whispered. He stared in reverence. "Death's Angel."

My dirtiest look went straight over his shoulder. "Specks and the other guy. We need a mechanic," I said.

"What for? You want an overhaul?" Malcolm sniggered.

I raised an eyebrow. Angelina belted him.

"She means if Blackjack ever floats, someone to make sure it's in working order," Jeff said.

"Blackjack? Yer off yer rocker. This is one dude that ain't going to sea again." Malcolm's jaw set, arms folded.

We found sleep impossible, our minds playing out scenarios of a showdown. I stewed in mind-lock, feared the worst.

※

Cris leapfrogged down the trail, gasping for breath. "They're coming. Get the hell up. Move it. They'll be around the point by now." He disappeared with the crossbow over his shoulder, clutching a dozen arrows.

I sucked a deep breath of chilled morning air, stared skyward. My heart hammered.

Jeff sounded the air horn to warn Angie and Zoë, who'd stayed overnight by the beach as lookouts. Fish and Millie rushed away to warn the islanders camped in the eastern vales.

Cris and Jeff headed for the strong points we'd carefully chosen, which were on the crest of each ridge flanking the gully. These were high, well clothed in foliage, and offered a good line of fire down the throat of the trail at its narrowest point. Cris cut away just enough brush to give each position a clear fire line.

Malcolm and I watched from the barricade. I fidgeted with the newest crossbow, conscious of its sensitive trigger.

The log barrier suddenly struck me as being flimsy, barely five metres wide and head high, clearly incapable of holding back a serious attack. I crouched behind the rock pile supporting its left side.

Water gushed under the logs, a blood red offering from the island's core. It reminded me of Mareva's tales of bloody battles and the anger of slighted gods. I stroked the charm's ridges, thick with sweat. I kissed it. Tasted salt.

We waited.

Above the water spill parrots raised riot as if stirred up. Malcolm and I looked at one another, thinking the same thing. We wouldn't hear Chun and company until they came well within view. The trail below still lay in darkness.

Jeff signalled from his position directly across and above us. He waved the glock pistol.

I wondered how Angie and Zoë were doing. If they waited until Chun landed and made a panicked retreat up the trail to their own high point, Chun's mob should take the bait. We shouldn't have long to wait. What if they split up? Still, there were only five. I guessed they would stick together. Thank heavens Wu wouldn't be there.

"This is crap, Bree," Mal grizzled.

"You're nervous?"

"Yeah. I'm a doer. Can't stand sittin'. I've run out of things to scratch."

Rat looked sickly pale, scrawnier, like a wind would blow him over.

I made a face. Strained to hear. Voices, high pitched and shrill, cut through the dawn chill.

"That's them comin' to the party," Malcolm said, cherishing confrontation. "Get yer twitchy finger off the trigger. Remember? We don't fire until Cris does."

His pushy I know best attitude burned me up. Why do guys have to be so macho in a crisis? I hid my anger. We peered into the shadows. I lost sense of time. The distance to the beach was a kilometre. They'd surely show up within minutes.

More shouts, much closer.

"That's Angie," Malcolm said. "Ain't she somethin'?"

"She's latched hooks on you."

"Angie's scarred, ye know, like inside, but she's cool. We're on one another's radar."

"So is Chun." I risked a peek. I whispered, "There's someone in the shadows." There was much chatter from the darkness beyond the turn in the trail.

A mother pig and five piglets emerged in haste, making for the barrier. They milled around, mother grunting orders. They began nosing about, uncertain what to do.

Our quarry arrived, muttering in dialect, oblivious of any need for quiet. Hak appeared first. He gripped a nasty looking automatic. They slowed, studying the banks, squinting into the first slash of sunlight entering the glade.

Hak waved the others on. Ming emerged, then the Gnome. They exchanged words. Ming laughed.

My heart sank, stomach knotted. Wu strode into view, bare to the waist, his neck and right hand swathed in rag bandages. He held a rocket grenade launcher. A satchel container of projectiles hung on his back. Wu radiated hostility.

Mal and I exchanged a pained look.

The mass of Chun laboured behind. They picked their way, slipping on uneven ground. Hak spotted the pigs and the maze of branches. He raised a hand.

Suddenly I caught the flicker of a shaft in flight. It disappeared in the bank by his head. Time froze. They looked at one another. Hak barked a command. Three scattered to the bank on Jeff's side, scanning the ridge.

Jeff popped off three shots. The vale resounded in the shock waves. Pig mayhem. Mad squeals. Frantic to escape, the mother dove into the stream and emerged thrashing on our side, wild-eyed. Her young tried to follow and were swept down the stream uttering shrill cries.

Hak and Ming opened up a barrage of fire across the ridges. Showers of tuff and branches rained on them. Chun's voice sing-songed commands. Hak swore.

Malcolm snap shot an arrow.

I jumped out and fired a shaft.

We felt a heavy *SHOOMPH* rip air open to our right, pitching both of us on our backs. Log splinters flew. Malcolm landed in my lap.

My eardrums rang, blown deaf. Dazed, I stared at a trickle of blood on my leg.

"Shee-it!" Malcolm grated, his hands on his ears.

I gagged on explosive stench. Our barrier smoked, now a jumble of splinters. The pig squeals faded.

"Reload, Bree. Make it fast."

I saw them rush towards us, but mud brought Wu down. Hak slid off the bank into the stream. His face screwed up.

I struggled to lever the string back onto the trigger latch and fumbled a bolt into the slot.

It was then Hiva and the islanders began beating the drums, building up a deep, steady rhythm. Their urgent pulse filled the air, sounding closer than they were.

Wu and Ming darted glances everywhere. Chun's guttural bark went unheeded.

Jeff fired two well-aimed shots. Hak yelped, held his head. He sprayed the slope above. Leaves rained like confetti. Malcolm fired low. Ming screeched, clutching his arm. He dropped to one knee and fired. Bullets clipped. Snapped branches.

I aimed at Chun's clumsy bulk obscured behind the others. My bolt vanished in the smoke and glare. Chun looked down in surprise. He abruptly spun around and ambled off with a peculiar, lopsided gait. The Gnome, who'd stood gob-stopped, dropped his weapon, overtook Chun and vanished.

I shook, fumbling, angry I couldn't load the crossbow quickly. My bolt discharged, disappearing into the mud.

Malcolm stared, his eyes dark and feral. "Cripes, yer really on a rush. Yer wired."

I frowned, torn by excitement and fear, sucked in air. The desire to kill fevered me as the drums intensified. Their chant rose and fell, wild and urgent, magnified amongst the crags.

Wu sent another missile into the hill directly below Jeff. A slab of waterlogged slope gave way in slow motion, carrying a tangle of greenery with it.

Shrieking rose over the din. Wu, howling like a banshee, fell back against the embankment. He thrashed, clawing at his chest, stiffened.

Hak and Ming bolted down the trail, firing as they retreated.

We made a dash for Wu. "They're on the run. Don't shoot." I cried. I reached him first. His eyes bulged, staring up beyond me. Face contorted, lips curled as if to say, "I don't understand," his throat gargled up blood. Surprise softened his face. A crimson stream pooled in his navel, pouring onto the launcher.

Cris joined us. "One dead," he said gazing, mesmerised by Wu's death rattle.

"Your lesson wasn't missed. Guess you'd call it a stiff one," Malcolm sniggered, "It went right through him."

I grabbed the launcher and ripped the warhead pack off Wu.

"You intend shootin' that thing?" Malcolm said in disbelief. "Watch where yer pointing it."

"How do you load it?" I said.

"Stop lookin' for a chamber. You stick the rocket thingo down the front end, you know, male to female," Cris said. "Then you sight your..."

Angie screamed. Her defiance told us they were close to the beach. A shotgun boomed followed by a mass of automatic fire. Malcolm raced off followed by Cris.

"Wait. You'll run into them," Jeff said.

We soon caught Malcolm's form, his feet wrapped in rags, limping double time. Cris ranged far ahead. This was the old Cris. He verified history repeats itself; may as well stick his ass in their faces.

Angie lay slumped against a tree fern, her head hanging over the stream's bank. Zoë held her head out of the water.

"She's fallen off the ridge. Knocked out," Zoë said. "I recon she peppered the bald guy. It's a wonder they didn't hit her. There was dirt flying..."

"I'm stayin' with her," Malcolm said, wheezing for breath.

We pressed on, stopping short of the open beach. Cris crouched behind fallen palms used as a lookout.

Chun's bulk limped beyond, his right leg scribing a jagged slash in the sand. Splotches of blood punctuated each footstep. I

266

saw the crossbow bolt wedged in the bone of his ham foot. It protruded from his heel. He wheezed, air expressing from the rolls of fat. Chun stopped, and pivoted, squinting into the sun.

Specs was already drifting out in the lifeboat. He waved both hands in the air. "Don't shoot. Don't shoot."

Hak and Ming struggled with the second heavier craft roughly a hundred metres away.

I aimed the weapon and fired. I shrieked and jumped as the projectile left the tube. A gush of water rose beyond the launch.

Ming slumped in the water, unable to climb onto the boat. His right arm hung useless.

Hak rolled into the craft. He fired, ripping off chunks of palm trunk.

My second shot struck the bow in front of Hak, sending him in a ragged back flip. An arm spiralled beyond his torso. Ming collapsed back in the water, struggling to stay afloat. Jeff and Cris sprinted to the boat and pulled him up on the sand.

I approached Chun who wallowed like a beached albino walrus. He studied the crossbow slung across my side, the smoking rocket tube. Drilling me, his eyes squinted hatred. "Bitch. You finish Chun off? He mocked, his face screwed up, his nose swollen out of shape.

The lust I'd felt evaporated. It was impossible to execute him face-to-face.

Chun's expression drooped, his breathing running ragged.

I tried to find something meaningful to say, to scorn him out, but words failed me.

I crossed to Ming, motioning Cris to watch Chun. Ming sprawled, belly bulbous above scrawny legs. He smiled, lips clenched. "You save Ming. I good to girls. Your flend."

"You've got a warped sense of humour," I said, furious he'd the nerve to lecture me how to treat him.

"I not hurt you. Please help now. Ming hurt bad."

I studied the perforations on his chest. His arm bore a surface wound.

Cris called, "hey! The big guy, he's not breathing." Cris nudged Chun's shoulder. Chun rolled sideways.

"He's dead as a doornail."

Specs came ashore. The Gnome materialised from a forest of pandanus, hands on the top of his bullet head. Both smiled for their lives. We rigged a pallet and made them carry Ming back to camp.

"So. You figured to kill us all? You two are deep in it," I said.

"Please. You not kill us. You don't understand," Specs said.

Chapter 37

We watched as Ming's condition worsened. Heavy buckshot made a mess of his shoulder and chest. Using tweezers, I probed, managing to remove a few. Ming gritted his teeth each time, no doubt cursing in dialect and the usual crude Anglo-Saxon. We were low of painkillers and the remaining antiseptic cream was precious. I sat with him as fever spread, his face flushed.

"You think bad of Ming. You never tell me your name."

"That's for my friends." I stared beyond him for a long time. "Bree."

"Blee. That is a good name. Strong," he grimaced. "What it mean?"

"Mum says it means on good days I patch things up. I'm a wilful bitch on bad ones."

Ming looked puzzled.

"I don't take crap," I said.

"Auh. You say other day, you born 1996. That Year of Rat. Very strong."

Rat? I thought it weird, ironic.

"My name mean 'bright light'," he cast a wry smile.

"That's seriously off knowing what you've done." A flash of recognition crossed his face. His breathing shallowed.

When I sensed he was going, I held his hand. To die alone was frightening no matter what level he'd sunk to. He once had a wife. Kids. He hadn't laid a hand on me except when I baited him - not that he wouldn't have eventually. It was some crazy mind game of his, like I was a toy girl. I wondered who'd won enough at gambling to claim me. A morbid thought.

❊

"He was sure fixed on you," Angie said. She cupping the bitter coffee we'd come to appreciate.

Malcolm limped on angry feet, sat close to her. She offered a sip. Kissed his shoulder. "Poor maggot."

Malcolm moaned, "somethin' terrible happened, man. Me dope's washed away."

"You're tragic," Zoë said. "You *are* the dope."

I smiled.

"Wuz growin' real good." Malcolm brooded. Angie busied placating him offering another addiction.

The boys, with help from Specs and The Gnome, placed Hak and Wu's bloated bodies into the lifeboat by rolling it up a log ramp. Chun's corpse, now blackening, was bloated with gases as if to explode.

"Lets torch them like the Vikings used to do. Pile it up with brush," Angie said.

"No burn them. Not burn." Fish stood, her dark eyes flashing. "No fire. Please."

"Why? What's wrong?" Angie said.

Fish opened up. "Bad men come to my house one night. They break in. Steal everything." Tears streamed, her voice neared hysteria. "They hurt my mamma and big sister. I hide under bed. They hurt Juanita terrible. She scream and scream." Fish's voice faded to a whisper, "my house on fire. I try to pull mamma from house. She too big." Fish spread her arms. "Fire too fast. I choke on smoke."

"You got away," I said.

"I run out front with kitchen knife. Cut one man in back. He hit my face. I ran into bushes."

"You found a boat and we found you."

"*Si.* Now you are my family," she said, her jaw set.

"There's nothing dry to burn them with," Cris said. "Let's have the sea swallow 'em. Is that okay?"

"No fire?"

"No fire," Cris said, his voice soothing. I watched him wrap her in his arms like a fragile flower, felt heat seep into the pit of my stomach.

✳

Specs soon lost his fear. The Gnome developed a smile to make up for his lack of English.

Cris and Jeff grilled Specs, discovering how they'd travelled from Celebes Island, along Northern New Guinea and through the Solomon Sea, eastward into the Central Pacific.

Specs described the horrors of the plague in his seaport town in minute detail, enough for word to get around amongst the islanders. All but Fau and Alili, being orphans, went to ground. I feared Niau already hunted high and low for the refugees.

"Chun promised us good pay. We look after engine. He not tell us where they go."

"Why couldn't you help the girls? Me."

"Hak say he would cut our throats if we talk with you. I know what you do with food," Specs beamed. "I say nothing to them. I hope you get away."

"You were outside the galley?" I said. I remembered many noises in the night's wildness. "Why'd they burn our boat?"

"Anger. They keep other boat, what you call Blackjack. I think Ming and Wu have plans to sail away."

Specs' real name was Antonio. He was from the town of Tarakan on Borneo. The Gnome came from Mindanao in the Philippines. Lope' by name, he was of Portuguese-Malay descent. Much to Fish's annoyance, He knew little of the language. She peppered him with insults in Spanish. He grinned, suffering the attention.

They were allowed to live on the ship and finish repairs. We soon found contraband below decks near the bow. There was a mix of weapons and ammunition, enough for a small army. Jeff found C-4 explosives as well as mines, fuses and detonators. Malcolm located their dope, blocks of opium, enough to stone all of Australia.

"That'd be made into heroin," Malcolm said, fingering a slab sealed in plastic. "Worth millions."

There was little argument. The ship must be moved into deep water beyond the reef and sunk. Malcolm hedged, sullen with the idea of so much waste. He gave in rather too easily, but Angie had him well in tow.

Talk about house cleaning after the big blow. Nobody wanted to work. We felt a fresh sense of freedom, like it was after first landing, so it took a fortnight to make the platform liveable.

※

I needed Mareva's wisdom. Niau's threat to kill innocent people weighed heavily on me, ruined sleep.

She sat under her tiny awning, stooped, her head tilted sideways, as if listening for some mystical notes. She grinned, peg toothed. I sat opposite, her gnarled hands grasping mine. Kalani preened nearby.

"I missed you. Too many days gone," I said.

"Mareva not miss you. My spirit always with you. Yes. Know your fears, old and new." She gazed across the lagoon, her grey hair swirling.

Mareva fingered my charm. "Spirit ghosts watch you."

Wu slashed so hard with the knife that dreadful night. The blade struck the amulet leaving a sharp imprint like a tattoo on my chest.

"The long haired one with the ear ring. He was cursed," Mareva said. "I have eyes."

I nodded, realised who her agents were.

"There is great danger you must face. You must find people from boat. Others on boat die of terrible disease. Hiva see body in water. Fever not of island kind. They bring it on island. You tell me once you have bad fever and live."

"That wasn't this plague. Just some bush fever."

"Find them before Niau does."

"And then what?" I stared, dumfounded, angry, too tired to think.

"Gods say signs right. You will know what to do."

Do? I felt prickly. Were they newly infected? We knew the virus took weeks from contact to begin attacking, melting body organs. I fought panic, resolved to hunt them down on my own.

"Hiva soon invite all of you to our feast. Rat Man is welcome. He very brave. A warrior with basket heart." She beat her breast. "His feelings come and go."

I laughed, "hero of sorts. The Gods must've hung around him for amusement. Is he forgiven for stealing the chicken?"

Mareva grinned. "Tell Rat Man he must do a chicken dance. Don't tell him Hiva will judge. He must dress."

"That's fantastic. He'll freak out. I'll tell Mal the Gods will be there. Angie can set him up."

"*Tupapa'u*, spirit ghost, always make mischief."

"Bree loves mischief. Life." I, yawned, beamed.

"You have more who are warriors. One has passion for you. *Lamoure*."

"Love?" I hedged. "Can't think of anyone worth the bother."

Mareva laughed, rocking back and forth.

Kalani joined us. She was dressed to kill. I'd begun to seriously suspect whom she intended as victim. Her black hair shone, accentuating a crown of yellow-orange flowers ringing her brow. I felt a wreck. We left for our camp hand-in-hand and rehashed our tales of escape. She went off with Fish, who adored her as a lost sister. I sensed Kalani's tension, desires stirring.

Millie lost her spirit somewhere in the maze of happenings. I dragged her away from camp on the pretext of escaping drudgery, but in reality, to have a good scrub and spill emotion baggage.

"Jeff says you were a great help with the radio."

"He's such a fusspot. I wish I could get around his front. He hedges, like you said."

"Still waters run deep."

"I'll drown trying."

"He's affectionate in small ways. Kept you warm at night. That's a big output."

"Had to wrap his arm around me." Millie's brow creased.

"He's a slow burner, Millie. He respects you."

"Jeff's not slow when Fau hits the scene," Millie pouted. "It's like she belted him with a mallet."

"It's a bit of P R. He prepares. They recite."

"Hah! More like..."

"Hey, Jeff won't go native, at least, not much. Maybe if she fires him up, you can burn him down. Maybe you'll become friends, that kind of close. Less complicated."

"Oh, Bree. I do like him."

I studied the supple sweep of her stomach, pink in the cold water. It appeared firmer. Millie looked older from all her worries and insecurities, more focused.

"Scab brain. Umm, Cris. He's still keen on you. You know how he tries to do clever things."

"He's awesome. He's not cutting you down so much."

"Every other day. I can dish it out too. Umm, I saw him climbing a palm. Zoë gave him heaps."

We laughed and hugged.

"Anything might happen - unless he breaks something vital," I said.

"That's not possible." Millie said shocked by the notion. "He's too..."

"It's true. Can't imagine one in a splint."

We locked eyes and shrieked.

Zorro and the twins joined us. Angelina arrived soon after with Fish on her shoulder. Seven's a crowd for showering. Angie's figure reminded me of Sascha's, only tall, proud, my height. We squeezed in under the cascade, ecstatic to be alive. Kalani was missing.

❋

Word of the feast brought a flurry of activity. The girls collected hundreds of shells. Zoë and I searched the highest ridges of the northern escarpment and gorges for feathers.

I hunted along the northern shores for the two survivors, and exhausted, realised there were too many places to hide. I remembered Jeff saying Zorro and Fish were up to no good. Noted the two toasted breadfruit and fish sandwiches she'd made, wrapped in broadleaf, much too big for their appetites; when confronted, said they'd put it down, lost it. Both played dumb.

Zoë collected fallen feathers from roosting birds. Ms Cliffhanger had the nerve to tell us she'd caught some bare handed and plucked "just a few tail feathers."

Kalani brought us tapa cloth to make skirts.

We used stripped coconut shells, burnt and scraped smooth to make bras. Soot and oil rubbed in made them shine. Seashells threaded on heavy twine linked them together. Jeff drilled the holes and insisted on helping to fit them. We egged him on, hoping to make him blush. Tongue-in-cheek, he offered to make a big hole in the middle to "lessen pressure." Zoë decorated by gluing a conical limpet on each of hers since she didn't have much to show.

Millie opted for a seashell bra. Cris bagged her; suggested thousands of shells might do for starters.

The boys were at a loss about decoration, but promised to come up with something big.

With a few days to go, our greatest headache was to find enough food. I wondered where the big porkers holed up. There were at least five groups on the island.

Cris fidgeted about, unusually nervy, even for him.

"You doin' anything?"

"What's up?" I said, offering cheek.

274

"Umm. A bit of hunting." He fiddled with smudge pots.

"What's the prey?"

"A pig or two. It'll take a while. Maybe all night. By the way, you're a great shot," Cris said. Winked.

"That's original Crissie. Thanks."

He smirked, rolled a blanket up. I sensed his mood, felt giddy.

We hiked to the high ridges by sunrise hoping to catch porkers nosing around before they went to ground. We scoured trails near Great Shark. Since the storm, a fresh tapestry of flowers bloomed across the meadows, fingering up the sides of the peaks. Goats grazed warily on the next ridge. A flock of red crested parrots screeched by, doing aerobatics over the cliffs.

Cris showed me his shaded hunting blind he'd set up overlooking a gully where an animal trail led to a series of tiny pools.

The air thickened in a thousand perfumes, softening senses. I leaned over, peering into the gully as a distraction, studied the cool water trickling over burnt lava. Cris leaned against the bank behind. I sensed his eyes exploring, so I gingerly loaded and sighted the crossbow, ignored him.

"Your back's beautiful. Poetry." His voice was deeper and soft. "I can count every vertebrae."

I laughed my dismay, braced for more, refraining from saying, "Oh. You think I'm skinny?"

He was beyond his usual furtive digs, couldn't imagine anyone finding beauty in a bony spine. I sensed there was more to his fantasy. I imagined his rehearsals, wondered how he'd coped with his frustrations.

His fingertips touched, tracing down my back.

I flinched. "What do you mean by poetry? Open verse or rhyme?" I watched a plover alight below and mince along the pool rim, pausing to stare at its reflection.

"Well, umm. Rhyming."

"Meaning I'm predictable and lumpy?"

"No! No. I think you're, umm, really different."

"Free verse? Up hill, down dale?"

"What? Oh, yeah." He chuckled. "Your curves are cool."

"Ice castle cool?"

Cris winced.

I mocked, "It's the same for guys, I mean, look at Mal's physique."

"Yer jokin', Bree. He's a weed. You don't think he's..."

"Why be so sensitive, Crissie?" I knew Cris soured when Malcolm actually volunteered to find me on the ship. "He's built like wire. Interesting." I flushed, glanced.

"Yeah? Girls are so different. You know. Temper. Feelings. What turns them, you, on."

"Crissie, is this a muddle in anatomy or psychology?"

"I just mean you're se..."

I clamped my hand on his mouth. Blushed. Felt hot and prickly. "I'm not. Mal thinks I'm too stuffy."

"He doesn't see you like I do."

"Meaning?" Thank heavens for that. Thoughts blurred and my stomach knotted. I avoided his gaze, studied the gully shadows.

Cris smiled. "I've got all twenty-five." He said, matter of fact.

"What? Oh. Okay," I laughed. "You want to buy me? It's not important. The wager's silly, a distraction."

Cris looked agitated. "Zoë's my witness."

I touched his arm. I knelt closer and kissed his cheek. He radiated heat.

"Thanks for wiping Wu. I couldn't bear to see him live."

"I picked him out. Saw the bandages and knew he was the guy you'd hooked. I was scared. Can't imagine what you went through." He shook his head. "I loved your braveness."

"I tried to wipe them and blew it," I sighed.

"Aw, come on, I'm amazed you had the guts to keep trying. Umm, stick to safe dishes now, maybe a touch of spice."

"Can't stand curry. Last curry set my ass on..."

"Fire? You've got all the ingredients I want," Cris said.

The sensation of bumbling into something new and dangerous made me jittery. My stomach growled. I resolved to be bold, since he was hedging around, and I wasn't helping. "I'm not prickly," I said. "I do care, want to know you."

"After all my pranks?"

"Yep. Remember the ice water raid?"

Cris grinned. "Never knew you could fly. I was chuffed."

"I had a cold shower after that. You really made me queasy. Didn't want you to know. Hey, you still had to pay for it."

"We're safe here. Nobody nosing around like Zoë." He brushed a wisp of hair from my face.

"Safe?" I laughed, nervous, and afraid he'd notice.

Cris suddenly kissed my nose. He nuzzled into my neck, blowing across my ear. I cringed. My cheek twitched. Everything suddenly felt fuzzy, too hot.

"I'm worried about - you know - don't want..."

"Neither do I. Look at the mess..." I stopped short of panning Millie.

He fumbled in his pocket, pulled out a condom. Cherry Brand. Deep ridged.

"Where'd you get that thing? How old is it?"

"Jeff and I got a pack from Papa's store."

"So. That's what Zoë and Millie cracked up about when they took a stock count. Hey. Why do you think I want to, you know, do it?"

"I've wanted you ever since the card night. You stirred me something awful. I read the signs right. Right?"

"Only one?" I mocked, balancing the condom on my fingertip. His eyes danced with mischief, pupils black, large. Cris shrugged, suddenly looked foolish.

"Cris, this doesn't have to be a Love thing. Hey, trying to stay in one piece on the ship. I never felt so alone. I do want, umm, I mean that whole stinking mess made me see life differently. It killed a few hang-ups about the past. What if I'd died? Never made love?"

"Umm. You mean..."

"Shush up. I'm just as nervous." I kissed him harder than intended, and pulled his lower lip back. Cris was awash in sweat.

Laughter in the distance warned us the girls were nosing about. "Zoë's a tart. She'll come undone," I whispered, exchanging small kisses.

Cris slipped behind me and snagged my back tie strings with his teeth. His hands brushed my side and spread across my stomach. I arched and leaned back against his chest. He toyed at the neck ties, which knotted.

"*Deja vu*. We've been here before, fumblefingers." We laughed.

Cris teased the tie end across my breasts, curling it around. They hardened. Ached. I closed my eyes, focusing, as his fingertips played in lazy circles around my navel, then radiated in growing sweeps, leaving a trail of tension.

"They're hot," he said.

"What?"

"They really stick out, like tiny towers."

"It's the family genes," my cheek quivered. I grabbed a shock of hair, thick and oily, pulling him around. We hugged. His tongue probed. I realised he'd popped the stud of my shorts, prised and pulled them down. The more he touched the more I found reason to help.

"That's so, so delicious. Don't stop," I whispered.

Cris hung over me, a hesitant musician searching on an untuned instrument. I closed my eyes, heard my shorts land on the crossbow, which snapped off, sending them flying into the gully. We stared at one another, stunned, and broke up laughing.

His hand brushed up my leg, shifted inside my thighs. My pulse compressed. I caught my breath.

He stopped, began messing with the condom.

"What's wrong?"

"It's hard. Haven't used..."

"Need help?"

"No." He turned away.

Fingers of cool evening breeze drove us together.

I wrapped the blanket around him. At that moment I recalled rumour said he'd done it before with damned Natalie Browning-Lee from the next street. She'd tarted their episodes through the school grapevine.

"The bitch!" I cried.

"What?"

The pain I'd expected came, more a twinge. We wrapped, fused. I fixed on the darkening sky and rocked, rapt in a sense of power. I bit his shoulder. He growled annoyance. I bit harder.

We nestled for ages unwilling to move. His heart pumped like a great machine, gradually slowing.

My stomach gurgled. I laughed, convulsed, and felt him swell.

※

A plover's evening cry woke us.

"You're something else," Cris whispered.

"It's so releasing," I murmured, "the afterglow."

"What if we made something grow?"

"Not in this bod. It's not in the scheme of things. I'm off limits tomorrow."

"What about tonight in camp?"

"Cris, you growled."

His face fell.

I lay staring at the eastern sky. Stars sprung anew, casting a ghostly halo on everything touched. The Milky Way was the signature of the Universe, and as it intensified, I likened the millions of sparks and galactic mist to sperm.

Voices filtered through the hiss of thermal wind, blending with the pulse of the reef. Zoë and Fish were returning unusually late from scavenging. Their chatter rose and fell in dreamy patches. "Where are they?" Zoë cut the ether.

They trooped nearby, Fish resonating, "I can see 'sometheeng' that begins with 'b'."

"Bum," I said.

Their steps faded down the opposite side of our ridge a dozen metres away.

"That was close," I murmured. "Time to hunt." I staggered off searching for my shorts, which hung impaled to a tree, stood shivering in the coolness.

"Wish you didn't have to dress. The moon makes your body glow like pale marble."

"I'm cold and my hair's shocking. It's all your fault. You know they'll smell we've messed around."

"Just say we chased a porker through the bushes."

We waited far into the night before a family of pigs ventured through the thickets. The boar emerged, halting to survey, sensing something wrong. He turned, hesitating in the shadows.

I shot behind his forequarter, ripping through the heart. The boar screamed a guttural protest and rammed into the bank, his legs flailing like pistons. The sow and piglets vanished.

"He's got a great set," I said.

"Set of what?"

"Tusks, silly. Wear them, after all, you're the hunter." I kissed him hard. His hands played, teasing.

"Hey, Romeo. That's enough. Later." But every cell hummed.

Chapter 38

We stumbled into camp. Jeff scratched his brow, eyeing me as if to say, "you're tried of everything, and found guilty. The prosecution rests its case."

Zoë smiled, tight-lipped, her smug look said it all.

Paranoia is a pain. I tried playing it cool, but blew it brushing my hand across Cris's bum. It was just a touch. Avoiding eye contact with Zoë was worse. I escaped to ground, exhausted.

✻

The feast called *Heheru* was held on the village rim near the beach. A large square marked where the dances would take place. Behind, covered in a heated pit of smooth stones, the boar we'd killed, and another the villagers had fattened lay. They were covered in a thick matt of pandanus over-layered with red-hot embers spread to seal them. Soil kept the heat in.

All of us, except Malcolm and Angie, arrived mid afternoon. She'd agreed to dress him without revealing the full extent of his dance debut. Mal would do absolutely anything to please her.

I spent ages on shell necklaces and wove the finest into a plaited belt, which hung low on my hips. The blackened coconut bra was rimmed with tiny pink shells. I'd made one thick garland of fine, red flowers. My hair, I pinned up and laced with red, pink and white blooms.

Millie stole the show with tiers of shells and little else, like a *Moulin Rouge* dancer, they clicked and shimmered as she gyrated.

We barely settled in when Angie arrived, red faced, gasping. She waved Jeff and me over.

"There's a couple at our camp. They look terrible. The girl's crook, like she's burning up. I've never seen anyone so stressed. She just dropped."

I felt my hackles rise, suddenly felt vulnerable, knew we'd no protective gear.

"Has she red welts? Blisters. Purple blotches?"

"She's pale. Her eyes are so bright. Saw blood."

"Blood. Where? Sounds like haemorrhaging."

Angie's face fell. "Cripes, not plague? I want nothing to do with it."

I dodged the question and made an awkward exit, apologising to Hiva, Niau and Mareva, muttering about Malcolm burning food we'd prepared. Jeff went about distracting the others. I saw Zoë and Fish squirming as if they already knew what Angie's message was. I eyed Zoë. She ignored me.

The girl, perhaps mid twenties, lay under a blanket below our platform. A young man who could pass for her brother sat nearby.

"How long is she sick?" I said.

He gestured confusion, appeared terrified. Neither understood English. I approached up wind, looked closely at her arms and legs for ruptured skin. Under firelight, I could see dark bruises and cuts, normal scrapes, but there were irregular patches of rash, like an allergy reaction and no blisters yet. Her face was mottled brown, yet strangely illuminated; eyes bloodshot. If the virus were active, she'd blister very soon, like a fractured road map, each intersection a boil-like rupture, claw-like as it spread. I seized up, couldn't decide.

It was then I swore, remembered the old Aborigine's brew sealed in oilskin months ago. I searched the camp in a panic, tore the platform apart before finding the pouch rammed under Jeff's carry pack used as a pillow.

Opening the paperbark, I saw several ingredients placed neatly side-by-side just as my tour guide Jake described. Some of the fungus-like materials were thimble sized compared to others. Roots. Grasses. It was impossible to tell what most came from. The old fellow must've mixed his brew in proportion, otherwise why did it all look so deliberately measured? How long he brewed the mix was a mystery. Whether she carried plague or not, there was no other choice.

I ground up and boiled nearly half, being careful to make the ratios roughly the same as the quantities, and left it more than an hour simmering. I placed two mugs of residue near him, gesturing they should drink all, and retreated, joining Malcolm. Angie fled to the dunny complaining of cramps. I suspected fear.

Malcolm perched on the ledge high above the couple.

281

He wore a strange comb-like piece on his head made from broadleaf, tipped red. A cluster of bound ferns stuck out of his shorts, which were neatly mended and patched. We had something in common.

Drums carried a hypnotic beat on the evening breeze. Strains of singing hung in the air. I wondered if Cris would dance the *pao'a*, Mareva described as sensual, and with whom. Kalani? For sure. She'd cast wonder struck eyes his way the morning we'd landed from the ship. He was beautiful, coiling the rope and his muscles stood out, glistening from exertion. He'd smiled, but I knew it wasn't just for me.

"Jeeze, Ice Chick, a cone for your thoughts."

"Do you mind? I'm worried. She's in a bad way."

"Yeah. It's spooky."

"We're missing the feast," I sighed.

"Yer face is an open book, Breezie, baby." He cast that cheeky look as if my whole being lay naked. "Rattie knows what you've been up to."

"You mean you saw us?"

"Yeah - No, dummy," he sniggered. "You just let the cat outta the bag. About time..."

"Shut up pox head."

"Bet you went off like a..."

"Rocket. I know." I blushed. Couldn't help smiling.

"And I couldn't give you..."

I cuffed him hard.

"Hey. Cool it. Yer prone to violence."

We lapsed into silence, watching the girl.

"When are we gettin' off this rock? I'd dig goin' back to Sydney."

"Funny, I thought the same, but it's not possible. You know that. Might be months. Years. Never?" I shrugged. "Thought you swore never to stick your toe in the ocean."

"I'm thinkin' flyin's cool. The Frenchies will come soon," Malcolm said.

"What for? Don't count on it. Besides, the airport's stuffed. They'd arrest you. Throw you in the can. Mal, you haven't got a passport, and we have. You might end up without a country."

"Aw, bull."

I kissed his cheek, noting he didn't turn octopus. "Thanks again for the rescue."

"I dug the danger. Makes me, well, you know. I owe you as much, Bree."

"You stirred up enough crap to last a rat's lifetime," I said. We laughed.

"Yer pretty bent for a bookworm. Keep it swingin'."

We left the two survivors sleeping. It was late when we returned to the feasting.

※

Malcolm walked in to a mass of clapping and cheers. Angie pulled him into the arena. She whispered in his ear. The drums began an erratic tempo. He stood looking the trapped victim, realising what was expected. He began mincing about and commenced moving his head back and forth with sharp, capricious jerks. Mal waved his behind like a mating display, and cackled as if choking. He bent over, using his hand to peck around bits of stick, throwing them in the air, as if to eat them.

The islanders clapped ecstatically. He pivoted on his gammy foot, hobbling right to left in a circle. We catcalled, giving criticism and encouragement, throwing anything at hand at him. He received a double ovation.

I joined Cris, who sat with Zoë. She crowded his space, treating him like a mascot; adjusting his grass *mo ray* she'd forced him to wear. Cris handled it well as an exercise in endurance, managed to laugh. Kalani kneeled nearby, pleased with herself, deep in a reverie. We exchanged smiles; mine forced, hers ecstatic, innocent of my pash with Cris.

Hiva and Niau removed the ashes and leaf from the pigs, which were stuffed with herbs and lemon. The thick crust of their skin was sliced off and spread above hot coals to make great sheets of crackling. Each was coated in oil and sea salt.

Seafood came first with a variety of reef fish and the huge ocean crayfish. A coconut based sauce with herbs made regular fare superb. We ate taro and breadfruit. I noticed Millie avoided the baked bananas. Worry turned my tastebuds to ashes.

We danced past the witching hour. Zoë and Fish egged the mass of children to join in, clapping and gyrating to drums and untuned guitars, each making their own rhythms. The village mutts skulked beyond the fire pit, sure of a good feed in the end.

Cris suffered cold feet when I tried to pull him up, so all of us teased him into performing. Even Jeff, who claimed he had "nailed feet," boosted his ego by showing sensuality and an imagination I never dreamt he possessed. Fau and Alili moved around him taunting, every instinct in me knowing they imagined a mating dance. I felt their heat in the pit of my stomach.

Being sore and stiff, I found hip swinging a drag. Kalani swept us away as she provoked the drums into wild rhythm. I swear. Her eyes smoked. Cris's mouth hung open.

＊

The feast broke up. Jeff tuned in as I struggled to explain my feelings about the woman's sickness to Mareva and Hiva.

"It's probably island fever," I bluffed, fearing Niau's murderous intentions, imagined him bursting into camp with a machete.

Niau went ballistic in dialect. Whatever Mareva screamed at him in Polynesian, fists shaking under his pug nose, he quickly backed down. We resolved all the villagers would stay a respectable distance until I knew better what the couple suffered from.

A tapioca orange moon sank westward. Emotionally exhausted, we made for home. Beyond the reef, gulls ghosted aloft before settling. Cris and the girls trailed behind exciting phosphorescence in the lagoon. I walked with Jeff, squelching wind-crusted sand between our toes.

"What do you think she's got?" Jeff said.

"I'm backing an exotic island fever." I raised my brow. I could lie, even to Jeff. "What choice have we got? Just hope."

"Radio stuffs dropped right off, eh." He scratched his scar. "A month ago we had the usual stations. They've cut back. Some only come on for a few hours."

I laughed scorn. "It's strange hearing Christmas stuff out of Tahiti and America; more hyped than usual; religious moaning too." I sighed, "The virus won't listen."

Jeff's brow wrinkled in thought.

"Jeff, it's important to know as much as possible. All viruses die down. This one's no different."

"Get wise, Bree. This bug's Mega. If we go back - that's what you're thinking, isn't it?"

"Well, yeah, maybe six months, by September, spring. I miss home."

"Forget it. Our world won't be the same. Ever. I reckon it'll sink back in some sort of primitive existence, eh."

I mocked. "At home with the Primitives. You know what I'd give for a latte coffee. Roast turkey. Cranberry..."

"Enough!"

"But there won't be much fuel at home; maybe no electricity; no market; if we've got a home left."

"It's a big If. Depends weather Blackjack's seaworthy. She's stuck. Needs manpower..."

"Female too." I pouted.

"And a high tide. The hull's damaged. We'll have to set a skin bandaid."

"You're so poetic, Jeffie. Any news from Australia?"

"When I can get it, it's chaos. Army units. Local militia ruling "Zones of Pacification."

"That means they shoot anyone first."

Anyway, from Sydney I picked up on "five million plus," then it all garbled. Couldn't figure if it was economic, about refugees, or deaths. Sure as hell isn't real estate, eh." He kicked sand.

"Graveyard realty," I said.

We sat watching the moon settle into the ocean. Blackjack's silhouette stood against the reef line. Far down the beach Millie shrieked, "leave my beads alone. Give them back." They splashed after one another laughing without a care.

Our two visitors disappeared by the time we reached camp at dawn. Both turned up several days later to wave thanks. Even at a distance the girl looked much better. They departed as hastily as they'd appeared. At first, I thought they figured they'd carried the plague and didn't want to spread it, but later I realised both feared the rocket launcher and weapons stack in full view hung up on a tree.

✳

Antonio and Lope' made good finishing the engine repairs. S-331 would move under power. They helped remove all remaining stocks of oddball tinned food and several sacks of precious rice. Chun's saki supply, two cases, and a bottle of twenty year old scotch proved a winner. Two large batteries and some safety gear were a major find.

We found the grizzly remains of the elderly crewman propped up in a cabin and promptly slammed the door.

I refused to speculate about cause of death.

Cris insisted we stock extra weapons and ammunition, including some C-4 explosives. I hoped never to be caught out by bandits, knew they infested the seas.

Specs informed us it was possible to use explosives for cooking, and a slice of it would burn slowly, but would blow up if a detonator were used. I registered extreme doubt and insisted he demonstrate while I hid behind a tree. He sat by a billycan and sliced a piece of C-4 off and ignited it. The water did boil. We kept several slabs. Cris asked if I intended heating water faster by using the detonators.

We watched from the headland first used to spy on the ship. She weighed anchor on a high tide, and blowing smoke, crept through the north entrance, rattling as if her innards were about to fall apart. Antonio set a long fuse and detonator into the remaining mass of C-4.

I watched through the glasses as they scrambled down the rope ladder, began paddling for their lives. Several minutes passed. S-331 began rolling side on to the swell as it turned, barely clearing the shallow reef ridge that spread a kilometre to the north.

The blast shockwave was deafening, resounding off the cliffs. We cringed under its impact. Millie fell. I dropped to my knees. The first massive pulse lifted the entire front superstructure skyward in a trail of flame and spiralling pieces, which impacted in foam geysers. A second deeper CARUMP blew her bottom out. Bits of ordinance roared like giant fireworks, flashing off in every direction. The stern rose slowly and slid into the sea leaving a boiling mass of smoke over the ocean's turbulence. Debris cascaded. Behind, the entire bird population wheeled about crying distress.

Antonio and Lope' landed. Blood streamed from Antonio's nose. Both waved from the beach.

Jeff raised a bottle of saki. "Here's to our future." He raised a toast. We shared, passing it around.

"Don't forget Antonio and Lope'," I said. ""We wish them good luck too.' Luck might come into it, but we'd have to learn to survive on our wits every moment if home was to mean anything ever again.

286

Chapter 39

"Millie. What's eating you?" I said. "I've seen more smiles on a corpse."

"Nothing, really."

"It's Fau?"

She shrugged. "Some. She's a darling. So's Alili. They're crowding Jeff."

"He's a big boy - and you don't."

"Crowd? Yeah. I know. I know! He can't be pushed." She frowned, pursed her lips.

I sensed Jeff was absent from camp exploring simply to escape pressure, avoiding too much company from the twins. I wondered if Millie would be wise enough to avoid being over attentive.

"Feed him a joke or two." I gave her a hug. "You're four months gone - if you're pregnant."

Millie's face distorted. "I'm so damned confused. I think I am. Mareva said so. My periods don't come, sort of."

"What sort of?"

"Well, it did, just a little."

"You can't be having it off with Mal."

"You've gotta be joking. Angie's his den mother. I'm scared something's wrong. I bled two days ago. Went for a shower. There's more today."

"Maybe the dance was too much. You put on a hell of a show. Silly, it's your menses."

"What? Millie gaped.

"You aren't pregnant, Millie. No baby."

"But, how can that be?"

I sat her down face-to-face, spiked a spidery purple orchid over her ear. "You puked and puked on the boat. Right?"

"Yeah, too true. I wanted to die."

"We nearly starved. Your body freaked out and cancelled your cycle three times. That's what stress did. Screwed everything up."

"You're not joking—I have felt queasy."

"How many sugar bananas?"

"Heaps, at least I used to; about a dozen a day. Loved 'em."

"I recon it's banana rash, like the one on your tummy, sweetie. It wasn't a lover's rash." I locked into her blueys, raising a brow. "Have a banana queasy, Millie. You're home free." I spread my arms.

"Oh, my gosh." Millie's face contorted in joy. She leaped up, began dancing in circles, arms swinging.

"Best not to play with dangerous equipment," I chided.

"Aw, Bree. You should talk. Can't wait to tell everyone."

"Tell? What? You'd better not..."

"I'm not carrying a bun. Oh, Zoë dobbed you in, sort of. said you were up to something. Weirdest noises."

"She's been up to secret mischief," I said, anxious to avoid Millie gossip. I resolved to find out Zoë's game.

"Once you get a taste for it," Millie sighed. "I'm starved now."

"If you need to, take a long, cold shower. Basket weaving."

Millie shrieked and ran off stopping to fly at Jeff, ruffling his curls, kissing him. "You beautiful guy." She launched towards the falls, vanishing in the undergrowth.

Cris shook his head, looked at me.

Jeff grinned, turning to scan for radio news. "What's the performance all about?" Jeff said. "She goin' wacko like she used to?"

"No comment," Cris said, spreading his hands in self defence.

"Millie's liberated. She'll tell you all about it when she lands," I said.

"That's what I'm afraid of," Jeff laughed.

※

In another late night radio vigil one medical report garbled on about "virus mutations", and the "seeding down" of infected areas with a new, less harmful virus to change the coding of the original contagion, like a biological marriage proposal.

"They're sure scrounging. What if it makes things worse?" I said. "Sounds nutty to me. Hey, Godzilla and Bo-peep. Get it?"

World economies, until now a vast interlocking global system, were in ruins. Everything from fuel and raw materials to the consumer market place was now driven by scarcity, inflated prices and fear-driven greed. Free trade had become free-for-all black market trade.

"It'll be backyard production," Jeff said.

"Yeah. Highest price gets it," Cris said. I can't believe petrol's over five bucks a litre—if you can get it. Makes you think."

"That we don't go home yet," I said.

"You could sell Zoë," Cris said.

"Why not pedal your wares, Crissie? You'll make a bundle," I said.

Cris opened his mouth.

Millie and Zoë jeered.

"What if it's all gangs? Vigilante," Cris said. He picked at the frayed denim of my shorts.

"Meaning?" I said, slapping his hand. "Behave."

"How're supplies supposed to move? They could nick anything. The strongest always survive that way." Cris said. His fingers pulled at the fabric.

"Paws off. No-go. Your passport's cancelled," I said, forcing indifference. "New developments, Cris."

"Someone's sure to rip you off." Angie said, grinning at Cris's discomfort. "Money talks."

"I ain't got no passport. I'm a no-mad," Mal drawled.

Fish giggled, "Rat *ees muy loco.*"

"Bet zone passes cost heaps," Cris said, sticking his tongue out at Angie.

※

Blackjack escaped the worst of the last storm.

She lay wedged between coral outcroppings. Jeff rummaged inside under the flooring where supplies were usually stored. "Can't figure this. The bilge has some oil. Not much water. There's nothing but dampness port side. Dry as a bone starboard."

I checked forward and found everything dry. "That's weird."

Cris banged on the hull. "She's got a second skin. Dead set, it's made of box compartments. How cool is that?"

We joined Cris and peered at a two metre long tear. Which exposed three sections of the hull.

"She's sound. A lot of muscle on big poles will get her afloat." Cris said.

"Hey, at high tide, eh." Jeff cautioned. "After the full moon."

"Then what?" Malcolm said, louder than usual. "Me and Angie ain't sailin' on something with a humungous hole, even if ye patch it. Man, a junk? Sounds like we're floggin' trash."

"Angie's not here. She'll tell you off," I mocked.

Jeff held his cool.

"Rat, get off your ass and do some scrubbing," I said. "You're only as good as your last deed."

"There's enough thin marine plywood inside to make a double patch. Screw it and glue it. No worries, she'll be seaworthy," Jeff said.

Jeff's methodical nature, and his confidence in the face of problems, made us feel stronger.

Angie and Millie swam alongside.

Angie applauded. "Sounds good to me, Jeffie. Get busy Mal, honey."

Millie stared.

Jeff picked up on her fear. "She's a faster boat, Mil. Should take half the time, eh." He kissed her nose.

✳

With three day's effort we levered Blackjack off the reef and beached her. Once canted at an angle to starboard the holed section was trimmed up and dried. The inside of each compartment received a coat of thick tree gum Hiva and Niau provided. Cris and I waterproofed the patch with gum.

"I haven't seen much of you alone," Cris said, planting goo on my nose.

"Mareva's ill. You know that. I've talked so much with her. She rambles on. They've left food for the refugees. Even built them a hut near the village. Both are too petrified to come near us for now. Poor things. Mareva thinks the brew I gave them is something special."

"Sometimes you rave on," Cris said, dabbing grease in my navel. "I don't get it. Did they have the plague? You shut up like a clam."

I sensed resentment. "The more I think about it, yes."

"They're okay now. That puts it up front. It's important. The virus hates that mix. You've got no right to sit on your bum. The stuff wipes plague."

"If. I might be wrong; anyway, we can't just sail off. We've got food problems."

Cris's face darkened. "Do you think it would've save mum?"

"No. She was too far gone. If I'd arrived two days earlier, maybe. Anyway, it was all a terrible shock, didn't think about the package."

"It should be analysed," Cris grumbled.

"There's enough left for two or three cups. It must be saved, Cris. I guess the answers somewhere in the Kimberley's, the Outback."

I sensed distance between us. Body language.

"Why your absence, Crissie darling?" I said casually.

"What do you mean?"

"Princess Kalani. You're both 'forty-five in the shade'. Her hormones pogo stick when you perform. Admit it."

"We. She's..." Cris dummied out.

I smeared grease across his forehead.

"If you've hooked into her, do what's right? Think how I feel. Work that one out." I slapped his hand away.

"You mean we're off? Finished?" Cris turned, waded ashore. "That's great."

I knew Cris suffered tropic fever. I ran cold, then hot, now feeling the need to cool out, except every time he brushed against me my stomach went to jelly, and the sticky sensations that went with it. Better he remain a friend, besides, a heated relationship crammed inside a boat? In the middle of the ocean? It'd come unstuck. Good will dies when you're in everyone's sweaty face, hormones screaming for action. Cris growling, the fiend that he was, that'd be the absolute pits.

I laughed, doubled over.

"What?" He stood on the beach, arms folded.

"Oh, nothing. Just a thought," I sighed, burst out, convulsing. Cris retreated, muttering about madness in my genes.

A stream of opaque fingerlings streamed between my legs. Was Kalani a good out for me, an instant solution? A cool dip in the lagoon made matters worse. No more emotional flip-flop, so I reasoned.

※

Mareva died a month later. She'd left us for her ancestral world, sitting, staring out to sea in her tiny lean-to. We attended the funeral, an elaborate ceremony and feast. Both chiefs spoke at length in dialect, punctuated with French and English. She was laid to rest by Christian custom and scraps of ceremony remembered from the time of the Old Gods. Fau and Alili were devastated; raked themselves; laid flowers and spilled their blood and tears on her grave.

I felt empty, uneasy, with the most peculiar feeling *Tupapa'u*, Mareva's "Rascal God," spooked in my headspace. The Spirit Ghosts of the Ancients hissed and moaned in the palms, tugging at me as cloud streams darkened, as if carrying her spirit to ancient ancestral lands far across the ocean. I was about to lay the amulet on her grave when Hiva grasped my arm.

"Medicine woman say you must wear charm. It is part of you. Bring good luck on *Moana*, what you call ocean." His hand swept in an arc westward.

❋

I sat alone on the western point as drizzle set in, and mulled over conversations Mareva and I shared. Her image appeared with that angular way of looking, teeth clicking, as if prying the lid off my inner thoughts. She'd been right about most things.

I bit my lip. "Fish and smoke." Laughed, remembering how she shuffled through the chiefs, bent on her own agenda. The power of age and her chest of knowing left them cowed. Above all, she was kind and so much alive.

Zoë crept up.

"Brat sister," I hissed. "What's your game?"

She made a face and wormed in, lagoon wet. "You okay, Bree?"

I made the customary scowl. "Zorro's stretching." I probed. "Found any strays lately?"

She grinned, remained indifferent. "Yeah. Hey, look. The curse of the Prices, nipples just like yours. Mums." Zoë smirked.

"Poor thing."

"I'll cope. You're snuffling."

"It's Cris. He's on the loose," I said.

"I know," Zoë said. Her voice deepened. "Let him go. He's into island mysteries and heaps more."

"I can't figure him. Spirits used to make him a wimp."

"What's he like?" Zoë grinned.

"Umm, for me it's tension release, sleeping all wrapped up; nothing's like it. More, lots more."

Zoë cast a sly smile, tilted her head, eyes probing, expecting detail. "When are we going home? Jeff's heaps cactus. Always says soon. How soon?"

"Months."

"Hot, dry places aren't getting plague."

I laughed, squeezing her leanness to me. Her curls smelled of coconut and sandalwood oil. "There's nobody out there, remember? Guess that makes Australia *tres paradisio*, what with the drought."

Zoë straddled my legs, facing me, her face sombre. "Motu-Riva is the bestest, awesomest island, but I'm desperate. I miss Ace. Mum. Dad. My bedroom. I could even like school. I'm sick of mossies and flies." Zoë sighed, rubbing a boil sized bite on her flank. "Forty-three bites. Fish counted."

"What else bugs Zorro?" I kissed her.

"Fish and me found those, umm, two. Oh - don't worry, we kept heaps distant. Cris said your brew saved them. He figures you should go back and see someone about it."

I wanted to chew her head off, but remained cool, smiled. "Cris is bossy. We will. The stuff's not my medicine. I'm just the caretaker. It's a bummer. Who's going to listen to a girl with a magic potion?

"Aw, you're Bree. You're not any girl. They'd better listen." Zoë's eyes lit up. "Wow. Imagine if it works heaps good," she gushed. "Mareva always said..."

"Remember, it'll be chaos back there. Our home might be a pile of ashes. When things quieten down."

"When everyone's dead?"

"It'll never kill everyone. We wait and plan. Bad planning equals disaster."

     ❋   ❋

It was a chilled, clear night in late September, over a year after departing Sydney. We huddled around the campfire, wrapped in tired blankets and pilled jumpers. I shifted upwind of Malcolm. He reeked of sweat and nocturnal hungers. The girls, presided over by Zoë, exchanged obscure jokes. She acted as the aerial extension high above the camp.

"Yer gunna lose yer virginity strung out like that," Malcolm drawled.

Zoë stuck her tongue out. "Have," she taunted.

"The death rates down in Singapore," Jeff said.

"Aw, Jeeze, feed us another. Pass the rice juice."

"They'd arrest anyone for dropping a gum wrapper. Even the mice have manners," I said.

＊

The previous fortnight brought patchy signs of improvement, but some countries like Bangladesh and China, whole regions, were as bad as ever. Still, the *United Nations* put the plague "in retreat." What could anyone say about a handful of better death rates? "Hope springs eternal from the human breast," so grandma Price used to say. I remembered how the Black Death in Medieval times came back a few years after the first slaughter and wiped out most of the next generation born since the first epidemic's end.

The whole perplexing mess argued to a head late in the evening. We'd toasted Angie's birthday too many times. "Leos had that effect on people," Cris said. "Scorpios are better."

"At copping out?" I said. "Moodier. Sneaky bums."

"Lets propose a toast to the death of the plague, *el Fuminante*," Jeff said, waving his cup, splashing wine on Fish.

"That mean to get small," Fish said.

"The Devil take the Claw." I said, feeling the sake's warmth.

"Who says we have to go? I like it here," Mal said.

"You wanted to go," Angie said. "Make up your blitherin' mind."

I knew she'd made his up already. "If there are seven of us," I said, looking around. "We could keep a pig or two on board in a cage. Feed them roots. Fruit."

"Some people drink pig's blood," Zoë said.

"Who's gunna slaughter it?" Mal said.

"Whoever's neat with a knife," I said. "Not me." I remembered the piglets terror on *S-331*.

Days before Fau and Alili caught wind we were thinking of sailing. Now, they stared at Jeff across the fire, their anxiety mirrored in the light.

"We must come, eh." Fau said, her jaw jutting out.

Jeff's brow creased. He cupped his face, becoming preoccupied

294

rubbing the orange fuzz on his chin.

"Hold on, you haven't passports," I said, looking at Jeff. He was no help. Fau took no notice.

Malcolm laughed his sarcasm.

Cris coughed. "Get real. There must be thousands already landed in Australia."

"We have no family. Like Feesh," Alili said, her voice wavering, yet all the more cutting. "We do any 'tings' you want. Cook. Work hard, eh."

Deep scratches across her chest and shoulders made her wraith-like, an orphan cast in a dark future.

Fau's eyes darted between Jeff's and mine. She was playing emotion poker and Alili held a full house.

"That'd make ten," Jeff sighed. "Too many."

"You can't abandon them," Millie said. "They come or I'm staying."

"Rat's waiting for a plane," I chided. "He'll stay."

"Jeeze, just a minute. I'm *in*."

"Err, umm, I'm not goin'. Count me out," Cris said.

Kalani edged closer to him, forcing a smile, her face taut. "Cris. He is my..."

"Lover. For how long?" I said, thrusting a stick, scattering embers.

Cris winced, flicked an ember away. The entire circle stopped breathing.

"I did not mean..."

"It's okay, Kalani. It's not your problem. I'm happy for you," I glared Cris down, raised a brow. "Then it's decided? We leave if things continue improving." I felt a deep pang of anxiety knowing the tensions and dangers we'd shared. Ignorance of what lay ahead is bliss.

"Super!" Zoë said.

"As soon as possible, I said."

"Jeezus Ice Castle, yer pushy."

THE END

295